THE

Throne of

DAVID

ANN FARNSWORTH

THE *Throne of* DAVID

SWEETWATER
BOOKS
an imprint of Cedar Fort, Inc.
Springville, Utah

This is a work of fiction. The characters, names, incidents, places, and dialogue are products of the author's imagination and are not to be construed as real. The opinions and views expressed herein belong solely to the author and do not necessarily represent the opinions or views of Cedar Fort, Inc. Permission for the use of sources, graphics, and photos is also solely the responsibility of the author.

ISBN 13: 978-1-4621-1714-7

Published by Sweetwater Books, an imprint of Cedar Fort, Inc.
2373 W. 700 S., Springville, UT, 84663
Distributed by Cedar Fort, Inc., www.cedarfort.com

Library of Congress Cataloging-in-Publication Data

Farnsworth, Ann, 1960- author.
The throne of David / by Ann Farnsworth.
    pages cm
A mysterious letter delivered to the Prince of Wale 32 years after it was posted hints of a secret royal marriage and the possibility of an unknown heir to the British throne.
ISBN 978-1-4621-1714-7 (perfect : alk. paper)
1. Monarchy--Great Britain--Fiction. I. Title.
PS3606.A7257T48 2015
813'.6--dc23
                              2015008590

Cover design by Michelle May and Kimberly Kay
Cover design © 2015 by Lyle Mortimer
Edited and typeset by Justin Greer

Printed in the United States of America

10 9 8 7 6 5 4 3 2 1

Printed on acid-free paper

This book and my life are dedicated to Dana, who taught me about truth. To Jody, who has class and loved my book anyway. To Michelle, who taught me to hug and gave us Roger and Eleanor. To Tracy, who knows how to sparkle and gave us James. To Stan, who never gives up. To Scott, who is effortlessly kind. To John, who is learning to slow down around corners. To Peter, who didn't want to put my book down to go to bed. To Samuel, who is too bright for his own good, and to Karen, who thinks I am pretty. To Roger, whom I accidentally killed off in the book, and to James, whom I steadfastly refused to put in the book in case his character had to die.

CHAPTER 1

The Wexford Middle School was set in a beautiful park in rural England. Shaggy grass, strewn with wildflowers, nodded in the breezes that swept up the front park to meet the brick and fieldstone exterior of the school. Huge mullioned windows rattled against sweeping winds and sent slivers of light glittering over the grounds. Trees, towering over the yards, presided in dignity over the picturesque courtyard.

The destiny of England was to be given an imperceptible nudge this afternoon. Even now, dust-bearing sirocco winds were riding Mediterranean ocean currents and racing toward the schoolyard. Originating in the Judean desert, the billowing clouds rose high above England in a hurry.

From across the Atlantic, the wind sent a chilled blast surging through the heart of New York City, following the jet stream toward Wexford. Galloping headlong toward the school, it rode just above the ocean, rising with the vast swells and plunging into the dizzying troughs. Set to tangle with the dry sirocco, it hastened to make the rendezvous.

In Wexford the school week was over and the final minutes of the last class were noisily playing out, the rumble of conversation competing with the banging in the boys' locker room as they changed from their gym clothes, getting ready to go home for the day.

Casement windows lined the top of the subterranean room, and to those glass portals came the winds. Cold gusts blew low across the grass and shrubbery, the darkening billows of the hot desert wind breathed above, and when they clashed, it was at the foot of a century-old oak tree in the front yard of the school. One powerful peal of thunder issued forth from the collision and the deep rolling clap shook the windows overlooking the basement lockers. A single casement window flew open in the blast.

As the winds hurled themselves upon the middle school, Eon McLeod finished dressing and gathered his books and backpack. His hair finger-combed and his shirttail half-tucked, Eon shivered as the wind swept over and around the lockers. Something was wrong. With only the vaguest disquiet to go on, he paused and looked around the room.

1

"Where is Huey?" he asked. It didn't make a dent in the noise so he slammed his locker and bellowed, "WHERE IS HUEY?"

The bang of the locker got the boys' attention and a gradual quiet settled over them. With the silence came the realization that there was a rattling in the locker at the end of the row. More of a wheezing, really. Eon glared around the room. Most of the boys were trying to figure out what he was all worked up about, and he quickly absolved them of any involvement. The guilty ones worked too hard at projecting a wide-eyed innocence that crumbled under his intense focus.

Eon launched himself at the gang of smirkers, even as they tried to laugh it all off.

"We couldn't pass up the chance to squish the little smart mouth, could we?"

Eon found himself in the midst of the group of bullies; targeting the ringleader with righteous anger, he grabbed a fistful of T-shirt. He was desperate to mop the smirks from their faces, but realized all at once that the wheezing from the locker was growing alarmingly loud.

"Someone go and get Mr. Morse," Eon ordered, and several boys were happy to flee from the simmering conflict to fetch the coach.

"Huey, are you okay? Are you in there?" Eon pushed through to the locker and tried to force it open without success. He wanted to slam a few heads against the door of the locker, but that would have to wait until he got his twin brother out.

"Breathe. Mr. Morse is on his way with a key." He could hear Huey muttering, calling down plagues on the heads of all the boys involved. Huey was a skinny, scrappy asthmatic, but his towering spirit never admitted to reality.

"Stop muttering and concentrate on breathing, or you aren't going to be around to whip anyone." Eon cautioned. His coolheaded wisdom was slapped aside; Huey only had ears for talk of sweet revenge.

Most of the boys had left the scene of the crime before Coach Morse could arrive, but a few lingered to witness the rescue. One of them, a new boy by the unfortunate name of Jerry Springer, shouldered his way through the tight crowd and gestured toward the lock. "Let me give it a try."

Eon vetted him with a fiercely protective look, which was pointedly ignored, and when Eon finally moved aside, Jerry quickly cleared the lock with a twirl and leaned in to press his ear to it. His fingers turned slowly, and then stopped and went the other way. All eyes were on the smallish crouching figure, and in the mounting silence, Huey's desperate scrabble became more frantic.

"Just a minute, Huey, settle down. You are almost out," Eon whispered into the vent. "This guy seems to know what he is doing. Just calm down and breathe." Jerry, who had paused impatiently at the disruption, went back to his task. Even Coach Morse charging in didn't deter him from one last move. He stepped back and with an offhanded confidence gestured for Eon to try the latch. It opened with ease and Eon threw Jerry a blinding look of gratitude as he managed Huey's topple from the locker.

"Let me rest up and we'll find the buggers that put me in that stinkin' hole," Huey huffed with determination. "Neanderthal thugs. Idiot goons, all of them! We can take them!"

"Stuff it, Huey McLeod," said Eon, with a gleam in his eye. He looked at Jerry and then back at Huey and, with a knowing look, grinned at them both. "Huey, I'd like you to meet your lock-picker extraordinaire!" The two brothers grinned at each other maniacally and Huey grasped Jerry's hand. "Would you give us a hand with one more thing, or do you have to go right home?" he asked. Jerry shook his head.

"I'm not supposed to exert myself when I can't breathe," Huey said. "Would you ride my bike home for me?"

"I would be honored to see you and your bike home," Jerry said.

The three boys sat with their backs against the lockers while Huey caught up with his breathing. Coach Morse looked Huey over with a jaundiced eye.

"I'd rather not prolong the school day, but if you want to spend an hour being checked out by Nurse Holmes, I'll take you," Coach said.

"Are you worried about me, Coach?" Huey asked, "I've never felt better."

"Good lad! Who opened the window? If I catch any of you lot climbing out those windows...!" Coach's mutterings descended into an incoherent tirade as he closed the window, locked it using a long pole and hook, and immediately escaped back to his quiet office.

"Would you teach us to pick locks?" Huey asked Jerry.

"I can try to teach you the trade my criminally gifted uncle and equally ruthless father passed on to me before they were swallowed up in the justice system, if you have the inclination."

"Is your father really in the pokey? What's he in for?" Eon asked with a curious awe in his voice.

"My uncle has an address at Newgate and my father is in for life. Fortunately, that hasn't stopped them from passing the family secrets on to me," Jerry answered with a serious mien. His black shaggy hair and his black slashes of eyebrows on a pale thin face looked mysterious enough to make his story credible, and the two brothers could read each other's minds. They couldn't believe their good fortune. Jerry was exactly the kind of friend they had been waiting for!

It was a grand ride home: Jerry rode Huey's bicycle and Huey rode on Eon's handlebars. The boys labored uphill most of the way to school every morning just for the thrill of an effortless ride home in the afternoon. The trio flew down the school road, alongside lovely rock fences and clusters of honeysuckle vines tangled and bursting with blooms.

They didn't talk at all on the headlong ride home, and when they turned into the drive, the twins didn't even consider ducking in the house for a snack but led Jerry straight past the house to the garage. A great hoary oak threw the lot into shadows and they leaned the bikes against its mossy trunk, right outside the padlocked garage door. Eon stood on his bike, reached into a knotty hole high on the trunk of the tree, and triumphantly pulled out a key. "We should conserve your special skills for what is inside," he said.

Eon turned on the lights inside the door. Fluorescents hanging twenty feet overhead flickered and hummed while the boys hurried through a maze of castoff rubbish. They passed a car up on blocks and a counter cluttered with tools. In the faint light, Jerry nearly missed a turn and bumped into an old wardrobe that emitted a distinctive odor of mothballs. The boys waited for him to catch up and they eventually reached the back wall together.

A row of lockers, very similar to the set opened by Jerry at school, stood dustily against the back wall. Eon took a moment to soak up the musty dreams that were part of the old garage while his eyes adjusted to the dimmed light. It was essential that Jerry understand the significance of this event and their new friendship.

Huey collapsed on an old brown couch and, through a hazy cloud of dust, nodded at Eon solemnly. "You tell, Eon, I haven't the breath."

The boys turned and looked at Jerry with an intensity that could have been a little scary, but it was obvious that Jerry had already bought in. He looked ready for an adventure and patiently waited for the boys to begin their tale.

It takes a lot of self-control for a twelve-year-old boy to sit perfectly still and listen. Self-control or a story so fantastic that you want to hold your breath to make it last. A story so incredible it leaves listeners believing that fairies are real, or that there truly are genies that grant wishes, or that mere boys could solve a deep, dark mystery.

"It's like this, Jerry. This old barn used to be part of the postal service, it was a big central hub, and all the mail was brought here to be sorted and sent out. These lockers were for the workers. When we first moved here we found all kinds of junk they left when the hub closed, most of it rubbish, but we found a notebook full of newspaper clippings and office gossip. It is mostly boring articles about the mail service, but there are a few interesting pieces. The best story is about a postman, a Mr. Andrew Higginbotham, who disappeared in June of 1980. He came to work but disappeared sometime before lunch. Never found a body, and if he ever showed up again it wasn't in the book. We were always looking for clues, hoping to find Mr. Higginbotham's bones and a bag full of money."

Eon and Huey looked at each other for a moment, knowing that they were one step closer to solving the case.

Eon went on. "One day at school in Social Studies, we were reading old newspapers for a project, and Agent Huey here happened to pick up a paper that had a report about the Wexford Bank Robbery—and guess what?"

Jerry was quick and the answer inevitable. "It happened the same day our postal worker disappeared?" The stakes were getting higher.

Eon and Huey nodded, pleased with the quickness of their pupil. Eon continued, "We aren't sure if anyone ever put the two events together. We have one more piece of the puzzle. Here, you can read it for yourself." He handed Jerry the notebook, marking the spot to read with his finger.

The entry was all about a prank pulled on one of the employees, Mr. Higginbotham. His locker was stuffed with Limburger cheese on a Saturday before closing, and by the time he got to work Monday morning, the obnoxious smell was radiating throughout the building. It was weeks before the smell subsided. The locker was listed in the story as #7.

Huey took over the story after he finished reading. "A few weeks after the guy disappeared, they closed this hub, and those lockers have been sitting there locked up tight ever since. We spent many an afternoon trying to break into that locker; we read a book on lock picking, but it's obvious we haven't your ear. We borrowed Dad's crowbar once, but these are quality lockers and we didn't stand a chance. And now here you are with a knack for larceny. Lady Luck has obviously fallen in our lap. I think it is time to find out just what is in that locker."

Together they paused until their excitement grew to fill the moment. Huey and Eon grinned identical grins and turned to include Jerry, and then the three boys stood as one and gathered around the locker. A faint whiff of Limburger cheese and an air of anticipation crept over the boys. Jerry's hands were steady as he paused over the lock.

"Are you ready?" he asked. He looked at the twins and they nodded in agreement. "Here we go then!"

After clearing the lock with a single twirl, he bent to press his ear tight to the mechanism. The brothers held their breath as Jerry spun the lock around once to a sure stop. He reversed and slowly felt his way, finally stopping again. He twisted the knob back around again and completed the final stop.

"Are you sure you've got it?" Eon asked.

"Why don't we see?" Jerry said with assurance. Echoing their experience at school, he stepped aside and motioned for Eon and Huey to do the honors. The boys stepped up and took the metal lever together, looked at each other, and gave a tug upward. Metal clanged and rattled: the lock was free. They pulled on it to open but nothing moved. Huey's eyes filled with disappointment and then again with determination and he kicked the bottom corner of the locker with an awesome bash and pulled again. This time the door came free, and they held their breath until it opened and bounced off the next locker with a bang.

"I think we need to call the police" were the first words spoken. It was Jerry, the criminal mastermind and surprising voice of reason.

"Come on up to the house then," said Eon, "and we'll ring up the constable."

Thirty minutes later Eon and Huey were explaining the events of the day to the town's new constable. Jerry was sitting in the shadows of the kitchen silently, letting his friends tell the tale. The boys' parents listened with growing amazement. They had heard bits and pieces of the story as the boys had dreamed and schemed, but hearing the whole thing with actual treasure hidden in the locker was astounding.

The constable stood tall in the kitchen with his pressed uniform, official badges, and holster, although the holster held a cell phone nowadays. He emanated practicality and was a good listener, letting the boys tell the story in their own way with little interruption. With a creaking of leather boots and equipment belt, he finally shifted a bit and peered into the dark corner, knowing there was one more boy involved.

"Son," he said, "is there anything you want to add to this story before we go out to the barn and see what we have?"

Jerry took a step or two into the kitchen light, with a sideways look at Eon and Huey. He looked up at the constable and then broke into a sheepish grin. "Hullo, Dad," he said, "it's just me."

"Well now, I'm glad to see you are staying out of trouble!" Constable Springer chuckled. He held out his hand and Jerry tucked himself under one beefy arm. They all walked out to the barn, there to discover all the secrets the mailbag contained.

The boys were given a citation from the police, which was instantly abandoned on the kitchen table, and a reward from the bank, which was put away for college. The mailbag was stuffed with banknotes on top of a load of very ordinary letters, meant to be sent out from that very town but delayed for thirty-two years.

Events quickly rolled forward. The letters were hand-delivered with an apology and a handshake early Monday morning. A few were undeliverable, but a flurry of bills, circulars, birthday cards, apologies, and one very special love letter settled into new homes that next day. Each a bit of history, one having power to shake the foundations of British rule.

CHAPTER 2

Ellen had worked for the Lord family as a housekeeper and cook for a little over twenty-five years in upstate New York, a couple of hours outside of New York City. She was cleaning up after dinner, and was wiping down the already gleaming kitchen counters and surreptitiously watching Elizabeth Lord give in to a black gloom.

I'm not putting up with her sulks tonight! Ellen thought. Davy would be home soon, and it wouldn't do to have his mother moping around when there was so much to celebrate. "Listen to this, Elizabeth," Ellen said as she sat down at the kitchen table. "This is the *New York Times* article everyone was calling about." She cleared her throat and started reading: "David Lord, renowned forensic accountant, was voted New York's most eligible bachelor this last fall. He has been untangling Behr and Son's convoluted books for months, and while the public waited skeptically for the results, we can now crown him the ultimate 'Behr slayer.' Two members of senior management are expected to be indicted for fraud this evening. Mr. Lord is well known in business circles, but he generally shuns New York social life, preferring to spend time at his family home upstate. His firm, Accountancy, Inc., only takes on two or three clients a year, and it has proven to be a profitable way to run a business. Not all accountants have the education or the intuition to succeed at forensic accounting, but Lord has brought a brilliant, methodical mind to his firm. His mother and half the single women in New York want to know when he will bring his brilliance to solving the problem of finding a wife."

Ellen watched Elizabeth perk up, her too-solemn eyes lightened as she focused on the triumph of her son instead of her own internal battles. Ellen continued her campaign. "I'll bet he is furious they used that picture. Remember that haircut? I never could cut his curls off!" Ellen watched carefully to see if the distraction had truly chased away the shadows.

"When I find a girl, you two will be the first to know," David said with a grin from the doorway. He filled the doorframe, and as advertised had a head full of loose black curls. "Do you realize how I suffered looking at that awful picture all the way home? I'll bet there were thirty copies facing me as people burrowed into their newspapers. Luckily all you can see are those blessed curls, so no one recognized me."

"Davy," his mother said, watching his face with apprehension, "are you still leaving tomorrow?"

"I have pushed it off for a week, if you'll have me underfoot for that long," David said with tenderness and a trace of concern for his mother's contemplative mood. "Come with me," he said impulsively.

"Ellen and I are underfoot enough, we don't need to follow you on vacation! Right, Ellen? Tell me, are you done with this case? Have you turned it over to the police?" Elizabeth asked.

Ellen watched as Davy knelt by his mother's chair and took her hands gently in his. He took in her beautiful, weary face and the exhaustion in her forget-me-not eyes and asked, "Mother, what is wrong? What are you worried about? You can talk to us. You can trust us with anything."

"Mrs. Lord, tell us what is troubling you," Ellen pled.

Elizabeth's face tightened into a bright smile, and with tremendous will her weary eyes cleared and radiated calm. She rose from her chair and said with a little of her normal spirit, "I am fine, you two old worrywarts. I am just fine."

David and Ellen watched her walk off with a regal dignity. She walked with head held high, shoulders straight, and a broken heart of some sort.

"Have you started packing, Mr. Lord? Could you use any help?" Ellen asked to keep the tears at bay.

"What's to pack?" he answered, distracted. "A swimsuit and a pair of sunglasses should take care of two weeks in Spain."

"Mr. Lord! At least take two swimsuits, for appearances' sake!" she answered and bustled off to get him a plate of dinner

One of the lost letters was delivered to Prince George at his office in London early Monday morning. It was addressed to *Mr. George Prince c/o Air Force Command, Wales*. The clerk sorting the mail that morning had figured out its intended recipient and had forwarded it to the prince, hoping to be lauded for his industry and intellect.

The envelope was delicate, a pale yellow notecard, and it was handwritten with a faint but decidedly feminine hand. There was even a blurred lipstick kiss still evident on the back.

Someone had written the prince a letter thirty-two years ago, and the carrier was convinced it was a thank-you note. "Right size and all that" was his brilliant comment to the reporter when interviewed on cable news. The receptionist who received the mail, quoted anonymously of course, was sure it was a love letter.

"I am sure I could make out a lipstick mark on the back. So lovely, really," she whispered to anyone who would listen.

Fortunately for the media, the prince was in the office that day, so the letter could be dealt with immediately. There had already been several calls that morning from the press, wanting to follow up on the contents of the mysterious note.

Roger Brough, the prince's personal secretary, carried a pile of paperwork into their morning meeting, with the mystery letter right on top, and when he came out of the meeting three full hours later, his paperwork pile had doubled, with the faint yellow note still right on top.

The little yellow note hardly seemed significant enough to cause the prince to pale and grow solemn and still. Roger had received a charge to follow up with the utmost discretion and haste. His directive was to delegate every other task until the author of the note was located. And it was understood that all of this was to be accomplished without arousing the curiosity of the press. The prince had given them a name, but little else to go on, and he seemed reluctant to give out even that much information and he wouldn't or couldn't say why. Still, the matter was imperative.

There was really only one man he could trust to be incorruptible and competent. The fate of the British nation would rest in the hands of an American, David Lord, Roger's one-time college roommate and the CEO of a highly respected forensic accounting agency.

In New York City, Mr. David Lord closed his eyes and leaned back in his office chair and relished the calm that physically echoed through the offices after the deadlines and reporting, the interminable ringing of phones, the hurry of interns and associates, not to mention the police and media siege that had strained everyone's patience this past week. He seriously debated taking the train out of the city instead of getting into a tuxedo and fighting traffic to the fundraiser tonight.

If only I hadn't asked Mimi to go with me, I could just skip it, he thought. He had asked her last month, and it would be impossibly rude to call and cancel this late in the day.

David Lord's company had just delivered the results of a nine-month investigation of one of the largest brokerage firms in the city. If you are a big player in New York City, then you are a titan in the world of investments and hedge funds. Behr and Son's was one of the biggest of them all, and it was inevitable that with all the money the partners made legitimately, some would feel the need to find a clever way to slide unreported income under the proverbial table. It was tiring really, finding again and again the trail that led inexorably to personal corruption and greed. Even though the details might differ from case to case, the human element was always the same, and David was weary of looking at wasted lives and the sadness of the corrupt players. The indictments in this latest case had been handed down today, and the scavengers that had been hovering around him had left to cover new scandals. His office was steadily lapsing back into the quiet of a typical boring accountant's office.

A chirping phone broke the lethargy creeping over him, and after a couple of rings he gave in and checked the number. He answered it determined to break away from the doldrums.

"I just have to grab my jacket, Arnold; can you pull around front? Give me three minutes and I'll be down," David said into the phone. "We have to pick up Miss Spencer before we go to the Met."

When the elevator opened on the lobby, the guard was waiting to speak with him.

"Mr. Lord?" the night guard said. "It looks like Enrique is back."

David gazed out the plate glass front of the building at the tent recently erected on a city steam vent at the side of the building.

"Have you talked to him yet? Is he sober?" he asked.

"Mrs. M. made it clear that I better not leave the building for any reason, not with your case so recently closed out. She said that you made some big people plenty mad," the guard said.

"Call Arnold then, would you? He should be out front shortly. Have him come and help me for a minute." David thought it all through. "And have him call Ms. Spencer and tell her we might be late."

Mr. Lord walked through the front doors and onto the streets of

New York, the wind slapping his skin with a fierce chill even though he was well bundled into a heavy coat.

"Enrique," he said as he stooped to see who was in the bundle of rags and blankets, "is that you?" Enrique had returned, back to his old haunt, but his breathing was shallow and fast and he was shivering in his sleep.

"Hey, Mr. Lord, there is no way we can make the trip uptown to pick up your lady and then back to the Met unless we leave right now," his driver said, indicating his watch.

"I can't leave until I deal with this. You pick up Ms. Spencer and meet me there." David met his driver's exasperated eyes. "I know she won't like it, but I can't just leave Enrique here in the cold!"

"Maybe he doesn't want your kind of help," Arnold said quietly. "How do you even know his name?"

"He called this spot of pavement his 'quarters' last summer, and I used to look him up during my lunch hour. I think he was army intelligence until something happened with a mission that sent his life off a cliff," David said. "Grab one arm and let's help him inside."

The wind, still bucking and biting any exposed skin, was burrowing into their warm coats, and both men hurried to get Enrique inside out of the wicked weather.

David Lord made it to the Met just in time. Striding up the stairs and to the ballroom, he caught Mimi's arm at the door and escorted her to their seats without missing a step.

She smiled at him without any hint of sweetness reaching her eyes. Mimi glittered. Her neck was draped in ropes of heavy pearls. Her ears were weighed down with antique pearl and diamond earrings that gleamed and sparkled in the soft lighting of the ballroom. Her shoulders were bare, her dress a deep black that glistened and shimmered over a body that could define perfection. Her skin was flawless, her hair a golden shade of blonde, and her eyes a mesmerizing blue. All in all, she was the most beautiful woman in the room, and she seemed sure of her tremendous worth. He might have felt honored by her presence at his side, but all he felt was anxious for this night to be over.

The tinkle of silverware and fine stemware recalled his attention to the event at hand as the army of servers brought out dinner and the evening began as they were seated. As dinner progressed, David forced his thoughts away from Enrique and leaned over to talk to his dinner partner.

"I am sorry I couldn't pick you up tonight," he said softly to her.

"I understand you were being a Boy Scout and doing your good deed for the day," she answered, toying with her drink and looking up at him. "Getting those dirty vagrants off our streets is an admirable service to humanity."

Her words echoed in his head. From a great distance, he heard the introductions from the podium begin, and he listened for them to call him up to make the presentation.

He heard his name being called and he stood to a swell of applause, leaning in close to Mimi to whisper, "Did I ever tell you that I have always wanted ten kids?" He didn't even crack a smile as he saw his words register on the calculator embedded in her heart. Instantly adding the cost, it was steeper than she would ever pay.

The audience in black-tie suits and shimmering dresses, the snowy white tables and opulence of the ballroom, while the Enriques of New York huddled in their need, seemed a slap in the face of honor and kindness.

A secretary laid the pen on his desk, not knowing that it was destined to become an instrument of destruction, the catalyst destined to change his life. An insider had planted the pen weeks ago but the battery had run down without recording anything of note. Only this morning were they able to charge said battery and place it in use again. The recording, obtained later, after the meeting was over, was disjointed. Someone in the meeting was nervously clicking the button up and down which turned the recorder on and off. The recording might have been intermittent, but the eavesdroppers quickly discovered that they were lucky beyond measure that they had recorded this particular meeting. The situation was dire and called for drastic measures.

An emergency meeting was called in London, three of them were in attendance, and in spite of the risks it was decided that the situation called for the elimination of the principal here in London.

Murder in cold blood was a drastic measure, but the consequences of doing nothing were so severe as to be unthinkable.

They had just the man in mind to do the dirty work, one Captain

Joseph Pillard of the SO14. The captain had just been promoted and would be anxious to prove he could handle the added responsibility. Manipulation was an art form they were very familiar with, and it wouldn't take much to set him in motion. For years they had watched the prince, and just as they had become secure in their position, it came down to this; it was unthinkable that anything would thwart them this late in the game.

Even the most remote possibility of disinheriting their children was a problem that needed to be dispensed with fast, hard, and decisively.

CHAPTER 3

David Lord arrived at JFK in plenty of time for his flight to London, as if he could speed his departure with his early arrival. Roger's phone call was urgent enough for him to catch the overnight flight. After boarding, he stared without seeing out the small window and remembered getting to know Roger their freshman year at Harvard, both of them serious in their absolute commitment to school and study. They had both been on the Harvard Rowing team, both roomed at Apley Court. Roger had spent Thanksgiving and Easter with the Lords and in turn had invited David to London.

Spending the summer in England with Roger's family after their junior year, David had fallen in love with the islands. His mother had been born into the poorest of Irish nobility, her family escaping the trauma of trying to keep up appearances by picking up and moving to the States when she was very young. David's trip to her homeland had been nothing short of magic. It was weeks and weeks of English manors, Irish castles, Scottish kilts, and the Welsh and Cornish coastline, all of it magnificent and charming.

Roger's call had come at an auspicious moment during the evening, after the program and before the dancing had commenced. It had sounded important enough for David to cut the evening short, pack a small suitcase, and hurry to LaGuardia in time to catch the overnight flight to London.

David yawned and looked at his watch. It was late when he leaned his seat back. Before long his eyes closed, his thoughts twisted and morphed, and he fell into an uneasy sleep.

Hours later, as the jet screamed into Heathrow and landed with a stomach-clenching lurch, David awoke. Leaving the airport, David walked without noticing where he was going, on autopilot. He easily caught a cab, stowed his bag in the boot, and settled in to enjoy the scenery. Although he eyed the passing view, his thoughts were already focusing on the meeting ahead.

Roger had asked to meet him at a café at the edge of Covent Garden, not too far from his office. It was typical London, stone and brick works of art disguised as architecture, crowding the sidewalks. Lost in thought and sitting on a bench, he didn't see his old friend approach until he sat next to him.

"Roger, my man, I'm glad you could make it."

"Isn't that my line?" Roger asked. "Thanks for meeting me here. I am trying to keep this matter out of the office and away from the prince."

"You look terrible—are you dying or something? Is that what this is about?"

Roger broke out in a real smile that lightened his decidedly haggard appearance.

"You don't know how to sugarcoat anything, do you? Well, that is why you are here."

A double-decker tour bus pulled to a stop at the corner.

"Come on, David, have you ever taken a bus tour of London?"

"Well, I suppose since I canceled a trip to Spain for this I should get something out of it," David said.

They were the last ones on the bus and found a seat on top, away from any curious listeners. Roger spoke in low tones, worry settling back on him in a single moment.

"First of all, thanks for going to all this trouble. I don't have much time, so let me talk and you can ask questions later." They leaned toward each other, David straining to hear.

"We received a letter…" Roger trailed off and then began again. "I have a list of women I have put together, women who traveled to the US in 1980. I need them investigated discreetly, so I can't hire anyone myself. I don't want to sound dramatic, but it could be dangerous." He saw the questions on David's face and held up his hand. "Just give me a minute," he said.

"It is peculiar that the prince didn't give me any more information. He asked me to find the women, between the ages of 18 and 26, who traveled between here and the US during the year 1980. An initial search on my end narrowed it down to these 16 women. They all came from the British Isles to America in 1980."

"I need to know if any of these women had a child 8 or 9 months after leaving here, and if they did, I will need a DNA test done on that child." Roger hurried his words, racing against something unseen. "This list could be worth both our lives in the wrong hands. Do you have someone you particularly trust who can investigate these women and not ask too many questions?"

David nodded, "I have a couple of firms I trust. If it is as important as you say, I'll have someone start on it immediately."

"I can't tell you why I need this done, not now, but it will be clear as we go along," Roger said. "And, as long as I am trusting you this far, I need another matter looked into, not quite as critical but just as important. It will need the same delicate hand." David was troubled by Roger's intensity and he shook his head slowly, as if trying to make it all come into focus. Roger was the very definition of brilliant, so it would all hang together somehow.

The tourist bus kept on its course, passing St. James, with a disembodied voice throwing out interesting facts over the loudspeakers as they traveled narrow London roads.

"I know it sounds crazy, but we are moving into the realm of kings, and the rules they play by are life and death," Roger said with a wan smile, the look of someone coming down with the flu.

Roger asked, "Have you ever heard of the Stone of Scone?"

David shook his head and Roger continued. "It is also known as the Coronation Stone or the Stone of Destiny, and I need you to find it and convince me that we have the right stone, without causing an uproar, mind you. This stone has been a sore point with the Scots for the last several hundred years." He barked out a humorless laugh. "There will be packs of baying reporters on your doorstep within the hour if anyone has breathed a word of this. I'm not telling you this will be one of your easier jobs!"

David picked his first question carefully. "Why do you want an accountant?" He felt sincerely puzzled. "I'm not the police or even a private investigator. Wouldn't they have the right resources to move quickly? Does this have anything to do with Prince George, or is it a private affair?"

Roger looked relieved. "I knew I could count on you asking the right questions, every time. This has to be completely off the books, I won't be able to pay you until this is all over! And you can't tell me that you are just an accountant! Following paper trails like a hound dog on the hunt is what you do."

Roger stopped and his eyes grew unfocused as he worked to gather his thoughts.

"The prince is tremendously worried about this matter, but his hands are tied for some reason and he won't or can't tell me why. He has told me little, I am speculating at every turn, and I am deeply concerned for him. The note has thrown us into the middle of a battle I never knew was brewing, and I am not entirely sure what course to take. How to protect the prince is my constant concern," Roger said, and then grew quiet again.

"Let me have the list then and I will get started straight away." David looked out the window and was surprised to see Hyde Park.

Roger handed over the papers and a set of keys. "I have an apartment you can stay in while you are in town; my Aunt Marge left it to me, so don't be surprised at all the chintz and lace! I want you to keep your head down for as long as you possibly can, and this apartment might help with that."

"I think staying in a hotel would be smarter, if you want to distance yourself from me."

"I am more worried about someone being able to track you, and hotels insist you surrender your passport. This apartment is still in my aunt's name, and only a few people know about it."

Roger looked silently at David. "I am sorry I had to bring you into this. I just had no choice; it is too important, and I had to have someone I trust," he said ruefully.

David grinned at him, "I was needing a challenge, I think, and this might be just the thing. Can I get a look at that original letter? Is that where you got the list of women?"

Roger considered. "The letter started it all. I suppose you could take a look. It is innocent enough unless you know all the players. It is in a safe place for now, and I don't dare bring it out just yet. Why don't we meet sometime this week at my office and I'll let you read it through? It might do you some good to understand the whole nightmare."

They watched out the bus window as the Dorchester Hotel came into view.

Roger breathed out a ragged breath. "We need to clean this up quickly for everyone's sake."

Their bus pulled up to a stop. "Let's get out here and walk; we are close to the apartment and I can catch a cab back to the office from there," Roger said.

They got off the bus, Roger looking cautiously about and keeping to the crowds. They walked to a corner, and while they waited for the light to change, Roger handed David a weighty disk, about the size of a silver dollar, dangling from a faded and shredded ribbon and engraved with an image of two oars. The words *Harvard–Yale Regatta* were engraved around the outside of the circle.

"Remember this?" Roger asked. "I found it in my glove box this week and wondered if it was mine or yours."

"My good-luck charm. I haven't seen it in years," David said, handing the medallion back to Roger. "I haven't relied on luck for a long time."

Roger took the disk and tucked it in David's shirt pocket. "Humor me, will you? I am feeling guilty about pulling you into this."

At the curb they heard an ominous squeal of tires, and Roger turned as if expecting someone. A gleaming dark sedan had pulled to the corner, idling. Its darkened windows obscured the occupants, its engine purred, and then deliberately, the door facing them opened. Without hurry, a pair of black boots appeared on the curb and a man in a uniform stepped out of the car. Meeting David's eyes, the man raised his arms above the door, a pistol held in two hands. He took aim.

All sound was stilled, all movement slowed, and David didn't even hear the blast that sent a bullet tearing through the crowd to his chest and knocked him down. He must have blacked out for an instant, but when he came to himself he was lying on the sidewalk and Roger was still standing, looking at the gunman. The gun bucked again and Roger fell hard, splattered in his own blood. The shooter climbed back into the car and the car pulled away.

The crowd around them erupted in panic, and David, worried that they might be trampled, managed to crawl over to Roger. Every breath was excruciating, but he was bewildered to find he was not bleeding. Roger lay on the sidewalk, pale and unnaturally still, blood pooling on his chest.

"Can you hear me?" David said, "Look at me. LOOK AT ME!"

Roger didn't seem to have strength left to even open his eyes, but he forced out a whispered command and it seemed to take his last breath: "Go…run…GO!"

David rolled to his side and took stock. He was alive, and, other than a wicked tenderness in his chest, seemed to be uninjured. Pulling his shattered cell phone and the regatta coin from his shirt pocket, David traced a burn mark running down the middle of the disk. Somehow, he had been shot in the only place he could be hit and not hurt. He cast one last look at Roger, crumpled and lifeless on a London sidewalk, and he got up and stumbled away.

CHAPTER 4

The doors stood open, welcoming worshippers and tourist alike, and Captain Pilliard entered the church and waited for a moment at the threshold for his eyes to adjust to the soothing gloom of the chapel. St. Martin-in-the-Fields Church was close by St. James, and the call to meet him here came at a most auspicious time. He would have good news to report to his benefactors. The sounds of emergency vehicles responding close by were shut out as the doors that led into the sanctuary closed behind him.

As his eyes adjusted to the dim lighting he could see that the chapel was empty of worshippers. Following the specific instructions he had received, the captain walked to the tenth pew and sat at the end of the aisle and waited for further instruction.

He had been honored to be selected for duty in this matter, and would give his all to serve the crown with his life, if necessary. It wasn't very many minutes before he heard the doors open again, the sounds of the city drifting in with the visitor, and he heard footsteps approaching him down the center aisle. The footsteps slowed as they reached his pew, and his contact sat down in front of him. She was wearing a dark suit and a hat with a veil that covered her hair and face to the chin.

The captain leaned forward, eager to report the news. "It is done, ma'am," he said. "I took care of it myself."

A note appeared in the lady's gloved hand; she stood then and turned to leave. He could sense her satisfaction with a job well done. She offered him the note, and as he reached for it she kept still for a moment—expressing, in the quiet silence, her approval and appreciation for his loyalty.

The captain took the note and watched the woman quicken her pace ever so slightly and leave the church. With a sense of reverence, he opened the note, smoothed out the folds of the paper, and read the words written just for his eyes.

"The threat has widened and now must be found and fought in the colonies." A list of names followed, and then the note continued. "One of these women may have had a child and that child is a clear and imminent threat to us. Not just the king, but the very throne of

England. We must protect what is ours. We are counting on you to do what is necessary on our behalf." It was not signed, nor handwritten: she was being cautious, which would protect everyone involved. He slipped the folded note into his pocket and then left the church. It was unfortunate that the elimination of the two in London had not meant the end of the threat, but no matter the cost, the threat would be neutralized.

Enrique Alonso Hernandez Gutierre hurried up 51st Street in New York City. A strong premonition pushed him along. Enrique had a conviction that if he could just make it to the ten o'clock mass, he would find his girls, and the need to find them was intense, even if he couldn't quite remember why. He was walking against the prevailing foot traffic and he was barely making headway, as if wading through knee-high molasses with crowds of New Yorkers rushing by him.

Finally he landed at the stairs of St. Patrick's Cathedral and was so rushed he barely glanced up at the beautiful spires or noticed the masterfully laid stonework. Enrique paused as he entered the shrine to let his eyes adjust in the sudden dimness and immerse himself in the stillness and peace of the chapel. He felt as much as heard a low-toned noise that rumbled steadily through the church.

Walking slowly up the aisle, his eyes sweeping the congregation, he thought, *Am I the only one that hears the noise? Could they be so deep in prayer that it doesn't intrude upon their solitude?* The rumble grew louder, and suddenly he realized with a sickening remembrance just what it meant. He looked around the church again and gasped as he saw that the patrons kneeling in supplication were covered with flies. He drew in a breath to shout at the petitioners and felt the absolute horror of flies brushing at his own face.

With a swiftly growing terror he watched layers of flies build deeply over each person in the church as they became statues of crawling, swarming parasites. He gathered together enough internal strength to rush to the closest woman and, shouting and brushing the flies away, yelled at her to run. His efforts gained nothing as the flies continued to swarm and gather. None of the people moved. None of them cried out. He rushed from person to person trying to wake them, willing them to move.

Enrique was abruptly pulled from the nightmare by the shrill ring of a phone. It took a moment for his pounding heart to realize that he wasn't in a church and the flies buzzing around human statues were gone. He lay in a bed, sweating out the fear and letting his intellect take over again, letting in the soldier and shutting off the dreamer.

Enrique pushed himself out of bed and turned on the bedroom lights, looking around, wondering where he was. He recalled being checked out of rehab and setting out to find his girls. He remembered camping out on the street vent, his old haunt. He even registered descending into feverish shakes, but that was all.

Remembering his family sent him into a frenzied search, with calm returning when he found the battered picture of the three most beautiful women now walking on this earth, although calling Sophia and Suri women might be stretching the strict meaning of the word a bit since Sophia had just turned six and Suri was four.

He found a change of clothing in his pack and a razor, a toothbrush, and a comb all sitting near the bathroom sink. He turned on the shower and turned to the mirror, confronting what his face had become. His eyes, no longer bloodshot or feverish, were dark pools of brown, deep and expressive, with straight, thick brows. His hair was longish and unruly, dark as night. His skin was brown, with a wide, fine nose. No longer stooped with pain, he stood tall enough, and though he was slim, the gauntness that he took to rehab had filled out with regular meals. The military bearing was returning, along with the angst his psyche fought against vigilantly.

Why can't I forget? he thought. *Why can't I let it go?*

The hot water heater was game but began to falter after a 30-minute run, and after a blast of cold to wake him up, he dried off, dressed, and went to find out just who his benefactor was.

Enrique could hear the phone ringing again as he opened the door. It opened into a smallish kitchen area, and through the open doorway beyond, he could see two guards on this side of a desk and beyond them the entrance to Mr. Lord's building. Mr. Lord must have been the one that had found him in the cold and brought him inside to recuperate. The two of them had spent many lunch hours last summer talking politics, war, and children—much of Enrique's portion of the conversations in a numbed and medicated haze.

"I think he has found the shower, Mr. Lord," said one of the guards into the phone. "Should we get him?"

"Are you looking for me?" Enrique asked quietly from behind them.

The guard turned to look and handed him the phone.

"Hello?" he said.

"Enrique! David Lord here! How are you feeling?" he said. The connection crackled and hummed.

"I am feeling better," Enrique said. "Thanks for letting me sleep off the fever in here, I owe you again." Enrique closed the door into the foyer and sat in the kitchen.

"I had to fly to London last night and I am staying here on an assignment for a couple of weeks. Listen, do you have anything like a job lined up?" David asked.

Enrique answered, "I have a couple of personal things to take care of but that's it."

"I want to hire you for a few weeks to help me out. I need an off-the-grid, military intelligence kind of guy and you seem to have shown up just at the right time," David said.

"What do you need me to do?" Enrique asked.

"This is so complicated and I don't want to talk too long on the phone right now. I need you to find some people for me, track their immigration to the US, and find out where they are now. You will need to talk to them face to face, and they are all women, so you may run into name changes. It might get dicey. It has become a deadly mess over here. Do you have a driver's license?" David asked.

"Somewhere; if I can't find it, I'll just make sure I don't get stopped," Enrique said.

"Can you keep your head down?" David asked.

"That is what I do best," Enrique said, which was quite untrue.

"I know you have a family, so if this gets too ugly I want you to walk away and I'll figure it out another way. I don't know exactly what is going on, but we are going to find out. It is important. Got it?" David sounded somber. "Communication is going to be a big headache. Can you buy a cell phone and let my secretary know the number? Listen, I have to go. Do you have any questions?"

"I might once I get more information, but for now I am good," Enrique said, sensing that David was hurrying.

"Good," David said. "Will you pass me to one of the guards?"

He was being handed a chance to get his life back without groveling or turning his back on the skills he had honed in the army. He would be able to take care of his family, if Alena would let him.

"Sure, Mr. Lord, and thanks for taking a chance on me," Enrique said.

Chapter 5

David gave the guard a few instructions, hung up the payphone, and started walking down the rich Mayfair streets. The area was filled with street-level shops and restaurants. Art galleries, banks, and investment companies took up the remaining space. The streets were clean and pedestrians pooled around window displays, providing cover and an illusion of normalcy.

Pulling out the keys Roger had given him, David was relieved to see an address on the keychain: 68 S. Audley Street.

Roger had said that the apartment was close to the bus stop. David looked up at the cross streets and back down to the address and saw that indeed he was close. He needed a place to lay low, make a plan, and draw in resources, and he needed, above all, to untangle this story so that Roger's death wasn't turned into a victory for the wrong guys, whoever they turned out to be. He needed answers.

As David turned the corner, he looked over his shoulder and saw two cars converging on the phone booth he had just left.

Why are they looking for me? he asked himself. *What is this all about?* He didn't know the answers, but he knew the right questions to ask.

A venerable stone-clad and brick building had the address he was looking for. It rose a modest four or five stories, with beautifully carved stone balconies and a rich brass and glass front doorway that seemed a beckoning fortress. He stood at the corner, watching for signs of official interest. A liveried doorman kept watch, opening the door for residents and looking ready to repel any salesman or riffraff if needed. David vacillated, but a quick glance behind him propelled him across the street and through the front door, past the doorman, as two black sedans rolled slowly down the street, emanating bristling aggressiveness that no one running from the law could miss.

The doorman called a cheery "hullo" as David started up the stairs; he wasn't labeled riffraff just yet, and the key fit easily into the lock of apartment 3B. Jet lag and the sudden realization that he had made it calmed the adrenaline surge that had been carrying him along since meeting Roger just a few hours ago.

David found himself in an elegantly lavish room, with walls soaring to meet embellished ceilings and the palest carpet thick underfoot. He made his way to the huge French doors overlooking the front of the apartment, drew the curtains aside, and looked out over the narrow stone porch. Sounds of the city met his ears, and shielded behind billowing sheer curtains, he could see that he had escaped the notice of the police; they were gone from sight. David sagged against the door as some of the pressing anxiety left him.

He pushed away his weariness as he shoved away from the door and went to find a computer. After coordinating with his office in New York and raiding Roger's cupboards for lunch, David borrowed some sweats and a T-shirt, glad that Roger had had a few things folded in the drawers. He then lay on Aunt Marge's couch and embraced the weariness that stole over him in an instant. He would rest for a few hours while New York gathered information and resources, and then he would figure out what to do next.

Enrique was up and pacing the lobby, waiting for Mr. Lord's secretary as they had arranged. He felt like a caged tiger, pacing and pawing the bars, anxious to be on his way. The guard watched his restless perambulations and was the first to spot Mrs. McCombs climbing out of a taxi. "There she blows, Mr. Rique," he said, rattling the cage just a little.

They watched the wind set its sights on Mrs. McCombs's hat as she hurried toward the door. She seemed the perfect picture of a grandmother, with her shirtwaist dress, sensible walking shoes, and hat pinned in place onto blued hair. If Enrique remembered right, Mrs. McCombs was a grandmother and the efficient dervish that kept Accountancy, Inc. operating at its frantic tempo.

Mrs. McCombs came through the double glass doors talking. "How he expects you to be up after you were so sick, I don't know." She sent a sharp look at him, demanding the truth. "Is the fever gone? Have you eaten anything?" she asked.

"I am more likely to be sick if I lay around doing nothing" was Enrique's answer, and it was the truth. "Did Mr. Lord send over a list for me?"

"Oh, Mr. Lord is one for lists," she answered. "Lists and addresses,

that's all he wanted to talk about." She handed Enrique a manila envelope. "There is a list of women, just names, and I assume you know
what he wants done with it?"

Enrique nodded, opened the envelope, and drew out the papers
inside.

She continued, "There is also a detective's report for you, with an
address and information about your wife and children. It was compiled
last summer, so I don't know how current the information is, but it will
be a head start for you anyway. I am sure Mr. Lord would want you to
have it now."

"Thank you" was all he said, his eyes locked on the report, burning
with a hot blaze of hope as he scanned through the pages.

Mrs. McCombs gave him a minute and then interrupted his reading. "Let me give you the rest so I can get up to the office and you can
be on your way," she said. She handed him a small backpack. "Davy
said that this would be a rush job and that always means money. Here
is a credit card and some cash. I don't know what this is all about, but
I know Mr. Lord and I know it is urgent, so don't spare the horses,
honey." She smiled up at him and pulled him down and gave him a dry
kiss on the cheek. "For luck," she said, and turning him around to face
the door, she set him on his way.

List in hand, money in the backpack, Enrique set out as the sun
began its ascent on the peaks and canyons created by the climbing sky-
line of New York City. The rising sun warmed the chill of the wind
funneling through the streets and lit the buildings with a gleam that
magnified and glinted brightly back at every turn. He knew that fate
was with him when he found a Big Apple taxi driver that could speak
English, and it helped again when he turned out to be a vet.

"Would you be for hire by the day?" he asked the taxi driver on an
impulse.

"How much is it worth to you?" the man countered, a sandpaper
voice matching his salt and pepper whiskers.

"How about $200 for your time and I'll take care of gas?" Enrique
asked.

"I usually work mornings and the evening rush hour, would you
need me all day?" the driver asked.

"I'll pay $300 to have you for the day, then, and I might need you
tomorrow as well, if you are free," Enrique said.

"I can do that." The cab driver leaned across the front seat to shake Enrique's hand. "The name is Bill, glad to make your acquaintance."

Enrique returned his handshake. "First stop is the NYC Public Library. I need to spend a couple of hours there."

Things were looking up, and there was a glimmering of happiness that might not have quite reached his eyes, but it had kindled in his heart. It had been months since hope had been a part of his life, and it felt good. Alena had been right to take the girls as far away as she could from him, a drunken ex-soldier with the right to carry. But he couldn't get them out of his heart, and he was going to find them and see with his own eyes if there was any way to rebuild what he had dismantled. Enrique was done playing the coward. It was time to blow the mistakes of the past and begin again to take care of his family.

But first he needed to sort out the whereabouts of these women for Mr. Lord, and to begin there was no finer facility than the New York Public Library.

They pulled up to this bastion of records, sitting low on the block, anchoring the towering buildings surrounding her. The Astor and Lenox lions were ever watchful on her front steps.

"Just call me when you get ready to roll and I'll pull up right here," Bill said, handing Enrique a business card.

Enrique asked directions to the Grand Rose Reading Room on the third floor and settled down to business using one of the computers available to visitors.

There are many reasons people want to stay hidden and many ways to stay lost, but for the average citizen, hiding isn't on their daily agenda. The first check he made was to see if any of these women were running and hiding or if they had stayed out in the open.

Army Intelligence is tasked with gathering and making sense of information on the ground and in cyberspace, with photoreconnaissance and actual informants, analyzing and presenting the information for use in national security and in war. Enrique had been part of a unique team that the Army relied on in hot situations for accurate, fast analysis, and Enrique had been the designated digital genius of the group.

Given a license to hack, finding backdoors into entities ranging from governments to schools, from databases of companies to terrorist organizations—anyone that had a computer was fair game. The government that made him an expert in hacking might not approve of what he was doing now, but then what did they know about right and wrong? He had made the decision to trust Mr. Lord and help him out if he could.

Getting in and getting out without being discovered was his genius, until that last foray, which ended up costing everyone, and he left the Army and ran. He couldn't outrun nightmares though, and today was the day he stopped running and faced the demons.

He started the search with a backdoor into the Immigration and Naturalization Service, and since he had names and a timeframe for their arrival, this part would be a cakewalk.

Any moderately intelligent spy could hire on to an office cleaning subcontractor and would routinely find usernames and passwords on Post-It notes on the back of monitors or inside the top drawer of most any desk, any night, and every night of the week. The more elaborate the security, the more available the reminders become to users. Plus, every top-level employee has an override code that will let him into the system, and that was the prize that Enrique brought with him out of Intelligence and into the private sector. He spent some time masking the search, keeping out of the open and away from any overt forays into the database.

Enrique went in through the front door into the Immigration and Naturalization Service and through to the back door of the website, creating a new employee that had clearance to sift through all mundane information. There was no need to get fancy for this data. He launched the search, typing in each of the sixteen names without setting strict search parameters. Better to cast the net wide and haul in too much, than to confine the search too narrowly and have to start over.

The computer whirred and churned, an overworked machine sifting valiantly through millions of pages of both useful and useless information. Just a few minutes into the search he became aware that there was a drag on the flow of information. The most likely reason for the slowdown was the inept computer he was using, but it might be that someone was sniffing around his search at the other end.

The Immigration Service is located in Washington, DC, not New York City, so even if a remote search was detected, they would have a hard time finding him here. It should take some time to launch the

New York City enforcement community and Enrique would be long gone before they could track his location and physically get here. It was a bother, though, and one Enrique couldn't ignore.

He got up, moved away from his table, and took up watch to one side of the room. The beauty of the wood, the soaring walls, and magnificent art on the ceiling were all just background noise to his alert and watchful senses. His eyes relentlessly scanned the room, watching for anyone with an open or covert interest in his spot at the table.

Enrique mentally prodded the computer to hurry. Every instinct was urging him to get out of the library. He could easily just print out the basic documentation and get lost in the vast crowds of the city; slip away to hunt down these women without calling any real attention to the search.

Enrique heard a distinct ding from the furiously chugging machine and sat down to see what information he had uncovered.

The search had returned thirty-six documents. He started pulling up each one and sending them to the printer. This could take a while. There was no time to winnow out the trash, so he would have to print it all and hope he had enough time before...before what?

Maybe I'm paranoid, he thought, but even as he tried to dismiss the premonition, he knew with a certainty that time was short.

Enrique sent document number eighteen to the printer and then knew, without question, that it was time to get moving, out of sight, somewhere less public. He pushed away from the desk, quickly putting distance between himself and the computer.

Pulling his backpack over his shoulder and looking casually around the room, he immediately noticed two men in blue huddled around the desk by the door, talking in hushed tones to the librarian. They hadn't sent parking police; these officers looked seriously capable, and Enrique was sure they were looking for him.

CHAPTER 6

Behind the librarian the communal printer was spitting out papers at what seemed an agonizingly slow pace. At this rate it could be too late before they were all printed, right under the nose of the police.

What have I gotten myself into? was his initial thought, immediately replaced by *I've got to get those papers and get out of here!* In that instant, Enrique realized that he was truly done running. He felt like he had woken up from a chemically induced coma, and he realized that he felt alive for the first time since the flight from Afghanistan earlier this year. He was ready to trust that this assignment was righteous, and it was what he was trained to do. He would finish it and begin to erase the memory of the failures during his last operation in Afghanistan. Enrique hoped he looked like an innocuous user of the New York library as he walked past the police and into the marbled halls outside the Rose Room.

"Excuse me, sir. I need to ask you to return to the reading room." One of the officers stood with a hand lightly on his hips, instinctively anticipating resistance.

Enrique peered at the officer, watching for signs that this was personal, that they had targeted him in particular, but there was no sign of alertness. He might have a chance to make this work.

"Yes, sir," Enrique answered. "It's just I have been feeling sick to my stomach and I need to get to the restroom . . ." Enrique turned with his hand to his mouth and walked quickly down the hall, heaving a couple of times to complete the illusion.

"Sir!" the officer bellowed, and from the sound of echoing boots on the stone floor, he wasn't buying the sick-stomach routine. "I must insist that you return immediately."

I need to stall, twenty minutes, thought Enrique, his mind racing. *I need him quiet and hidden. Just twenty minutes . . .* As he staggered toward the bathroom, he hoped that his strength was up to grappling with this cop. The men's bathroom was at the far end of a very long hallway and Enrique ensured that the strapping young police officer was close on his heels as he barreled into the bathroom.

In any combat situation, soldiers are taught to execute orders issued by their chain of command. They are trained to obey orders, without questions and without second-guessing. Single-minded obedience was a highly sought after trait in 99 percent of military personnel; however, Enrique was valued for thinking on his feet and making adjustments when plans went awry. Enrique had the mental agility to deal with any situation, and he had the training to use whatever resources came to hand.

Enrique turned as the officer came through the bathroom door and slammed his shoulder into the door, wedging him between the door and bathroom wall, using the door as a tool to incapacitate the policeman. Before the officer could throw him off, he reached up to his carotid artery and, pressing firmly on the vein, counted slowly as the officer quit struggling and began to droop.

Enrique counted meticulously to sixty and then released the pressure, opened the door, and caught the officer as he slumped to the floor.

He knew that he only had a few minutes before his partner began to wonder why this officer wasn't back, so he quickly pulled the police-issue handcuffs out and cuffed the officer to the exposed plumbing under the sink. The officer, Officer Riozo, as his nametag said, would be out for just a minute or two, and Enrique needed twenty. He unzipped his backpack and fished around at the bottom until he found a prescription bottle containing the last of his sleeping pills from rehab. These babies were powerful narcotics, capable of inducing sleep even when he had been terrified of closing his eyes.

Enrique, none too gently, opened the officer's mouth and pushed the pills as far as he could reach down his throat. He put his hand lightly on Riozo's neck as his automatic response kicked in, and Enrique could feel Riozo's throat constricting, convulsively attempting to swallow the pills.

What if they aren't after me at all? Enrique paused to consider. *If they weren't before, they are now*, he lectured himself. *Just get going and finish the job for Mr. Lord.*

Enrique propped Officer Riozo up against the bathroom wall, leaning him against the sink. He turned off the lights, opened the door, stepped into the hallway, and walked away from the reading room to the stairs. Although he felt a target painted on his back, he gained the stairs without anyone shouting him down and descended as quickly as possible without actually running. Going back for the papers was out of the question, but there had to be some way to print off his research.

Enrique walked quickly down a wide hall, and although his eyes were busy scanning the halls and open doors, his mind was engaged reviewing all he knew about the library, considering and discarding possible scenarios. He was passing offices, restrooms, stone alcoves, and lush meeting rooms. The beautiful stone halls were liberally lined with murals and leaded windows to let in light.

He needed computer access if he was going to have a chance to catch the tail of whatever force had initiated the operation against him, and he needed access immediately, before they withdrew and the trail grew cold. Information was power, and the pursuing force left trails that an information-age warrior could follow. Like the tracker reading barely perceptible signs of footprints, broken plants, disturbed dust, and quieted birds, Enrique was trained to follow trails of computer records, phone calls, and deleted emails.

Enrique followed the hall to the end and down another set of stairs, wide with worn marble treads. Down to the lower floors, where the workers more at home with materials than patrons were housed in utilitarian offices. The floors changed from elegant marble to polished red brick and he knew he had reached the bowels of the library. He started to pass an office marked Materials Recovery with only one female worker in evidence but decided that this would be it.

Enrique swung his backpack off his shoulder, kept it hidden by the door, and poked his head in.

"Is this Materials Recovery?" he asked with brisk authority. The woman in the office jumped slightly at the sound of his voice. She was young with hair and skin so pale she looked almost diaphanous; even her eyes were pallid blue.

"Can I help you?" she asked, finally, her voice whispery and pale as well, as if she were an apparition and not real at all.

Enrique continued the game, his booming voice designed to drive the woman out of her office.

"Larry, up in the maps room, is having a meltdown and sent me to get help. A bird has gotten loose in his room and has not only defecated all over a 17th-century Russian map but has also started a nest in one of the uppermost cubbyholes. Let's get a move on before Larry's fit turns into a coronary." He clapped his hands as if to wake her up, and, starting into the office, walked around the right side of her desk. She kept her distance, backing up twice for every step he took, which herded her right to the office door.

"I'm going to the Map Room?" she asked. "Do I need any equipment?"

"Larry just wanted a consult and some help clearing the room; janitorial will catch the bird," Enrique said encouragingly, willing her to walk away.

She looked longingly at her violated office, wanting to stay at her desk. "Uh, I'll be on my way then," she said, and turned and hurried down the corridor toward the elevator.

Enrique watched her until the doors of the elevator closed and then grabbed his backpack and shut the office door, locking it just in case she came back before he was finished. He sat at the desk and found that the skittish office worker hadn't logged off her computer.

Logging back into his previous search, he began printing the documentation again. Watching the clock and allowing himself a full twenty minutes, he then began the back search. He was going to grab the tail of whoever it was that had tracked him here. The officer dozing upstairs in the men's room and the others likely searching the building must have been handed some sort of story to get them down here so quickly. That story could be tracked and traced. They had picked the wrong guy to mess with if they had wanted to stay anonymous.

Minutes later, Enrique had what he needed in hand. Now he needed a way out of the library. He pulled out the taxi driver's card and dialed Bill's cell phone.

"Bill? I am getting ready to quit here. How is traffic looking out there?" he asked, hoping that the police hadn't cordoned off the streets around the library yet.

"It looks like something is going on inside the library and I haven't seen anyone come out the front door for some time. There are a couple of squad cars parked in the front with lights on, but I could meet you on the side instead of out front," Bill said. Enrique could hear the sounds of traffic through the phone and wished he could just crawl through the connection and avoid walking through the minefield ahead.

"I'm done here. Isn't there a loading dock on the west side of the library? I think I am close to that side of the building right now and I'm in a bit of a hurry, if you could be waiting," Enrique said.

Bill said, "We aren't going to be running from the law, are we? I don't think three hundred a day covers that kind of trouble." He paused, and Enrique could hear more sirens in the background. "I think you'd better hurry. Another cruiser just pulled up to the library."

"I'll be there in just a minute," Enrique said, and he hung up the phone. Grabbing his papers and stuffing them in the backpack, he paused at the doorway to the office. Looking up the corridor away from the stairs, he noticed a lighted exit sign and just below it a fire alarm. Just what he needed for a diversion and a way to get out of the library without notice, hopefully with a panicking crowd to distract the police.

Walking quickly, his shoes noiseless in the hallway, he was halfway to the alarm when he heard the echoing ding of the elevator. Within a step he was at a full sprint, and he lunged to pull at the alarm as he heard the elevator doors opening. Spinning around the corner as the reverberating clang of the alarm began sounding, he decided that a quick look down the corridor to see whom the elevator had disgorged would be worth the risk of exposure.

Keeping low to the ground, he took a quick look around the corner, into the corridor. Four armor-clad policemen with weapons drawn covered each other down the wide hall. They visually swept each office and were quickly heading his way. Enrique pushed to his feet and turned to beat a hasty retreat to the loading dock.

It seemed that the fire alarm had triggered further firefighting mechanisms. He could feel the rumble of a massive metal barrier that was descending quickly at the end of the hall. It was moving fast, and Enrique had the full distance of the hall's length to cover before it blocked his escape. He mentally blasted his luck as he ran full out at the looming barrier.

Head first and without conscious thought, Enrique slid, with his arms full out, toward the rapidly approaching steel wall. The carefully polished brick floors were slick and his head and shoulders cleared the barrier. Unfortunately his slide stopped abruptly as the backpack caught on the dropping barrier as it moved relentlessly downward. His feet scrambled frantically, seeking purchase on the polished floor. Pure instinct caused him to twist to the side, shoving through just seconds before the resounding sound of metal meeting stone echoed through the hall.

He lay for a moment, just breathing with his cheek against the cool floor, and reflected on the magnitude of the force brought to bear against him, against the search for these women. He might not know what this search was all about, but someone else did and was willing to go to fantastic lengths to stop him.

Enrique stood, unconsciously brushing off imaginary dust from his knees, checked to make sure the backpack was all on this side of the barrier, and followed the exit signs to the loading docks.

He found his taxi patiently awaiting his arrival, and they drove away from all the chaos unleashed inside the library. Inserting themselves into lunch-hour midtown Manhattan traffic, they inched their way slowly across the city down Fifth to Broadway and on to Yonkers. Enrique knew that his small head start would evaporate once officials got their hands on the surveillance video. He cursed himself for not taking the precaution of wearing a hat and keeping himself anonymous. He was leading them straight to Alena and the girls, so he would have to be careful and wary, but he needed to see them before he went any further.

CHAPTER 7

Camryn Lavender sat as still as death on what could be claimed as the most uncomfortable seat in Lancashire, waiting for the 6 p.m. train bound for London. The rail station was small, not even a ticket booth or attendant. Just a covered spot to sit and take in the feeble sun and watch the wind play with the grass and ruffle the hedges. She was alone waiting for the train and she cherished these last few minutes of solitude, enjoying the stillness and peace before trading it all for a week in London with her big brother and only sibling, Roger Brough. She was composed, and the views from that particular seat rolled over her still figure without reaching her at all. She looked without seeing and heard without hearing, her back erect, her mouth set in a vague resemblance of a smile, her eye the gray of an overcast sky. Her skin bore the marks of illness, pale cheeks accompanied by a vague bruising about her eyes.

Right on time the train swept down the tracks, finally piercing her reverie. She checked the time and, gathering her purse and bag, waited at the edge of the platform for the train to stop. As the train screeched and groaned, Camryn saw herself reflected in every passing pane of glass, every window and door mirrored back to her the paleness of her skin, her honey-colored hair pulled back in a ribbon, her eyes too old. She had secluded herself, seeing no one, for far too long, and her mother and brother would be shocked to see her in this frail condition.

She wasn't officially in mourning, her husband was only 'missing in action' and not 'presumed dead,' but the year had taken a toll on her health. Waiting for him to return to her had been the hardest thing she had ever done, and battling general opinion, she wasn't ready to move on without him yet. She wasn't ready to accept that he wasn't returning.

The train finally ground to a halt, and the doors all along its length pushed open. With a look back at the eternal stillness behind her, she stepped into the real world. Pulling her bag behind, she found a window seat. The conductor pushed her bag into an overhead bin. The train sat for a moment, waiting sufficient time for other passengers to appear, and then, starting slowly and gathering speed, it coursed southeast toward London.

As the train snaked its way through small towns and stone-walled fields, Camryn found herself becoming more and more interested in the landscape rolling by her window, taking notice of laundry hung out to dry and dogs sleeping on stoops. She watched with little flutters of interest as cars bustled around larger and larger towns, buses picked up passengers and trundled through traffic, and businessmen in suits ate supper in cafés, framed in picture windows for anyone to watch.

It was late when the train rolled into London's Victoria Station, and with a final huff, the doors opened once more. Camryn found herself outside in the chill spring air. She breathed in London, brick and cement, glass and pigeons, the river Thames, and felt through her purse for her cell phone to call Roger.

"Roger, where are you? I'm at the station. I am going to take a taxi, so I'll see you at the apartment." She disconnected and hailed a taxi: "Mayfair, please." Leaning back onto the seat, she watched London roll by. Roger had asked her to come and spend the week, knowing it was time. It was silly, really, to hide out in Lancashire.

She had the world's best brother. She had been born when he was eight and no one would have blamed him if he had resented her for interrupting his life, but he had adored her from the minute he saw her and treated her like she was his very best friend and not just a constant nuisance. Which she surely was.

I can't wait to see him, Camryn thought.

Pulling up to the Mayfair apartment, Camryn paid the taxi driver and paused at the front door, waiting for the doorman to let her in. "Hello, miss." The doorman doffed his cap and offered to carry her luggage up to the apartment.

"Thank you, but it's not heavy. Is Roger in?" she asked.

"I haven't seen him today, Miss, but I just couldn't say for sure." She had her own keys to the apartment, but the door swung open as she pushed against it, not even shut properly. This door had always been a little tricky to close, but still, Roger was fanatical about security. When Roger left the apartment to take the trash down the hall, he locked the door and carried his keys.

"Roger!" she called. Leaving her luggage, Camryn walked cautiously through the dimmed light of the living room. Glancing into the kitchen she could see there was a dish in the sink and a glass on the counter.

She was feeling edgy, unnerved by the feeling that someone had been in the apartment and that something was very wrong. She called again with no stirring of response. She settled herself a little. *Well, Roger is probably sleeping at his own apartment, I'll see him tomorrow,* she thought, a little disappointed.

She checked the front door again and locked it up tight. Checking the apartment more thoroughly, she headed down the hall to the guest room for some much-needed sleep. Morning would come quickly. As she turned down the hall, passing the overly fussy parlor, the greenish glow of the television caught her eye. She walked cautiously into the doorway.

Immediately, she sensed the presence of someone in the room and she walked to the back of the frilly cabbage rose couch. A man lay stretched out on the couch, sound asleep, and it wasn't Roger. He was beautiful, with huge black curls, a straight Grecian nose, and flat-planed cheekbones. She crept closer, not wanting to wake him as her traitorous heart took him in. The TV murmured softly in the room as Camryn battled and stared.

You have a husband, what are you thinking? she lectured with her head while her heart beat double time in her chest. *Lucas, I am waiting for Lucas.* All the while she drew closer and her hand reached out to this man in front of her. He was so still it was hard to tell if he was even breathing as she quietly leaned over the back of the couch and gently placed her hand on his heart. Her fingers took up the frantic rhythm of her heartbeat instantly, and his eyes opened. The instant awareness and the bluest of blue eyes sent Camryn back just a step, out of his reach.

She fought a rising panic, and she stammered out a verbal assault. "Do I know you? Where is Roger?" She sounded defensive and that stirred her into anger. "What are you doing here?"

He looked at her and something like sorrow blazed from his eyes. Camryn recognized sorrow and pity; she had seen it before.

"What is going on?" she said. The television murmured in the background. Its light, the only light in the room, flickered and faded.

As David looked at her, he saw her eyes fly to the screen and widen in shock. He turned and saw his passport photo emblazoned on the screen, WANTED scrolling beneath the picture. He was the headline story, and the image of Roger followed, lying on the Mayfair sidewalk.

"What is going on here?" Camryn asked again, not looking at the man but watching the television. Understanding dawned. "Where is Roger? What have you done?" She closed her eyes while reality penetrated her already broken heart, and when she looked up, she could feel hate take root. And when she looked at this stranger, he recoiled from what he saw there in her eyes.

"Why are you here?" she said, with a towering calm.

"It wasn't me," he spoke quietly, "but yes, Roger is dead. He was shot in the street yesterday morning, I was with him and..." Camryn was cringing as he spoke, like he was bludgeoning her with his words, and he finally ground to a stop.

"I'm going to call the police," Camryn stammered.

She drew her phone from her purse and tried to turn it on. It was dead. She backed farther away, wanting to get as far from him as possible. She reached for the phone on the end table, watching him steadily, and knocked the phone to the floor. The stranger reached to help her and she moaned in fright. She scrambled to the door, searching through her purse as she ran. Then turning, she looked right at him.

He had risen to his feet. There was something kind in his beautiful face, but she hardened her heart and pulled the spray from her purse. Pointing it at those kind eyes, she pulled the trigger and watched him stagger to the floor and crack his head sharply on the fireplace stone. She watched him carefully but he didn't move.

Camryn stood over this stranger, her sweater drawn up over her mouth and nose so as not to breathe in the pepper spray; she was still drawn to him but finally left the room and made the call.

She was shuttled from operator to sergeant and placed on hold for a long time, but finally a policeman came on the line and listened to her story of the fugitive murderer in her apartment. He said that someone would be coming around to the apartment presently. He took down her address and instructed her to meet them at the door.

CHAPTER 8

Camryn took the telephone cord and wrapped it around his hands and tied them as tightly as she could. As Camryn tied the limp and unresisting man, she couldn't help but think that his face looked familiar.

Where have I seen him? she thought. It wasn't from the story on the news and she didn't remember ever meeting him, but slowly she realized that she did know him. She looked at the time and ran into Roger's little study right off the bedroom. There on the desk was a picture of Roger and this man. Years younger, but it was him. She turned the photo over and found it marked in her mother's handwriting: *Roger and David—2001.*

Camryn tapped the picture and furiously thought. She hurried back to the sitting room. He wasn't stirring; she had sprayed him full in the face, and he had a goose egg swelling on the back of his head from knocking his head on the stone. She touched his shoulder and tried to get him to sit up, but he was out.

"What should I do?" Camryn asked an unconscious David Lord. She had heard a hundred stories about David, but they had never met. She should have recognized his name, but she was only fourteen when Roger had brought him home for the summer, and she had been shipped off to spend that summer in Scotland with her nannie and Duke. Her heart sank. She knew he would never hurt Roger, never.

She looked at the time. "Wake up!" she pled. Camryn grabbed his shoulders and tried to pull him to a sitting position, but he was a dead weight and wouldn't budge. She sat and memorized him. She was just reaching out to finger a blue-black curl when there was a violent pounding at the door.

"Wake up," she begged. The pounding at the door intensified. "Just a minute," she called, and watched David, willing him to wake up. He just lay there, barely breathing, looking like a classic statue in Roger's favorite Rugby shirt. The pounding intensified again as she considered what to do.

Maybe I can tell them he escaped! she thought as she walked as slowly as possible to the door.

"Ma'am, are you all right in there? I am here from the police; you need to let us in!" someone bellowed at her through the door.

"I don't need help anymore," she called back.

"Ma'am, once a call has gone out we have to verify your safety. I can't leave here until I talk to you and file a report." He sounded reasonable.

Hesitantly, Camryn opened the door an inch. That opening was just what the prying official needed. He pushed through and scanned the room. He breathed through his mouth, in excitement or exertion she didn't know, and looking past him to the door, she became confused.

"Where is your partner?" Camryn asked, wishing she could block out the sound of his heavy breathing. This wasn't right, and she wasn't sure just what it meant.

"Sir," she asked politely, "can I see your badge and ID?" He wasn't dressed in uniform, though she had no doubt that he was a member of law enforcement—he was all that was official. He was starting through the room and turned when she spoke, drawing a leather wallet from his shirt pocket, flipping it open, and thrusting it toward her.

She reached for it as he snapped it shut and shoved it away while barking at her, "Where is Mr. Lord, then?" When she didn't move, he walked into the apartment and she trailed behind, willing him to stop. He asked no more questions, not even asking her name. When she looked back at him, all that was in his hands was his gun. Something was terribly wrong.

"He escaped just a minute ago," Camryn stammered, unbelievable even to her own ears. "He did! He just got up and walked out," she insisted, although the man didn't even pause to listen. His mirrored glasses masked his eyes. He moved quickly through the grand living room, dismissing it and quickly reconnoitering the kitchen.

"Sir," she tried again, "there is no one here anymore. Please stop." He ignored her completely. Moving into the hall and through the parlor doorway, Camryn skirted by the completely rude official. His flattened nose, mirrored eyeshades, pockmarked skin, and sour-looking mouth proclaimed him a brute, and she moved toward David, hoping he would just stay out.

David groaned a little and sucked a hard lungful of air. He was coming around. She stood in front of him, shielding him with her slight frame.

The man charged toward her, pointing his weapon. "Down there, out of my way," he said, gesturing to her to get out of his way. His heavy breathing quickened as she memorized his face, and his manner, and suddenly she felt a towering anger. Camryn knelt and felt wildly for her purse and the pepper spray, still blocking the prone David. She felt him struggling to free his hands and the deadly officer aimed a weapon once more at Camryn.

"Out of my way," he yelled again. Just then, David Lord shouldered her aside and she watched him stare the man down.

"Afraid to look me in the eye while you shoot me?" David challenged.

The man wavered and then lowered the pistol; he reached up with thick fingers and pulled the glasses off a pockmarked face. Slick with sweat and flushed with heightened emotion and with an ugly grimace, he raised the gun once more. Camryn again felt wildly beneath the couch. She pulled the pepper spray from where it had rolled, raised it, and sprayed without hesitation. As the man staggered, David freed himself from the cord that bound him. He grabbed a thick ceramic vase and smashed it over the man's head, ending his blind lurching and sending him out cold.

Camryn reached up to the couch, pulled off two pillows, and used them as a shield against the lingering pepper spray. She handed one to David and they fled the room, slamming the door and the nightmare behind them. Leaning against the silken oak, they paused while their pounding blood began to slow and cool.

Camryn reached out and took David's hand. "I am so sorry for not recognizing you," she said. "Who was that?"

David's heart started a wild surge the instant she put her hand in his, all while feeling the prick of a rather large diamond ring that made his reaction to her out of bounds. He carefully removed his hand from her grasp.

"That is the man who killed your brother." David stopped talking then, and they leaned against the door, giving the room time to clear before they went in to search his pockets.

Alone in his head David added it all up. The murder of Roger, two attempted shootings, and the shifting of blame to an American accountant meant someone was making this important. He wondered how Enrique was coming along in New York and hoped no one yet realized that Enrique was engaged in this conflict as well, whatever it was. He looked over at Camryn, her burnished gold hair hiding her face. Baby sister Camryn. How was he to get her out of this right this instant? Maybe he could tie her up and she could somehow convince the magistrate that she had been forced to play the aggressor in front of the police back there.

"Don't even think about shutting me out," Camryn said from behind her curtain of hair. "And I won't be shuttled off to safety. He was my brother and I want to help with whatever you do to find out why he was killed!" He continued to watch her and the curtain parted as she looked back at him intently. She was too pale, but if anything it made her prettier, the fragile look casting an aura of mystery about her. But her cheeks were flushed from all the excitement and her eyes were flinty with determination. The fragile appearance might just be misleading.

David needed to find a safe place to stash her. "We'll need to find somewhere to stay in London, then, and a car," he said in a big-brother fashion. "And I should say 'thank you.' Roger always did say that you were a wicked good shot."

"My husband bought that pepper spray for me. I think I might have just broken the law, but Lucas insisted I keep it with me at all times and to shoot first and ask questions later. Sorry about that," she said with the smallest and saddest smile David had ever encountered. "I think we should search our mystery man in there and then get out of here before anyone else shows up to back him up."

"Okay," David said, pushing off the wall, "let's get this done!"

CHAPTER 9

The New York portion of David's endeavor was parked outside of a sad little house that was snuggled between two rough-looking apartment buildings in Yonkers.

"The Empire State," Bill said, "doesn't quite seem to describe Yonkers, does it?"

They had been sitting in the cab, parked on this street, for going on three hours now, and the deep dish meat lover's pizza from Papa Romano's was long gone. Bill knew how to sit without talking, so they sat and Enrique read through his printouts. He could see the beginnings of the trail to lead him to these women. He hadn't heard a word from Mr. Lord, but he had his orders and would start as soon as he settled with Alena and his girls.

The time passed quickly until he ran out of study material. Enrique leaned against the cool window, the chill setting him shivering. His fever was still waging war against the invading illness. It was apparent that he wasn't quite as healthy as he had proclaimed to Mr. Lord's secretary only this morning.

He closed his eyes and let his thoughts drift to the lazy warm days of his childhood. He remembered palm trees, pineapple plantations, the white Panama hats of the men. He thought of the bright colors of the long skirts his mama wore. He thought of four black-eyed sisters, spoiling and coddling him, the long-awaited precious male child. He remembered terrifying his sisters with a fierce fighting look, and they would cower or squeal and run from him. He was petted and loved but he was the only one of his family that still lived. He had no new memories; only the sweetest childhood remembrances remained.

He could not forget the hard home of his uncle Ramon, the women always quiet and subdued. No singing or shouting or laughing. He always thought of Miami as cloudy and dreary. The sun didn't shine in his Miami memories. He joined the army when he turned eighteen, escaping a hard home for an even harder ten years in the military. He relived memories of assigned missions, shortened friendships, and faraway places. Almost immediately he found himself reviewing Afghanistan, where his carefully built life finally fell apart.

He opened his eyes and cleared his head, then lay back against the chill, shook remembrances of war away with a shudder, and remembered meeting Alena. He could see her serious jet eyes, smiling only for him, and he could see her standing with her father and brothers at their wedding. Carlos, Eric, and William, his closest military brothers, wearing dress uniforms and raising toast after toast to the happy couple. Eric and Carlos, dead now in Iraq, and William lost in the drug flotsam of Chicago. The greatest waste of manhood he could imagine, and all for nothing. He opened his eyes again, the happiest memories swallowed up by the more potent horror stories.

In the front seat, Bill rolled down the window and a light breeze blew through the stale air.

"It's going on 6:15; if we are going to be much longer I should call my daughter and let her know I'm alive, and it might be nice to know if we were on the evening news or not," he said.

"All right, let's give it another ten..." Enrique could see a begrimed city bus making its way to the corner and slowly coming to a stop, the folding doors opening and allowing passengers to disembark in a darkening night. He leaned forward, blinking a little to focus into the gloom. It looked like Alena was getting off with two little girls, each one holding her hand, skipping and hopping and pulling their mother toward home.

"There's Alena!" he said.

Enrique could feel Bill watching him through the rearview mirror. Hunger and nerves warred in his heart, along with a fair amount of pride.

"What is your plan?" Bill asked. There was complete silence in the cab.

"I have been gone for nine months," Enrique answered, "nine months and twelve days, to be precise. I am sure they will be happy to see me."

"And you are just going to jump them here on the sidewalk, after all that time?" Bill asked quietly. "You plan on getting your face slapped?"

"They'll be happy to see me," Enrique said again, fully convinced.

Enrique could see Bill's eyes staring at him in the mirror. They were alive, boring into his doubts. The girls skipped in circles, the streetlights turning on in the dark as they made their way down the sidewalk toward him.

47

"What? What do you know about anything?" Enrique said, clipping every word into a razor-sharp thrust. Still Bill watched in the mirror and Alena and the girls came closer. They could hear the chatter of the little girls through the window now. Enrique couldn't take his eyes from the trio. Finally, Enrique could stand no more. He threw open the cab door and stepped out onto the sidewalk. The girls' chatter stopped abruptly, and Alena pulled them in closer to her. Enrique stood in the shadows for a heartbeat or more and then ducked back into the backseat of the cab and shut the door firmly.

What was I thinking? Enrique raged at himself. The girls continued cautiously on their way. The cab was silent as they watched Alena usher the girls up the sidewalk. Onto the sagging front porch and using multiple keys to open the door, the girls disappeared into the safety of the little house. Lights flared on as they scattered about inside.

"Well, that was a bust," Enrique said.

"A man has to have a plan, that's all I'm saying," Bill said.

"I am done with running away, and I want to come back, if she still wants me. I will never leave them again." Enrique meant every word.

"Well, showing up without warning and wanting commitment from them without giving anything in return sounds like a taker and just another problem for that pretty girl to solve. If I were you, I would try being the man instead. I would do something to make her life better, right away, tonight." Bill turned the key in the ignition, pulled away from the curb, and continued pointedly: "Where to?"

"I'm thinking," Enrique said, and he was. They pulled up to a stop sign. Down the street to the right was a grocery store. Not nearly enough. That grimy city bus passed them by, and with that in his sights, he knew what to do. "Pull down here to the right," he said. "I remember seeing a car dealership just a few blocks before we pulled into their neighborhood. Maybe they are still open."

Bill grinned into the rear view mirror, pulled onto the main drag through town, and said, "Now you're talking sense."

An hour later, Enrique sent Bill home to his daughter. "Thanks for helping me see what's what," he said.

Enrique handed Bill a bundle of bills for all his help that day, and with a quick handshake they parted. Bill pulled out of the parking lot in his cab and Enrique drove the newly leased SUV back to the little yellow house, parking again in front of it. He picked up a paper cone cradling the daisies Bill had insisted he buy at the corner grocery store and breathed in the hope they represented. Picking up the all-important backpack as well, he slung it over his shoulder and let himself through the sagging metal gate that led to the steps of the porch. He knocked softly on the door, a reassuring knock, and waited patiently. His earlier pride was subdued. He'd knocked softly on the door and waited on the mercy of his family.

He could hear someone through the pitiful hollow-core door; there was no peek hole. "Alena?" he said. "It's me."

There was no answer, but he heard a bolt being thrown back, a chain rattling still in place, and saw his black-eyed Alena peering through the crack at him. He smiled at her through sudden tears, his desperate emotion at seeing her warring with his worry that she would send him away. She didn't have an answering smile for him, those serious black eyes weighing, thinking, and the door closed without her saying one single word. Hope collapsed with that decisive click, but how could he walk away? He leaned his forehead against the door and felt his fever again in the coolness of the wood.

The seconds ticked by and he turned, laying the flowers in a forlorn arrangement on the porch where she would be sure to see them in the morning. He walked to the edge of the porch. He stopped, imagining the sound of the chain rattling against the front door. But then the door rattled again and he turned to see it burst open.

Alena ran to him, throwing herself into his arms and holding him. "Oh, my Rique," she said, over and over.

It was many minutes before they disentangled themselves and he got to hold his little girls, but he never let go of Alena's hand. He talked to the girls and answered their questions, but his eyes never let go of Alena. It was over an hour before he came to his senses and remembered the force that was certainly out probing for his whereabouts. They were packed and driving away from the curb in thirty-five minutes.

"Anything left in the dryer?" he asked Alena as they packed the car. "Do we have their favorite stuffed animals?" She shook her head sharply yes.

"Why are we leaving? Are you in trouble?" she asked, looking at him with concern. The two little girls, mimicking their mother's grave face, looked at him with mournful eyes, waiting to hear the bad news.

"I'll tell you everything once the little ones are asleep; you need to know everything," Enrique promised.

They found an obscure, quiet motel and registered as Mr. and Mrs. Garcia. He paid in cash. There was a little diner next door; they ordered and took the food back to the motel to eat. Suri was drooping before too long and Sophia was yawning as well.

"Can I put them to bed?" Enrique asked. Alena just smiled and squeezed his hand.

Enrique tucked the girls into a huge king-size bed. "Tell us a story, Papa!" they pled, laying little girl heads in the crook of his shoulders. He relished their closeness and began telling them a story about his papa while they still lived in Panama.

"When I was a boy, we lived in the smallest little village, right on the edge of the jungle. Monkeys would sometimes swoop down from the trees and take treasures from our yard. Butterflies as large as my hand lived there too. There was also an old jaguar that roamed the hills near our village, and when we were naughty, our grandmother liked to scare us by warning us of El Jaco, the cat.

"Late one summer night, when the moon and the humming of insects were keeping small boys from sleep, El Jaco walked boldly into our village. He slunk into our neighbor's hut and stole out with their small baby, taking him from his cradle. El Jaco was black as night and nobody saw his raid. It wasn't long before the mother found the empty cradle, her wail curdling the tranquil night and continuing until the men of the village organized themselves to track down the huge cat.

"His paws were easily the size of salad plates, and he was crafty and stringy and mean. The men spent the night tracking El Jaco. Papa was slightly ahead of the rest when a blinding blackness moved on the trail, and the cat's glowing eyes appeared before him, his mouth still lightly carrying the baby in a bundle in his teeth. El Jaco turned and Papa taunted the huge jaguar, drawing his yellow-eyed attention, while the rest of the men spread out and surrounded the cat.

"El Jaco dropped the baby in the tangled roots of a mango tree and leaped through the air to attack his pursuer. He knocked Papa to the earth, a rumble deep in his chest. Papa let out his own warrior call right back as he felt El Jaco's heated breath on his face. With an angry lunge, he thrust a knife deep into the ancient heart and immediately felt its life drain out.

"The men of the village had to lift the monster off Papa. They laid the baby in Papa's arms and celebrated their way home to return the baby to his mother. I was with the women and children of the village, and we heard them coming for a mile. We waited at the edge of the road, surrounding the mother of the baby. Though we heard the singing and jubilation, no one dared hope until they caught the howl of the hungry child on the wind.

"My mama kissed Papa's wounds, deep gashes from fetid claws. She cleaned them and bound them with calico. My papa wore the bright bandages for several weeks and was the bravest guardian of our village. He is still my hero."

Enrique finished the story while two little girls burrowed into his chest, sound asleep. He slipped out from the bed and covered them to their chins with a thick blanket. Turning to leave, he found Alena watching at the darkened doorway.

Enrique pulled Alena from the room and held her close, leaning on the back of the couch. He breathed in her scent and felt her hair brush against his chin. When she reached up and put her hands against the sides of his face he opened his eyes and looked into the dark pools of her eyes. A quiet but forceful love was in them, a bottomless, fathomless force. He didn't deserve it, but it fed his soul and cheered his broken heart. As he leaned down to her and kissed her, she tightened her hold on him and held him with all her might.

"I missed you every minute," Alena said softly. "I didn't know if I would ever see you again. Tell me everything, please, Rique."

Enrique started at the beginning: living on the streets, entombing himself in a drunken numbness, Mr. Lord talking him into checking himself into rehab and tackling the echoing memories of that last battle.

"You were right to throw me out," he said, "and I promise you right now that I am done with hiding from that war. I am here to be a husband again and a father to Sophia and Suri. If there are horrors to face, we will do it together." Alena looked at him seriously, watching him, searching him. Everything burned deep in Alena and her happiness was all bound up in two little girls and a certain warrior that wouldn't quit trying.

"Now, I want you to tell me, why you were riding that bus? Did you get rid of the car?" Enrique asked with hesitation, not wanting to hear all the reasons his leaving made her life harder.

"That devil car!" she exclaimed. "He never will start, and if he does, he tries to buck me off, lurching and throwing us all over the city! He is parked at Sam's place, and we ride the bus. Sam wanted me to sell the car, but I wanted you to come home and take us for rides. You are the only one who tames him." Alena picked up her purse, and pulling out a key chain, she took two off and handed them to Enrique. "Here is the key to the garage, *mi amor*, and one for the devil himself. Sophie can stay home from school tomorrow and we can—" She saw him shake his head. "Can't you stay?" she questioned.

"Alena." Enrique loved her name, loved the way it sounded coming from his mouth, and when he pled with her, it was with a caress. "I have a job to do, it should take me a week or so, but I have to leave soon. It is for Mr. Lord and I owe him. We owe him plenty."

"Can you stay tonight and start tomorrow?" Alena asked.

"If I stay, I'm afraid I'll never leave," he said. Then he told her all that had happened at the library. "Once I knew where you lived I couldn't stay away, but I might be putting you all in some danger. Can you miss work until I come back? Sophie can stay home from school. We'll be moving schools anyway once this is over. Right?" Enrique couldn't regret finding them first, but they would have to be careful.

Alena had listened thoughtfully. "Who are these women you need to find? What about them is so dangerous?" she asked.

Enrique shrugged. "I asked that myself, and I not sure that even Mr. Lord knows. I can quit. He can find someone else."

"Well," she said, "it's only a week. We can pretend we are on vacation, this place is nice enough. We can live in the pool and watch movies and eat popcorn. And we have a car I can actually drive! We'll manage. Just don't forget to come home when you are done."

Enrique gathered her close and just held on. "Let me tell the girls goodbye then," he said, and pulled away. In their hotel beds, piled with stuffed animals and books, two little girls slept. Long black hair fanned the pillows, and Suri had her thumb in her mouth. He brushed a kiss on both little cheeks, and as he turned to leave, Sophia called out to him, "Daddy, are you going away again?"

"Not for long," he answered. "Is it okay if I come back to be with you and Suri and Mommy?" Sophia, half asleep, answered him as she turned over in her bed and drifted back into her dreams, "Only if you bring us a kitten." He heard her breathing deepen and he slipped out of their room. *A kitten!* he thought. *The price of redemption is a kitten!*

Alena let him go, but hung onto his hand until he walked out the hotel door. "See you in a week," he promised.

Enrique jogged the four miles to Sam's house in the dark. He needed to get in and out without talking to his brother-in-law. There would be words eventually between them, but now was not the time to fight over Alena's honor. Sam would need a long afternoon and enough space to pace and thump Enrique's chest a few times. There would be some hollering and yelling about leaving his sister, he would need to get it all out of his system before they could be friends again, but Enrique didn't have the time right now. So he was going to sneak away with his car tonight.

It wasn't easy getting into the garage carrying a sixty-pound battery without waking the dog. More important, he didn't want to chance waking Sam; they could talk it all out next week. He fumbled to find the keyhole, but once he did the door opened quietly. He found the light switch by the door, flipped them on, and found his prized car, a Dover white '69 Z28, still covered with a dusty gray painter's cloth. He was lucky Sam had pretty much left it alone.

There were ladders leaning against the car and paint buckets and a few tools piled on the hood. Enrique cleared the rubbish away and carefully pulled the tarp off the lovingly restored car. He used the sleeve of his cotton jacket to wipe off dust covering the hugger orange stripes on the hood. The car was originally ordered to match the 1969 Indy 500 Pace car, and played a significant role in Enrique's former life.

Enrique reached under the seat, his hand feeling for a small metal gun safe and hoping it was still tucked away. It had shifted farther under the seat but he groped until he felt a hard corner. It was heavy as he pulled it forward, out from under the seat, and pressing a finger to the lock, the safe recognized his fingerprint and opened. The pistol was still inside.

It only took a few turns of a wrench to take out the dead battery and replace it with a new one. Closing the hood of the car, he stood in the silence for a moment, listening for any noise from his brother-in-law's house.

The car turned over without firing the first time he cranked it, and then the engine caught and the 30/30 roller cam hummed its familiar tune. It was clear she was as anxious as Enrique to run a street again.

"I hope I don't need this," Enrique thought as he pushed the gun box back under the seat.

He rubbed a hand over the seat and could feel the herringbone pattern playing over his fingertips and remembered when this car used to mean everything to him. Then he rolled through the gears with the clutch in to feel them tumble. Oh, yeah; it would do.

Raising the garage door was an eerie task. The screeching and groaning of rusty hinges could have raised the dead. Enrique heard Sam's dog wake up and begin to growl and lunge at the back door of the house, but either Sam worked nights or was an extremely sound sleeper. Porch lights were coming on up and down the street as the neighbors heard the racket, but Enrique backed out of the garage, put the car in neutral, and set the brake so he could pull the garage door down. He hurried, and jumped back in the driver's seat like a fighter pilot in his cockpit, gripped the shifter, turned on the headlights, and raced through the Chevy's gears until there was nothing left to see but red taillights at the end of a dark, quiet street. This time he was running toward something instead of away from his fears. He was an hour away from the beginning of a challenge. It would take him a week, and then he had a family he needed to get home to.

CHAPTER 10

In London, as dawn crept over the horizon, David and Camryn juggled keys as they pointed the clicker at parked cars along the streets of Mayfair. They had searched their felled policeman, but his pockets had been sanitized before he had come to finish off David. No wallet, no I.D., no receipts: all they found was his badge number and a set of keys, so they searched the streets for his car while he was safely tied up in Aunt Marge's sitting room.

On the third street over, they finally got a response to their continued pressing of the little button. The lights of a car chirruped and the doors unlocked. The car was spotless, as cleaned out as the man's pockets had been. They put the keys under the driver's seat and locked and closed the doors. David wrote down the license number in case they could track him with the police, and they called the deed done.

Camryn was yawning and fighting sleep as they turned back to the apartment to track down Aunt Marge's old red Bentley. It was parked in a lot behind the apartment. They loaded Camryn's suitcase and David's borrowed gym bag into the trunk. One tire looked low, but the car started right up, and they drove away.

"So," said Camryn, breaking the silence, "what in heaven's name is going on?"

David looked over at her, leaning against the elegant old car's interior. "I am going to tell you everything I know," he said, "but that isn't much. Your brother didn't have time to tell me the whole story, but I think there is a letter somewhere in his office that will explain why he was desperate for me to come over so quickly. You've been to visit Roger at work. Do you think we will be able to get into his office?"

"Most of the guards at Clarence House treat me like their little sister, so I think they will let me in to clean out his personal belongings, and I'll take you along as my driver," she said, clearly making it up as she went along. "We need a place to stay until we can get some time in Roger's office, then," she continued. She closed her eyes, and with a weary smile, her eyes popped open. She looked around, and pointing at the intersection, she said, "Turn right here and make your first left."

David worked his way through the mounting morning traffic, and they found themselves in a small courtyard in front of a discreetly elegant building, announcing itself as the Dukes Hotel.

"Let me out here and I'll be right back," Camryn said.

"It says 'no waiting,'" David protested. "And won't I need to surrender my passport? My picture is all over the news."

He was working himself into a slight panic. But the door was shut and Camryn was climbing lightly up the front steps, cool and elegant. A liveried doorman opened the door and escorted her to the front desk. David watched as she talked to the desk clerk, who tapped on computer keys and then picked up the phone and spoke for a minute. Camryn watched with studied attention. He could hear traffic outside the little courtyard; London was waking up. "Come on, come on," David tried to hurry her. A car turned the corner and moved into place behind him, drawing unwanted attention to the illegal parking job.

Come on! he thought. Finally, the clerk paused in his tapping and fished out a key, handing it to her with a flourish. Watching in his rearview mirror, a uniformed guard approached the car parked behind him, gesturing vehemently at the 'no waiting' sign. He slouched a bit in his seat. *Camryn!*

As he watched in the mirror, the guard watched the other car pull away. David put the Bentley into drive and watched his side mirror, ready to make his move. He glanced one more time at the hotel doors.

Just then Camryn stepped through the glass doors, escorted by the desk clerk.

"I'm sorry, sir, I didn't think I would be so long." She took the guard's hand and let him lecture her about minding the rules. She smiled sunnily at him and walked him away from the car. David relaxed and slouched a bit more. Camryn let herself into the car.

"That was close," she said. "But we have a room!" She seemed a bit drained by maintaining the façade of cheerfulness. "A friend of mine works here and he comped us a room. It won't be on the books, so we can hide out until tomorrow, I think. Tonight is a reception of some sort at Clarence House. Roger was invited and he insisted I attend with him. He promised to come personally up to Lancashire and drag me to London if I didn't get here on my own. So I was included on the invitation, although I have the feeling that the invitation is sitting on the mantel in Aunt Marge's sitting room right now, and how we will get it, I couldn't begin to tell you. Roger's office is right off the main entrance at Clarence House, but I'll bet his keys are at the morgue." Camryn leaned her head back against the headrest and spoke once more with her eyes closed, fatigue written all over her expression. "This is all going to work out, isn't it? Let's park, and you can tell me what 'this' is."

He couldn't help but want to protect Camryn from the brutality of what had happened to her brother. He watched her cope as they pulled around to the back of the hotel and turned their car keys over to a valet. The room was a suite at the top of the hotel with a rooftop terrace and a view of St. James Park. Usually reserved by visiting dignitaries, it was not used much during the week and was regularly comped by the hotel during the week to favored guests and special friends.

"Okay, David Lord." Camryn sat on a brilliantly white love seat, picked up the phone, and curled her legs up on the cushions. "You can tell me everything, about Roger and, well, everything. Are you hungry?"

It wasn't quite dawn, but she ordered a huge breakfast and then sat back into the pristine cushions and waited. Sitting in the stillness for a moment opened the floodgates of sorrow. The reality of Roger's death finally seemed to catch up to her. David sat quietly and let the heartache have its way. He would have taken her hand, but the ring on her finger acted as an arctic shield, pricking his inclination to ignore that fact that she was married.

"What is your husband's name?" David finally asked.

Camryn looked at him, and the anguish welling out of her stormy gray eyes was painful to look on. He closed his eyes against the emotion. "Sorry," he said. "I withdraw the question."

"Will you sit by me?" Camryn asked. "It will be easier to listen if I don't have to watch you tell it." She patted the seat cushion and moved over a bit to make some room.

"All right, stop me when you have had enough." Camryn nodded and David continued. "Roger called me just two days ago. He asked me to come and said he needed my skills to solve a mystery. I figured that someone was fiddling with the Crown's accounts, and they needed an outsider to look at the books. Since we'd just finished a huge project in New York, my people were scattering for a thoroughly deserved vacation, and it was the perfect time for me to take off, so I left that evening. I landed in London yesterday morning and met Roger near his office.

"It was curious, but from the moment we met I knew that something was off. He kept looking over his shoulder, and then he took me on a tour bus instead of meeting me at the office or somewhere for breakfast. Something was wrong, and he mentioned a couple of times that I would be in danger if I helped him. He told me that some sort of letter was delivered to the office that could stir up a firestorm of trouble. He needed an outsider to track down sixteen women. All of them had traveled or immigrated to the States in 1980. He wanted me to find them and check to see if any of them had a child born that next year, and if they had a child, he wanted me to go so far as to get a DNA sample.

"He also asked me to find a stone, the Stone of Scone. He wanted me to find out if the stone known as the Coronation Stone is genuine or a fake. He didn't give me much to go on and it didn't seem like that one task had anything to do with the other, but they must be connected in some way. Roger was worried and anxious for me to get started. He intimated that there might be those willing to kill to keep this information hidden. He did indicate that the letter that launched this adventure is somewhere in his office, and he wanted me to read it. I'm sure Roger's office has been searched by investigators by now, but we have to try to find it or we will never know what we are really looking for and why." David paused.

Camryn sniffed and dragged her sleeve across her damp eyes and runny nose. She moved a little and tucked her feet under David's leg; they were chilled. If she were just his best friend's sister and not a woman that made his blood sing, he would have held those feet and warmed them, but all he could do was scold himself into remembering she was married. He held himself still for a minute. Her lightest touch set his heart galloping off on some headlong journey that he didn't control in the least.

"Okay, I'm ready. Tell me about the rest," Camryn finally said, and David took a deep breath and continued.

"Well, Roger and I got off the bus near the apartment. We walked a ways together, still talking, and at a corner, we waited in a crowd for the light to change. A car pulled up to the curb, and that policeman got out. I will never forget his face. He shot at us. His first shot hit me in the chest. My shirt is scorched, but somehow, he hit something that deflected the bullet. The second shot hit Roger.

"I don't know how they found us, maybe they were tracking Roger's phone, maybe we will never know, but they knew where we were and drove right up to us.

"Anyway, I tried to help Roger, but with his last breath he told me to run. Out of pure instinct I got away from there, but I have replayed that moment again and again, and I am not sure I did the right thing. Instead, he is gone, and I am not sure how to move forward or even if it is important now." David grew quiet. Camryn's sleeve was now a sodden mess.

It seemed a tremendous effort but Camryn straightened and opened her eyes. With quiet deliberation she said, "Well, we aren't going to let that man get away with shooting my brother and blaming you. Even if we can't figure out all that Roger wanted, we have to go on and figure out why Roger is dead and why they are after you. Whoever 'they' are."

They heard an elevator ting and a trolley in the hall. David didn't open the door until after peering out the peephole and deciding it was just their breakfast. He turned off the overhead lights to cloak his features and opened the door. The trolley was filled with dishes and a stack of *Daily Telegraph* newspapers sitting in one corner, David's picture above the fold. Dipping his head, David scrawled a signature on the bill, adding a substantial tip to the total. He avoided the gaze of the bellhop and carefully locked the door. When he finally wheeled the trolley back to the sitting room, Camryn was curled up on the loveseat, sound asleep.

CHAPTER 11

David was ravenous and ate all the pancakes and most of the fruit before slowing down and leaving the rest for later. It was about six in the morning. If they could get into the reception at Clarence House tonight and into Roger's office, if they could find this letter...a lot of ifs, but if they could manage to make this work, they might be able to figure out why Roger had set him on this course. And, in David's experience, if you could figure out the why, then who and what would line up right behind it.

He let Camryn sleep. There was nothing much to do until the reception anyway, and in wandering around the suite, he found his way onto the expansive rooftop terrace. The space covered much of the hotel roof. It had a huge hot tub and was covered with wooden decking. Outdoor furniture was placed in groupings looking over St. James and the city. Oversized white umbrella canopies were anchored to the floor and could be raised or lowered by remote control, to catch or block the weather. It was peaceful up in this aerie, with the sounds of the city waking up, a little muted at this altitude above the traffic. It was designed for privacy and relaxation, the perfect spot for some quick study.

Leaving the French doors open, he set up Camryn's laptop on a teak coffee table and watched the sun rise in inches over the city. The shadows shortened and faded as the morning sun painted London with light. He imagined Roger watching them from the throne of God.

"Help us if you can," he said into the heavens.

He started up the laptop and began his hunt at the very beginning. He started with how to spell the Stone of Scone, also known, as Roger had said, as the Stone of Destiny or the Coronation Stone. The chill morning air and the warmth of the new sun vied for supremacy on his skin as he settled in to read the story of this mysterious stone.

After a couple of hours of searching and reading, things were just getting interesting. He was beginning to understand how important the Stone of Scone was to Roger and to England. The story had many permutations, and it began long ago, before written history. It is generally believed that the stone, called Jacob's Pillow, was a part of Hebrew history and that the stone came with the descendants of Jacob to Ireland and was then given to their kinsmen the Scots to establish their right to rule in Scotland.

According to official Irish history, the true Lia Fáil never left Ireland for Scotland. They say that the true stone is a large pillar stone that still stands on Tara in Ireland. The stone in Scotland is either a portion of the original Lia Fáil or another stone taken to Scotland as a symbolic gesture of the growing power of the Dál Riata dynasty, the stone is said to be shaped like a chair or a seat.

In spite of official records, it is generally believed that the Stone of Destiny was given to Scotland to be used in their sacred coronation rites. The stone was then stolen by the English King Edward I 700 years ago. With it still a powerful symbol of Scottish independence, many people believe that King Edward stole a false stone from Scone. The real stone was switched out by the monks that knew he was coming. The genuine Coronation Stone was hidden in the wilds of Scotland, the knowledge of the location lost as the monks died off, the secret carried to their graves.

To add another twist to the story, the coronation stone taken to London by Edward was stolen on Christmas Day in 1950. A group of four young Scottish separatists took the stone from Westminster Abbey, planning to return it to Scotland. They broke in a side door of Westminster Abbey, and during the theft, the stone broke into two pieces. After burying the greater part of the stone in a Kent field, they camped for a few days, waiting for the heat of the search to cool down. When they felt it was safe they uncovered the buried stone and returned to Scotland. The broken stone was passed to a senior Glasgow politician, who arranged for it to be repaired by a stonemason.

A search for the stone was conducted by the British government, but they were unsuccessful. The students eventually left the stone on the altar of Arbroath Abbey on 11 April 1951, in the symbolic care of the Church of Scotland. London police were contacted and the stone was returned to Westminster four months after it was taken. Afterward, rumors circulated that copies had been made, and that the stone returned to the British was not the original.

Since the time of Edward I, the Scots have occasionally demanded that the stone be returned to them, and eventually, on St. Andrew's Day, 30 November 1996, the supposed Coronation Stone, the Stone of Destiny, was given back to Scotland and installed in Edinburgh Castle. Much of the city lined the Royal Mile to watch the procession of dignitaries and troops escort the stone from Holyrood Palace to the castle. In a service at St. Giles' Cathedral, the Right Reverend John MacIndoe formally accepted the stone, saying it would "strengthen the proud people of Scotland."

Once inside the castle, the stone was placed on a table sitting in the Great Hall. The Scottish Secretary of State then officially received it from Prince Andrew, who represented the Queen.

Outside the castle, a twenty-one-gun salute was fired from Half-Moon Battery. And the celebration began. The Scots celebrated the return of the symbol of their nation, but it was returned conditionally. The Scots had been compelled to promise that the British crown could make use of the stone during future coronation ceremonies.

As helpful as it was to understand the confusion surrounding the more recent history of the Coronation Stone, David was anxious to research the beginning of the story of the Pillow of Jacob.

The beginning of the story is ancient history. The importance of the stone to those who possessed it is hard to imagine. The mere possession of it was used throughout the ages to support kings and kingdoms. But, although the stories shifted and changed with almost every teller, the beginning was the same, every time.

It began in the dusty, rocky plains of Israel. Everything in that land began with Abraham and quickly moved on to Isaac and then to Jacob. Of course, Ishmael had his role to play.

Isaac, Abraham's son, and Rebekah, Isaac's wife, had suffered through twenty years of marriage without having children when, like Sarah, Rebekah found herself with child at last. Rebekah inquired of the Lord and was told that there were twins in her womb, wrestling. They would continue the fight all their lives and their children would carry on after them.

She was told that from her two sons would spring two great nations and those nations would contend with each other. The prophecy also said that "the elder shall serve the younger." At birth, Jacob was born with his hand grasping Esau's heel. As the eldest, Esau claimed the birthright as his inheritance.

From the days of Adam, in much of the world, the firstborn son received this birthright or an extra portion of the division of the family inheritance. This inheritance is what Esau sold to Jacob for a bowl of pottage when he returned hungry from hunting. Esau gave up the extra portion of his inheritance for a single bowl of red bean stew. This is why it is written, "And thus Esau despised his birthright."

In addition to the added inheritance, the eldest child could also be given the patriarchal right, the right to govern the family after the father dies. This blessing was not always bestowed on the eldest, but generally he would receive this right and responsibility. So, when Rebekah was told by God that "the elder shall serve the younger," she interpreted it to mean that Jacob would receive the right to rule. In the womb, before birth, the Lord had designated Jacob to receive the birthright, but as Isaac grew old and blind, he was wont to bestow the blessing on Esau. Isaac asked Esau to make a dish of the savory meat that he loved, and then he would bless him. Esau went to the hills to hunt, but Rebekah overheard the conversation and instructed Jacob to take two goats from the herd and bring them to her. She would make the savory meat that Isaac loved and Jacob would receive the blessing.

There was clearly subterfuge involved, since they tricked a blind and elderly Isaac into thinking that Jacob was Esau and Jacob received the birthright blessing. But they weren't beguiling God, who had pronounced that Jacob was to receive the blessing of governing.

Soon after Jacob had departed his father's tent, Esau returned with the meat properly prepared, and Isaac realized that he had been tricked. So, Rebekah sent Jacob out of his brother's reach, to her brother's house in Haran. This is where the stone first gains its importance in the annals of history.

Jacob stopped for the night at a place called Luz or Bethel on the way to Haran and "took of the stones of that place and put them for his pillows, and lay down to sleep.

"And he dreamed, and beheld a ladder set up on the earth, and the top of it reached to heaven and beheld the angels of God ascending and descending on it.

"And, behold, the Lord stood above it, and said: 'I am the Lord God of Abraham thy father, and the God of Isaac. The land whereon thou liest, to thee will I give it, and to thy seed (his children).

"'And thy seed shall be as the dust of the earth, and thou shalt spread abroad to the west, and to the east, and to the north, and to the south. And in thee and in thy seed shall all the families of the earth be blessed.

"'And, behold, I am with thee, and will keep thee in all places whither thou goest, and will bring thee again into this land. For I will not leave thee, until I have done that which I have spoken to thee of.'"

When Jacob awoke out of his sleep, he said, "Surely the Lord is in this place." He was afraid, and said, "This is the gate of heaven." Jacob took the stone that he had used for his pillow and set it up for a pillar and poured holy anointing oil upon the top of it.

So, in 1950 BC, almost 2000 years before Christ, a man made his bed on a rock and dreamed of his God and heaven. He called the rock the gate of heaven. His family kept the stone for the next thirty-eight centuries as a reminder of the promises made to their father Jacob.

It became a symbolic throne and provided water in the desert; it became the symbol of the right path and the coming of a deliverer. It traveled with them for forty years in the wilderness and was preserved and brought with them to Ireland, taken to Scotland, and finally to England. Some experts believe the stone came to Ireland by way of the north, Scandinavia. Others track it coming through Spain and the Strait of Gibraltar. But regardless, the Coronation Stone of England is thought to be the most sacred stone of the Hebrew nation.

Irish legend says that the stone would roar with joy when the rightful king stood or sat on it. One tradition states that the stone Jacob used for his pillow at Bethel was then set up as a pillar, and it became the pedestal of the Ark in the Temple of Solomon in Jerusalem. But that was just one act in the history of this sacred stone.

The blaring of a siren down on the streets below pulled David away from the ancient land of Israel and back to London. Leaving the land of caravans and patriarchs behind, he got up and stretched his back, stiff from sitting in one place too long.

He looked down to the street at the front of the hotel, cautious about any sign of police activity and curious about the siren. The police car had moved down to the end of the street and turned the corner, harmless this time. David glanced at his watch: it was nearly two in the afternoon.

As he turned to go back to his research, a blinding glint drew his eye back to the street and he thought he saw an antique red car turning the corner at the light down the way. There couldn't be two of those vehicles in all of London, let alone on this stretch of the road.

David packed up the laptop and pushed the button on the remote to lower the umbrella shade. As the mechanical device retracted, it shimmied and shook, like it wasn't quite fastened correctly, but gradually it deflated. David quickly moved through the open patio doors and checked the hotel room. The television was turned on, muted, to the cable news. Camryn was gone.

CHAPTER 12

Worried, David checked the suite for a note. She hadn't left anything for him, but her luggage was still on one of the beds. *Maybe she saw something that spooked her*, he thought. *But why would she leave without telling me? Surely she isn't afraid of me again?*

Watching the television while contemplating all the reasons why Camryn would leave without talking to him, he noticed that the murder of Roger was no longer the running highlight at the bottom of the screen and his picture wasn't shown as the top story of the moment.

It would be a good time to catch up with Enrique; it was still morning in the States and he could use the hotel phone. He dialed the States and listened to it ring.

"Enrique!" he said when the call was connected. "What is that racket? Can you hear me?"

"Mr. Lord, can you hear me now?" The din faded somewhat. "I'm watching the *Times* roll off the presses right now. A friend from the army let me bunk here last night. We are going to run current addresses on these women this morning. I should be able to start seeing them in person after lunch, the ones in New York at least. My search yesterday stirred up a storm like you wouldn't believe. I did a reverse search on the call that went out to summon the police to the library and found that it was a terror alert, and it came from London. Someone from SO14. We aren't terrorists, are we? We aren't fighting a government, are we?" Enrique tried to talk above the machinery static.

David answered, frustrated, "I was hoping that you would escape notice, but for whatever reason, I have stumbled into that same kind of trouble here too. You might well find me a murder suspect in this morning's news. I am going to try to get access to my friend's office tonight; if luck is on our side, we will have better information tomorrow. You should probably change phones. Find some burner phones and send me the numbers."

Enrique answered, "The email address I gave you is encrypted, which won't keep out a determined hacker, but if we are careful, we can use it for a while. Try to remember that the NSA has access to whatever we say. I'll pick up some phones and shoot you the numbers."

"Stay safe, Enrique."

"You too, Mr. Lord."

David hung up and watched the clock for a minute. It was almost three, and Camryn was still AWOL.

He grabbed his overnight bag and went into the vast master bathroom. The shower had several heads. The towels were huge, white like the rest of the suite. He figured out how to turn on the shower hot enough to billow steam. He pulled off his shirt and examined the blooming bruise on his chest, a bother enough to remind him of the shot that thumped him in his chest yesterday, that shattered his cell phone but didn't even draw blood.

I wonder where I put that medal, he asked himself. Rummaging through the bag, his fingers found the metal disk quickly. It was as he remembered it, with a dent that burrowed a ridge through it from top to bottom. This disk was truly a lucky talisman. After a win against Yale his sophomore year he had made sure it was in his pocket during every one of the Harvard rowing meets; the whole team considered it their team's lucky coin. And now it had deflected a bullet and saved his life.

Stepping into the piping-hot shower, he let the water beat against his bruised body. His jet-lagged, bullet-punched, pepper-sprayed, wearied muscles absorbed the heat. He adjusted the water to a pummel and let it beat up and down his skin. After he felt his muscles finally relax, he washed his hair and figured out how to turn all the faucets off. Unfolding one of the huge towels and drying off, as the dripping water slowed and quiet returned to the bathroom, he could hear someone moving around in the hotel room.

He dressed silently, shook his wet hair, and opened the door into the hotel room. With heightened senses and a vivid remembrance of present danger, he moved quietly. He hoped that Camryn had returned, or a maid, but it could be the police if the porter delivering the food had recognized him this morning. David paused at the threshold and listened. Someone was walking, but quietly, stealthily.

He left the shelter of the doorway and turned to the right, walking barefoot and without making noise, making his way into the main room. No one was there. There was another bedroom, and David silently opened the door, standing to one side. A quick tour of the room and bathroom revealed no intruder, but a tuxedo and formal dress were hanging in the closet. Camryn had returned.

He found her on the terrace. "Where have you been?" David asked.

She grinned and held out an elaborate envelope, a corporate-embossed packet. It looked like an overdone wedding invitation.

"You went back to the apartment? You could have been killed!" he exclaimed. "Of all the mad, witless, addled, brave...," David sputtered at her. Her grin just got bigger and brighter.

"It was all that," she said. "I woke up, and you weren't in the room. When I saw you so absorbed in your research, I decided that we would need to get this invitation sometime today, and really, the sooner the better."

"You're a daredevil," David said, almost to himself. "And tell me why you didn't invite me along? Why didn't you leave a note?"

"The keys were just sitting there tempting me, so I grabbed them and drove over. The apartment is just as we left it. There is a rabid policeman still tied up in Aunt Marge's sitting room. I think I woke him up and he raged at me when I took the invitation from the mantle. Completely unhinged," Camryn said.

"Do you think he knows what it was you went back for? Would he have been able to read the envelope?" David asked.

Camryn shrugged. "Come and see what else I brought." And with a crook of her finger, she disappeared down into the hotel room. He followed, wondering how much further she had tempted fate. Standing in front of the closet, she pointed out the black tuxedo and a dress made of the palest of blues. Pointing to the tux, she said, "You can wear this tonight."

"Oh, and one more thing." She paused dramatically and pulled out some barber's clippers. "We need to disguise you a bit. You will have to trust me to cut your hair. I used to practice on my dolls."

David let out a skeptical snort.

"Really!" Camryn said. She looked closely at his hair. "Shorter should just about do it."

"Okay, where do you want me to sit?" David asked.

"Aren't you afraid of my barbering skills?" Camryn asked, amused.

"If you mess up, we'll just shave it all off," David answered, completely unworried about the fate of his hair.

"Sit here in the kitchenette, then, and I'll see what I can do." Camryn held out a towel, and once he was sitting, she wrapped him up and combed out his still-damp hair. With sisterly ease, she tilted his head this way and that, combing out the snarls and parting it here and there, all the while commenting and carrying on a one-sided conversation. David, however, found to his distress that he couldn't speak.

With her first touch, his heart began cavorting. His blood was pounding in his veins, and although he heard the murmur of her voice, he couldn't pay attention to any single word she uttered.

This has got to stop! he lectured himself silently. *She will never be yours, she belongs to some aristocratic warrior. GET A GRIP!* For all the good it did, he might as well have told himself not to breathe; his heart was singing, his blood was dancing, and he couldn't think straight.

Without warning, David stood. He took Camryn's arms and held them still.

"Please, can I just catch my breath for a minute?" he asked, too politely.

She looked at him, comprehension dawned, and she nodded. He moved to the counter and leaned against it and looked at the floor. David continued the internal lecture until his blood slowed and his hearing returned. Gingerly, he sat back in his chair. Camryn started combing and cutting, carefully keeping her distance and without the carefree chatter of before.

In silence, his hair was cut. The heavy black curls fell to the kitchen floor, the squeak of Camryn's shoes and the rasp of the scissors the only sounds that broke the stillness. Finally, she combed it out, making a few adjustments around the ears, and then she unwrapped the towel and brushed off his neck.

"Well, it isn't much of a disguise, but you look a little older and a lot wiser," she said, trying a light note.

"Thank you, Camryn, and not just for the haircut. You are a genius," David answered. "Have you looked at the invitation yet?"

"Dinner is at nine," she said, opening the invitation. "It says there will be dancing too, so with all the commotion, it should be easy for us to disappear and get into Roger's office. I found a spare key in the apartment."

"I don't really expect to find the letter just sitting in his office. I am sure it has been thoroughly searched by the authorities. But we have to try," David said. He found a mirror by the door and examined the haircut. "Not bad, for a Barbie scalper," he said with a weak little smile.

Chapter 13

Aggie E. Danforth
Alyce Eliza Woolen
Bailey Elizabeth Milford
Bernice Eli Dodge
Elizabeth Helen Lewis
Eleanor E. Miller
Eliza Cici O'Malley
Beverly Ella Ellsworth
Kalli Lizbet Ramsey
McKenzie E. Durrett
Liz Juliette Lawrence
Beth Maeve Larson
Paige Beth Newland
Eliza Poppy Barton
Violet E. Tennsdale
Tessa Lizzie McCellewan

Enrique's fever had finally broken during the night and he had spent the morning using the Times's vast resources, looking for the life stories of these sixteen women. They had all entered the US from England in the year 1980. They were all in their early twenties at that time. Two of them were married before they came over. The rest were single, and all but one had married subsequent to their arrival. Finding marriage records was the first hurdle to cross. Luckily, the Times carried most wedding announcements, college graduations, and local announcements for the area, and they kept great records.

They also had access to enormous amounts of information, used to investigate and report news of all kinds.

Two of the sixteen women had died, but he still needed to find out if there were any children born at the right time. Six had married and then divorced. One was in prison.

"Hey, Nixon, I'm about done here," Enrique said, over the clatter of machinery. "Let's go get something to eat before I take off."

"Sure," Nixon answered. "You want a gyro?" Brought up in New Jersey, Nixon had been born with a bad case of wanderlust and, as the oldest of seven kids, had no one to bankroll his dreams. He joined the reserves right after high school, worked at the Times on the loading dock until he was called up, and had been in Enrique's team early in the deployment to Iraq. After spending two years on the ground in Iraq, fighting the heat, the wind, and the sand along with the revolutionary guard, he had just wanted to get home to New York. He landed right back at the Times, and he was happy to stay put.

His office was a cubbyhole in the warehouse. It was small and rank, but it had the world's most comfortable couch and vending machines right outside the door stocked with candy bars and ice cream. Nixon ran the machines that ran the Times and wielded his power with military precision and a thick New Jersey accent.

"Something quick and I'm out of your hair," Enrique said.

Nixon ran both hands over his shaved scalp. "In a manner of speaking," he said. "Let me finish up here and we'll head down the street a ways and get the best gyro in the city. You can take off from there." Nixon was putting tools away and cleaning up the shop.

Enrique, idling outside the loading dock in the Z and waiting for Nixon, read through and studied his list of sixteen women. His world now relied on his absorbing the details of their lives down to the smallest element. He needed to find them, speak with each of them, and identify their children, if they had any. He would need to collect DNA, report, and turn it all over to Mr. Lord.

He started with the addresses listed on their immigration papers. Some would still be there, but most of them would have moved on, either with marriages or jobs. The inmate should be an easy one to find at home. First stop, seven addresses in New York City and the prison. It should take two days to find and talk to each one.

Nixon slid into the front seat. "Nice ride!" he said. "This is the car you and William rebuilt when we were on furlough? Did you really blueprint the engine?"

With a lurch of his heart, Enrique nodded. "That we did, and William lost his license street racing because of that engine. We had some great times before he got caught up in drugs and whatever. It was the war that did him in, no matter what else gets the blame."

"Sorry, Rique," Nixon said. "There's a Greek eatery right up the street. Take a right on Astoria and then try and find a place to park."

They pulled up to the restaurant. The long line of customers and the smell of meat roasting on a spit met them the instant they opened the car doors. They ordered, and when their plates arrived, they were piled high with roasted lamb, cucumbers, shredded lettuce, and feta spilling out of the pita bread. Eating those gyros was a two-fisted proposition. They tucked in and ate leaning over their plates. Nixon finished first, leaning back in his seat with his hands behind his head, watching Enrique clean up.

"So, Rique, you're on a mission? Are you going to need any backup or are you flying solo?" Nixon asked.

Enrique wiped his mouth, swallowed the last of the lamb, and said, "Do you keep in touch with any of the guys?"

"Yes, I do. Is there anyone in particular you want to talk to? You know, we all heard about the botched mission. You think you have to carry it all yourself?" Nixon asked, solemnly.

"I know, Nix. My head knows it perfectly. It is just my dreams that get me in trouble, and I can't stay awake forever. I tried, but all it got me was sick. I'm not hiding in a bottle anymore. That's something."

"The powers that be don't have a clue what they ask us to do when they decide for us all and drag us into a fight," Nixon said, a slow-simmering anger flushing his neck and ears. "Anyone that decides to start a war should be the first in line to go and fight it. It wouldn't happen often, and it wouldn't last long if the brass and politicians had to spend one single night sleeping on patrol."

"Well, all I know is it's a new day and I'm still breathing," Enrique said, to convince himself as much as his friend. "Let me drive you back to work. Is there a Best Buy or a Wal-Mart anywhere near here?"

A short hour later Enrique found himself the new owner of eight burner phones, a state-of-the-art GPS, and a topped-off gas tank.

Violet Tennsdale, one of the women, lived right in College Point, about forty miles from the little Greek eatery. He decided to drive over without tracking down a phone number and see if anyone was home. The neighborhood was wooded, with roads that wandered, paved-over cow trails without shoulders. The house was a comfortable tan cottage, with overgrown bushes and trees standing magisterially over the lot. There was an SUV in the driveway.

Enrique pulled in behind the car and made for the front door. He rang the doorbell and waited, listening to a dog barking wildly at the door and finally, footsteps. A woman of about twenty opened the door, her eyes red rimmed, dressed in a black pantsuit. The dog was nowhere in sight.

"Can you come around the back?" she said, tonelessly.

"Sure can," he answered, and he followed the sidewalk around the garage and waited by the back sliding door. The women in black slid the door wide and he stepped into the kitchen. The counter was covered with papers. He had been so focused on physically finding the women on the list that he had never thought about how he would get the information they needed. If Violet's family still owned this house, then this could be a daughter. It was hard to estimate her exact age, but, if he had to guess, she looked too young to be who he was looking for.

"Miss," he started, interrupting her as she began talking.

"My mother is just through here," she said.

How did she know he needed to speak to her mother? Thoroughly confused, Enrique started again.

"Miss, I'm looking for Violet Tennsdale," he tried again.

"Yes." She sniffed. "She is right through here." And she turned and walked through the doorway. Enrique followed her down the hall and into a nice bright living room, ending up in what should have been a small dining room, but it was filled with a hospital bed, a walker, and the odds and ends of an invalid occupant. Someone, he assumed it was Violet, lay on the bed with a beautiful patchwork quilt pulled up, covering her face. Enrique turned to the woman, the black clothing now making sense, and asked, point blank, "Is she deceased?"

The woman looked at him quizzically. "Aren't you here to take her body to the mortuary? You're not, are you?" Her voice rose and took on a little hysteria.

Oh, crap, Enrique thought, but remained calm. "Let's go back to your kitchen, ma'am, and I'll explain why I am here. I'm sorry about your... is it your mother?" The women nodded and then turned and walked stiffly back through the house, arms folded protectively across her chest.

"Who are you?" she demanded.

"My name is Enrique Gutierre and I was sent to find your mother." He tried to convey an officious, matter-of-fact manner. He took out a pen and small notebook from his pocket and waited for her to start talking.

"She just got home from the hospital yesterday, and when I came down this morning she was gone, dead!" she said, every word raw, new, and cruel.

"I am representing a party that has an interest in finding your mother and any heirs. I just have a few questions. It won't take long, and you may find that it is to your benefit to answer," Enrique said politely. He started right in to the questions, assuming her acquiescence. "I understand that your mother came from England in June of 1980, is that right?"

"I think that sounds right. I would have to check to make sure," she answered.

"Can I ask your name?" he asked, pen poised over the notebook.

She must have been reassured by his demeanor because she answered without hesitation. "Amy, my name is Amy Johnson. What is this about finding heirs?" Her interest was piqued.

Enrique said, "I've been sent to find out if your mother had any children that may answer the description I have been given. What year were you born?"

Amy was no longer hesitant about answering: "1989."

"Do you have any other siblings?" he asked.

"I have a brother born in '85 and a sister born in '86," she said.

"Do you know when your mother and father were married?" He was thinking on his feet.

Amy thought for a moment. "I believe they were married in 1985. They used to kid that my brother's birth was just barely respectable. He was born nine months after they were married."

"Perfect," Enrique said, "those dates are just what I came for. Did your mother have a sister or best friend I could speak with? Someone who would have known her well before her marriage?" What he didn't say was that he needed someone she would have confided in if she had discovered she was pregnant out of wedlock.

"Aunt Susie and Mom have been best friends since college," Amy said. "She is coming over this morning to be with me. I could call her and see if she could come over right now if you'd like?"

They waited in the kitchen. Enrique asked questions about her mother while they waited. Violet had been hospitalized for shock, no one knew what had brought it on, but the neighbors had found her wandering outside at one in the morning. She wasn't responsive, wouldn't talk to anyone about why she was outside in a robe and slippers at that time. She was released to her daughter and there was no indication that there was anything physically wrong with her, nothing to cause a sudden death like this. Her daughter was obviously confused, and the full extent of grief was being held at bay by the business of a funeral and all the arrangements to be made.

Soon enough there were signs that Susie had arrived. It seemed that the sound of a dog barking was a mechanical device meant to scare away troublemakers. She came around the back and through the slider, without knocking. She gathered Amy in a hug and held her; motioning to Enrique to sit tight, she took Amy upstairs and, after a bit of knocking about, came back downstairs alone.

Susie sat heavily on a kitchen chair. "Amy said that you are searching for an heir to an estate? How can I help?"

"I am looking for an unwed mother from England, traveling to the states in 1980, so I need to know if Violet could have had a baby before she married."

Enrique could feel her thoughts churning, looking back over the years and considering the issue. "That would have been impossible," she said firmly. "Vi and I roomed together at New York University that year. She wouldn't have been able to hide something like that."

"Well, thank you for your time. I'm sorry to intrude at a time like this, but I am grateful for your help." Enrique walked to the kitchen door and slid it open. He stepped through and was turning to shut the slider when something occurred to him.

"If you find anything unusual about Violet's death in the next few days, will you call this number and leave me a message?" He wrote down Mr. Lord's number in New York on a scrap piece of paper on the table and handed it to her. Susie took the paper and tucked it into her purse. Enrique walked back around the house. He was getting into the car when he noticed a suburban parked down the road, idling. Vi's death, a nagging suspicion that it wasn't all as it should be, and now an idling suburban. He started the car and watched in his side mirror for a minute.

Without touching his brake or turning on a blinker, Enrique threw the car into reverse. Hitting the pavement, he shifted into first and laid a heavy foot on the accelerator. He flew down the road leading out of the sedate subdivision. The road was little more than a path, winding through the heavily wooded area. Homes set back into shady lots and a car parked here and there turned the road into a one-way obstacle course. The suburban pulled out without hesitation and gave chase. Their speed topped seventy miles an hour as Enrique pushed the limits of the road and his car's ability to stick to the pavement.

As they came up fast over a small rise, Enrique lifted his foot slightly off the gas pedal. A two-car caravan from the mortuary was stopped side by side in the middle of the road, windows down, conferring. They took up the whole road.

Purely on instinct, Enrique stood on the brakes, and then, shifting down into third, he left the road and took his flight up on the side of the road, taking out bushes with abandon and then fishtailing back onto the asphalt on the other side of the roadblock.

The suburban, with all its muscle, hit the soft, uneven shoulder and, instead of being thrown back onto the road, was flung into a stand of trees and over onto its side. Enrique saw the high-speed calamity in his rearview mirror as he poured on the speed and left the wreck behind.

One down, fifteen to go.

Enrique charted a course to Forest Hills Gardens in Queens on the GPS and took off. He had found Aggie Danforth Ellis there. She had married in 1985, and property tax records pulled from the Times databases from last year indicated that they lived in a townhouse near Station Drive. It was only an hour drive, but he made it in fifty minutes thanks to a slightly heavy foot and moderately light traffic. He knew something was wrong when the GPS directed him to turn right onto an avenue that was filled with fire engines, emergency vehicles, and the blackened shell of a townhouse still smoldering and belching thick black smoke into the pale sky. All about him there were lights flashing, bystanders watching, and spectators talking in tight groups. He knew what he would find, but he parked the car out of the way and walked toward a small group of middle-aged women.

"Is it Aggie's home?" he asked. The women all nodded—in shock, he would guess.

One of them spoke. "Only one of that whole family survived," she said. "They had company in town and they have been carrying out children. Dean and Aggie…" She choked up and couldn't continue.

Enrique stood with them, watching the scene for a minute longer, and then moved closer to a remaining ambulance. The driver was sitting in the cab of the truck with the door open. Enrique moved just a few feet from the driver's door and waited until the driver acknowledged him. All the while, Enrique was watching the burned-up shell of a home. He couldn't seem to make himself look away. Firefighters had battled the blaze until it was only a smoldering sodden mess, and they were stomping through the wreckage and talking in huddles.

"Are they waiting for the arson investigators?" Enrique asked, and the ambulance driver gave a nod.

"Did you know them?" he asked Enrique.

Enrique shook his head. "No, I didn't," he said, "but I had an appointment with Aggie to talk about an estate. We are looking for the heirs and she is, or was, on the list." He paused, so as not to seem in a hurry, and tried to act offhand. "Who survived?" he asked.

"I guess that would be your business, if you are looking for an heir," the driver answered, looking at the destruction before them. "I heard that the family had gathered for a grandchild's baptism. Everyone but one son is dead."

"Do you know what hospital they took him to?"

"They took the victims right to the morgue. The son wasn't home and I haven't seen him here. He may not even be in town. Poor guy." The driver shook his head.

Enrique walked back to his car, wondering how he was going to find this son and interrogate him about the 80s. A heavy weight was ripening and fermenting in the pit of his stomach.

It can't possibly be a coincidence, he thought. Violet and Addie dead on the same day. Someone or something was wreaking destruction and making sure that none of these women were alive to tell their story. What kind of a person would kill children to keep a secret?

He got on one of his phones and dialed Mr. Lord, hoping that he was still at the hotel in London. It was seven in the evening in London, but it wouldn't have mattered what time it was. He was asking Mr. Lord as a courtesy, but like it or not, he was going to get some help.

"Mr. Lord," he said when the call connected. He couldn't help sounding steamed. "Can you hear me all right?" As he talked, Enrique scanned the crowd, watching for...what was he watching for? Pure evil? How do you spot that in time?

"I am going to need to call in a platoon of men, this minute," he said. "Well, I won't get a platoon, but I need ten to fifteen right away."

"What is happening?" David asked, reflecting Enrique's serious tone.

"There is a killer hunting these women. The first two on my list are dead, with anyone else in the way being taken out as well," Enrique answered. "We need to get them and put them somewhere safe until we can figure out which one is the heir. That is what this is all about, right?"

"It might be, but I don't know yet. I trust your instincts," David said.

"Maybe we should go to the police?" Enrique asked, already knowing the answer. "There just isn't time to sort it all out for them. I'm not sure they could do anything without proof, and we don't have time to investigate and then act. We need to get some protection for these women."

David agreed. "I want to tell you to lay low but I need you, so be as careful as you can. We should know in a couple of hours just what we are doing and why, so we'll talk tomorrow."

"I bought some burner phones and sent you the numbers; just call through from the top until you get me," Enrique said.

Sitting in the car, Enrique called in the troops. He called on the men in his former unit, and they responded just like he knew they would. No questions, no hesitation—they were willing to trust him and willing to act quickly. He gave each team two women and sent them to find them and safeguard them. If there were any children born in 1980 or 1981, they needed to convince them to go into hiding as well. The teams were moving to Florida, Colorado, Seattle, New York, and Virginia. Most would be in position within a few hours.

If the force that was killing these women came from the States, Enrique's team would lose. With all the resources of the military or police available to them, even a crack team of experts couldn't withstand the efforts they could bring to the situation. But, if the force was coming from England, they had some hope. There would have to be a cover and a line of command. They wouldn't have infinite resources. His team could compete.

He did not tell them the end goal, he just sent them to find and protect. Enrique set himself to figure out how to find the only living member of this family in Forest Hills. His first thought was to locate the mortuary. They might know where he was or when they expected him. He drove out of the neighborhood, and idling at the corner, he looked both ways and thought.

Across the street and down the road a bit, a steeple soared above the strip malls and car lots. It was worth checking, so he bullied his way into traffic and ended up at a church. He walked into the chapel, and as his eyes adjusted to the dimness, he saw a youngish back bowed in prayer in the middle of the sanctuary. He walked quietly forward and hesitated, but finally need impelled him to sit down at the young man's side. The face that lifted and found his was agony personified. Enrique had found his man.

"I was just at the house," Enrique said to him. "I think it was torched, and I want to find out who did it and why. Will you help me?" He put out his hand and pulled the man to his feet. "My name is Enrique Gutierre."

"Dean Junior," he said. He was young, not more than twenty-five, short and stocky with coppery red hair.

"Tell me how you are related to Aggie, how everyone in that house was related, and it could help us to find the devil that did this." They walked together down the aisle of the sanctuary. Enrique pulled from him the tangle of relationships that are family and found that there was one other member that had escaped the fire. Dean had a grandmother, Aggie's mother, who was currently residing in a nursing home. Her mind was serenely addled, although she had lucid moments from time to time.

Something of the urgency Enrique felt kindled in Dean, so they drove to The Meadows right from the church, leaving Enrique's prized car parked in the church lot and driving Dean's truck. Aggie's mother hadn't been told about her daughter's death, and after a few minutes with her, it was obvious that even if she did learn about the tragedy, she wouldn't remember it for long.

Dean sat beside her on the couch in her little room and tried to catch her hands. Her aged, wrinkled, bird-like hands fluttered as they clasped and unclasped, over and over, washing and wringing. She didn't seem anxious or worried and she didn't seem to notice that Enrique was even in the room.

Dean asked her the all-important question: "Grandma, could Mom have had a baby before she and Dad were married?" The words didn't register and they got no answer. Dean had been born in 1990. As they left, Dean told the matron of the nursing home what had happened that afternoon, fending off her sympathy with curt, short answers to her questions, and asked them to keep an eye on Grandma, just in case.

It was quiet in the car as Dean drove back to the church. "Who are you?" he finally asked, "You're not from the police, so how do you come into this? How did you find me?"

"I was hired to find your mother and ask her the questions I asked you. If she had a child born at the right time, I am supposed to locate that child and do a DNA test and send it to my employer. Pretty straightforward, right? But it has turned into an unholy mess, and someone thinks it is worth massacring an entire family over."

"Is my mother the only one you were sent to find?"

"No, there are several women, and I think they are all in trouble." Enrique could see the spire of the church up ahead.

"I want to help then," Dean said simply. They turned into the parking lot and he pulled his pickup truck next to Enrique's racecar. It was dusk.

"It is too dangerous," Enrique said, with rigid finality. He wouldn't be responsible for hurting this boy.

"It was my family and I want to help—no, I need to help." Dean was the personification of reasonableness. He just didn't know the lengths these villains would go to. Well, actually he did.

Enrique was reaching for the door handle, leaving Dean no choice in the matter, when the truck was rammed savagely from behind. They were thrown forward, Enrique had no seat belt on and his head hit the windshield, stars skittered around his brain and he started to black out.

Dean threw the truck into gear and flew across the parking lot, lurching over an island and then taking out the parish fence. He floored the accelerator and turned onto the road that ran in front of the church, running a couple of minivans to the curb as they swerved to avoid hitting him. An SUV tried to run up beside Dean's truck from behind them, but he swerved and blocked them. So it rammed them soundly from behind, and they locked bumpers.

Dean didn't hesitate; he slammed on his brakes and swung the truck around facing oncoming traffic. The SUV, locked to their bumper, swung with them. They could see the two men in the vehicle cowering as it broke loose and slid out of control across oncoming traffic. It was hit several times and they could see it careening across all four lanes, finally hitting a cop car head on and stopping dead in the street. Steam poured from the hood and no one emerged from the car.

Enrique watched until they turned the corner and left it behind.

"Welcome to my world," he said.

CHAPTER 14

David tried on Roger's tuxedo. It was a little snug, but he was able to button up and still breathe with only a little effort. They had eaten a late lunch, killed several hours, and then gotten dressed for the reception. David used some of the time to do a little more study.

The mystery of the Stone of Scone was shrouded by thousands of years of history and it was going to take some work and a great deal of luck to find what others had tried, without success, to uncover. He wondered how much Prince George knew about what Roger had set in motion.

Camryn called to him from the bedroom, "Why don't you fill me in? What did you find out today while I was asleep?"

He walked out of the bedroom. "Here, do you want to see all the references I found?"

He picked up his notes. Camryn appeared next to him in the formal blue dress, smelling just like a girl. Concentrating on his notes and shifting away from her, he turned the paper so they could both see.

"Look at all the Hebrew symbolism that traveled from Israel to Britain. The flag of Ireland used to have a red hand on it, overtop a star of David and under a royal crown. The symbolism is explained by two stories. The first is that the kingdom of Ulster had no rightful heir and they agreed to settle the issue with a boat race. The first man to touch the shore of Ireland would be king. One of the men who was behind in the race cut his hand off and threw it to shore and so became the king."

"I thought the red hand had something to do with twins," Camryn said.

"That story is about Israel's fourth son, who was called Judah. He had twin sons called Zarah and Pharez. During birth Zarah put his hand out of the womb and the midwife tied a red cord around his wrist to mark the first-born. He withdrew his hand and his brother Pharez was born first, so we have the symbol of the red hand."

"I don't remember a flag like that," Camryn said.

"I think it was changed in the 70s. An even earlier Irish flag featured David's harp, and it was also used in their heraldry—that is definitely Hebrew symbolism. Some scholars think that even the term

'Union Jack' refers to the flag being symbolic of the union of the house of Jacob."

Camryn looked at clock on the laptop. "Look at the time!" It was going on nine o'clock.

With all their possessions already stowed in the boot of the car, Camryn grabbed her purse, tucked the invitation into David's coat pocket, took his arm, and turned to go. "Let's go do a little breaking and entering."

At the door, David reached for the doorknob, but the ding of the elevator stopped his hand, and they both hesitated. They could hear several footfalls in the hall and then an ominous pump of a firearm as a bullet was chambered into a clipped revolver. Camryn whirled, her blue filmy dress fluttering like she was twirling on a dance floor.

She took hold of the bureau beside the door and tugged it toward the door. David, once he realized what her intent was, pushed as she pulled and they wedged it in front of the door beneath the doorknob.

"Come on," he whispered.

"There is no place to go!" she said. But she followed along when he took her hand and ran, up the short steps and out onto the terrace.

"Help me," he said, when they stopped by a huge umbrella at the edge of the deck. David grabbed the base of it, and remembering this afternoon when he had tried to lower the canopy how it wobbled and shivered, he worked the clamp that seemed to be holding it all in place. One side was loose and it swayed precariously as he worked the other clamp free.

"Hold it steady," he said.

Down in the hotel room they could hear the battering of the door, wood splitting, and a relentless banging. They would break through soon. David grabbed the remote from the side table and pressed the open button. The electrical connection was still in place, and they watched the umbrella slowly bloom before them.

"What is your plan?" Camryn whispered. "I can't do what I think you are planning on doing!"

"Just try to hold this up for another few seconds," David said.

"I . . . well, never mind." She faded out and just held on. They could hear someone break through and shove the bureau aside; they only had seconds.

David hoisted the umbrella, twisting hard to pull out the wiring,

and threw it hurriedly over his shoulder. Camryn lifted some of the
weight and they hurried to the side of the hotel and looked over. They
were over a narrow alley. David didn't want to think it through too
much, so he balanced the umbrella on the stone ledge. It was wide and
sturdy but four stories high.

"Climb on." He helped her climb up, with one arm helping steady
her and one arm around the umbrella. "Grab onto the spokes on the
umbrella. You are going to have to balance it all for just a second—can
you do that?" Camryn gave him a curt nod.

"Ready?" David clambered up onto the ledge, reaching for the
spokes opposite Camryn to try and balance the weight.

"Don't let go," he said. "Ready? Jump!"

They jumped out into the air. The umbrella fell too fast, a free fall.
The ground was flying up to meet them when their downward motion
was stopped with a lurch. They were caught. The umbrella had opened
enough to catch on a protrusion from the hotel and the building across
the way.

Gripping the aluminum spokes, David bounced and his efforts sent
them plunging down again.

"Hang on!"

Camryn's dress fluttered and rippled as they dropped further. The
umbrella canopy was barely holding together, one side straining against
the rough stone exterior.

This time they seemed to catch some air and slowed for an instant.
David's hands were slippery with sweat. They went into a free fall once
more, but their fall was abruptly stopped. They swayed over the alley
and could clearly hear the police storm the terrace. It was too far to
drop. Without warning, the umbrella ripped and flung them sideways,
closer to the hotel façade, down another three or four feet.

"You trust me?" he asked Camryn. She gave the barest nod, and
at that David let go. It was dark in the alley, and he couldn't gage the
ground rising up to meet him. He landed heavily on his feet, bent his
legs to absorb the impact, and tumbled. He lay there in the grimy alley
and then bounded to his feet. He moved quickly and placed himself
under Camryn and whispered to her.

"I'll catch you, Camryn. Let go!" She let go, no sound escaping her.
Her blue dress fluttered as she fell, and David moved a foot to be right
under her. It was only a few feet, but it seemed she fell in slow motion,

and hit his arms hard. He bent his flexed legs to keep his feet and then helped her stand and take stock. Her face was a ghastly white and she held her purse in a death grip.

A radio from the terrace squawked a loud blast up on the roof of the hotel, and a voice answered in muffled tones. No one seemed to be aware that the chickens had flown the coop. They walked cautiously to the end of the alley and took their bearings.

There were no visible guards posted nor could they see anyone patrolling the street, so they turned toward Clarence House and started walking, without talking. They were about a block away from the hotel when Camryn opened her little purse and shook out the keys to Aunt Marge's car.

"I parked on this street when I came back from Mayfair this afternoon, instead of waiting for the valet. Should we pick it up now or just walk over?"

"Thank God for small favors," David said, relieved to have the car still available to them.

A few minutes later, they were safely in the garden ballroom outside Clarence House. They had walked a gauntlet of guards and security checks, even a receiving line. They had ducked out before reaching the dignitaries that would recognize Camryn and passed unnoticed through the archway that led into the courtyard.

Camryn sat him in a seat shrouded in the cover of shadows and moved a potted plant slightly to shield him even more.

"I will be right back. I want to find out who the guards are over in the west corridor, near Roger's office."

"Stay put," she said over her shoulder as she walked off.

David watched her walk away. She didn't call attention to herself in any of the usual ways and yet a wave of heads pivoted to watch as she made her way across the garden. Once there, she slipped quietly out the door.

It took only a few minutes and she came back through the same door, fought her way through throngs of well-dressed, important people, and approached his darkened little corner.

"We are lucky. The guards tonight are my favorites and they said they would let me spend a few minutes in Roger's office." She looked around as the lights dimmed. "It looks like they are starting dinner, so let's hurry."

Guests were finding their seats and moving with purpose instead of milling about aimlessly. David kept his head lowered. It wouldn't do to be recognized now when they were so close. They were halfway through the courtyard, the throng scattering nicely, when they heard someone call.

"Cami!"

Camryn did not turn around, ignoring the greeting. Again, an insistent voice called, "Cami!"

Camryn paused and then, bowing to the fates of the evening, turned to see who was calling.

"Uncle Leon!" she said, shooting David a concerned look. They were right in the middle of the garden courtyard, and Uncle Leon seemed determined to have a word with his niece. And to put it mildly, he was stone deaf: everyone was going to hear exactly what her uncle thought.

"Cami, what are you thinking of? Showing up tonight, when your mother needs you!" He bellowed his disapproval in the loudest of tones. "It's bad enough that you have hidden yourself in that desolate pile of stones these past few months, but to be out on the town now when Roger has been murdered? What are you thinking, child?" His bushy-white brows bespoke his disapproval, moving higher and higher on his enormously broad forehead. The courtyard had quieted somewhat and those close enough were listening and taking mental notes of the speech to share with those not close enough to eavesdrop.

Camryn gaped at him, her mouth opening and closing without a sound issuing forth. This was the worst thing that could happen right now and she did the only thing that would let them flee the room. She burst into tears and retreated, David following at a respectable distance.

When David caught up with Camryn in the hallway outside the ballroom, she was wiping her eyes and worrying.

"My favorite uncle and he thinks me a thoughtless, vain girl. He had to bring up my mother," she wailed. "And he is completely right!"

"Listen, Camryn, let me have the keys to the office. You go straight to Aunt Marge's car and go home. Console your mother and mourn your brother. You shouldn't be mixed up in all this. Roger would have never wanted that to happen," David said. "Let's go find the office and we can call your mother from there."

As an answer, Camryn turned and walked down the long corridor.

The carpets were red and gold, and the walls hung with priceless paint-ings. Office doors were closed and two guards stood at a relaxed atten-tion near the end of the corridor.

"David, these are my friends Benedict and Chum. When Roger first started working for the prince, my mother and I would visit Roger here once a week or so. They were kind enough to try and entertain me while the grown-ups talked."

Camryn nudged him and gave a significant look at the guard's bulging coat pocket. To David's rapidly emerging cynicism, it resem-bled nothing less than a gun-size weight pulling down one side of the jacket.

"This is David, my driver. He is going to help me clear out a few of Roger's personal things. Oh! We didn't bring a box," Camryn rambled and felt for the keys in her purse. "Where are those keys?"

David took the purse, fished out the keys, and handed them to Camryn. Her courage appeared to be pure bluster and wouldn't hold up under much more pressure.

The guards regarded them intently. Chum stood about six foot five, dwarfing David, and could have measured five feet across. In short, he was a giant, and he didn't look gentle. His visage was forbidding, but it yielded somewhat as he gazed on Camryn. Benedict looked like a bantam dandy. He sported a single white carnation in his coat pocket and his hair was slicked back in a pompadour style.

Chum took Camryn to the office door and watched her open it with Roger's keys. She nudged the door open. As Camryn turned to look at back at David, he was standing behind her with Chum's scarred hands gripping his shoulders.

"We are going to visit the storeroom and find you a good box, aren't we, sir?" he said.

Camryn looked at them uncertainly. David didn't look afraid, Benedict seemed his usual affable self, and Chum didn't seem any more threatening than usual, but something was off.

She hesitated until David motioned her inside.

"We'll just be a minute. Wait right here and I'll be back," he told her. Chum, a beefy hand on David's shoulder, turned him around and steered him to the storeroom. Camryn must have given up, because he could hear the office door close.

The guards took him down just a few yards, opened a storeroom door, and helped David inside. Benedict indicated with a short nod of his head that Chum should remain just inside the door.

There were no boxes piled in the storeroom, so David waited. Benedict shut the door and came to stand aggressively in front of David and pulled a billy club from a simple holster.

"What's up, guys?" he asked them calmly. They might be bristling with hostility, but he instinctively felt no fear. Maybe it was all the drawn guns he'd dealt with the past twenty-four hours, but these guys didn't worry him in the least.

"We thought that we might have a little chat." Benedict was the spokesman, Chum the muscle.

"I'm just the driver, you know," David said. For that, he got an index finger in the chest, right in the middle of his blooming bruise. It didn't help his mood.

"Hey guys, what do you want?"

"We know who you are," Benedict said. "And we want you to leave Camryn alone. She trusts you, so I know you didn't hurt her brother, but she shouldn't be running around with a wanted man either. You are putting her in danger. And we don't like that." He looked a dandified pit bull when he spoke of Camryn, and Chum stood behind him, menacing by his mere presence.

David told them the barest outline of all that had unfolded these past two days, so they would know Camryn had been pulled into these events by circumstance and not by his design.

"We aren't here to collect tea cups or family pictures. Roger told me of a letter I needed to read just before he died, and Camryn came to get me in the office, that's all. I don't know exactly how to get rid of her safely. Has her involvement been on the news?"

The big guy shook his massive neck from side to side, and the little one answered. "No."

Benedict barred his teeth and gloated, "We've already taken care of how you will leave Miss Camryn." David looked at Chum. His mouth was formed into a fierce smile as well, or something that would pass for a smile in other circumstances.

"You haven't called the police, have you?" he asked politely. "Because I won't be able to stay long enough to be collected by them if you have."

"Oh, no," Benedict answered, "it's much worse than the police. We've called her mother and she's on her way over as we speak."

"How long do I have then?" David asked.

"They live outside of London. I don't think anyone has seen or heard much from Camryn for over a year, so they will be in a bit of a hurry to get here. I'd give you about forty minutes."

"Plenty of time," David said. "Do you guys really have a box for me? If we are going to be playacting, then I will need my props."

Chum manhandled a box of office paper out of the corner, dumped it out onto the floor, handed the empty box over, and pointed David out the door. They followed behind, and just before David reached the office door he turned back to them, a question on his lips.

"What is up with her husband? Something isn't quite kosher, am I right?"

The two guards, poker faces on, consulted each other with a sidelong glance. Benedict, of course, was the one to speak. "What did Miss Camryn tell you?" This guy should be an ambassador.

"It's just that whenever she talks about him a wave of something wallops her. It makes me wonder if he is..." He realized he was talking too much and stopped short.

Chum took this one. "Our Miss Camryn is loyal to a fault, and until she admits Mr. Lucas... Well, never mind. You'd better ask her."

David stepped into the office and shut the door firmly on the two protectors. Time to get on with the search. It was obvious that the office had been scoured. Files were piled on the sideboard, papers were scattered on the desk, and file drawers were opened. Roger would never have left his things like this.

"Oh, well," David said, "I didn't really have any hope that we'd find anything."

"Well, I was just waiting for you to come in before I opened the safe. It is well hidden, so maybe they missed it," Camryn said.

She got up and pulled aside a picture, revealing a small safe set in the wall. A pull on the handle drew the weighty door open. It had already been well searched, with no attempt made to hide it. David leaned over the chair and looked in the safe. There was a small stack of papers in the bowels of the unit. Leafing through them, he could see there were several letters, but not knowing what he was looking for, it wasn't clear if any of them could be the right one. He read them through, just to be thorough, but nothing mentioned the Stone of Scone, and they were all either from or to a male, no women. He placed the papers back in the safe, turned to the file cabinet and, leafing through them at random, wondered how best to conduct a quick search.

Camryn was on her knees fiddling around with Roger's desk. She had the top drawer out and was examining the underside of the workings of the drawer.

"What are you looking for?" he asked.

"I assumed that he would put anything important in the safe, but I remember once when we were visiting, Roger told me he had a hidden compartment in his desk. If there is a secret compartment, then I can imagine Roger would consider a secret hiding place more secure than an office safe."

"Maybe we have a chance then. If someone searched the safe and didn't find the letter, they might have assumed it is gone or that no one else will be able to find it. They didn't chop the desk to pieces, so they probably didn't know about any secret compartments," David said.

Camryn was circling the desk, considering, weighing, and looking at all the angles. The desk was quite ornate with a full front. Two pillars reaching from the floor to the top of the desk were about a foot apart in the middle of the front panel. Each pillar was about six inches in width and about three inches deep, carved in a fanciful garden theme. Trees, fruit, flowers, and birds frolicked all over the desk. It was made with rosewood, oak, and black walnut interlocking with each other. David watched Camryn come full circle and then kneel before one of the pillars, pushing and pulling on each piece of wood as it connected with the whole.

The pillars looked solid as she finished with one and started on the other. At the very top of the second pillar a piece of walnut moved when she gave a twist. They heard a decided metallic click somewhere deep in the depths of the desk.

David circled the desk now, taking out drawers and looking for loose pieces. When he took out the top drawer, a long piece of wood had shifted, he pulled it back, pushed it forward, and finally lifted it sharply, and at that, he felt something move and heard Camryn gasp.

David leaned over the desk as Camryn pulled at a section of one of the pillars. It came loose in her hands. The box was the width of the pillar, three inches tall and about five or six inches deep. The section was rosewood, a carved eagle with wings spread wide to sweep the air.

The carving was beautifully intricate, her talons stretched out, ready to clasp the branch of a scrubby mountain pine. Lying innocently inside the box was a note-sized envelope, pale yellow, handwritten. The script was feminine. It was addressed to *Mr. George Prince c/o Air Force Command, Wales.*

Carefully, Camryn turned it over, opened the flap, and pulled out a small note card. This was it. This note was the catalyst that had set in motion the events of the last couple of days. Camryn read it out loud.

"My Dearest George: You looked at me, from the beginning, exactly like every woman wants to be looked at by a man. To be thoroughly seen and then loved is all I ever longed for. I guess that dreams sometimes do come true.

"I know I promised to meet your ship on the tenth, but I have to go home. My grandfather is ill and is not expected to live much longer, I must go. I wish there was some way to talk to you before I leave. I know you will wonder why I am not at the docks when you arrive; just know that I am missing you more than I ever thought possible.

"Please call as soon as you get on shore. My grandfather's address is 300 Braddock Park in Boston, and his phone number is (857) 666-0111. I realize as I write this that I don't have your address, my husband! I am dreaming of you far away across the ocean."

The note was signed with a flourish, impossible to decipher.

David took the note and read it all again, taking all of twenty seconds. If George Prince was really Prince George, if this happened in June of 1980, if there was a marriage, if there was a child, then the mission they had been given was paramount. It all made sense. Even the killings. Any number of royal factions could be responsible for the attacks in America, and any of the current heirs would have an interest in keeping this a secret. Even the whisper of an event such as this, the smallest hint, and those that give their lives to protect the king would be set on course to contain the rumor.

Prince George may have been married. It would have been unapproved and unknown by all but a few people. How they had evaded publicity must have been a miracle. If there was a child, then there must be an heir to the throne, although David wasn't any great expert on succession to the throne of England. Any number of parties could have an interest in keeping this unknown and hidden.

"Our Prince George has never married, but he broke many a girl's heart," Camryn said.

She was quiet, studying the floor as David looked at her. This might be the last time he saw her. He would eventually go back to the States, she would be reunited with her husband, and they would be here in England. He studied her, trying to read her thoughts.

"Tell me about Lucas," he said. "Where is he now?" Why hadn't he asked these questions earlier?

Camryn looked up at him, through a golden curtain of hair. "I don't know what to say." She thought for a second and then continued hesitantly, clearly unsure of what to share. "I have known Lucas since we were children. He was my age and my best friend all through school. He was a rugby player and a risk taker and he promised to always cherish me. He is in Afghanistan." She looked down and the golden curtain closed David out. It hid her storm-brewed eyes from any scrutiny. "I haven't heard from him in a while."

David tried again: "Why does talking about him make you so sad? Were he and Roger friends? Does he treat you well?" He knew he had gone too far when she looked up sharply.

"Please don't ask me anymore," she pleaded. "I just can't." Her eyes were a well of tears, brimming but unshed for the moment.

It really was none of his business and the sooner he got her out of this the better. Now that they knew why they were in this investigation, he would do better on his own.

"Do we take this letter or put it back?" David said out loud. "Let's make some copies to scatter around but leave the original here. It withstood a full-out search already."

The copier was in the office, and it took a minute to warm up and make several copies. Finding an envelope, David addressed one to his office in New York, folded a copy, placed it inside, and sealed it. One copy he folded and handed to Camryn to put in her purse, and the last copy he folded and placed in his suit pocket. Camryn placed the note with its innocent yellow envelope back in the hidden panel, and they worked at fitting all the pieces back together and finally fit the desk drawer back in place.

Easing the door open, David checked the corridor. Benedict and Chum were nowhere in sight. Walking warily, they made their way back to the party. Every corner was a nerve-wracking deliberation.

David could hear the large, loud party, music playing, voices raised, and a radio squawked. With utmost caution, he took a quick look around the next corner. A familiar figure, talking into a radio, stood not ten feet from them. The official from the apartment was on the loose and had tracked them here. As David listened, he finished his radio command: "Spread out!"

CHAPTER 15

David turned, and pulling Camryn along, he sped back down the corridor. "That cop is here," he whispered furiously.

Every door was locked up tight. The corridor seemed endless, and they ran so fast there was no time to look behind them. At last they gained another corner, and urgently checking all the doors, they found them, every one, locked tight. They ran and turned like rats in a maze until, finally, they were lost and beginning to wonder if they were going around in circles.

At last, they chanced upon a set of stately double doors that gave way into a beautiful, soaring library. A fire burned low and gave the only light in the room. Walking carefully through the dim glow, they watched for a place to hide, a way to escape. The carpet was thick underfoot, and as their eyes adjusted to the dim light, they were able to avoid rattling against the tables and other furnishings.

Reaching the far wall, David silently drew aside a heavy curtain that covered a wall made almost entirely of glass. It overlooked the courtyard where revelers still made merry. An elbow dug into his side, and David was pushed farther into the curtains. Camryn mouthed to him and pointed down to the party, "My mother!"

He finally spotted Lady Patricia Brough, driver in tow, circling the courtyard. At that instant, the huge double doors burst open and lights were thrown on. David heaved Camryn deeper behind the curtains and grew still. The heavy brocade trailed the floor, hiding their feet. The carpet muffled sounds as someone, several someones, swept through the room and moved closer and closer to their hiding place.

Abruptly, from near the fireplace, a man's voice challenged, "What is this? How dare you intrude in here?"

All was silent, and then a deferential voice answered, "Your Royal Highness. We will leave you at once, sir." David stood still. Of all the rooms in Clarence House, they'd chosen the one with the prince in it?

"What is this? I want an answer," Prince George said.

"Sir, we have reason to believe that Mr. Lord gained entrance to the party tonight," the guard answered, reluctantly.

"Very well, do what you must, but there is no reason to fear Mr. Lord. If you find him here, I expect an immediate report. Send my guards in at once." George dismissed them.

Camryn's nails dug into David's arm. They daren't breathe or move. Prince George must have been asleep by the fire all along. They heard sounds of a log being heaved onto the fire and a rustle as someone settled into a chair. They scarcely breathed, but it wasn't long before a door opened again.

"So, they sent our Goliath. Does this mean there is concern that Mr. Lord is after me as well; killing my personal secretary wasn't enough? Preposterous!" No one responded, but David and Camryn held perfectly still behind the curtains.

"Well, I will turn in for the night. Will you see me upstairs then?" They heard someone rise and muffled footsteps retreating, doors opening, the lights were extinguished, and they heard the sigh of the huge doors closing.

Camryn felt her way out of the curtains, David following in her wake. They were trapped, royal guards on one side, Lady Brough on the other. David sat by the fire, thinking furiously, while Camryn perched on a stone window ledge in the dark and watched the celebration in the courtyard.

"Is your mother still out there?" David asked her.

"Yes, and I am selfish," she said, "thinking that mine was the only heartache."

David barely heard her, so deep in thought her words barely registered. These killings weren't by the order of George, he was sure of that after overhearing him speak tonight. But Prince George must know the importance of what had been set in motion by that stray little letter. He was caught up in the events of the years as well as them. Someone with a lot of pull was trying to protect the prince from the past. Or trying to protect their own position in the hierarchy of succession.

There was no proof, just instinct, yet he would bet his life on that as solid truth. Maybe it would be wise to get caught here where the prince seemed to think him guiltless. No, not yet. But he wasn't inclined to run around the maze anymore. At that thought, the library doors again opened, though the lights stayed out this time.

This is it, he thought. As the doors slowly closed, they both tensed.

"Miss Camryn?" someone whispered into the room.

"Benedict?" Camryn scooted off the ledge and met Benedict at the fireplace.

"It was you! Chum came in to take Prince George to his quarters and all he could see were two lumps in the curtains. He sent me to take you out of here." Benedict was cheery.

"Thank you, Benedict, though I'm not sure there is a way out of here. My mother is in the courtyard. Could I see her before we go?"

Benedict grinned at David and spoke to her. "We'll have to see about that."

"Let's see if I remember how this goes." He walked around the right side of the fireplace. "Could one of you turn on the lights?"

David turned on a table lamp, but the feeble light only threw the mantle into deeper shadow. He walked to the door and flipped on the overhead lights.

"Someone is outside this door," he whispered across the room. He could hear a door opening across the way, and he opened his door a crack and peered through it. A guard was posted in the corridor. Noiselessly, he closed the door and looked for a way to lock themselves in.

Outside the library, Sergeant Cooper, stationed in the hall, saw a flicker of movement at the doorway. Immediately, he spoke quietly into his headset warning the team they had found someone. Even as he spoke, he distinctly heard two bolts being thrown into the floor of the library, locking the doors.

"Someone is in there, we've caught them!" Sergeant Cooper said, pounding on the door.

"It might be the prince, he was in there reading earlier this evening," someone cautioned.

A more respectful Cooper knocked and called out, "Sir, we need to clear this room."

There was no response. The team of guards huddled and considered and finally radioed Captain Pillard.

"Good work, Cooper," the captain said. "I'll be right there. Send two men outside to guard the windows. He will not escape us again tonight!"

"Yes, sir!" Cooper dispatched two of his men. They strode down the corridor to stand outside the library windows.

Barreling down to rendezvous with the team outside the library came the captain, behind him a half a dozen men following quickly in his wake.

"They are in there, Captain. I am sure of it!" Cooper exclaimed. "Someone threw the bolts and locked themselves in. I was standing right here."

"Excellent job, men." Captain Pilliard rubbed his arms, as if kneading out a knot.

"Did Mr. Lord really tie you up in the victim's apartment?" Cooper asked. All ears tuned in to the captain's answer. Everyone had heard the rumor, but only a longtime associate would dare broach the subject with the dour captain. He shot Cooper a look of pure venom and the rumor was verified.

"Take your places," the captain said. They snapped to attention and encircled the double doors. A flurry of footsteps sounded through the thick library doors. They would have them in custody soon. There was nowhere to go but out the windows or through these doors.

"I demand entrance. Open up this instant!" he shouted through the door. Another scrabble of footsteps sounded close by the inside of the door.

"We are going to break down these doors at the count of ten. Open up!"

"Okay, okay, I'm coming!" a voice said from the inside. They heard bolts release with a solid click. The door was thrown wide open and tensions immediately deflated as the guards realized they had only captured another guard. Still, to be sure, they entered the room with guns drawn, covering each other and searching every corner. The captain was the first one to the windows and called out to the guards outside.

"Any sign of the suspects?"

"No, sir, no one has come this way."

Turning back to Benedict, he asked, "Where are they?" The captain steamed, about to boil over.

"Who are you looking for?" Benedict asked, yawning widely.

"You know who I'm looking for!" the captain raged, a twitch throbbing in his temple. "I will have your job for this insubordination!"

"I'm sorry, Captain, but I just had a little lie down and woke to someone pounding down the door. I don't know what you think happened in here, but make your search, and if you have an accusation, then let's make it a formal one and you can prove I did something wrong."

Benedict's congenial mask slipped and the steel that lay underneath the happy exterior flexed and swaggered a bit. Everyone knew that he had the ear of the Prince and his complete trust as well.

"I don't see anyone in here and there is no way to get out but through that door," he continued.

The guard team thoroughly searched the library, with Benedict looking lazily on.

As Benedict faced down the captain, David and Camryn fled behind a hidden panel door, just to the side of the fireplace. Benedict had heard whispers of a passageway between Clarence House, Buckingham Palace, and the House of Lords for years, but only last year had he actually seen someone open this panel. So, he knew about where the latch was located, but he had never used the actual mechanism.

David had searched the courtyard from the wall of windows while Benedict had fiddled with the fireplace. *Maybe we can jump, or climb down a rainspout, or something equally as stupid in a tuxedo and ball gown*, he thought. His mind churned through possibilities. His contemplations had been interrupted by the unmistakable sound of a lock opening and a door sliding open.

"Here we go." Benedict's voice sounded relieved. David looked over his shoulder and saw a panel next to the fireplace slide sideways.

There was a new, imperious sound of movement at the door.

"I can't go with you," Benedict explained, ushering them into the opening. "Someone needs to be in here to welcome these guards. This is a tunnel from here to the palace and the House of Lords. If you keep to your right, you should come up in Parliament, somewhere in the basement I have heard. I think that Chum may be able to meet you there and let you out. Otherwise, sit tight, and tomorrow morning someone will come." Benedict spoke quickly, openly trying to hurry them on. He took a lethal looking cylinder from his belt and handed it through the opening. David must have looked quizzical, because they heard his whispered shout through the closing panel: "It's a flashlight!"

Chapter 16

The tumult and light from the library was shut off when the panel clicked into place. David fumbled with the flashlight and turned it on. A bright light illuminated the stone passageway. It was surprisingly roomy. The path sloped down, and a draft of chilled air accompanied them. The passage went on to the edge of the light and then turned into darkness. David shrugged out of his jacket and handed it to Camryn.

They walked quickly through the dusty corridor, their only light the powerful flashlight bequeathed to them. The stone path led them steadily downward, and when they came on another passage, they kept to the right and before long the slope turned upward and they began a gentle climb. They had only been traveling ten or fifteen minutes when they reached the end of the passageway. Anxious, they listened with ears pressed tightly to the doorway but heard no sign of anyone on the other side. There was no doorknob in the roughhewn wood door, and rather than knocking or announcing their presence to just anyone, they sat with backs to the portal and waited.

"What do we do next?" Camryn asked David, when the silence grew heavy. "It sounded to me like Prince George isn't the one chasing you down. I would guess that he knows exactly what Roger set in motion but just can't be steering the helm publicly. The more I think about it the more it seems reasonable that Roger would have only acted on these matters under Prince George's direction."

Hunkered down at her side, David agreed with her assessment. What to do next?

"We need to get out of London, and it is either to Edinburgh or Ireland. If we are following the path of the stone, then Ireland seems to be the place to go next." David turned and looked at Camryn. "What about your mother?"

Before she could answer, they heard the clatter of keys and the turning of a lock. The door opened, and Benedict and Chum stood before them, motioning them out of the passageway. Behind them stood Lady Brough, though she was no longer the casually elegant woman he had met on his first visit to England. Grief had plowed over her face and etched itself into the lines and planes of her skin. It had rendered her into someone he hardly recognized.

"Mother," Camryn cried out, and gathering her up, the women stood pressed together.

When, at last, they pulled apart, Lady Brough turned to David. "What is happening? Why do they think you're responsible for Roger's death?" Benedict pointed discreetly at his watch and shook his head. They didn't have the time for a recitation.

"Mother"—Camryn interrupted the oncoming harangue—"I am starved! Can we finish the interrogation in the car?"

Lady Brough seemed appeased with the thought that she would be able to feed Camryn. They followed Benedict, with Chum guarding their backs, and made their way on echoing marble floors to a side door. As Camryn and her mother leaned toward each other, holding hands, talking non-stop, Benedict held David back and spoke softly.

"The captain doesn't yet presume to put out a warrant for the likes of Camryn, but he seems to have developed a passion for hunting you down."

"I think all those hours he spent trussed up in the apartment turned him against me," David said.

"So, you really did that." Benedict threw David an appraising glance. "Well, our captain can't bear any swipes at his ego and I am afraid that this battle is escalating. He isn't going to let it go until he has you in cuffs," Benedict said.

As the sound of sirens leaked into the historically hallowed halls of Parliament, the group picked up their pace, remembering that the man pursuing them had endless resources and very few limits to his power. Benedict and Chum opened the doors of a roomy sedan parked near the side door of the House of Lords, Camryn and her mother slid into the backseat but David hesitated, realizing that anyone who helped him was at risk of falling into the sights of the enemy. And at the moment, that included Lady Brough.

Toying with the keys of the old Bentley in his pocket, David leaned into the car. "You go on. I am going to take the Bentley," he said.

Mrs. Brough took his arm and gently, but firmly, said, "I am sure you think you are protecting us by leaving, David, but now is not the time for heroics. Let's just get out of London and then we will decide how best to help you. Besides, I think I deserve some answers."

The driver was given terse instructions about dodging roadblocks and waved on. They followed a contorted path through London and finally passed beyond the city proper and into a quiet country road leading north out of town.

On the outskirts of the city, remembering the copies of the note, they made a short stop to drop the envelope addressed to David's office into one of London's distinctive red mailboxes. It would be a week before it reached the New York office, but it would be safe there. A short twenty minutes later, and end of a long day, they finally pulled through a stone arch, across a stone driveway, and up to the back door of the Broughs' home in Henchley Downs.

It was late when they piled out of the car and headed into the cavernous kitchen, but Lady Brough put flame to pan and within minutes spread a feast of leftover roast chicken, roasted new potatoes, and a salad onto a scarred slab table occupying center stage in the kitchen.

"David," Lady Brough began, pulling up a chair and sitting next to him, "can you tell me what happened?"

David recounted his story yet again, but this time, knowing the backstory, the reason why Roger needed help, and why he was so brutally murdered, it seemed a different tale. The path forward seemed clear, and the imperative nature of the task he had given Enrique dwarfed the investigative task he'd been asked to do.

"I know the whole country is after me, but I think it is only a lone royal guard convincing everyone of my guilt. His story won't hold up," David said.

"What will you do?" Lady Brough asked kindly.

"I need to get out of London, and I suppose cross the channel to Ireland and, after that, to Edinburgh. I am just figuring this out as I go."

"Well, let's get you settled in for the night, and you can take a car tomorrow and be off." She leaned in and took David's arm. "I knew you had nothing to do with hurting Roger."

"I know you want to help, Mrs. Brough, but I can't involve you any further. I don't want you in any danger."

With an airy wave of her hand, Lady Brough dismissed his objections. Turning to Camryn, she grasped her hand and said, "We have a busy schedule tomorrow." She looked at her only daughter closely. "You are too thin, Cami. I am so glad you came home."

Upstairs, settled into the room he had used when visiting the Broughs so many years ago, he made a quick detour into Roger's room, pulled some clean clothing out of drawers and closet, and packed another small bag for tomorrow. He needed to be able to make an early start.

His thoughts turned to memories of Roger and his prior visit to England as he drifted into a deep sleep. He was pulled from sleep abruptly, it was the dead of night, and by the faintest light of a cool silver moon, he sensed a huge beast looming over him, pawing at the covers.

CHAPTER 17

It was too late to pay a visit in New Hampshire. Enrique and Dean watched outside the home of Mrs. Juliet Knowles, formerly Juliet Lawrence, but they would knock on the door anyway. Seven of the women on his list had been shepherded to safe locations; his team was functioning with precision. Juliet lived in a cedar and glass home with a view of Claremont Junction. She lived with her husband and had two grown children living away from home. They were about to deliver bad news, and they would do it fast. They finished their cold supper, drained the last of a flat soda, and walked quickly up the drive and to the side door.

Dean gave a solid knock on the kitchen door, which brought the sound of deep-chested *woof!* and skittering nails clicking over kitchen tile. A woman called out a welcome "Come in!"

Enrique opened the door and they stepped through until a growl deep in the throat of the dog brought them up short. The woman sitting at a kitchen table and her husband standing at the sink both called to the dog, "Heel, Baylee!"

Enrique looked down at his watch; they were in a hurry, but each family needed to be gentled before they would believe and act. So he put on a pleasant smile.

"How are you this evening?" He began in salesman-like tones: "Is this the Knowles home?" The woman nodded. "Are you Juliet, by any chance?"

She looked at her husband and back. "Yes, I am. Can I ask why you want to know? It is a little late for callers," she said pleasantly.

Enrique turned to Mr. Lawrence, "I'm afraid we have some bad news." He let that sink in.

"Is something wrong with Kim? Travis?" Juliet waited in a slight panic and then walked to the sink and stood by her husband.

Enrique walked toward them. "No, no it is nothing like that," he said. "Did you travel from England in 1980?"

"Yes, my American cousins came to stay with us in Lancashire after winter term that year, and we backpacked all over the islands that spring. I came with them when they traveled home and stayed. I became a citizen right after college." Her face reflected her building confusion.

"I have to ask you something pretty personal. I'm sorry about this, but it is enormously significant, I promise." Enrique looked at the floor, "May I ask how old Kim and Travis are? Was either of them born in 1980 or 1981?"

Mr. Knowles shot a look at his wife. "Who are you anyway? And why in the world should we tell you anything like that?"

Enrique jumped in to explain. "I started this off badly. We have been asked to track down several women that traveled to the US in 1980. I assume it is a matter of inheritance and there has been some trouble. Someone else is looking for the same women and is killing off not only the women on the list but their families as well." He passed to Dean.

Dean was composed. His role was to bring credibility to the situation. "My parents' home with most of my extended family was burned down yesterday." His matter-of-fact demeanor brought a look of horror to Juliet's eyes. She was quiet for a moment as she contemplated the risk for herself and her family.

Juliet then asked a most astute question. "Why? Why are we being targeted?"

"Like I said, I believe it is an inheritance matter and that stakes must be high for someone to go to all this trouble to get rid of possible inheritors," Enrique said. "Mrs. Knowles, I know this is an intrusion on your privacy, but did you have a child in 1980 or 1981?"

"Well, not a child, but I did miscarry in 1980." She didn't look at her husband, but she didn't lie either. "I was young and foolish, and I got pregnant that spring, didn't even realize it until we were here in the States."

"Who was the father?" Enrique asked.

"I'd rather keep that to myself, if you don't mind," she answered, looking a little miserable.

Watching Juliet's husband, Enrique could see that they had worn out his patience for questions; they would need more answers, but for now they needed to get them somewhere safe. Enrique plunged right to the point. "Mrs. Knowles, we need to get you and your children, even you, Mr. Knowles, to a safehouse this minute. We are not far ahead of whoever is doing the killing. I don't think you will need to stay out of sight for long, a week or so, but we do need to hurry right now."

Juliet went into a full-out panic, but in thirty minutes, they were packed and following Dean's truck out of town. They were headed for Concord, a big enough city to hide in easily. The children lived locally and they had been convinced to join their parents for a few days.

This woman might be the one they were after, the first one to admit to a pregnancy. Enrique took special care with this safehouse, renting a complete floor in an Embassy Suites hotel and setting out three hired guards to keep them alive. Twelve down, four more to find and protect.

Captain!"

Captain Pilliard woke at his desk as the knocking at his door persisted. Captain Pilliard, a Royal Protection Officer of the SO14, rubbed his wrinkled face, smoothing out marks caused by sleeping at his desk. He stopped at the small bathroom in his office and straightened his hair and his shirt collar. It would never do for his subordinates to see him off duty in any way.

"Yes, man, what is it?" The captain opened the door without inviting him in.

"We've found out who the woman is with Mr. Lord. She is the victim's sister, Camryn Lavender."

"We can trace him through her then. Find out where she lives and where she might go if she couldn't go home. Good work, Knibbs."

"Her husband, Lieutenant Lucas Lavender, is missing in action in Afghanistan. Their residence is uncertain. We think they sold an apartment in London last year. But her mother lives just outside of London. In fact, her mother was seen at the reception tonight by several people."

This was it then, another chance to get rid of David Lord, an imminent threat to Prince George.

"Load up your men. I want eight of our best men ready in thirty minutes," the captain barked, and shut the door. His voice was still hoarse and raspy from the shot of pepper spray he had inhaled early this morning.

The memory of lying trussed up on the floor of that apartment would keep him going until he took revenge. "I will avenge myself on David Lord if it costs me my last breath!" he swore to himself.

The captain took out a heavily starched officer's uniform and a pair of gleaming boots. In a carefully established ritual, he dressed himself for battle. While he dressed, he murmured the words of his personal creed:

All threats made to the king will be answered upon the heads of the aggressors.

The House of Windsor will be protected at all costs.

The price of victory is eternal vigilance.

August, 27, 1979: A stain upon the SO14 that must be erased by the diligence of every officer.

He was ready now for combat in every detail. He paused before the mirror and pressed out the tick that twitched unceasingly now to the side of his right eye. For just the barest breath of a moment the words of Poe swept unbidden through his mind; the eye 'a dull blue, with a hideous veil over it that chilled the very marrow in my bones.' But no! His was not the evil eye of 'the tell-tale heart.' It might be blue, but it was unveiled and clear. As clear as his purpose, he aspired, no; he must clear the ancient and noble name of Pilliard.

This is the deed that will resurrect the family honor and erase the lingering whispers of fault attached to my family upon the ignoble death of Lord Mountbatten.

27 August, 1979, will be forgotten in the glory of this singular act of protection, this heroic dedication to the crown.

Looking at the clock, he decided there was time to make contact with his benefactor before they left for the Brough's. Taking out his personal cell phone, he composed a short message: "Found Mr. Lord again and will have him in my sights within the hour." He entered a phone number he knew by heart and pushed send. The message was delivered. He would chance one more use of this phone before destroying and replacing it.

The call was placed to the States and answered immediately. "Captain?"

"Do you have anything to report?" he asked.

"Yes, sir. Two of the sixteen we have taken care of, but someone is ahead of us now. We had some collateral damage, but it cannot be traced to us in any way. It could not be helped."

The captain spoke, "This mission is imperative, you must remember that, and you must succeed. You must find these women and eliminate the threat they pose to our nation."

"Yes, sir, I understand."

Captain Pilliard ended the call, straightened his uniform one more time, and then walked stiffly, purposefully, out to his men.

"Come," he called, "let us storm the manor now while Mr. Lord sleeps."

Chapter 18

David rolled to escape the beast pawing his covers and it took a moment to figure out where he was. As he recovered, he recognized the huge mastiff, who was whining with urgency. David could hear the sound of a telephone ringing downstairs. He didn't hesitate. He pulled on some jeans and a t-shirt and then scooped up the bag he had packed the night before from Roger's room. The dog moved with him like a shadow.

In the kitchen, Mrs. Brough was just hanging the phone up when David walked in.

"That was Benedict," she said. "The captain is on his way here; they left London twenty minutes ago."

"I need to be gone before they get here then," David said, regretting his decision to come home with them last night. "Is Roger's Austin still parked in the garage?"

"It is up on blocks, and I don't think it has been started for a while," Lady Brough said, choosing a set of keys from a board in the pantry and handing them to him. "You are welcome to try to start it."

As David neared the back door, off the kitchen, another huge mastiff thrust his cold nose into his hand, and to his dismay, Camryn joined him, all dressed in black and carrying a small duffel bag.

"I can't believe you would really leave without me!" she said.

"Camryn, stay here with your mother, please."

"I don't want to be safe. Playing it safe has gotten me nothing. Lucas was supposed to be safe..." Her voice broke as she fought back tears. Then, her eyes steely and determined, she said, "I am going, whether you want me to or not. Roger might have been your friend but he's my brother!"

Behind Camryn, David could see Lady Brough in her housecoat and slippers. She watched Camryn plead for a moment and finally interrupted.

"Cami!" she called out. "Leave us for a moment, will you?" Camryn resisted but finally sat in the morning room facing David, who would not be able to leave without her seeing him go.

"Lady Brough," he said, "I need to be going, now!"

"We have a little time. I think you should take my Cami."

"This man murdered your son, Lady Brough, and you want to hand over Camryn as well?" David was flummoxed.

"I don't think you will quite hand her over, as you say, but she has been in deep mourning for over a year, and to see her so alive and almost happy, well, if helping you find out why someone killed her brother is the cure for heartbreak, then let's give her a chance to recover completely, shall we? You will protect her?" Lady Brough replied, in no hurry at all.

"Lady Brough, I'm not sure you understand that I am likely to be shot on sight in the next few minutes. Surely you don't want your daughter running out with me," David pleaded.

David tried to speak, but Lady Brough didn't let him form much more than a sputtering beginning before she continued as if she was in charge.

"We have a few minutes before they arrive, go and see if the Austin will start. If not, you can take my car."

The phone rang, disturbing the tensions David was sorting out.

"Benedict?" Lady Brough said into the phone, "Yes, yes, I understand. He's leaving right now. No, I won't make breakfast!" David could hear Benedict give a few words of instruction, and then she hung up the phone with a terse "Goodbye, then."

She turned to David. "The captain has called in the local constable, so we don't have any more time to talk. Take my car..." Mrs. Brough said, her voice fading into silence as the sounds of wailing sirens penetrated into the uncertain shelter of the kitchen.

David left the kitchen and ran to the garage, and turning on the overhead lights, he found the little Austin at the back of the fifth bay, up on blocks and covered with a thick coating of dust.

Unlocking the car door, he crammed his shoulders into the driver's seat and, fitting the key into the ignition, he pumped the gas pedal a couple of times. The sound of pulsing sirens grew louder. David turned the key but it only clicked once and then fell silent. Again, he turned the key in the ignition and again there was no spark. Reaching for the hood release and popping it open, David unfolded himself from the small car, knowing that it was too late. He looked at Camryn, standing near the door of the garage, as the sound of the sirens came closer, he could hear them slow and turn into the driveway to the estate.

"Mother said to head toward the Alberts' grass airfield if we can't get Roger's car started. I think it's a lost cause," Camryn said, looking at the little, dusty car. She reached up and threw the light switch off, plunging them into darkness as they heard the sound of tires pull up to the back door of the home. The only light in the garage was the swirling colors of police lights. "Do you know how to fly a plane?"

David just shook his head absentmindedly. As he walked back to the door, he wondered what to do to get away from the Broughs' before the captain and his men arrived. Mrs. Brough would handle the local officials, if any handling was needed.

"Let's just get out of the way and let Mother talk to these guys; they won't let the captain bully her. Come this way." The garage door opened at the side of the structure. Camryn pulled David into the shadows thrown by the police lights and into the barn, which stood at the back of the driveway. The dogs sensed them moving and followed like shadows, one on either side of Camryn. The barn was unlocked and half a dozen horses stood drowsily in their stalls, aging polo ponies. David recognize Mr. Brough's black that must have stood sixteen hands, a family legend. Camryn pulled him out of his stall and then chose another dark horse for herself. David slipped a bridle into the black's mouth, wincing slightly at the noise and watched as Camryn did the same.

"There is no time to saddle them or anything, but we can get out of here faster on horseback than on foot, before the rest of them get here," Camryn said. It was now or never. David swung up onto the horse while Camryn pulled the huge sliding doors open and lightly mounted the chestnut roan. David loosened the reins and the horse was out of the barn, following Camryn, close at her heels. The dogs ran beside them and then pulled out front, the horses followed trustingly, moving quickly over mown grass and around flower beds and skirting around a bench and then a wheelbarrow filled with mulch. The darkness hid them from sight and the grass muffled any noise the animals might have made.

They were gaining on a wooded area when he heard the sound of shrieking sirens and, looking over his shoulder, he could see a line of headlights pull into the driveway.

Once inside the relative safety of the forest, they relaxed their guard. The horses slowed to pick their way carefully over an uneven terrain. The dogs moved with them, eyes gleaming in the darkness. It was the deepest night, insects harmonized, and there was no moonlight to give them away.

After traveling about a quarter of an hour, the comforting darkness began to lighten, and they reached the edge of the forest. The dogs stopped and pricked their ears. They sat and then lay in the grass just inside the line of trees. David nudged his horse out into the open. "Do you know where we are?" he asked hopefully.

"Maybe if we follow this road a little further I will recognize something." She kneed her horse and the horses cantered beside the road and up a small rise. Before the crest of the hill, they dismounted and stayed in the shadows of the forest. They walked carefully to the top of the hill and looked out over the road beside them. The road sloped downward, over a small brook, and then intersected with another lane small enough that there was no stop sign facing either way.

"Our neighbor with the airfield is that way." Camryn pointed down the road they were on, right through the intersection.

"Let's get back undercover and make our way around them then. You don't know how to fly a plane, do you?" David asked.

"No, I was hoping you did," she said. He could barely make out a serious smile in the gloom of the night.

Just then the sounds of a truck, laboring and shifting up a hill, sounded on the air. "I wonder if someone is coming to help us," Camryn said, under her breath.

"Your mom did tell us to come this way; did she make any more phone calls while you were listening?" David asked. Camryn shook her head.

They left the shelter of deep forest and edged closer to the road so they could see who came into sight and saw an old farm truck stop in the middle of the intersection. One of the horses whinnied, and the truck flipped its lights on bright. The light didn't quite reach them but they backed further into the woods to remain hidden.

"Let's send these guys home, okay?" Camryn asked, indicating the horses. "We are about a half mile from the airfield."

They pointed them in the right direction and gave them a good slap on the rump. Once started, they picked up speed and thundered down the side of the road toward their nice quiet barn and where they were sure of a bucket full of oats.

Whoever was in the truck must have heard the horses, because it backed up a ways and then rumbled up the road toward them. Just before the top of the hill, the driver seemed to reconsider and squealed to a halt parallel to them in the woods. The dogs, still shadowing Camryn, barked, and David peered, trying to see into the cab of the truck. They didn't dare move for fear they would be seen.

"Miss Camryn? Mr. Lord?" a deep-throated voice called from the truck. "Are you there? Chum sent me to shift you to a safer neighborhood."

They stayed still, numbed into indecision.

"Miss Camryn, he said to tell you he is still waiting for a rematch at backgammon." Camryn knelt and hugged the dogs. "Home, boys," she whispered, and they took off.

"It's okay. Chum always let me beat him at backgammon."

They left the shelter of the forest and squeezed into the cab of the truck with Chum's brother. Camryn was straddling the gearshift, and the windows were opened to allow for shoulder room.

"I'm glad to meet you. We weren't sure you would be able to get outside the net they closed over the area."

"Are we to call you 'Chum's brother'?" Camryn asked.

"You can call me Toms," he answered. "Where do you want to be dropped?"

"We need to get to Ireland, so I guess we should head west," David said.

"We will need to fill the tank then. It would be a five-hour trip to Holyhead in a car, but in this beast, it may be a bit longer," Toms said. "They seldom ask for I.D. if you are traveling across British borders."

With that welcome news, he ground the truck into reverse and backed into the intersection. Pointing west, they bucked through first, whined through second, and finally found their stride in third gear. Topping out at 50 or so, the truck bounced and swayed its passengers down the back roads until they merged onto A40 and then the M6. Even with Toms's foot to the floor, the truck labored while all other traffic passed them with little effort. But with every mile they moved farther from the captain and closer to some answers.

They ignored the growls of empty stomachs until mid-morning and then stopped to fill the truck and eat in a petrol stop lunch counter. Back on the road, tires humming, Camryn drifted into a daze, leaning on David's shoulder and then falling sound asleep. David tried to back away as his traitorous heart did its best to convince him to hold her close and never let go. Finally he escaped her closeness the only way he could, and he shut his eyes and began a logical, reasoned review of the facts in their search. Before long he came to himself again and found himself holding onto Camryn like she belonged in his arms. He made himself move away from her, back against the door. Then he turned and stared out the window.

CHAPTER 19

Toms wrestled the battered truck across England. He plotted a circuitous route to avoid large cities, steadily eating up miles, until the road ended at the edge of the world. Holyhead Island was barren. A half a dozen cars parked tidily against a lowered barrier told them the ferry was due shortly.

Although he was willing to take them farther, they sent Toms home and waited with the small group of commuters. The wind blew steady as gulls rode invisible currents and shrieked at the sun. The sea lapped against the island in tireless waves as David and Camryn found a bench on which to wait. Presently the first cars started their engines, and the ferry churned into sight and maneuvered to the dock.

A lone resident of Holyhead appeared to secure the ferry and raise the barrier. Twenty minutes later, the ferry was released from its moorings and backing into the channel. They started on the two-hour trip to Dublin.

David watched the shore with some anxiety from the top deck. If they could just leave England without notice maybe he would be able to figure out this riddle of the Stone of Destiny. Although he knew that their departure on the ferry was untraceable, he couldn't shake the feeling that the captain was hot on their heels. Over the last three days they had barely escaped capture twice, and the feeling that their pursuers must be close by was constantly nagging at him.

Arms resting on the railing with the wind blowing at his back, David watched as the island receded. Just as he was losing sight of the dock, a car came into view. It could have been a reflection, but he thought he saw the flashing lights of a police vehicle. He squinted and looked again, but he could only watch the island fade and finally disappear from view.

David walked with Camryn to the enclosed deck at the top of the ferry and looked out over the ocean. The channel was busy. A rusty tanker headed south. A good-sized yacht, blue and white cushioned seats strewn over the deck, passed by on the starboard side. Three sleek sailboats hove to and fro in an intricate dance with wind and waves.

Gusts from the channel blew in from doorways and cocked windows. Camryn's gold hair swirled, twined, and trailed across David's face and arms. He sat down on the bench and leaned back, with eyes shut against the day and the wind. They were alone on the deck for some time and savored the quiet peace and the sunshine that bathed the benches.

Over an hour into their journey, David walked to the window looking out over the back of the ferry, and memories of Roger ran through his head as he watched the curling wake. They were interrupted by the sound of a door opening into the deck. Two men in uniform walked toward them, their shoes striking disturbing footsteps on the decking as they drew closer.

"Are you alright, Miss?" one of the men asked, while alternately peering at a clipboard and back at Camryn.

"Yes...," Camryn started to answer.

"It is them," the second man interjected, pointing to David.

"Excuse me," David said, motioning Camryn to come. As she stood up from the bench, the taller of the two men reached for her.

"Don't move," he ordered.

"Camryn," David said. He moved quickly to her side and looked toward the door leading to the outside deck of the ferry, considering their options.

Knowing that the captain had come for them, but wanting to make sure, David asked, "What is this about?"

"We've had word that we have a fugitive on board. Are you David Lord?" he asked. "Miss, we mean you no harm."

"You have the wrong man," Camryn said. "He has done nothing wrong."

"We need you to come with us; the police will be meeting us at the port in Dublin and we can sort this out there," he said.

"Watch him up here," said the ship's captain to his assistant, "while I get our passengers ready to disembark. It is a little early, but we don't want to take any chances with a fugitive aboard. Miss, there is no reason for you to stay in here, you are free to go."

David watched the two men confer, quietly, and saw a gun pass discreetly from the captain to his subordinate. That gun changed everything; the time to get away was now while the captain was busy.

As the captain turned to leave, he said again, "Miss? Will you come with me?"

David watched her eyes turn mutinous, and she shook her head sharply. "I told you, you are making a mistake. I will be fine here."

The ship's captain left them, they heard his footfalls across the wood decking and then an announcement came over the loudspeakers informing the passengers it was time to return to their vehicles and get ready to make port.

The remaining officer stood by the doorway, watching them closely and saying nothing. His hands played with the handle of the gun.

"I can't let you hand me over; you don't know what you are doing," David finally said. When the man said nothing, David stood and walked to the doorway, Camryn following close at his heels.

"Come on," the officer said quietly, "you aren't going anywhere; we are in the middle of the channel and there is nowhere for you to go." He gripped the gun but did not pull the trigger.

David walked by the officer and then reached for Camryn's arm. They started toward the outer deck, away from the ship's officer and toward the back of the ship. He could hear footsteps behind them as they reached the doors.

David whispered to Cami, "Run!" Opening the door, he pushed her before him and they ran down the width of the ferry. He could feel crosshairs on his back, and sure enough the deck was plowed into splinters to his right. Still they ran. Just as they made the corner another bullet punched into the wall. Then a single shot exploded into his shoulder, the impact knocking him forward into Camryn. They collided with the railing, and a line of bullets stitched across the railing and it gave way. Camryn grabbed at the deck, fighting the force of the impact and the rolling deck beneath her. She slid to the very edge of the ferry, her legs dangling precariously over the side.

David clutched with his good arm for the rail but it disintegrated, and he fell into the churning waters of the channel. Camryn, watching from above, tracked his fall and without conscious thought let go and tumbled immediately in his wake.

The channel was rolling, the swells carrying them high enough that they could see the port of Dublin, the troughs pulling them down where all they could see was the billowing ocean and the bluest of skies. The sea calmed somewhat as the ferry moved farther away. David, floating helplessly on his back, watched the ship disappear as it headed toward Dublin. Camryn kicked off her shoes and, holding onto his good arm, began a side stoke toward Ireland.

She was a fair swimmer, and the rolling current swept them toward the shimmering green horizon, but they were still a good distance from safety and before long Camryn grew tired. David passed in and out of consciousness and his feeble efforts to help subsided. He dipped under the surface of the ocean and slipped from her grasp. He reached for her and she grabbed onto his injured arm. She hung onto his dead weight for an instant but lost her grip, and he slid down further into the cold embrace of the ocean.

Camryn dove beneath the waves, the murky salt water both stinging her eyes and blinding her vision. Coming up for air she looked frantically about for help, and finding herself alone, the ferry growing small in the distance, she allowed herself one desperate sob and then filling her lungs she dove deeply and found nothing.

CHAPTER 20

Across the Atlantic, Enrique waited at a stoplight, when the car in front of his finally started rolling. DC was no place to be in a hurry. So Enrique crept across town, his thoughts worrying at the puzzle he was set to solve. He was finally approaching the turn off when his cell phone vibrated in his pocket.

"Mr. Lord, is that you?" he asked, answering the phone.

"It's just me, Enrique," Dean said. "Warden Prejorovik called me earlier. From upstate New York, you remember?"

"Tessa McCowen?" Enrique asked.

"Exactly. One of their prison guards was caught unlocking Tessa's cell door about an hour ago. The guard had a rope with her and she lawyered up without talking. I got to talk to Tessa, though, and she said she didn't have a baby until two years after her immigration, so she isn't the one we are looking for," Dean said. "Don't worry, I got her sister's number and her mother's address so we can double check the facts."

"I still haven't found anyone home at the Larsons'. Their windows are shuttered, so I can't see anything inside. I have been watching and no one has come or gone. I really don't think anyone is home. It is probably time to get in somehow and make sure everything is all right," Enrique said.

"I'm on my way," Dean said, "so don't go in without me!"

"We'll wait until morning," Enrique replied, but he was talking to thin air; Dean had already disconnected.

Three hours later, Dean pulled his truck behind Enrique's car.

"I ate on the road, so I'm ready to go," Dean said.

"Let's go and see if anyone is answering the door yet. It's not too early if they are home," Enrique answered.

Beth Maeve Larson and her husband lived on Beall Creek Court, not far from the Potomac River. Lush green grass, old hardwood trees, and blooming azalea bushes lined the meandering little lanes. The homes were roomy old estates with acres of fields between them. They found the right address on a charming mailbox. Enrique motioned for Dean to park in the grass off the lane, and he pulled into the drive and behind the house. It was early and no one was home.

No security stickers on the windows, no dogs, nothing but a peaceful silence settled on the would-be housebreakers. Dean joined him at the back of the house and watched Enrique try the door and a large porch window, but they were locked. The gravel driveway underfoot was the only sound carrying on the pastoral air as Enrique moved to the garage door. Opening the keypad, he studied it for a moment and then punched in a quick succession of numbers. The quiet was broken as the garage door slowly rattled open. An ebony cat crouched on the hood of an SUV, her tail twitched once, and she jumped lightly to the floor and leisurely disappeared.

"We'll hide the car in here; we just need a few minutes to do a proper search," Enrique said.

"How did you do that?" Dean asked.

Enrique showed him the worn number pad. "These guys only take a four-number sequence," he said, "and it is obvious what numbers are used over and over. So, a few educated guesses and we're in. And no one locks the door into the house from inside the garage."

Sure enough, after pulling into the garage next to the SUV, they found the kitchen door unlocked. Enrique stopped and pulled his gun safe from underneath the front seat of the car. Unlocking it he unpacked the gun and holster.

"Just in case," he said to Dean as he strapped the holster around his hips, checked the gun for ammo, and then, punching the button to close the garage door, they stepped into a silent home.

The fridge hummed in the corner and an old-fashioned clock ticked time above them in the doorway; dust motes drifted lazily in the afternoon sun. All else was still.

In an undertone, Enrique said, "We need to clear the house. Take the upstairs, I'll do this floor." The office was on the main floor, just inside the front door. The marble floor of the entry gave way to coal black slate as he crossed the threshold into the office. Lined with mahogany shelves and cabinetry, the far wall boasted an enormous slate and river rock fireplace. Two oversized armchairs were placed to gaze upon the fireplace.

Enrique looked for a desk calendar or an address book. The desk was unlocked and neatly organized, but held nothing that would help. As he powered up the computer, he could hear Dean upstairs checking rooms. Enrique searched the cabinets along the wall while the computer finished loading. It was password protected, and without knowing more about this couple he didn't have a hope of getting a look at their calendar.

Enrique searched the main floor, all the while thinking about how a home was usually organized. He called up the stately curved stairway, "Hey Junior, anything interesting up there?" There was no answer, and he had his foot on the first step when it came to him and he made his way back to the kitchen. There on the fridge was a calendar, and on the calendar was marked out most of the month of March and a week into April. Across the dates was scrawled *Vanuatu*. Maeve and her husband were in the South Pacific until tomorrow, safe and sound he hoped.

"Junior?" he called, and, grabbing the calendar off the fridge, Enrique took the stairs two at a time.

"Dean Junior! They are out of town until tomorrow." Enrique paused and then called again while climbing the stairs, "Dean?"

The upstairs was immaculate. Enrique looked into bedrooms, bathrooms, and sitting rooms, the sound of his movements muffled in deep pile carpets.

The last room, the master bedroom, sprawled before him. A king-size bed to the right, a wall of glass leading onto a stone deck, and to the left a looming master bath and closets. Dean had disappeared. Enrique took a quick tour through the closet, nothing was out of place. Next he looked out over the deck, there was a hot tub but no Dean. Enrique turned to leave the bedroom when the door flew open. Dean stood in the doorway.

"There you are!" Enrique said. "Where have you been?"

"You've got to see this!" Dean said, and he disappeared back into the hall, leaving the door open for Enrique to follow.

Enrique followed him to the alcove at the top of the stairs. Creamy white cabinets lined the room, waist high. Shelves filled with books and trinkets sat on the cabinets and stretched to the ceiling. One of the sections was ajar and Enrique followed as Dean stepped through into a hidden room.

"The latch didn't quite catch the last time they used it, so this section of the cabinet was just a bit askew. When I opened the base I felt a draft of cold air. It caught my attention, and when I looked more closely, it swung open and I found this!" It was a media-infested room, with six flatscreen monitors mounted on the inside wall. Views from cameras all over the house shuffled on and off the screens. A tall tower encased a computer underneath the desk and ran the show. There were no windows in the walls, but the room was bathed in light from two large skylights. A door led into a cramped bathroom; a shower spigot was set in the tile wall without even room for a shower curtain. Another door opened to a miniscule kitchen, a European-sized fridge running next to a microwave and a bar sink. Still another door opened to a closet filled with canned food and four cots stood stacked on the floor. The room had been built as a hidden shelter—a pretty sophisticated setup.

"Well, this is interesting," Enrique said. "But I found the goods tacked to the fridge. Our elusive Maeve is in the South Pacific. The calendar is blocked off until tomorrow, so we just need to watch this place until they show up. We can sleep in the truck so we don't miss them."

Dean was fiddling with the mechanism of the hidden door. "I don't see how this works!" He seemed entranced by the puzzle of it.

"Come on, it's time we are off. We've found what we came for." Enrique nudged Dean away from the enigma of the hidden room.

Stepping into the alcove, Enrique pushed the section of bookcase closed behind him. It shut with a quiet click, and Dean turned to inspect the door. The passageway couldn't be discerned by any seams or hinges; it was beautifully designed to be completely hidden. Scanning the room, it was impossible to see the camera that streamed video in the hidden alcove.

Enrique started down the central stairs, his hand lightly sweeping the velvet grain of the balustrade. Steps curved toward arching windows positioned over the entry, and Enrique turned to take the curling steps. Caught in the frame of the window, a posse of vehicles turned sharply into the drive.

Turning on a dime and sweeping Dean before him, Enrique ran out of their line of vision, thinking furiously. Dean stepped quickly to the alcove and again began to look for a latch, some way to open the door to the hidden room.

The sound of tires on gravel filtered to them and then car doors opening and closing. Six times they opened and closed.

Dean searched methodically, his forehead damp with heightened nerves. There had to be a lever to work the latch, but it would be well hidden. Enrique was cool, cat-like in his attention to the front entry. He drew his gun and held it loosely by his side.

Men disgorged from the vehicles and moved around the home, rattling doorknobs and looking in windows. One of the men called to the others, and they heard gravel crunching underfoot as they all moved to the back of the home, and then all was quiet; they could hear no more.

A tinkle of broken glass sounded in the kitchen and then sounds of a latch turning—and the men were inside.

Enrique, focused on the stairs, raised his gun and sighted the curve of the stairs.

"Rique!" Dean breathed. Enrique heard only the blood pounding in his ears. Dean touched his shoulder, breaking his concentration.

"Not now!" Enrique said and lifted the gun again.

"We're in!" Dean said. He reached around, took hold of the pistol, and turned Enrique toward the alcove. The shelf was ajar. They heard the squeak of rubber soles on marble and the feedback from a radio receiver as they noiselessly slipped through the opening, pulled it shut, and heard the lock catch.

Dean held up a tiny silver remote control. "This is the key."

"So they won't be able to get to us," Enrique said. "But we are stuck in here, and I won't just watch as Maeve and her husband are slaughtered tomorrow."

"Good," Dean replied, "because I wouldn't want to go out there alone."

Enrique pulled out the calendar. "They don't know when Maeve is getting back, so we have an advantage, but I don't see them leaving; we have everyone else stashed away. Well, most everyone," he said, remembering Dean's family.

Dean confronted this reminder of what he was doing here with Enrique by moving to the wall of monitors. They spent the next few minutes studying the enemy, side by side. After watching the leader mouth instructions and trying to read his lips, Enrique opened the cabinets beneath the monitors and studied the equipment. Flipping a switch and turning a knob slightly, sound poured from the system. He adjusted the switch so the squelch died, and instead every monitor was speaking on top of the other. Eventually, they figured out how to move between the screens, listening in on some conversations and ignoring others.

The men had British accents. Enrique watched as the team methodically searched the home. They had all the calling cards of a military unit. They didn't trash the place but weren't afraid to announce that someone had been looking, which was not good news for Maeve and her husband. They took their time but eventually finished an unsatisfactory search, even a young man working on the computer gave up, and they collected in the kitchen for their orders.

"George, Collin, and Archer, take the trucks into town, stash two of them, and pick up some food. We can hide one vehicle behind the shed. We may be here for a while." Three of the men found keys, checked wallets, and walked out through the broken kitchen door.

"Carter, I need you to set up a sniper position. You and Byron will take shifts." Carter followed the three drivers out. Enrique tracked them on the monitors. Carter took a rifle case and a large duffel bag from one of the vehicles. All three drove out the front drive and out of view.

Enrique weighed their options.

"Two on two are odds I like. We only have a few minutes before the shooter is set up and may come back inside."

Dean agreed, catching up.

"We will need some way to tie them up," Enrique said. Quickly they searched the cabinets—nothing. Dean moved to the closet and rifled through the shelves.

"Bingo!" he said, holding up a bundle of zip ties. Enrique put a few in his pocket and handed some to Dean as well. "Just in case," he said.

"Mr. Larsen owns a security firm, and with this setup I'll bet he was intelligence before he got into security," Enrique said. "They might not need our help at all!"

Locating the two remaining soldiers on the monitors, Enrique considered how to split them up.

"Enrique, listen to this," Dean said. "He is sending his man up here to sleep."

From the kitchen monitor they listened in on the conversation.

"I'll wake you in three hours," the commander said.

They watched the soldier walk up the stairs toward them. The commander watched him leave and then he walked out the back door. They saw him walk through the backyard and off the screen.

"He's gone to talk to the other soldier. Let's take care of this one then," Enrique said.

They watched as Byron crested the stairs and moved away from them, down the hall to the master bedroom.

"What are we going to do?" Dean asked.

"I want you to go into this first bathroom and flush the toilet. Then hunker down in the bedroom and wait."

Taking one last look at the monitor, Dean quietly opened the door and slipped across the hall and into the bathroom. Enrique watched Byron on the monitor, then he too slipped out of the room and down the hall toward the soldier. Enrique heard the toilet flush, and standing behind the bedroom door, he caught the door as it flew open. Byron led with his gun, so it was easy for Enrique to snap it out of his tensed grip. The greater prize was the phone clipped to his belt.

"I wouldn't make a sound," Enrique whispered as he pushed the gun into a freckled neck. Dean, listening at the door, appeared with a zip tie in hand. With a gun pressing into his neck, Bryon was docile as they tied his hands behind his back and did not resist as they pushed him toward the alcove.

CHAPTER 21

Dean held the door open as they herded the soldier into their lair. As Enrique passed him, Dean reached out and grabbed the gun. Knocking the soldier to the floor with a solid shove, he knelt on his chest and put the gun to his head. Enrique stilled his struggling legs and bound his feet.

Dean seemed mesmerized by the soldier's cornflower eyes. He looked the part of a country innocent, and yet this man was part of the team that firebombed his family.

"Not yet, Junior," Enrique said, trying to stay calm. "They will pay for what they have done, but right now we have to stop them all, not just this little one."

He reached over, took the gun gently from Dean's clenched hands, and pulled him to his feet.

"Dean," he said, then gave him a few seconds for his heated blood to settle down to a simmer. "Can you do this, Junior? I need you to watch the monitors while I search this guy and see if we can use this phone somehow."

Dean nodded once and turned blindly to face the wall of monitors. Gradually his vision cleared and he watched the monitors.

Enrique studied the phone; it was a smartphone that could also be used as a walkie-talkie.

It needed a fingerprint to unlock the screen. "We'll figure these phones out later. One of these guys will talk to us," Enrique said, with a studied look directed at their captive.

The commander sent the sniper into the house. Keeping an eye on the monitors they watched the soldier key the mic on his phone. The phone on the table buzzed, but the screen stayed locked. The phone buzzed a second time as the soldier walked toward the stairs. He was coming to them.

"Byron!" he said into the phone. Enrique looked at the clock; it had only been thirteen minutes since the trucks left for town. He would love to be able to interrogate the men, if they had time.

"We will lure him into the bedroom the same way, what is he

doing?" Enrique asked, coming to stand by Dean at the wall of monitors. He kept his voice low, just in case.

"Here he comes," Dean said, watching the monitors. Enrique sent Dean into the bathroom and then disappeared into the bedroom to wait. He heard the toilet flush and listened for footsteps in the hall. Again, the soldier led with his gun and Enrique snapped it from his hands. The soldier resisted, but Enrique fired a shot at the ceiling and he gave up. They secured his hands behind his back, led him to their command center, and sat him against a wall, opposite the other soldier.

"Keep quiet, and I won't tape your mouth shut," Enrique said. Laying the gun on the desk, he grabbed a chair from the desk and turned to sit, watching the men thoughtfully. Looking from one to the other he considered their options. Dean was engrossed in fiddling with the controls in the cabinet that adjusted the cameras monitoring the outside of the home. On one of the screens the stand of fruit trees was barely visible.

"What are you doing?" Enrique asked, distractedly.

"Nothing much, just watching this guy," Dean answered.

Enrique watched him focusing, and then adjusting the frame of the picture, and focusing again; he honed the view closer and closer to the shooter's position. The camera was placed high in the eaves of the house and looked over the back property.

They both scanned the camera views. Dean seemed intent on viewing everything happening on the property. Two children walking a dog down the street near their driveway caught his attention.

"Enrique…," he said, and trailing off he seemed anxious as he watched the two boys.

The outside camera system only carried a visual signal, but the sudden sound of frantic barking carried from the kitchen speakers as the children's dog raced up the driveway, toward the back of the house.

Jumping to his feet, Dean ran to the door. Shoving it open, he flew heedless down the stairs and out the back door.

Enrique started after Dean, but a look behind him caused him to stop. He couldn't leave these two unguarded.

Enrique returned and watched Dean charge around the side of the house trying to head off the children—he ran full out, with no weapon.

Watching on the monitor he could see that the dog had gotten as far as the backyard and was running straight toward the grove of trees, barking madly. Enrique watched the boys follow the dog at a dead run. Dean rounded the corner of the house as they came up the last bit of the drive, and Enrique watched as he struggled to stop the boys from going farther; they were obviously anxious to follow after the dog. He didn't hear any shots fired, but something caused the boys to quit struggling and instead run to take cover behind the shed at the end of the drive.

The commander was in a precarious position; he was trapped by civilians, treed in a neighborhood that would not welcome military action. Would he flee or fight? The unit had already proven their willingness to accept civilian deaths. Enrique knew he needed to act before the rest of the soldiers returned to reinforce their commander.

Checking the ties on their hands and feet, Enrique left the soldiers secured in the hidden room. He ran downstairs and found guns and ammunition on the kitchen table. Picking one of the rifles, he checked to see if it was loaded.

His heart was racing, remembering the disaster of his last mission. Fighting panic and focusing on how to best handle the situation, his thoughts kept pace with his racing heart. High ground, that's what he needed.

Enrique took the stairs two at a time and found a bedroom that looked straight down on the grove. Leaving the curtains closed, he peeked through a small opening, and estimating the distance, he carefully opened the window. Jerking the barrel of the rifle, he tore a hole in the screen, and, counting on the commander focusing all his attention on what was happening in the yard, he knelt and sighted the stand of trees.

Dean was having a difficult time keeping the boys behind the shed: the dog was frantic, circling the tree under the soldier, barking and sounding the alarm. Enrique could only imagine where the soldier would be set up in the tree. He focused on slowing his breathing, took a deep breath, and pulled the stock of the rifle tight to his shoulder. Peering through the sight and centering the crosshairs, he pulled the trigger. The rifle coughed twice and Enrique watched through the target for any movement, any sign he had hit the target.

Nothing moved.

"Dean," Enrique called out the window. "Junior!" he called again.

Dean looked up at the house and, realizing Enrique was watching them, pointed and whispered to the boys.

"Stay where you are unless the other members of the unit come back. Can you see down the road a bit?" Enrique asked. Dean nodded and spoke to the boys, motioning to the road and then giving him a sign that they understood.

Turning back to the job at hand, Enrique brought the gun back into shooting position. Peering through the sight he watched the foliage for signs of the soldier. Inch by inch he inspected the tree, the dog still circling beneath.

I got you! he thought, finally spotting what looked like an elbow. Then he watched as a gun came into view. Enrique took a deep breath, pulled the rifle tight to his shoulder again, and gently squeezed the trigger. The bullet struck flesh, the gun jerked, and the man fell partway out of the tree, dangling precariously from his perch.

Immediately, the dog quieted. Enrique watched as he approached the stranger. The dog was whining and sniffing.

"Get those boys out of here," Enrique shouted out the window.

Dean pursed his mouth and let out a loud whistle, calling the dog. One of the boys called him by name and the dog came running. Bounding over the tall grass and leaping up to lick the boy's face. Enrique watched Dean kneel and talk to the boys. He saw the boys vigorously nodding, their faces full of delighted excitement. Dean pointed them down the road and the boys immediately took off for home.

The commander was struggling now to right himself, but instead fell out of the tree completely and grew still. Enrique saw three black shadows jump lightly from the same tree and make their way through the field toward the house.

That cat we saw in the garage, Enrique thought, *I wonder if that dog was barking at the soldier or the cats.*

He watched Dean march the commander through the house and up the stairs, and then turned to see them step through their door. The commander was disheveled and a bruise was blooming on one eye. His arm was bloody and made a sickening click as he moved. He was unnaturally pale and fell rather than sat in the chair offered to him. Dean zipped his feet and good arm to the chair and then deposited the rifle, a small ankle pistol and holster, a radio, and a wicked big knife onto the desk before sitting down and acknowledging Enrique.

"Hey." An understatement.

"What in the...," Enrique started to ask, but was interrupted by the arrival of the mother cat with her two tiny black kittens. Trustingly, they walked through the doorway, straight onto Enrique's boots, and proceeded to claim him by rubbing their little faces against his ankles.

Recognizing emotion in someone you know well isn't hard, but the vengeance that coursed from Dean as he watched the two dusty kittens wasn't hard to read even though they had just met. Dean turned to the soldiers, and then stood with a look of complete contempt. The soldiers flinched, but Dean just turned and left the room to sit in an armchair in the alcove.

Enrique found him there, with his head buried deep into his arms.

"Junior," he said, pulling up another chair, "what happened out there?"

Lifting his head and sitting up, Dean explained. Enrique deposited a sleeping kitten into Dean's lap; the other clawed a trail up Enrique's shoulder and stood sentry while Dean told his story through to the end.

"I didn't think," he said. "Something wouldn't let me watch while that devil hurt one more bystander! I turned into a raging brute! I turned into them." Dean gestured toward the hidden room.

Enrique answered forcefully, "You are not anything like them. We are on defense here, not offense, and if we can stop them from hurting anyone else, we will do whatever it takes. What did you tell those two children?"

"I told them we were playing a game, and I think I convinced them it was a great adventure," Dean said. "I can't imagine the police being a help just yet. Maybe later..."

As they spoke, knee to knee, the sound of tires moving over gravel filtered up to them. Enrique stood, steadied the kitten balanced on his shoulder, and said, "Three down, three to go."

CHAPTER 22

Camryn bobbed helplessly with the ocean swells. She dove into the murky water over and over, hoping to brush up against David because under the surface she couldn't see anything. He was gone.

The sailors later said that it was the sun glinting off her hair that drew their attention and they maneuvered their sailboat beside her in the channel. When a wave threw her at them, they caught her and lifted her over the railing and into the boat.

"My friend is still in there!" She pointed to the channel. The weekend sailors tacked back and forth for over an hour until the wind blew them toward the shore and even Camryn gave up hope. Wrapped in rough wool blankets and sitting in the bow, Camryn watched the Dublin Harbor come into view.

When they finally docked the vessel, she realized that she was on her own again.

David drifted in the cold waters of the channel, down where light doesn't reach and raging currents race. Unconscious—until he found himself in the sky above the channel, wishing he could help Camryn, but unable to do anything but watch her struggle. There was much he regretted about leaving his body and life behind. He watched Camryn repeatedly diving for him and then saw her giving up.

He heard someone call his name. It sounded like his father. He turned to find himself in a darkened library, his footsteps echoing on stone floors. Bookcases soared beyond his sight into blackness, filled with books. A light flashed ahead and he tried to quiet his footsteps as he made his way toward it. A ghostly image floated in the dark as he passed a faintly glowing stone bust.

A wizened old man, muttering under his breath, emerged from a row and followed the main corridor. He carried a single oversized book under one arm and a flickering lantern in his hand. David followed behind and watched as he placed the book carefully on a table. The old man turned to David with pale, unsettling eyes and motioned David to come closer.

Still speaking in a sibilant tongue, hardly above a murmur, the bent old man leaned over the book and pointed to the title. David looked past the gnarled finger and the yellowed, chipped fingernail to the embellished title, *Before the Book of Kells: The Lost Books*.

The aged scholar looked up, watched David eagerly, and then disappeared into thin air.

David waited in the dimness. Soon he noticed a light again flickering, tracking rows of books; again he heard the hissing speech of an old man and his shuffling journey to the table. He placed the book again on the table and drew his attention to the title. David struggled to hear his speech. He tried hard to understand what he was saying, but he recognized nothing. This time, the old man cupped his ear, and motioning toward the distant aisle, he bared worn-down teeth in a mirthless grin and disappeared.

David moved the distance and waited by the aisle for the light to return. A shuffling footstep, a muffled voice, and the old man returned with the lantern and commenced looking through shelves of books. Finally, with a jubilant whisper he pulled the familiar book from the shelf and started the short journey to the library table. He laid the book on the table and opened it to the first page.

Written in an unfamiliar script, the pages had been painstakingly decorated in the Kells style, but the pages were loose in the book and marred by water and creeping mildew stains. David looked up for just an instant, meeting the old, rheumy eyes, and the man disappeared again.

David walked to the aisle he had last seen by flickering lamp light. At the end of the row he reached down to the bottom shelf and pulled out the leather-bound, oversized manuscript.

Under an arched window a low-slung leather chair stood against the wall. David sat and examined the curious book, anxious to find out what it contained. The pages were tough and worn at the edges, each one decorated in a Kells style with jeweled colors tracing the first letter of each paragraph and symbols lined up at the edges of the page. A preface was written in English, explaining the contents of the religious manuscript.

BEFORE THE BOOK OF KELLS: THE LOST BOOKS
Preface
The 'Lost Books,' including the 'Book of Understanding,' are generally thought to have been in circulation among religious houses from 550

AD, and teachings thought to have originated from the book surfaced until about 1430. After that, history is silent on the subject and we are left with pure speculation. The 'Book of Understanding' begins a little before the traditional scriptural accounts, when mortal men fell from heaven to inhabit the earth.

Eagerly turning the page, David read on.

The Book of Understanding

In the beginning, the Gods looked upon their children, knowing the time had come for them to take on mortality and they, the Gods, looked upon the coming days with joy and sorrow. Earth had been prepared for the experiences to come; it was beautiful and fruitful and would provide much for their children.

Gifts were bestowed upon the children, gifts that would encourage and bless, but there would be no coercion. The gift of choice, valued beyond all else, would prove the downfall of many and the unveiling of the noble…

David finished the page and paused, his mind busy with the truths written in the battered old manuscript.

Turning several pages he paused and read.

A True and Careful History of Jacob's Pillow

David read yet again the story of Jacob and his dream of a ladder that reached into heaven. Skipping a few pages and starting again he was plunged into the middle of ancient stories concerning the stone.

He found the book beautifully illustrated with drawings of the life of King David. Intricate pictures drawn in jeweled colors drew him into the story of the young shepherd, a desert scene depicting a flock near a well, the shepherd drawing water for his sheep. An afternoon sun burned heavily in the sky, and he could almost feel the heat rising in waves from the rocky earth. One of the lambs had moved out of the protective shelter of the flock.

The artist had carefully drawn a tawny lion crouched and hidden among the rocks, a lamb wandering from the herd marked as prey by the predator.

The next illustration showed the shepherd and beast fighting, the lamb now running toward the safety of the herd. A knife glinted in the shepherd's hand, ready to plunge into the heart of the lion.

The last illustration showed the triumph of the shepherd, standing with his sandaled foot on the neck of the lion, victorious.

Turning the page, the next story depicted the prophet Samuel anointing the young David as the King of Israel. David was depicted kneeling submissively before the prophet, his brothers looking at him in disbelief.

Turning the thick vellum pages again, he found a series of illustrations depicting the battle of David and Goliath.

The first picture showed two armies camped on either side of a vast plain, set against low, flat-topped hills. Buzzards circled high in the sky, and a dry riverbed scarred the valley floor.

Across the valley, a giant of a man stood on the plain, clad in full armor. He was truly a giant and he held a spear loosely in hand. The evening sun glinted orange sparks off flinty armor. The young shepherd stood with a sling and a single stone whipping through the air.

The next depicted David with his foot on the chest of the fallen Goliath; he had hold of Goliath's battle-worn sword, and his severed head lay in the dust. The Philistine army ran and the Israelite army pursued the conquered invaders.

Drawn into the finely illustrated stories, David turned another page and read the story of David and Bathsheba. He read of the king's treachery in taking Bathsheba for his own and ordering Uriah, her husband, to be placed in the hottest part of battle, causing his death as surely as if he had slain Uriah himself.

He turned another page and found an illustrated depiction of King David seated before a hearth fire, the light dim, the figures thrown into deep shadows. The story beneath was one he had never heard before. The prophet was Nathan and he brought a grievance to the king.

There were two men in one city, one rich and the other poor; the rich man had exceeding many flocks and herds. But the poor man had nothing, save one little ewe lamb, which he had bought and nourished up. And it grew up together with him and with his children. There came a traveler unto the rich man, and he spared his own flock but took the poor man's lamb and prepared it for the man that was come.

King David's anger was greatly kindled against the man and he said to the prophet, "As the Lord liveth, the man that hath done this thing shall surely die."

Nathan, the prophet, said to David, "Thou art the man."

Nathan continued, "Thus saith the Lord God of Israel, I anointed thee king over Israel and I delivered thee out of the hand of Saul.

"I gave thee thy master's house and thy master's wives and gave thee the

house of Israel and of Judah and if that had been too little, I would have given unto thee more.

"Why hast thou despised the commandment of the Lord? Thou hast killed Uriah the Hittite with the sword and taken his wife to be thy wife, even Bathsheba."

King David cried unto the prophet, "I have sinned against the Lord."

David shut the book, wondering what these stories could possibly have to do with the history of the stone.

CHAPTER 23

Camryn woke from a heavy sleep at the jostling of the sailboat against the dock in Dublin. Her clothes had dried stiff with salty residue, and her skin was chafed from wind and salt. Her heart ached when she remembered that David was still out there, at the bottom of the channel.

The sailors spoke to her with thick Irish patter, but she kept on forgetting to pay attention and quickly got lost. They finally let her rest alone in her own thoughts.

Then a policeman arrived at the head of the dock, or maybe it was just a hired guard; either way, it sent Camryn into a panic. She grabbed onto the thick arm of the oldest of the sailors. "Please, help me," she begged.

"Well now, we won't leave you, we'll help," he reassured her. "We pulled you from the sea, lass, and aren't looking to throw you to the wolves now that we are on dry land."

"I don't think it's a good idea for me to meet with the police just yet," Camryn said. "There is a chance someone from London might be trying to find me and my friend."

"The Irish know all about being down on your luck," one the younger sailors said, and taking her hand he held it with great gentleness.

"Not now, Bobby!" the older gentleman said.

"You three," bellowed the seaman, "off the boat and stand at attention!" The younger men stepped off the boat and blocked the view from shore while Camryn slipped off the boat, followed closely by the older sailor. He beckoned to her and they swam around the back of the boat. He shielded the top of her head as she ducked under the dock and came up inside. The tide was low and they could tread water with plenty of headroom. Footsteps echoed on the dock above them, walking toward the sailboat.

Finger to his lips, the sweet old sailor shushed her and motioned her to follow. The lapping of the water and the creaking of boats tied to docks covered any sound they might have made as they made their way toward the land from beneath the covering of the dock. Soon enough, they could walk and then crawl through the ooze of harbor mud, and finally the sailor ducked out of the cover of the dock and then back to get Camryn.

"Come on, let's get out of here," he said. She scrambled out from under the dock and followed him up a slimy cement boat ramp to a truck parked in the lot. His formerly white pants were now a mottled green and brown and she picked a strand of seaweed out of his hair.

"You are my hero," she said. "May I know your name?"

With the slightest bow he said to her, "Neal O'Brien, miss, and glad to be of service. Where are those boys of mine? It shouldn't take all day to throw the coppers off the trail!"

The boys and the boat weren't visible from the truck, but they waited in companionable silence for them to come. When the boys emerged from the dock, they had a policeman trailing them. Instead of heading for the truck, the three of them took off at a saunter toward a ramshackle bar sitting right on the pier. They disappeared into the bar and the policeman stood outside for a moment, believing that something was up but not being able to put his finger on just what it could be.

"Okay, lassie, I'm going to take you home for my daughter to fuss over. You can tell me what happened on the way."

"What about your boys?" Camryn asked. "How will they get home?"

Neal waved her question away. "They'll figure a way home, and they'll be there in time for supper, just wait and see!"

Neal pulled out of the lot and headed northwest. "Okay then, I'm listening. What happened out there and why don't you want to talk to the police?"

Camryn started at the beginning, telling him all about the killing of her brother, the case the royal police had against David, and the attack on the ferry.

"Have you ever heard legends about the Irish Coronation Stone?" Camryn asked. "That is what we were coming to find."

As she talked to Neal, Camryn realized that there was really no valid reason to continue the search for answers now that David was gone, but she didn't know how to stop.

"We have the Giant's Causeway, Biddy Early, St. Patrick, the Blarney Stone, fairies, and likewise, we have Lia Fáil, the Stone of Destiny," he answered. "Our Irish Isle has magic in every cupboard and corner. Now, what might you need the Stone of Destiny for?"

"Isn't there some controversy about the stone the English took?" Camryn asked. She sat back in her seat and waited as old Dublin rolled by through the window.

"It was a long time ago," he began, "when we had the Lia Fáil. There is no love for the stone that sits up on Hill Tara nowadays. It marks a sacred place, but that is all it is, a marker. The real stone left for Scotland long ago." She turned again, surprised, to look at Neal as he spoke.

"Are you sure?" Camryn asked.

"It is common knowledge, at least with the common people," he answered.

Camryn was quiet for a moment.

"Is there someone I can ask that would know where it was taken?"

"There is always the Trinity College library, or you could go to the Hill of Tara itself; it isn't far from Dublin," Neal said.

They had turned down a residential street lined with row houses and mature trees.

"Wych Elm," Neal stated, watching Camryn's interest in the beautiful climbing trees. "Wait until school lets out: they are filled with children all up and down the street." He pulled over and parked in front of a townhouse with an orange door.

"You live here?" Camryn asked.

"My daughter Eileen is rehabbing it, just painted the door last Saturday," Neal answered. "She should be home."

They walked up the stoop and Neal banged a couple of times on the door and then walked in, calling out to his daughter as he pulled Camryn in with him.

"Eileen!"

"Dad?" someone answered from upstairs. "What are you doing here? I thought you and the boys went sailing?" Eileen ran lightly down the stairs and was hugging Neal around the neck by the time she finished her sentence.

"I want you to meet Camryn, she came sailing with us today and spent some time in the channel. Lost her purse and shoes. Can you fix her up?"

"Which one of my brothers brought you home?" Eileen looked at

Camryn appraisingly. "Bobbie? Connell? I think I'd bet on Frank," she said with a conspiratorial grin.

Camryn opened her mouth to try to explain, but Eileen had taken charge and was leading her up the stairs before she could begin.

"Put some tea on, will you, Dad? I'll be right back down."

The stairs let them off onto a large landing still in the throes of construction.

"I'm rearranging this floor into two spaces, bedroom, sitting room, and bathroom on each side. It is slow going," Eileen apologized.

"You are not doing the work yourself, are you?" Camryn asked.

"My dad is a master carpenter, so I come by it naturally," Eileen answered. "You'll want a shower first thing to rinse the salt off."

They walked through the half-finished bedroom into a bathroom of immense proportions. Standing her before a full mirror, Eileen took stock.

"I am too tall for you to fit in my clothes; why don't you get in the tub instead of the shower and I'll put your things in the wash?"

"Thank you! Tell Neal I'll hurry."

"He won't want to leave when he sees what I'm working on down-stairs! I found a dumbwaiter in the wall and I'm trying to get it work-ing. That should keep him busy until you are ready to go," Eileen said as she turned on the faucets and handed out towels, shampoo, and such. She turned her back to Camryn and held out an imperious hand.

"All right, let's have you down below your skivvies then!"

Camryn stripped, poured a bit of shampoo under the faucet, handed Eileen her bundle of clothes, and stepped into the bath as it filled with bubbles.

"Come down to the kitchen when you're done. I'll put a robe on the bed," Eileen said as she shut the door.

The hot water melted dried salt and stung her sunburned skin. It took several washes for her hair to feel clean. Camryn turned off the faucet, lathered her hair with conditioner, and, closing her eyes, rested against the back of the tub. It didn't take long until she was drifting off.

Camryn found herself in an enclosed garden wearing a filmy pale dress, her feet bare. The grass was cool and lush underfoot and she wandered, following a narrow brook. It babbled, tripping over river stones and flowing into meadow byways.

As she soaked in the peace of the garden, Camryn became aware of a light shining in the distance; someone moved within its brightness and she felt hurried to reach it.

"Cami!" a low voice called to her.

"Lucas? I'm coming!" She ran, and the faster she ran the farther away the light seemed. She ran and yearned and ran faster still. The light was getting dim and soon she could barely see its gleam in the distance. She ran until she was exhausted and was gasping for air, then she ran some more.

She stumbled and fell to the grass, panting from the exertion. With her heart pounding in her ears, she gave up the race and, looking about her, found a little stone bench sitting beneath a flowering tree. Pale pink blossoms covered the ground and fluttered in the air as the tree shed.

"Cami!" she heard again and instead of running she sat on the little stone bench and listened.

"Lucas?" she whispered and there he was standing by the bench.

"Are you really here?" Camryn asked. Tall and beautiful, it was his crooked grin that made her believe it was really him. She leaned toward him, but he put up his hands in warning.

"I can't hold you, Cami. We're in different worlds for now," he said.

"I love you, Lucas," Camryn said.

"But . . . ," he prompted.

"What do you mean? I love you!" Camryn declared.

"Do you need me to tell the whole truth?" Lucas asked. He paused for a moment and then continued.

"I wasn't ready to be a husband. I could have gotten out of deployment after we were married, but I wanted to go and I didn't think about you, just myself. I played at being a hero to my unit but didn't work at marriage. I've watched you waste away this last year and you are grieving someone that never existed. A figment of your imagination—the man I could have been but wasn't."

Camryn was silent as she considered the thoughts rolling through her heart. "I still love you," she whispered.

Lucas knelt by the bench and looked up at her. "You love me in spite of me," he said, and stood again.

"Now listen to me, Camryn Lavender, I don't want to see you worrying one more minute about how I died or why I died or even how I lived. Look at me! I am figuring it out. Have a little faith. And if I look in on you, I want to see you finding happiness again."

"How do I do that?" Camryn almost whispered.

"Just hang on to the things that last the longest," Lucas said. "Is it a deal?"

She drew a breath to protest but something light had settled inside where tangled knots of darkness had long been, and she realized that Lucas had been standing beside her all along this last year.

"Now that is the face of an angel!" Lucas said, looking at her. "I need to show you two things and then it is time for me to go."

He pointed and as Camryn followed his gaze, she saw a rocky mound the size of a man under a lone pistachio tree in the middle of a great desert plain. A trail ran by the grave. A village could be seen quivering like a mirage in the distance.

"The women in that village came upon my body when their men were away in the mountains and they had compassion and buried me."

"Do you want me to bring you home?" she asked, knowing the answer before he spoke.

"This is me, my body was just a gift, a tool and covering. It is safe enough and I do not need it here where I am," he answered her tenderly.

"Ready?" he asked and she nodded.

He drew her attention again and this time they were on a sloping cliff. Down below them the surf pounded into a crescent harbor and wooden stairs carved a treacherous path down to a little beach. A weathered sign pointed up the path to "Greystones." The moon hung low in the sky.

"Will you remember this if you see it again?" Lucas asked her.

"I think so," she muttered. She looked about her to memorize the spot.

"I need you to be here at 9:55 tomorrow night, can you do that?" He asked her intently.

"Is this near Dublin?" she asked him.

"We are just south of Dublin, not far at all," he answered.

"I'll be here then. What will I need? Will you be with me?"

"I can't stay, Cami. I wish I had treasured you like I should have while I was with you, but if I try to stay in your world I won't be grow-ing in this one, and I have some growing to do, some things to work on," he answered softly.

"You won't forget me?" she whispered.

"If I could do this all over again, you would never even think to ask that question," Lucas said, his voice trembling with regret. "Don't forget, 9:55 tomorrow night. Take care, my love!"

Camryn reached for him and found herself in a lukewarm tub, con-ditioner dripping onto her nose. She rinsed, pulled the plug, wrapped herself in a towel, and brushed her hair all in a daze. Finally, she shook herself out of her thoughts and, finding tears salting her skin all over again, she reached for the feeling of perfect happiness and peace she had while dreaming of Lucas. After wrapping herself in a robe, she set off to find the kitchen.

CHAPTER 24

Downstairs, following the sound of a tumbling dryer, she found the hallway that led into the kitchen. She found Neal with the boys abandoned at the wharf seated at a granite island, the remains of sandwiches crumbled on white plates. The dryer buzzed as she paused in the doorway and Eileen walked into the kitchen carrying a small basket filled with her clean clothes.

"Camryn, pop in here and change and we'll get one of the boys to make you a sandwich," Eileen said. Four sets of male eyes watched her walk across the kitchen and disappear into the washroom.

"Your tongue's hanging out, Frank!" Eileen smirked at them all.

"What time is it?" Camryn called from behind the closed door.

"It's close to five," Neal called to her. "Come and eat and let's figure out how to get you home. I've been telling the boys about your troubles."

The washroom door opened and Camryn emerged. "I'm starved!" she exclaimed, "I haven't felt this hungry in over a year!"

Three boys scrambled to their feet, offering her their seats, and Neal placed a gleaming white plate in front of her with a mile-high sandwich on it.

A warm lightness had settled into her heart and her eyes glowed with happiness.

"Thank you, darling boys, for taking care of me." She looked at all of them. "Did you find out why the police were at the dock?"

"They were checking to see if we had picked up someone that fell overboard from the ferry! They are asking everyone that comes in," Bobby said.

Camryn picked up the sandwich with both hands. "Now, about getting me back to London, I'm not quite ready to go home just yet. Whoever it is that was chasing us thinks that we are at the bottom of the channel, so I should poke around for a bit while I have the chance to do it without being watched."

"Why are you interested in the Lia Fáil?" Frank asked. "It is an old story."

"I am not really sure, I just know that two good men are dead because someone doesn't want us asking questions. That is a good enough reason to keep asking them."

"What is going on?" Eileen asked.

Camryn sat up in her chair, took a long look at Neal, considering, and finally answered. "The only reason I hesitate to tell you the whole story is to protect you all."

Neal answered for them all, "It seems like fate has brought us this far, so we can walk a little farther. Or do you think that our finding you in the channel was just dumb luck?"

"No, it couldn't have been that," Camryn answered. "Well, where do I start?"

"The beginning might be a good place," Frank said solemnly.

"All right, you asked for it! It really does start with the Coronation Stone thousands of years ago. Do you know that story?" Camryn asked, looking around the table.

"Isn't that another name for the Lia Fáil?" Eileen asked.

"I think so," Camryn said.

"I remember that the Lia Fáil is one of the hallows of Ireland. There was a cauldron that filled itself with food, an unbeatable sword, a powerful spear, and a stone that revealed their kings."

"It seems that the legend of the stone takes many forms, but it begins with the prophet Jacob using the stone as a pillow and having a dream of his destiny," Camryn said.

"Didn't Scottish students steal the Coronation Stone from under the throne in Westminster Abbey a few years back?" Bobby said. "There were rumors that the students switched the real Coronation Stone with a fake."

"If what we have learned is right, then the stone they stole was a fake as well," Camryn answered.

"And this is what someone is trying to kill you for? Asking questions about an old rock?" Eileen asked.

"Exactly!" Camryn said. "Who cares? Right?"

"Someone obviously cares," Neal said.

"There are prophecies about this stone, which if the rightful king is crowned upon the stone, it will actually roar of God's approval of the coronation. So our king would have a vested interest in being able to claim the stone for himself and for his children," Camryn said.

"Although the stone hasn't been said to make a sound for many hundreds of years."

Neal said, "These same questions have popped up again and again. Why would someone feel threatened now? How did you get involved in this?"

"My brother works, or rather, worked for Prince George and started asking questions, though on behalf of the prince or on his own, we don't know. He called in a friend to find the answers for him. His friend is the man that I was on the ferry with—the one that was shot and left in the channel this morning. My brother was killed on the streets of London two days ago," Camryn said.

"Who is your brother?" Neal asked, softly.

"Roger Brough. And David Lord is the friend he called in to help. David is from New York. They were friends in college. I think Roger felt that getting someone outside the English establishment would be better than stirring up controversy within official circles," Camryn said.

"David Lord, you said?" Neal asked with a long look around the table at his children.

"Yes, he is some kind of special accountant in New York," she said.

"His mother wouldn't be Elizabeth O'Brien Lord, would she?" Neal asked.

Camryn looked up from tracing water lines on the table. "What are you talking about?" she asked.

"My father's brother left Ireland with two of his children in the late 70s, one of his daughters married a Phillip Lord. I know they had one son and while I have never met the American side of the family, I believe that his name is David," Neal said into a shocked silence.

"You are cousins to David?" Camryn said. "And just happened along to pull me out of the channel?"

"That settles it then, we are in this with you, Cami. What do you want to do and how can we help?" Neal sat solidly in the timeworn oak kitchen chair and looked at Camryn with green eyes that burned with a solemn fervor.

With an effort, she put aside her hesitation to involve them and accepted that they had been sent to help.

"I don't want anyone to know that you are helping me," she said, "so we'll have to be careful." She sent a piercing look at Neal, until he gave a short nod, accepting the terms. Leaning on her elbows, she talked low and fast, explaining what they could do to help.

The moon hung low in the sky before the meeting ended and they separated until morning. Nestled in the second bedroom, Camryn stared dreamily out the window, memorizing the face of the moon. She succumbed to slumber without a fight, no longer seeking the forgetfulness her dreams brought and no longer afraid of waking to a remembrance of her sorrow.

It was two hours past breakfast before Camryn caught the highway that led from Dublin to Hill Tara. Scattering last night and reassembling this morning, the O'Briens helped bring the pieces of her life back together. Clean clothes and a toothbrush, a cell phone and a borrowed car and she was good to go.

The M3 thoroughfare cut through mint green fields and reduced the time to Tara down to a mere forty-minute drive, though all of the charm of traveling in Ireland was sacrificed for convenience. Until she pulled off the highway and everything slowed back down.

Neal had warned her to leave the cell phone off, so she had to find her way around a small village and down a country lane, which was so old that a strip of grass grew right down the middle of it. Huge hedgerows grew along one side of the old road with a rock fence on the other. She passed only one other car driving slowly along the narrow road. With her windows rolled down, she called for directions as they inched past each other.

"How far to Tara?"

The woman in the mini turned and pointed down the road. "About an Irish mile I'd say. It's not far at all." The mini crept by and tooted as she sped up down the lane. Camryn continued on toward Tara, and when she gained the roundabout, the hedgerow ended and before her a stood a lush, green hill. A small brown sign pointed up the road: 'Hill of Tara.'

With the wind blowing through the car, she rolled up the gentle incline to the crest of Tara. A hawk circled lazily high above and all birdsong had quieted in respect. At the crest of the hill she parked in a graveled spot, turned off the car, and soaked in the soul of Ireland.

Although the climb had been gentle, it added up to something substantial, and the broad, flat top of Tara seemed far removed from the valley below. Cattle quietly lowed and the leaves of the grasses jostled as a light wind brushed across the hilltop. From below came the muted sound of a truck changing gears on the lane. Camryn made her way to a simple footpath. It led to a stone church and a sign that announced she had found the visitors center.

The church doors stood open, inviting visitors, and as her eyes adjusted to the dim light, a woman in sensible shoes walked toward her.

"*Dia duit*, welcome to our Hill of Tara," she said briskly.

"Are you open?" Camryn asked, "Are you a tour guide?"

"You are here a little early for our big season, but I am here tending the graveyard this morning, and it would be lovely to show you around Tara," she said. "My name is Mary. Let me wash up and put my tools away; it will only take a moment. You can look around the graveyard if you want or you can sit in here and wait if you'd rather."

It was warm in the little chapel; the light filtered in through thick old windows and lit up clouds of dancing dust motes. Camryn waited in the peace, quiet thickening around her minute by minute. Seeing Lucas, even in a dream, had served to wake her up and make everything feel different. She found herself feeling joy for no reason at all.

The sound of a door and the squeaking of sensible shoes announced Mary's return, lifting the curtain of quiet but not disturbing the peace in any way.

"Well, dear, just how much do you want to know about our Hill of Tara? What did you come to see?" Mary asked.

"I'd love to stay here all day, but I came to see the Lia Fáil for myself," Camryn said.

"Let's go then, it's just this way."

Leaving through the front doors, they started down the gravel path.

"Ireland is an ancient land and Tara is even more. She is the very soul of Ireland."

They walked through awakening green fields, making their own path toward the Lia Fáil. Mary continued: "Our Hill of Tara has been a sacred place for centuries. Looking over her shoulders you can see half the counties in Ireland. One hundred and forty-two high kings ruled in the name of Tara, and the most powerful kings held their feasts and celebrations here."

Mary continued, "There are several different and conflicting legends in Celtic mythology describing how the Lia Fáil is said to have been brought to Ireland. The Lebor Gabala, dating to the eleventh century, states that it was brought here by the semi-divine race known as the Tuatha Dé Danann. The Tuatha Dé Danann had traveled to the Northern Isles, or Norway, where they learned skills in four cities: Falias, Gorias, Murias, and Findias. From Norway they traveled to Ireland, bringing with them a treasure from each city—the four treasures of Ireland.

"Have you heard of 'the hallows'? From Falias came the Lia Fáil. The other three treasures are the Claíomh Solais or Sword of Victory, the Sleá Bua or Spear of Lugh, and the Coire Dagdae or The Dagda's Cauldron. Many scholars believe that the Tuatha Dé Danann could be the tribe of Dan from the twelve tribes of Israel.

"Others are convinced that the legends that tell of the prophet Jeremiah bringing the stone to Ireland, along with his granddaughters, heirs to the throne of David, are the true history of the Lia Fáil."

Mary stopped walking and turned to look at Camryn, "Am I boring you?"

"Not at all," Camryn said. "This is exactly what I hoped to find. Wasn't the stone sent to Scotland for the coronation of their kings?"

A black raven landed in the grass in front of Camryn. Cawing raucously, he cocked its head and picked up a white feather from the rustling grass. They watched him as he spread his wings, lifted into flight, and floated lazily over the edge of the hill.

Mary looked at Camryn for a long moment. "Who are you?" she asked.

"My name is Camryn Lavender," she answered. "I am pleased to meet you . . ."

Mary wasn't listening. She had turned toward the Lia Fáil again, walking quickly, this time in silence. Camryn followed, cursing herself for being an overreaching fool. Her question about the stone traveling to Scotland, too hastily blurted out, might have ruined any chance of finding out what she needed to know.

Reaching the Lia Fáil, they stood before the light gray edifice. Finally, Mary seemed to come to a decision, and looking about her as if making sure they were alone, she asked, "What is it you came to see?"

"I am trying to trace the true history of the British Coronation Stone and it seems that most scholars believe that it used to rest here on Tara; that it was taken to Scotland to be used in the coronation of their kings, who were close cousins to the Irish. Which means this stone is something else, maybe even something special, but it isn't the Lia Fáil."

"I was born in Navan," Mary said, "next door to Tara and I have heard every tale of our Lia Fáil, good and ill. Some say it was Jacob's Pillow, brought to Ireland by the prophet Jeremiah. Here it became the Lia Fáil or 'Fatal Stone,' used as a mystical throne of Irish kings and proving them worthy to reign under God. It was also said to be the deathbed pillow of St. Columba on the island of Iona. Legend says it was moved to mainland Scotland, where it served as the preserver of royal succession and was called the Stone of Destiny.

"It is said that when the King of Munster sent an army five thousand strong to support Robert the Bruce in his defeat of the English at Bannockburn in 1314, a portion of the historic stone was given by the Scots in gratitude—and was returned to Ireland.

"Others say it may be a stone brought back to Ireland from the Crusades. If so, it could be the 'Stone of Ezel,' behind which Jonathan advised David to hide when he fled from his enemy Saul. A few claim it was the stone that spewed water when struck by Moses with his staff. I have heard it all, do you want to know what I think?"

"I do, very much," Camryn answered.

"The official story is that this pillar here is the Lia Fáil, but I think we are venerating another stone entirely. Regardless, every single legend of the Lia Fáil begins with the house of Israel; every thread winds back to a single beginning. And that beginning is the Hebrew nation," Mary said, a little breathlessly.

"Do you think that the stone went to Scotland? Do you think it is the British Coronation Stone that used to sit under the coronation chair in Westminster Abbey?" Camryn asked.

"I don't know anything about where it is now, but I believe that it left here and went to Scotland. And, most important, all the old records describe the Lia Fáil as a polished oval stone. Elaborately carved and glowing with light. Mind you, I would be fired if I talked about such things to our visitors!" Mary said. "Tell me again, why do you want to know about these things?"

Camryn didn't know how to answer her but tried again, "A simple letter set events in motion that have propelled me here to ask questions. Two good men have been killed to stop us from coming here."

Mary looked uncertain. Camryn watched her eyes close. She might have even been whispering under her breath.

"Excuse me?" Camryn asked, in case she was supposed to be following what was happening.

Mary squared her shoulders and motioned for Camryn to follow as she struck out toward the chapel. Camryn hesitated only a moment, unsure of what was happening, and then hurried to catch up.

"Where are we going?" Camryn asked.

"I am an O'Donnell, the caretakers of Tara. Trustee of the history of this hill of the High Kings, keeper of the ages. I have something to show you that I think will help you understand. We have been given the sign of the raven! And I am not second-guessing that!"

Mary spoke without slowing her pace, speaking almost to herself. Camryn matched her stride and her serious mood and, when they reached the chapel, followed her up the steps and into the warmth and security of the stone walls. The timeless dust motes still hung in the ancient light of Tara, and they danced and swirled around the women as they walked quickly through the main hall and into a small anteroom.

"What do you mean 'sign of the raven'?" Camryn asked. "That raven we saw is a sign of something?"

"In Ireland the raven is an oracle; they foretell the future, and his appearing that way can only mean one thing," Mary said.

Here, Mary seemed to pause once more and then, gathering herself, pulled open a file cabinet. Fingering through the files, she pulled out a bulky manila envelope, and after reaching in, she solemnly handed Camryn a key. It was old with an ornate top and a simple configuration on the bottom and it was a bit greasy with age.

"In the graveyard there is a headstone for Mick McCabe. This key opens a portal on the north side of the grave marker. Inside that hollow is the record you want, kept by my people as keepers of Tara through the years. It has been foretold that our words will help to usher in the reign of one who has the right to rule in Ireland."

"I don't know what to say," Camryn said fervently.

They both turned at the sound of a creaking door and suddenly other sounds became obvious: sounds of a scuffle and a shot.

Chapter 25

Camryn slipped the key in her purse and they waited by the solid oak door. When it was obvious that all was quiet, they opened the door and left the miniature room.

It seemed impossible for the captain's men to have tracked her here; it was nothing but providence that saved her from drowning in the channel. Still, if they were watching her mother, they might have found the bank transfer and tracked her to Neal somehow.

As Camryn followed Mary, she marshaled her thoughts; she needed to get the papers quickly and get away from this place. It was imperative that she be at Greystones by 9:55. There were no further sounds of an intruder or a fight. They paused at the doorway leading out back to the graveyard, surveying the scene in front of them and then Mary slowly poked her head out to check on either side of the doorway.

"Ony McCabe! You gave me a start!" she exclaimed, her hand to her heart, obviously feeling every one of its galloping palpitations. Camryn ventured a look out the doorway and found the man called Ony holding a long handled shovel. A man in a suit and glossy shoes lay at his feet, a bloody knot on his forehead.

"I was watching for any of this fellow's friends who might be sneaking around after him and saw you two skulking about. Didn't know who it was for a moment," Ony said.

"Is he dead?" Camryn asked, not really wanting to know the answer.

"No, but he'll have a powerful headache when he wakes up," Ony said. "I came to relieve you, Mary—thought I'd find you in the cemetery so I brought my shovel and a rake. You weren't here so I went in the back way and caught this bloke with his ear pressed to the anteroom door and a gun in his hand. I must have made some noise because he turned real cat like and shot a hole in the wall an inch from my head, so I knocked him silly with my shovel. Dragged him out here and waited to see if anyone showed up to find him."

Camryn had a thought. *Can I look in his pockets before we call the Guard?* Without waiting for an answer she knelt and started going through his pockets. Coat pockets clean, even the inside ones, no keys in his front pockets and no wallet in his back pockets.

He groaned sluggishly as she rolled him on his back after the search. Ony nudged him firmly in the chest with a muddy work boot.

"It looks like this fine boy came prepared to do mischief, probably had lots of practice leading up to an attack in broad daylight and on the sacred Hill of Tara, for heaven's sake!" he said, his words rising in a lilting tune the Irish learn at their mother's knee.

"Mary, do you have your knitting with you? You'd better hurry up and fetch it if you do. Or I might have to knock him about again."

Mary bristled as she walked toward the garden shed. "Thick old idiot," she muttered loud enough to send a sly smile across Ony's jowly face. "He thinks I have nothing better to do than knit in my free time. Blathering bogger!" She was rough on the shed door but seemed to settle to a simmer on her return as she pointedly refrained from slamming it shut and had decided to laugh at her own temper by the time she returned offering Ony a fine length of rope and a sweet smile.

"You do set me up, and I go for it every time." She laughed. "Let me see to this lady and her tour." Mary turned to Camryn. "I don't see any reason to involve her in our bit of violence any further, do you, Ony dear?"

Ony nodded slightly in agreement and asked, "Do you think there are any more with him? Why don't we tie him up and I'll go and take a look around." Ony bent and wrapped him tightly with the long length of rope, arms to his sides, legs whipped together with a sailors knot in a sweep at his ankles.

"Keep his gun with you and I'll take the shovel. Stay here!" Ony left them then, disappearing into the little church.

Mary started to fit the gun in her dress pocket but instead thrust it at Camryn and rather than touching the brittle chill of the handle, Camryn held out her purse and Mary dropped it in.

"Is the safety on, I wonder?" Camryn asked.

"I wouldn't know, dear, just try not to jostle it around too much," Mary said airily. Then with a meaningful glance, Mary said, "Let's hurry and get the record out now, before Ony comes back!"

Camryn shushed her, indicating the trussed up intruder.

"Where is the grave?" Camryn asked in the barest whisper.

Mary took Camryn's arm and they walked together through the new spring grass, trimmed low after a winter's nap. The graveyard was not large and Mick McCabe's headstone was of new black marble. Mary stopped at the back of his stone and knelt to brush away the debris of windblown leaves and loose soil. Camryn watched as the buried receptacle was uncovered and then fitted the key into its lock and turned. With a decided click a lid popped up enough for her to pry it up and open. Mary reached into the box and pulled out a sheaf of papers, and Camryn dropped the top into place and locked it. Camryn helped Mary to her feet and they smoothed the dirt back into place over the box.

"There," Mary exclaimed, "I've gone and done it!"

Ony was just coming around the side of the church when they returned to their post. The dark-suited gentleman was wide awake now and was watching them with sharp eyes.

"Well now, the cute hoor decided to wake up," he observed. "I think we need to have some words about where his friends have run off to."

Mary looked at Camryn nervously. "I think you had better be off, my dear," she said. "Ony, there isn't any need for the young lady to stay, is there?"

"I don't want you here either, Mary, until we find out how many villains we have roaming about Tara. Both of you go along and ring up the Guard when you get down the hill," he answered and the look he cast at the man at his feet sent a ripple of trepidation up Camryn's spine. She wanted to be far from this ugly struggle. If only she could go back to a London where Roger and David and Lucas still breathed and she could lean on them.

Maybe they would leave me alone if I just walked away, she thought. *I could go back to Scotland!* Her memory lingered over golden mountains, shaggy ponies, and the sweeping, endless wind.

"And waste our sacrifice?" someone seemed to whisper. No, it wasn't echoes of their voices she heard, but her own lagging determination to see this to the end, whatever that would bring.

"Are you quite all right?" Mary peered at her with a quizzical frown.

"I was just woolgathering, and so sorry to think that I somehow might have brought trouble upon you!" Camryn said.

"You! How did you cause any of this trouble? I thought you said you didn't know him!"

Rather than explain her outburst, Camryn took Mary's hand and asked, "Is there a pub close-by that makes a decent sandwich?"

The satisfaction of feeding someone as thin and pale as herself seemed to be universally appealing. Mary instantly forgot Camryn's odd behavior and the two women left after promising to call the guards when they got down off the hill and into town.

Mary did know a quiet lunchroom, although she refused to talk business until after huge bowls of steaming Irish potato soup had been set before them. But once Camryn had swallowed a few creamy spoonfuls, Mary broke down and spilled the whole story. Camryn leaned across the table and listened intently to the Irish story of the Lia Fáil.

W̄e tell the story of the Hill of Tara hundreds of times during the big season," Mary said, "and most of the guides know that we are telling tales when we talk of the Lia Fáil. The Hill of Tara has been a sacred place for thousands of years. A place where the high kings of Ireland were crowned and held their celebrations and were buried. Legends concerning the Lia Fáil take three paths, some say that the stone came from the north countries. Viking people came and went as they pleased, raiding and marrying, so it is a possibility.

"Others say that a great ruler came to Ireland about the time of the exodus of the Israelites from Egypt. Kin to Moses, he brought with him the Lia Fáil, the Coronation Stone, the Pillow of Jacob.

"Others tell a tale of the prophet Jeremiah. Jeremiah was a prophet in the Old Testament and lived at the time King Zedekiah last ruled, in fact, some think that Jeremiah was Zedekiah's grandfather, although he might have just been of the royal house. He was a prophet and he was sent to call the king to repentance and for this he was imprisoned. When the land was conquered and the king slaughtered, the conquerors found Jeremiah in a dank prison. They let him go free because he obviously was not a friend to the former rulers.

"Legend has it that Jeremiah took his two great-granddaughters and traveled out of Israel with the Stone of Jacob and ended up in Ireland. Some say he became the great lawgiver in Ireland called Ollam Fodhla and one of his great-granddaughters married the king of Ireland. The name of Tara, adopted at this time, hearkens to Israel. *Torah* and *Tara* are both words that mean 'the law,' you see?

"Regardless of how the stone got here, it is sacred because of where it came from and what it is to remind us of." Mary finished her tale and Camryn sat deep in thought for a moment.

"There doesn't seem to be any other story here but that this stone is, indeed, the stone that opened the heavens for Jacob in Israel, thousands of years ago. Is that true?"

"That is the beginning of every story of the stone," Mary said. "There is a prophecy in the Bible about all of this. It is in here somewhere..." Mary turned the pages, scanning them quickly. "Here it is, in Psalm 89: 'I have made a covenant with my chosen, I have sworn unto David, my servant, Thy seed will I establish forever, and build up thy throne to all generations.

"'His seed also will I make to endure forever, and his throne as the days of heaven. If his children forsake my law, and walk not in my judgments; if they break my statutes, and keep not my commandments, then I will visit their transgression with the rod, and their iniquity with stripes. Nevertheless my loving kindness will I not utterly take from him, nor suffer my faithfulness to fail.

"'My covenant will I not break, nor alter the thing that is gone out of my lips. Once I have sworn by my holiness that I will not lie unto David. His seed shall endure forever, and his throne as the sun before me. It shall be established forever as the moon and as a faithful witness in heaven.'

"And one more in Jeremiah: 'For thus saith the Lord; David shall never want a man to sit upon the throne of the house of Israel.'"

"So King David's throne was promised to his children forever?"

"That is what it says."

"So where did the stone go from Tara?" Camryn asked her elderly guide.

"Why, that much is clear!" Mary said, "Dunadd in Scotland: that is where it went from here, of that there is no question.

"And remember, miss, this stone has become a 'Holy Grail' to many throughout the ages. Men and women have fought wars to possess it or to keep it from those deemed unworthy to lay claim to it," Mary said solemnly. "If you are caught up in a quest for the Lia Fáil, you will need heaven's grace!"

Camryn was loath to take the original records, so they stopped and made a copy. By the time Mary and Camryn parted ways the village church bells were tolling two o'clock, sending a flock of ravens to blacken the sky. Twittering joyfully, they rocketed through pale blue skies. Soaring and then diving, they settled back in the bell tower before echoes of the last chime died in the chill air. An omen for Mary to record in the history of the Hill of Tara. Camryn headed south, back to Dublin. Lost in thought, it took a while before she noticed the black motorcycle that was boldly trailing her at every turn.

CHAPTER 26

The new Virginia day dawned chill and sweet. Enrique yawned, his eyes heavy and gritty, trying to bring the clock into focus.

Almost nine, time to take over guard duty, he thought. They had divided the night between them, watching over the little troop of prisoners. The men had struggled surreptitiously for hours to free themselves; their heavily-bandaged leader was offered a painkiller, which he declined. But the need for sleep and the futility of getting free of zip ties and yards of duct tape had finally won the night. The men slept where they lay, immune to the cool night and the slate floor.

Maeve and her husband were due back in town this morning. Although confident they had rounded up all the soldiers, they were being rigorously careful until Maeve and her husband were home. Once she and her husband were safe, they would turn these soldiers over to the police.

The sun was filtering through a cloudy morning fog, illuminating the kitchen more as it climbed into the sky. Enrique sat at the kitchen table watching the news and eating a bowl of cereal, compliments of the British soldiers' foray into town. Two black shadows rubbed against his leg and licked creamy white milk from their whiskers. Their mother dreamed under the chair. The kittens were a reminder of his promise to Sophia.

"I see our little friends are still following you around," Dean said, in the pale morning light.

"Hey, Junior," Enrique said. "I guess they don't know that you are the crazy fool that saved them. How are our guests doing?"

"I think they have given up trying to escape. They are sleeping right now or are at least doing a good imitation of it," Dean said.

"I want to talk to their leader," Enrique said. "It would be good to figure out how many of them came to the States and who sent them."

"You mean we might not have them all rounded up!" Dean said. Enrique shrugged.

"I scrolled through their phones, so tying them to the murders will be easy for some prosecutor with all the information I found. Only the crazy guy with the broken arm—London—we can give that info to Mr. Lord. We'll see what information they give up to an expert," Enrique said. "Why don't you eat and shower, I have guard duty until Maeve gets here."

When Dean was upstairs and out of the way, Enrique moved the wounded leader into the kitchen. His arm was swollen and blood had seeped through the bandages. Without painkillers, he had to be in a great deal of pain.

"What is your name?" Enrique began, and expecting no response, was not surprised when the man was silent. "Listen," Enrique continued. "You are obviously military, and here on a mission. Here without informing your ally, the greatest military power on the earth, that you are here or what you are up to."

Enrique let that settle in.

"It must be important. It will go better for you and your men if you tell us why you are here and how many of you are running around threatening murder. Committing murder."

The man smirked just a little, as if he knew something he wasn't going to tell.

"If you think we won't find out the whole story eventually, you are crazy." Enrique held up the box of phones. "We have all of this, we have your vehicles, and if you think that all your men will hold steady once they are in custody, well, someone will talk, and once one does, you all will."

The man's look of amusement held. Enrique watched him then and fell silent.

Finally, the silent treatment worked; the man spoke. "You will get nothing from me," he said. "But I will warn you. If I were you I would watch my back, and your family's backs and your friends' backs. Only those of us who have nothing to lose are here, and we are willing to give our lives for the people who sent us."

Enrique heard what he was saying and understood that they had not caught them all.

It was a little after eleven in the morning when a taxi pulled in the drive and around the back. Enrique had pulled the car out of the garage and he waited in full view for them to step out of their cab. Dean was standing in the shadows of the car, watching for trouble. Motioning for Maeve to stay in the taxi, her husband stepped out.

"Mr. Smith?" Enrique asked, politely.

"Who are you?" Maeve's husband asked aggressively.

"I am Enrique Gutierre, Mr. Smith. And this is Dean Ellis," Enrique said, nodding toward Dean. "We need to talk to you and your wife before you go inside."

"She stays in the car," Mr. Smith said, on edge.

Enrique nodded once in agreement. "I apologize for waylaying you this morning, but I was hired to locate a group of women who traveled to the US under specific circumstances. Your wife is on that list."

"Who hired you to find my wife?" Mr. Smith demanded. His eyes were cold and all business.

"Someone who wants to protect Maeve and everyone on that list. We have discovered that someone else was looking for them as well—someone who wanted them eliminated," Enrique answered civilly, reigning in an answering coldness.

Dean walked over, sensing that the conversation was turning into confrontation. "Mr. Smith, we aren't here to cause you any trouble. In fact, we have the men tied up in your study right now and if you look in the trees on your back lot you will find them set up to ambush you. They were waiting for you."

"Buck? Honey, this is silly." Maeve got out of the taxi and stood by the back of the car. "Pay the driver please, I'm going inside to unpack and do some laundry." The driver opened the trunk and started removing luggage.

"I don't think you want her to go in there by herself," Enrique warned him.

"Do you have some identification? And I need a number for someone that will confirm your story." Buck Smith thawed enough to keep the peace in front of his wife. "Maeve, will you wait just a minute while I call and check on them? Then we'll go inside." He paid the driver while Enrique wrote down the phone number for Mr. Lord's company.

The taxi drove off and Mr. Smith called Accountancy, Inc. and talked to Mrs. McCombs. The ice in his demeanor had thawed just a degree or two by the time he was finished.

"She seems to think I would be smart to listen to your story. Let's go inside, Maeve, and hear them out."

They went in through the kitchen door this time; the pizza boxes on the counter, the milk in the fridge, every detail added up to trouble.

"All right, I am listening," Mr. Smith said, standing stiff with controlled tension.

"Me too," Maeve said, equally alert.

Enrique began at the beginning. Dean played his part well, and when they got to the part about the invading forces, Mr. Smith went into the study with Enrique to take a look.

Maeve had much to tell them too. It turned out that she hadn't traveled from England in the time frame they were concerned with, but had traded tickets and passports with a girlfriend who needed to get home quickly. She had stayed for several months, coming to the States after the New Year.

Much later, after close questioning on both sides, Maeve's husband placed some calls to various officials, none of them the local police.

"I take it you would like to be on your way before the authorities show up?" he asked them.

"We had hoped we would be finished once we talked with your wife, but since we have one more woman to contact, it would be best if we could skip explaining all this to the police and got on the road back to New York," Enrique said. He handed Mr. Smith a bundle of cell phones, wallets, keys to the black Suburbans, and incidental trash gathered from the soldiers.

"Do you have a card?" Mr. Smith asked Enrique.

Enrique grabbed a pen and wrote his name and the phone number at Accountancy, Inc. on the calendar on the fridge.

Mrs. Smith watched their departure, holding the mother cat and stroking her fur. The kittens followed Enrique, working hard to stay clear of his boots but sticking to him like he was their mother.

Dean looked from Enrique to the kittens and back.

"Are you looking for a home for the kittens?" Dean asked.

"Would you like to take the kittens with you?" Maeve said, surprised. "They are weaned, and we can't keep them. We travel too much to take proper care of the little darlings, so I am afraid they will turn wild if we don't find a home for them soon."

With a box and the two kittens, they walked out to the car and climbed in. Enrique started the Z28 and they pulled to the end of the drive and dug out the map.

"We need to get back to 95, I suppose; I'll follow you in the truck," Dean said, tracing a route out of the winding country roads to New York City.

A left turn out of the driveway started the final leg of their journey.

CHAPTER 27

Just outside of Dublin, Camryn stopped for petrol. Consulting the GPS on her phone, she charted a course to Trinity College library.

As she pulled out onto the highway her phone buzzed on the console. Camryn pulled over abruptly and answered the phone.

"Hello? Camryn are you there?" Neal shouted into the phone.

Watching through the side view mirror, Camryn saw a dark motorcycle swerved to miss her. She heard the distinct whine of brakes as it came within inches of hitting her fender.

"I'm just outside of Dublin, I thought I'd go somewhere quiet to study what I've found."

She watched the motorcycle as he drove away.

"Let me get through this traffic and I'll be right back," Camryn said into the phone. She tossed the phone in the passenger's seat and pulled out slowly, driving on the shoulder and then merging into traffic.

Once she was out of traffic, Camryn picked up the phone again. "Sorry about that, I was hoping to spend a few hours at the library and then head down to Greystones. I have to be there before ten."

"Right. Eileen wants to meet you now and Frank or I will go with you tonight, we need to leave at 8:30 or 9:00," Neal said.

Hanging up, she topped a small rise and fixed her sights on what was ahead of her, following the GPS instructions to Trinity College Library. She couldn't help watching for the motorcycle, but she didn't see any sign of him or anyone else to trouble her.

Eileen was waiting for her at the entrance to the library long room.

"Did you ever see Star Wars?" she asked Camryn. "The Jedi archives are said to be modeled after this room. The Book of Kells is downstairs."

Camryn interrupted, "Could we go and see it? Is the book itself displayed?"

"Does this have anything to do with the stone?" Eileen asked.

"I don't know. I am feeling my way in the dark," Camryn said to her. "But the Lia Fáil left Tara and was taken to Scotland, and eventually the Scottish kings were crowned at Iona with the stone. Iona is also where the Book of Kells was partially written and kept. I don't know if this will help me understand why we are chasing the stone, but since we are here and the line is short, let's see what we can find out."

During the tour they were able to view a few pages from the Book of Kells, under glass for protection. They learned that the Book of Kells is an illustrated copy of the four Gospels, written and illustrated by Celtic monks in the eighth century.

The pages displayed were breathtakingly impressive. Camryn and Eileen spent several minutes examining the intricate design and brilliant colors of the illustrations, before the guide began speaking to the group.

"Historically, the book was thought to have been created at the time of St. Columba—many believed it to be the work of his own hands. These beliefs have long been discredited on scientific grounds. Our best evidence suggests a composition date about 800 AD, long after St. Columba's death in 597. Eventually, Viking raids dispersed the monks and their holy relics into safer retreats within Ireland and Scotland. There are other traditions, which have gained growing belief among Irish scholars, that suggest that the manuscript was created to honor the 200th anniversary of St. Columba's death."

The guide continued, "Although the question of the exact location of where the book was written and illustrated will probably never be answered to everyone's satisfaction, the theory that its beginning commenced at Iona and finished at Kells is currently the most widely preferred explanation. Scholars are convinced that the Book of Kells was produced by Columban monks."

"Any questions?" the guide asked the group. "Yes?" she said, indicating a gentleman with his hand in the air.

"Who is Columba?"

"St. Columba was an Irish monk who was banished from Ireland for inciting a war over the copying of a manuscript. He built a monastery in Iona, Scotland, was descended from the Irish high kings, and renounced all rights to the throne in order to preach the gospel of Christ. He was one of the twelve apostles of Ireland.

"Have you all seen the Book of Kells? Then our next stop will be the oldest Gaelic harp in Ireland, it dates back to the fifteenth century." The guide moved on with the group trailing behind. "Did you know that David's harp is the symbol of Ireland and Guinness beer?"

"Excuse me!" Camryn interjected. The guide turned to see who had interrupted so vehemently. "You said 'David's harp'? You mean King David from the Bible?"

"Well, yes," the guide said. "We have harps on our coins, on our postage stamps, on our passports, and on the official seals of Ireland. Even Guinness uses the harp as its symbol."

"Why?" Camryn asked.

"Why?" the guide rejoined, "That is a good question, and one I don't know the answer to. Maybe we can ask the curator when we get to the next exhibit."

"To continue, the harp is the oldest of its kind in Ireland and probably dates from the fifteenth century. It is made of oak and willow and has twenty-nine brass strings. It is the model for the emblem of Ireland."

Stopping the group at the displayed harp, she called on a handheld walkie-talkie and an official in a dark gold jacket joined them.

"Someone had a question about the harp's history in Ireland?" he asked, rocking back on his heels and rubbing his hands together.

Camryn raised her hand a bit and asked, "Why would David's harp be the symbol of Ireland?"

"Ah yes, great question. In short, Ireland and Scotland have deep and tangled roots in Old Testament traditions. The settlers of these islands were said to have come from those tribes of Israel, the word *Saxon* comes from a shortening of 'Isaac's sons.' *Brit* means 'covenant' in Welsh and Hebrew.

"If you look at the Irish flag and other symbols used in Irish life, you will notice a red hand. That story hearkens back to the story of twins born to Tamar and Judah, one of the sons of Israel.

"During birth one of the boys stuck a hand out (they named him Perez) and the midwife tied a scarlet thread around his wrist to identify the firstborn, but the other son (Zerach) was born first. So the family of the first was identified by the red hand. King David was descended from Perez, and descendants of that family were said to have settled these islands. If you look closely you will find symbols of the house of Israel all over Ireland, Scotland, Wales, and England.

"David's harp is just one symbol and stands as a reminder of the covenant God made with King David. That his throne would not fail, that a descendant of David's would sit on the throne until Christ comes personally to reign on the earth."

An older man from the group interrupted to ask, "Shouldn't the throne of David be located in Israel?"

"You are right. Since King Zedekiah was killed and the kingdom of Israel taken captive, there has not been a descendant of David on a throne in Israel. But the English monarchy can trace its beginnings back to the house of David." He paused.

"Many Irish believe that someday the Lia Fáil will be brought back to the Hill of Tara and the true king will reign over these Isles and unite forever the lands of Britain."

Camryn stood in a daze, putting together another piece of this singular puzzle. The group moved on but still Camryn stood and considered. The arched library hall echoed muffled library sounds. Finally, she looked around as if everything was just coming back into focus.

"Can we sit outside near the river and look over these papers I brought back with me from Tara?" Camryn asked.

They turned, walked out of the library, and slowly joined the throngs of students and professors enjoying the finale of warmth on this fine spring day.

"Isn't it funny that I have never heard any of this before now?" Eileen said.

"You'd think that something this important would be general knowledge," Camryn said. "I wonder just how far it is from London to Jerusalem."

Eileen did a quick search on her phone. "It says that it is about 3,600 kilometers; kind of far if you were walking, but it wouldn't be a bad trip by water."

"Here's a bench, can we just sit for a little while?" Camryn said.

The bench had absorbed warmth from the afternoon sun, and while chilled breezes cavorted down the Liffey River, Camryn and Eileen were snug on their little bench. Before long the sun tipped below the western horizon, casting long shadows across their reading. When it was too dark to read, the girls gathered their things and left the river promenade for Eileen's home.

"Do you think all this is true?" Eileen said.

"It's pretty convincing, isn't it?" Camryn said. "But what makes it important is the lengths someone is willing to go to keep us from learning about it!"

Camryn followed Eileen home, watching for a moment outside just to make sure it was safe.

Neal and Frank were waiting for them and Bobbie and Connell showed up as Eileen pulled a large pot of Irish stew from the oven.

Neal voiced the question on everyone's mind, "What did you learn today?"

"Well, it is pretty obvious to me that Ireland was settled by colonists from Israel. I guess it is common to find that many believe that the Lia Fáil, or the Coronation Stone, is really the Stone of Destiny from Old Testament times and came from Israel. When it came is in dispute but they seem to agree that it is Jacob's Pillow."

"So the stone on the Hill of Tara now is what?" Frank asked.

"According to what I read today, the true Lia Fáil was taken to Scotland for the coronation of King Fergus (son of the Irish king) and was never returned. I don't know where the stone on Tara right now came from, but it isn't the stone that was a part of the coronation of the high kings of Ireland. Every drawing or description of the Coronation Stone depicts it as oval, with intricate carvings. It has been described by some as marble," Camryn continued.

"On the summit of the Fort of Dunadd in the Kilmartin Valley is a footprint carved in stone and next to it a bowl-shaped hollow and the figure of a wild boar. The hollow contained water used in ceremonial bathing. While Fergus was being crowned, he sat on a stone with his foot in the footprint. Tradition says that the newly crowned king would place his foot in the footprint as an indication that he would follow the precepts of his forefathers.

"Listen to this. 'A book entitled *Chronicles of Scotland* adds some details: Fergus was first King of the Scots in Scotland and brought the chair (the stone is sometimes referred to as the chair or throne) from Ireland to Argyll, and was crowned on it.

"'There is an old prophecy that says: Wherever the stone is found the Scottish race will reign.'

"Have you ever heard of any of this?" Camryn asked them.

"They didn't teach this in school, at least not while I was listening," Eileen said.

The men inhaled the stew and Camryn watched with a faint smile as it seemed to disappear before her eyes. Neal listened to the last of her story and then, dishing up a bowl for her, placed it before Camryn.

"You had better eat something, we might have a long night ahead of us," he said.

"I've read nothing of Greystones in any of these papers, so I don't have a clue why Lucas wants me to go there," Camryn said, before taking her first bite.

The conversation swirled around her as she ate: When to leave (9:00), who to take (Neal, Frank, and the dogs), and speculation about why they were going.

At nine sharp they piled into Neal's truck, dogs sitting amongst the tools and buckets behind the seat, and headed south along the coast. The sun had set long ago; the night was soft and inky black. Their headlights revealed a faint path into the darkness and they followed trustingly. About halfway into their journey a filmy layer of fog crept over the road and settled in to fill every dip and turn.

Neal slowed as the dogs whined and strained to see out the side windows.

"Are we going to make it on time?" Camryn asked.

"We are coming up on Bray right now, we don't have far to go," Neal reassured her. "How will we know where to stop?"

"I should recognize the place when I see it. There will be a low rock wall running along the road, on the left, and a path that follows the coast. We should be able to see a small beach with grass running down a hill, if the fog lifts. Oh! And there will be a brown weathered sign that says 'Greystones.'"

"Okay then, let's watch for the sign and the path once we get out of Bray. Until then, I am going to concentrate on getting through this fog," Neal said, leaning forward and peering out the windshield.

It was slow going that foggy night as they followed the coastal road from Bray to Greystones. Every twist and turn was cause for alarm as they lost the road in the swirling fog and cause for relief as they found themselves still on the road down the straightaways. On a quiet stretch of road between the two towns they finally came upon the sign announcing they had arrived. Neal put Frank in the driver's seat, stood outside in the fog, and directed him onto the shoulder.

There was a path and a knee-high rock wall. The beach butted up to a length of steep cliffs. The sea welcomed them with an exhale of breath which gently blew the white tendrils of fog away. As Camryn eased open her door, the dogs stood at attention, noses quivering and alert.

"Should I let them out?" she asked Frank.

"This old truck is perfect for hauling messy dogs, let's let them explore a bit, shall we?"

Camryn joined Neal at the wall, looking over the stretch of tall grass growing right up to the beach. The sand was only a meager pale crescent in the distance; instead, boulders littered the cove.

"Well, here we are! Do you know what to do next?" Neal asked.

Camryn pulled her phone out of her pocket and checked the time.

"It's 9:40 now, I guess we wait here and see what happens. Lucas said to be here at 9:55."

The dogs were following unseen trails through thick waves of beach grass; only their tails could be seen above the vegetation. They watched those tails swerve in unison and an explosion of frantic birds emerged from the grass, lifting out of the reach of the two bounding predators. The baying dogs followed the white birds to the ocean. Distracted by the water, the dogs turned their attention to charging waves. Leaping into the water and retreating as waves rolled onto the beach, the dogs played tag with the waves.

Slowly, but surely, the dogs moved down the beach and their observers stood on the hill waiting for what was to come. Camryn surveyed the scene, scanning the road and turning to the coast. Finally, she checked her phone again.

"9:54...," she said, almost to herself.

Neal and Frank quit fidgeting and Camryn watched and waited.

Down on the beach the dogs had abandoned their romp with the ocean and followed a trail that disappeared behind a craggy gray boulder. A few seconds passed and urgent barking erupted, the dogs calls echoed over the cove. Frank gave a loud whistle, calling them back, but the sound of his voice only increased the fervor of their barking.

"They are probably just excited about something washed up on the beach, but I'd better go and check on them," Frank said. He dropped over the small wall and made his way through the grassy dunes.

Neal divided his time between watching his son's progress along the beach and Camryn's anxious waiting. Camryn fidgeted, watching the road, turning to observe the path and beach area, and finally, checking the time. Her nerves were taut with the wait.

On the beach, Frank finally reached the craggy gray boulder. The fog had entirely lifted and the moon cast a cool clear light over the silvery sand. The labs must have heard Frank coming because they raced to meet him, barking and bounding back to the boulder. Frank followed close on their heels and disappeared behind the rock.

The dogs quieted, the tumult was stilled, and in the deep silence Camryn began to sense a curious pounding. It began in her veins, but soon her ears felt the pulsating thrum and lights began dancing at the edge of her vision. The sound started out as a gentle drumbeat but within a short time it had swollen, drowning out every other sensation completely.

Vaguely, she heard Frank call to his father. She felt Neal touch her arm and then she was alone on the hill. Her heart accelerated, her stomach lurched, and her hands shook. Something real pulsed through the night air, something light and wild and full of joy.

It was a surreal dance of emotion and her heart tapped in time with whatever was echoing through the air and something in her recognized it.

"David?" she whispered.

As she reached for an answer, Neal appeared at a run. She could see his mouth forming words and his urgency almost moved her but she was unable to respond, incapable of doing anything but feeling what was happening all about her. Neal reached the truck, and opening the door, he put her inside then ran around and hurriedly got in.

Firing up the truck he ground down into low gear and with a heavy lurch they were off the shoulder and picking their way through the sea of grass. He talked to her, but although she could see him speaking, nothing seemed able to penetrate the barrier of what had engulfed her.

Finally, they were on the packed sand and steadily picked up speed until they saw Frank and skidded to a stop. Neal twisted in his seat and reached awkwardly behind the bench. He opened the door and looked in the back from the side and found a small bundle, then threw a 'wait here' to Camryn and hurried off. Sitting in her seat, Camryn was immersed in the shock of unexpected joy. A tangle of feeling swept through her.

As if in a dream, she opened her door and walked around the truck. She saw the two labs sitting at attention. Neal stood watching. Frank knelt in the damp sand, covering something with the rough blanket Neal had brought from the truck. Unbidden, Camryn walked to them, knowing what she would find.

Kneeling in the sand, she drew the blanket off the body beneath it. David's face lay still and pale, his curls lay soft on his head.

"David?" she whispered, not to him but into the liquid air shimmering about her.

'Camryn' was the silky refrain she heard ringing through the air. Her vision was veiled but something hovered just beyond her ability to see and hear and feel. It pulsed and danced just beyond the horizon of her vision.

She framed his face with her hands and felt his chill spread through her, leaning closer she pressed her lips to his eyes. Did she feel a flicker of warmth? She laid her cheek on his, and his alabaster skin chilled her own living pulse. Pressing closer, she found his mouth and pressed her warm lips to his. Salty and shivery, they soaked up her warmth but only returned a bleak cold.

Her warmth wrestled with his glacial stillness.

It could have been a minute, it might have been an hour before she looked about and found Neal and Frank at her side. As she focused on their worried faces, the shimmering pounding in her veins subsided and the sounds of the ocean's roll became clear to her again.

"Are you okay?" Frank asked. Camryn nodded. "Is this David?" he asked curiously.

"This is David. He can't be dead, you know," Camryn said.

"You mean he can't be living, don't you?" Frank said.

"There is too much life here for him to be gone," Camryn stated, and as she made the declaration a wave of shimmering joy washed over her again.

"I can see where he was shot, but the saltwater must have helped clean it up. It looks like it went clean through and is healing well." Frank said.

"Are you a doctor? I don't know enough about you all!" Camryn answered.

"I'm a vet—better hours, you know."

"What do we do now?" Camryn asked, certain that fate was carrying them along.

"Do you really think he is still alive?" Neal asked. "I can't find a heartbeat and he is as cold as the morgue."

"I don't think he is gone, I think he is right here with us," she said.

"Well then, my lady, I think we'd better load up and take him home—or do we take him to the hospital?"

"I don't know! Let's just get on the road and hope we'll know what to do," Camryn said.

CHAPTER 28

Neal and Frank carried David to the truck and carefully placed him on the seat, leaning against the passenger's door. He looked like he was sleeping. Camryn straddled the gearshift and Frank and the dogs hopped into the truck bed. Back over the packed sand and through the sea grass, up over the shoulder and back onto the road to Dublin. The truck whined a little at the last rise but seemed content to be back on firm footing once they got onto the road again.

Forty minutes later they pulled up to an old Georgian manor.

"Where are we?" Camryn asked with a yawn.

"This is our family place, just a mile or so from Eileen. I thought it would be easier to take care of your gentleman friend from here," Neal said. "Is he warming up?"

"I think he is," Camryn said.

"Have you felt him breathe at all? Because if he is dead, we are all in load of trouble," Neal said.

"I might have a problem facing death in general, but I don't think David is dead," Camryn said. "Why else would Lucas tell me to go to that particular place at that particular time?"

"Let's get him inside and warm him up then." Neal opened his door and banged sharply on the side of the truck, Frank sat up in his sleep and followed the dogs as they jumped down onto the driveway.

"Ready, Dad?" he answered, a little groggy.

"Let's put him in the guest room off the kitchen, shall we?" Neal said.

As Neal and Frank carried David across the driveway, through the kitchen, and into a small bedroom, Camryn opened doors and turned on lights. The dogs watched as David lay still on the bed, covered with a thick duvet. As sentries, they each took a post, and resting but alert they watched over David Lord. Camryn, Neal, and Frank stood to the side and watched as well. Their patient was lifeless and still.

"What do you want to do now?" Neal spoke into the thick silence.

"We can't do anything until he wakes up so why don't you sleep. I will stay with David," she said.

"If something happens during the night, we are just down the hall and up the stairs," Neal said, already at the door. "Or send the dogs—they will find us."

The dogs had found their way onto the bed and were curled up on either side of David, watchful and alert.

"Goodnight, and thank you for all you've done to help me. I will never forget it," Camryn said as they left.

Camryn closed the door and turned out the lights. The curtains were open and moonlight filtered in through the windows. She watched David and remembered standing above her father laid out in a coffin. This wasn't the same at all; David was no waxen, lifeless corpse. She took a pillow from the head of the bed, and crawling beneath the bottom of the duvet, she curled her warmth around his cold feet and fell headlong into sleep.

Standing slightly above the ground, David looked over the panorama before him. He looked on his own body, lying so still on the bed. Camryn's bright hair was in a tangle on a pillow at his feet. He could see her breathing in and out—a miracle.

"Why does this woman trouble me so?" he despaired, knowing that she would never be his.

Unbidden thoughts trembled in the air about him, and when he looked up, he saw Phillip Lord, his father. "David, it is time for you to return to your body that you may finish your work upon the earth."

"Father? Is that really you?"

"Yes, my son."

"Is this death? Am I dreaming?"

"I don't know all things," his father said, "but I know you have work yet appointed to you. And that work is upon the earth."

"How do I do this then?"

"Open your heart to what you know is right and you will find your way. Have faith in the Lord, David."

The light that had enveloped David since his tumble into the channel began to dim and soon he was left to himself. Contemplating his body, knowing the burdens and limits as well as the majestic sensations associated with that body, he approached the bed.

The dogs woke as he drew near, but Camryn didn't stir beneath his searing gaze. For a moment, he lingered. The desire he felt for this woman, his need to touch her and hold her was a towering reality unchecked for just this moment. And then, reaching within himself, he mentally put all the longing back into its proper place and he looked at his own face, his own form. With a fierce thrust of will, he opened his heart to returning back to this life once more.

With a gasp caused by an exhilarating bolt of pain, life coursed through him once more. He drew in a burning breath and felt his body like a heavy encumbrance, lumbering as it picked up mortality again. Blood began its cycle, sluggish and cold. He felt warmth tingle as it moved from his heart, radiating through his veins.

He became aware of a raging thirst, yet he could not move. David concentrated on opening his eyes. They were closed and all his efforts did not generate even the tiniest flicker.

"Calm down," he admonished himself. Concentrating on one part of his body at a time, he spent moments with the raw newness of living in his body once again.

Without conscious effort he realized that his eyes were open and gritty with salt. He needed water.

Concentrating on moving his fingers, he flexed and stretched them, and reaching up, he pushed the covers to the side. He then worked at drawing his legs up, but they would not move. He panicked then for just an instant, but recalling Camryn sleeping at the foot of the bed, he steadily pulled until they were free from her grasp. Sliding them to the floor he sat up and surveyed the room while Camryn sighed, burrowing down into the covers and falling ever deeper into sleep.

I am truly alive! he thought. The two Irish labs sat at attention, watching him curiously. David stood; he was stiff and briny.

"Come on, boys," he called to the dogs softly.

The kitchen was right off the bedroom. He rinsed a cup from the sink and drank until his thirst was slackened. A clock over the oven told him it was midnight. He was sitting at the kitchen table in a bit of a daze when the kitchen lights flickered on.

"What the...? When did you wake up?"

David lifted his head and again concentrated on opening heavy eyes. He moved and caked salt scattered all over the kitchen floor.

"Sorry about that," he said to the stranger. "Have we met?"

"After a fashion," the man said. "We fished you off a beach earlier this evening. We thought Camryn was mad, but she insisted you were alive so we brought you home. My name is Francis O'Brien, and I think we are your Irish cousins. Can I get you something? I am sure we could find something to eat."

"Cousins? I guess Camryn has told you who I am. If I could get out of these clothes and wash up, I would be forever in your debt," David said.

"Come upstairs then, you can wear something of mine and use the shower."

David followed Frank down the hall and up some stairs and into a bedroom. Frank pointed him toward the bathroom as he searched through drawers for clothes.

"Am I in Ireland?" David asked from the bathroom. "How did Camryn find cousins I didn't even know I had?" He could hear a drawer closing and Frank appeared at the bathroom door with a pile of clothing and a first aid kit.

"We were sailing Thursday and fished her out of the channel. We searched for you until even Camryn gave up, and later we helped her avoid the authorities. She told us about everything, I think," Frank said. "Here, it takes a while for the hot water to get to this part of the house. Let's get it going." He turned the water on and showed him how to work the knobs. "Why don't you get cleaned up and I'll dress that wound for you," he said. "I'll be in the kitchen when you are done."

It took David quite a bit of effort to get his salt-encrusted clothes off. His shoulder was stiff and sore, but he could move it with little effort. Sand, salt, and even a bit of seaweed littered the floor of the bathroom by the time he was in the shower. The hot water and a good lathering of soap seemed to restore him to some level of normalcy, although he was as weak as a newborn. David finished and dried off, truly weary now that he was clean. He dressed in borrowed sweats yet again and used his damp towel to wipe up the grime of his exploits from the floor and dropped it all in the hamper.

The bedroom was large; a low-slung sofa sat before a blazing fireplace and David had no defense against its siren song. No sooner had he laid his still damp head on the arm of the couch than he tumbled into a deep and dreamless sleep.

Frank found him there and examined the gunshot wound without waking him. It was healing nicely, so he turned out the lights and left him sleeping. The house settled into repose again, as the household slumbered and sighed.

CHAPTER 29

Camryn stirred as a company of birds jostled and twittered on the window ledge. The sun was gradually loosening nights grip on Dublin and a shadowy light filtered through bedroom windows.

For the first time in over a year she woke to joy instead of sorrow. Seeing Lucas had set her heart free to feel happiness again, and finding David brought hope.

"David?" she spoke softly into the dusky shadows.

Sitting up in the bed and peering into the emerging dawn, it was clear David was gone.

"David!" she called, emerging into the kitchen. Neal was sitting at the table, a mug of Earl Grey curling steam at his elbow and a newspaper rustling as he unrolled it out on the table.

"Have you seen David?" she asked, shaking. "Tell me last night wasn't just a dream!"

"Mr. Lord is gone?" Neal asked. Camryn nodded, too worried for mere words.

"Where could he have gone?" Neal asked. He rose out of his chair and checked the bedroom himself. Pulling open another door in the bedroom suite, he looked into the powder room as well; no sign of David.

"I didn't take him anywhere, I promise," Neal said. "He must have woken up!"

Camryn hadn't even considered that David might be up and about.

"Call the dogs. They haven't left his side since we collected him from the beach!" she suggested.

With a sharp whistle, Neal called for the dogs. Almost at once, they heard the padding footsteps of the dogs answering his call.

"They are coming from upstairs!" Camryn said as she started down the hall. Neal caught her on the stairs as the dogs waited for them on the landing. Whining and nuzzling Neal's hands, they led them directly to where David was still deep asleep.

Her heart lurched when she saw him laid out on the couch in front of the glowing fire. For a moment, fear elbowed hope aside. He looked so still and pale that she thought him dead again. But as she watched him she could see life. His face was no longer as pale and she could see his chest rising and falling with precious breath. His limbs conformed to the contours of the couch and an arm curled as a pillow under his head. Someone had dressed the bullet wound in his shoulder.

She watched Neal move to the couch and gingerly touch his forehead.

"He is warm!" Neal announced in a murmur.

Camryn started toward the couch but paused just past the doorway.

"Let him rest," she mouthed to Neal, and motioning toward the stairs, she retreated to the kitchen.

"I honestly can't believe he survived," Neal said when he joined her. "I wonder how long he was in the water?"

"I don't want to think about that! When he slipped under the water..." She shivered in remembered distress. "I'll just play Scarlet and think about that tomorrow."

"Can I make you some breakfast, Neal? My mother makes the world's best oatmeal. Have any oats?" Camryn asked.

Neal pulled out a box of McCann's from the pantry and a saucepan from the cupboard. Camryn melted butter in the pan, measured out the oats, and mixed them into the melted butter. Within a few moments the smell of toasted oats filled the kitchen.

"Do you think he will be able to travel? We need to get to Scotland as soon as we can," she said while stirring. "Do you have any buttermilk?"

"Maybe Frank talked to him last night. It looked like he had showered and changed," Neal said.

Camryn added some water, buttermilk, and cinnamon. Once it was simmering, she handed Neal the wooden spoon.

"Can I make some more tea while this is cooking?" she asked.

Neal reached out and lit the fire beneath the teakettle.

"This was hot just a few minutes ago. I have a cup on the table that is probably just about cool enough to drink now. You go ahead and I'll make another. There is lemon and sugar on the table."

The tea was just right, as it warmed her hands and cooled her blood. *David is here!* was the refrain that played over and over in her mind.

The morning newspaper was unfolded on the table and she was careful to keep the saucer away from the pages, her thoughts swirled around and around in mad convulsions of happiness.

Neal finished the oats and put out bowls and brown sugar, all without feeling the need to make small talk.

I will tell David everything today; there is so much to tell, she thought to herself.

Without any fuss, Neal set a bowl of creamy oats in front of her. A lump of brown sugar melted into liquid gold and a crock of cold cream sat close at hand.

Neal half turned, but pausing, he pointed to a headline.

"What is that about?" he said.

Focusing on the page, Camryn read the title out loud. 'David Lord Feared Missing in Ferry Mishap'. Neal pulled up a chair and both of them scanned the article.

" 'Thursday's morning Holyhead Island ferry pulled into Dublin on time but seemed to be missing a passenger or two.

" 'Sometimes our passenger counts can be off, but we have double checked and Mr. David Lord, wanted for questioning in the murder of Prince George's private secretary, is believed to have fallen overboard sometime during the trip.

" 'He was reported to be traveling with an unknown woman, who may be missing as well.

" 'Officials are searching the coast south of Dublin, following the currents. It is no longer a search and rescue but is now officially a search and recover operation. See story on page B-13 for a related story.' "

"Can you see which section is B?" Camryn said, pawing through the paper.

"Here it is. Can you find page 13?" Neal turned the pages. "This must be it." Neal paused and laid the paper out on the table. *Beauty Queen Swears David Lord Didn't Do It.* A large picture of a young woman in an evening gown and a sash reading 'Miss Connecticut' sat beside the article.

Neal read: "Speaking by phone from her home in New York City, Ms. Mimi Spencer told the *London Press* that there was no possibility that David Lord could have murdered his longtime friend Roger Brough.

" '*We were together the night he left to fly to London*, Spencer said, *and he told me that he was traveling on business.* Roger Brough, assistant to

Prince George, was shot in the street in Mayfair on Wednesday. *How would David have gotten a gun in London anyway? You can't travel with weapons. And it is almost impossible for a foreigner to buy a gun in the UK.* When asked to comment about Mr. Lord's trip to Ireland after the assault in London, Ms. Spencer broke down and revealed that she and Mr. Lord had just become engaged. *He told me that he wanted ten children. It is very difficult to believe that he is gone!' "*

Neal folded the newspaper and said, "They just needed a few comments as an excuse to print that picture."

Camryn pushed back from the table, feeling sick to her stomach. David engaged! All this time she thought he was such a gentleman, but he was really just in love with someone else. Her cheeks flamed at the memory of touching him when she first saw him lying on Aunt Marge's sofa. She had put to rest her devotion to a husband buried in an unknown grave in Afghanistan only to learn that David loved some beauty pageant princess in New York; it was heartbreaking.

"You look ill, Camryn. Why don't you eat your oats?" Neal said to her.

Camryn pressed her hands to her cheeks—they were hot to the touch.

"Would you mind if I pass? I'm feeling a little sick just now," Camryn asked. She didn't hear his response but fled to the little bedroom and shut the door before she disgraced herself by bursting into tears.

Sitting on the bed, she made a vow to herself. *He will never know I love him, then.* Camryn sat in the little bedroom and fought a mighty battle for control over her own heart.

She allowed herself a forty-minute reprieve, huddled alone in abject misery, before she decided that she was strong enough to face everyone. How carefully she entered the kitchen. Neal and Frank sat at the table eating oatmeal and talking.

David, his back to her, was at the sink. In the instant she knew it was him. Her hard-fought defenses were breached.

Did she call his name? Or was it just her presence that impelled him to turn around?

"Camryn! I'm just getting caught up with my long-lost cousins," David said, moving close to her.

Neal and Frank started to excuse themselves but Camryn motioned them to stay.

"I told them everything," she said to David. "Do you remember falling into the channel?"

"All I remember is watching myself sink. I saw you dive for me and then I was in a hurry to get somewhere and was gone."

"You watched yourself drown?" Frank asked.

"It is weird, I know. I watched my body drift down into the channel but that body wasn't me. Does that make sense?" David said.

"So where were you if you weren't in the channel?" Camryn asked.

"I was in a library and was shown a book. It was a religious book and the writings told the stories of King David. Stories my mother told me as a child because of my name."

"I wonder what King David has to do with the Lia Fáil. I guess if the stone really does come from Israel there might be a connection," Neal said.

"If we are looking for a link between them, that is the only one I can see." David said, "But it is reaching."

"Did you see us at all?" Camryn asked.

"No, not until I realized that my body had washed up on the beach and found you there," he said. "I know that the O'Briens pulled you from the channel, but what else have you done?"

"I went to Tara—was it just yesterday morning?" She looked to Neal for confirmation.

Camryn continued, "I found that the stone did lie on the Hill of Tara and the high kings of Ireland were crowned sitting on the stone. When the king sat on the stone during the coronation ceremony, it let out a roar that signified to the people that God approved of the choice."

David interrupted, "Did they have a description of the stone?"

"I talked to a lady at Hill Tara who knew the history of the Lia Fáil and she gave me a copy of a written history that has been kept for many years by her family," Camryn said, avoiding his eyes.

"It seems that there are many people who believe that the stone now at Tara is not the ancient Lia Fáil," she continued. "There are traditions that tell of St. Patrick blessing the Lia Fáil. And many accounts say that the stone is oval in shape and is intricately carved."

"That sounds nothing like the Coronation Stone of England then," Neal said.

"I know!" Camryn said. "Mary said that the stone was in Ireland from roughly 400 AD. Let me read you some of my notes." The papers she had taken from Tara were secured in the bedroom, sitting under her purse on the dresser.

"Okay," she said, coming back to the kitchen and spreading out papers over the table. "When the Irish talk about the Lia Fáil it means the same thing as the Stone of Destiny, so don't get confused!" She scanned through the pages. "Here it is. 'Andrew of Wyntown in his book *Chronykil of Scotland* gives an account of the stone as it came from Spain.

" 'The king had at that time a famous stone which was used as his throne, and was regarded as a priceless jewel in Spain. He gave it to Simon, and directed him to take it with him to Ireland and win that country for occupation, and to hold the stone perpetually.'

"A book called *The Chronicles of Eri* says this about the coming of the stone to Ireland from Spain. 'And Erimionn (came from Spain to Ireland) was seated on the Lia Fáil, and the crown was placed on his head, and the mantle on his shoulders, and all clapped and shouted. And the name of that place, from that day forward, was called Tara.' It says here that the word *Tara* comes from the Hebrew word *torah*, which means 'the law.' "

"Do they say the stone left Ireland and went to Scotland?" David asked. He turned a chair about and sitting on it laid arms across the back and gazed down on the papers scattered across the table.

"Yes. An Irish king sent it to his son to give him authority as a ruler with the people of Scotland," Camryn said.

The dogs, lying under the table, came to attention then and after a moment they heard a car turn in the driveway and pull around to the kitchen door. The dogs barked and raced to wait expectantly at the door.

"That is probably Eileen," Neal said, sensing their nerves. "Are you thinking that this captain is still searching for you?"

"I don't know how he could know where we are," Camryn said, "but when I was at Tara someone took a shot at one of the guides in the church. They seemed to think it was an attempted robbery, but I wondered about it. I thought someone was following me when I left Tara but I was probably just imagining it."

Eileen walked in, balancing parcels. Frank leaped to his feet and helped her transfer a few groceries into the fridge and cupboard.

"I wondered if you came here last night. It must have been a late night, or I would have heard about your trip, right, Dad?" she said, with hands on her hips and a slight scowl on her face.

Camryn jumped in, "It was too late to call by the time we got here, but look who we found." She turned to David. "David, this is Eileen O'Brien."

"No! I don't believe it. This is why Lucas sent you to Greystones?" Eileen asked. She turned to her brothers and began complaining about their treatment of the only girl in the family.

"No one takes me seriously! There I was, up most of the night pacing the floor and worrying and no one even thought to call and let me know you were all right." On and on and on she went; the girl had evidently kissed the Blarney Stone at some point in her life, because she barely took a breath between complaints and exaggerations. When she began to run out of steam she abruptly changed the subject.

"Camryn, have you told them about the papers you got from Tara?"

"I was just reading some of our notes." Camryn found her place and burying herself behind the papers began reading again.

"Where was I—Scotland, right?" Her finger moved over the paper for a moment and she started reading again. "There was a time when a colony in Scotland found the old Pictish inhabitants too strong to conquer. After suffering many reversals at war, the colony sought help from the high king at Tara. It says here: 'Ambassadors were sent to Ireland (from Scotland) to complain of the treason and danger done by the Picts, and to seek support against them. Ferquhard, who was at that time king in Ireland, became angered by the harassment received by his friends in Scotland. He therefore sent his son Fergus, a wise and valiant prince, to their support.

"'Also, to give the Scots the appearance of permanent fortune, Ferguhard sent with his son the Stone of Destiny. Fergus was warmly received by the Scots because their very existence was in great danger. After his arrival, a council was held where they chose Fergus to be the king because of his noble blood and excellent virtues. Fergus was crowned upon the Stone of Destiny, which he brought with him by the will of the Gods to stabilize the realm in Scotland.

"'It was first taken to Dunadd and it was moved to Iona when

St. Columba inaugurated King Aidan at the command of an angel. It was moved to the Scottish mainland when Viking raids grew troublesome, the stone transported to Dunstaffnage.'" Camryn quit reading and looked around the table.

"So, how do we get to Scotland then?" David asked.

Eileen leaned forward. "I have someone I'd like you to meet first if you have the time. When I was going to school I waitressed part time at Mulligan's and one of my professors was a regular. He would sometimes hold forth on the subject of the Lia Fáil. We could stop by and see if he still comes in." She looked at the kitchen clock. "Mulligan's opens in about an hour and the professor was usually there with his morning paper when we unlocked the front door."

CHAPTER 30

A little over an hour later, David, Camryn, and Neal approached the no-nonsense eighteenth-century pub, located just off of the river and down a small side street. Following Eileen through the old wood doors, they were met by a cast of regulars and a complete lack of modern airs.

It was dark, the floors were old, and the wood was rich, shellacked ages ago. It smelled of stout.

"Might the professor be in this morning?" Eileen asked the barkeep. He moved a toothpick in his mouth from one side to the other and nodded toward the back of the establishment.

The group followed Eileen and paused before a table halfway down the room, one chair occupied by a gentleman partially hidden behind the *Times*.

"Professor?" Eileen began. The paper rustled and a pair of eyes peered over the top of the paper, looking them over carefully. His observation ended with Eileen. "Professor," she began again.

"Where have you been, lass? Pull me a pint, will you?" the professor said. He was wearing a plaid wool cap and a thick cable-knit sweater. A cane leaned against the wall behind him.

"Guinness?" Eileen asked.

"Is there anything else?" the professor said, behind his paper again.

"Sir," Eileen said, pulling out a chair, "we were hoping to ask you a few questions about the Lia Fáil. May we join you?"

When he heard the words *Lia Fáil*, the professor snapped his paper, folded it, and laid it on the table. He motioned for them to sit and said, "What do you want to know?"

Eileen stayed standing. "Let me get your pint while they explain. You might need something to keep up your strength once you hear their story!"

David listened as Neal spoke with the professor, laying out why they needed to know the story of the stone. When Eileen arrived back at the table with a pint, she was sent to find paper and pencil, then to ask for a whiteboard. "The one behind the bar will do," he said.

Henry, the barman, wrestled the whiteboard down from the wall, still filled out with the daily specials. He handed an eraser and markers over to the professor, who stood at their approach. Taking a long drink, he emerged from the pint with foam in his mustache. They watched as he vigorously wiped the board clean and began making a list, muttering to himself. David strained to hear and understand, but it was gibberish, so he concentrated on reading what the professor was scribbling on the board.

Jacob's Pillow
The Stone of Destiny
The Fatal Stone
The Lia Fáil
The Stone of Bethel
The Stone of Jerusalem
The Stone of Egypt
The Stone of Samothrace
The Stone of Portugal
The Stone at Tara
The Stone of Mora
The Stone at Iona
Columba's Pillow
The Stone of Scone
The Stone in London
The Stone in Edinburgh
The Blarney Stone
The Coronation Stone

At the bottom of the list, the professor wrote in large letters: *Known Names of the Stone!!!*

Jabbing at the list, the professor began.

"These are the names by which the Lia Fáil is known. It is a remarkable story, and one that the Irish should be familiar with but are generally ignorant of. Oh, they are vaguely aware that the stone that sits on the Hill of Tara is not the legendary stone, but they couldn't tell you where it has gone, or where it came from either." He paused to take another dip in his pint.

"It is somewhat remarkable that while the Scottish legend tells of the stone coming to Scone from Ireland, the Irish legend tells of the stone at Tara originating from Scotland. Our people are kin and the old ones knew it."

He continued. "The Lia Fáil was believed to be magical. When the rightful High King of Ireland put his feet on it, the stone was said to roar in joy. The stone is also said to have the power to rejuvenate the king, to endow him with a long reign. Cúchulainn is said to have split it with his sword when it failed to cry out under his protégé, and from then on it never roared again, except for the coronation of two Irish kings: Conn of the Hundred Battles and Brian Boru.

"Any questions?" The professor looked at each of them, only Camryn raised her hand. "Yes?" he said to her.

"What does the Lia Fáil look like?" she asked.

"An astute question, young lady," the professor said. "All early historians described the stone as elaborately carved and decorative, durable and handsome. In contrast, the Westminster Stone is identical with that of the local building material, almost certainly dug out of a Scone quarry, and is composed of soft red sandstone. Moreover, venerated sacred stones were nearly always made of meteorites, hard and capable of a hard polish, which may have been called marble. Ancient Great Seals of the early Scots kings, up until 1296, all depicted the Stone as of a different shape and size from the present one. These seals were meticulously drawn; surely the artists would not all make the same mistakes in depicting the stone—over a period of centuries, mind you! All of them drew the stone of seat height, almost as high as it is broad; the Westminster Stone is shorter and longer than depicted, eleven inches high and twenty-six inches broad.

"Like this..." The professor drew a sketch of the stone.

The professor paused. "Does that answer your question, my dear?"

Camryn smiled at him and nodded. David then spoke. "There is something that has been bothering me. Can you answer how the stone came to be in Ireland?"

The professor began to pace, gesturing wildly and muttering to himself.

"Henry," the old man finally shouted, "I need eight bottles of your finest brew."

"He's just getting started," Eileen muttered, watching Henry come toward them with a tray and a collection of bottled beer.

CHAPTER 31

Clearing the table off and snatching the tallest bottle from the tray, the professor slammed it onto the table.

"This is Bethel, about ten miles from the temple mount in what is now called Jerusalem. Jacob spent the night here and had a dream of heaven; you know this part of the story, yes?

"Good," he continued. "Then my job will be easier." Picking through the remaining bottles, he chose one and slammed it on the table close to the first. "South and east from Jerusalem is Egypt. That is where the stone went next. Jacob's sons carried it to Egypt." Another bottle was plucked from the tray and slapped onto the table. Straight east this time, and slightly north. "And then to Spain with King Gathelus."

Pointing at each bottle, in turn, the professor named them again. "Bethel, Egypt, Spain, got it?

"If the stone traveled with Gathelus, they next hauled it to Scandinavia and then to Ireland, where Scota was slain in battle and her eldest son, Eremon, was crowned upon the Stone at Tara." A bottle was banged on the table well north of Spain, representing Scandinavia; the last bottle was brought down with a bang that rattled the table, south and still further east to represent Ireland. David watched Henry wince as each bottle was slammed down on the table.

"Got it?" the professor asked them. David nodded and, pointing at each spot, named the travels of the stone. "Bethel, Egypt, Spain, Scandinavia, Ireland. Right?"

"Very good, excellent marks for your memory!" he said, gathering up all of the bottles except the first two. "Now, an alternate version of the story claims that Moses and the Hebrews kept the stone and that during the Exodus carried it out of Egypt with them. That it was the very stone that Moses struck to provide them with water when they were thirsty."

Banging another bottle on the table, he continued. "The stone passed over the Jordan River and into Canaan with Israel. It was kept in the temple along with the Ark of the Covenant, the stone tablets written by the finger of the Lord. Many centuries later, the prophet Jeremiah and Princess Tamar Tea Tephi of Judah brought the stone with them to Ireland, where Jeremiah gave it to King Eochaid as Tamar's dowry. Eochaid set up the stone at Tara and called it the Lia Fáil.

"Anyone else want to give it a try?" the professor asked.

Eileen pointed at the bottles in order. "Bethel, Egypt, Canaan, and then Ireland, right?"

"Very good!" he said, and then continued. "There are certain scholars that hint of another tale, one that tells of the stone being brought to Ireland by King David himself." The professor looked hard at the bottles. "The bottles remain in the same position for this story.

"King David had a son named Amnon that became sick with love for his own sister, Tamar, and forced himself upon her. He then hated her as vehemently as he had loved her before. When David discovered what had happened, he took his daughter and traveled to Ireland. There he gave his daughter in marriage to the high king of Ireland and with her he also gave the stone."

Pointing to the bottle representing Ireland, the professor went on.

"A few centuries later, Cúchulainn angrily split the Lia Fáil in half after it refused to acknowledge his friend, Lugaid Red-Stripe, as King of Ireland. There are those who would like to connect the Coronation Stone with King Arthur and Merlin, but that is pure fancy. But it is a beguiling fancy if I ever heard one.

"Around the year 500, the Irish prince Fergus took the stone with him to Scotland to found the kingdom of Dál Riata. Some legends state that the stone was discovered by King Conn of the Hundred Battles, or that it was brought by the Tuatha Dé Danann, the Irish faerie-folk, from Scandinavia before coming to Ireland." The professor grabbed the last two bottles and again rattled the table, placing them on the imaginary map marking Ireland.

The professor stopped suddenly, seemingly out of breath. David was stunned into silence by the sheer volume of information they had just been given.

After a moment, the professor took strength from his draft.

"Well, do you understand?" he asked.

"I can see it is an unholy mess, but yes, you have helped us untangle the stories," David answered. He reached over the table and offered his hand. "Thank you very much for your time, professor."

"Just a moment!" the professor said. "I am sure, as bright as you are, you must have another question or two."

"Well...," David said, thinking quickly. He looked at the others; they looked as confused as he felt. "Not at the moment. I think you have told us what we need to know. And I thank you for your time."

The professor took David's hand then and said goodbye. "I'm sure I'll be seeing you again. Good luck with your...search? Or might I call it a quest?"

Somewhere in Pennsylvania, driving in tandem, Enrique and Dean had to stop and fill up the truck. They ate at the Dairy Queen next to the gas station and let the kittens out to romp on a tiny strip of grass. They bought some water for them and a plain hamburger and watched them play tug of war with the patty. Twenty minutes later they were back on the road. Another hour north on 95 and Enrique realized how close they were to Mr. Lord's office.

Maybe they had heard from him, or know how to get him on the phone. It would also take him closer to Alena.

The exit for Newport was coming up, and after cutting across two lanes of traffic, he took it. Dean followed and came over to talk while they waited to be loaded onto the ferry for New York City.

"I'm hoping that his secretary might have heard from Mr. Lord," Enrique said. "His office isn't far from the ferry terminal."

"I wonder if he has been getting any of the messages we've been leaving," Dean said.

"If he could call us back, he would. When we get to his office I'll see if I can use a computer and check for emails. I wonder if Mr. Lord's employees are in any danger."

There was a parking lot close to the office, and for fifty bucks they parked for twenty-four hours and walked the long city block to Accountancy, Inc. Dean carried the kittens that were curled up together in their box, fast asleep.

"Hey, Mister Rique! What you doing back here so soon?" the guard called out as they walked in the front door.

"We were just in the neighborhood and thought we'd drop by. Is Mrs. McCombs still here?"

"Oh yeah! She's running the show while Mr. Lord is gone. Let me call upstairs and tell her you are here." He picked up the phone and murmured into it for a moment.

"Go right on up to the fourth floor, she will meet you there."

"They know me a lot better than I know them," Enrique said to Dean while they waited for the elevator. "I was medicated out of my mind all last summer and evidently talked my head off to one and all."

When they reached the fourth floor, a diminutive Mrs. McCombs stood with a wadded, soggy tissue clenched in one hand.

"Oh, Mr. Gutierre! We have been so worried!" Dean stepped back as she pulled Enrique to her side and held onto his arm.

"We are just fine, Mrs. McCombs. This is Dean Ellis. He has been helping me these last few days."

"You haven't heard, then. Come with me." She pulled them into the foyer. A television was strapped into one of the corners; the sound was on, and several employees watched helplessly and wept as they listened to the news.

The story was local: a sanitation workers' strike seemed to be imminent in the city. Puzzled, he looked to Mrs. McCombs. Patiently, she pointed to the screen, and when he still didn't see, she began reading from the clip running at the bottom of the screen.

"David Lord, a New York City businessman, has been reported missing from an England-to-Ireland ferry and presumed deceased."

Enrique turned to her, "When was the last time you heard from him?"

"Only once since he sent me that list for you. He needed some research started, but he hasn't called back since then. We were worried and then we saw this awful news!"

Enrique thought, *And I don't have a clue to why we are searching out these women. I certainly don't know what to do if I find who we are looking for!*

"Can I use a computer?" Enrique asked. One of the teary associates had wrapped her arms around Dean, assuming he knew her boss. Dean was patting her back as they watched for updates. Enrique raised his eyebrows at him as Mrs. McCombs led him down the hall to an office with a computer. Dean just shrugged and stayed behind to comfort the young woman.

Mrs. McCombs logged into the computer for him and turned to leave. "I'll just leave you to it, I should be keeping vigil with the other employees." As she left to join the others down the hall, he heard her murmur, "I wonder if anyone has called Mrs. Lord?"

Enrique was stunned. *What should I do with all I have learned? And what do I tell all the women we've put in protective custody?*

Pulling up their shared email account, he logged in and hoped for a message of some sort. Nothing in the inbox. Nothing in the sent or deleted files. Clicking on the 'compose' button he began writing, putting into words all he had learned the past few days, listing all the women, what they had told him, and who was protecting them. He was just finishing and ready to send it when a message flashed at the bottom of the screen.

"Is anyone there?"

"Who is this?" Enrique typed.

"The rumors of my death have been greatly exaggerated!"

"Boss! We need to talk."

"I have to leave to catch a flight. Twelve hours—can you wait?"

"I'll be waiting, and I'll have some answers by then, I hope."

"I have to go."

"Wait, what about Mrs. M.? Can I tell her you are all right?"

"Yes, but she needs to keep it to herself for a little while. Just ask her to keep on praying. I've got to go now. I'll find you soon."

"Wait! I have to talk to you."

There were no more messages, and after a few moments Enrique idly pushed send; the almost-finished saga disappeared from the screen and then reappeared in the inbox. Mr. Lord would be able to catch up on their undertaking at his leisure. He stepped to the door and eyed the employees congregated in the foyer, considering the consequences of easing their heartache.

"Junior," he called. Dean turned and found Enrique motioning him to come into the office. When Mrs. McCombs turned he motioned to her as well.

"I want to show you something." Enrique sat at the desk and moved the mouse to reveal the text conversation in black and white.

He gave them a minute to read and absorb the import. Mrs. McCombs shuddered with relief.

"He trusts you to know who to tell," Enrique said.

"It would be best if people thought he was dead, right?" she asked.

"I think that is true," Enrique answered.

"Have you found what Mr. Lord sent you to find?"

"I think so, we have one more woman to track down and the address we have for her is upstate. If we could use your bed downstairs for tonight we will leave at first light."

"Certainly. There is a couch in the foyer you can move after everyone leaves for the night."

Mrs. McCombs left to announce that she wasn't going to believe the news reports completely.

"Let's not borrow trouble, people. I can't believe Mr. Lord is dead, and until I hear that they have a body and identify him, I won't believe it."

Accountancy, Inc. employees grasped on to her optimism and her hope buoyed them all. Tears dried, worry abated, and everyone gradually left the foyer and prepared to go home.

"Mr. Enrique, Mr. Ellis, come downstairs with me, will you?" Mrs. McCombs asked.

They closed office doors and waited for an elevator. "I probably won't see you before you go in the morning." She continued, "There are some granola bars in the cupboards downstairs, and whatever has been left in the fridge you are welcome to eat. There is a small washing machine in the dining area. I'm not saying you need it or anything, but please make yourself at home."

Downstairs she showed them the accouterments. "You can't take those little guys with you," she said, peering in the box at the kittens. "How long will you be upstate?"

"Only for the day, unless something comes up," Enrique said.

"Well, leave them here then, they will be fine for a day or two with us."

"Mrs. McCombs, you need to be careful until this matter is resolved. Someone threatened harm to anyone connected with Mr. Lord."

With a considering look and a slight nod, she acknowledged his concerns. After letting the guard know they would be staying the night, she left through the front doors, hailed a taxi, and was absorbed into the press of cars pushing toward home.

"I'll be here till 10, Mr. Rique. If you need anything, just ask," the guard said. "I am going to watch Wheel of Fortune at 7 if you want to bring some popcorn."

It was well past midnight when Enrique woke in a cold sweat. A black foreboding shadowed his thoughts, and with sudden certainty he knew that something evil was stalking the night and its target was Alena and his girls.

Flipping the light switch and stumbling toward his backpack, Enrique pulled out the report compiled on his wife and girls. Somewhere in this mass of papers was the address and phone number for Sam, his brother-in-law.

"Here it is…" Enrique folded the stapled pages back and held a finger to the number. He found the phone on the wall in the kitchenette and quieted his shaking hand enough to dial the number.

Pick up, Sam. Pick up was his mantra. It went to the machine.

"You have reached…" Enrique hung up. Dialing again, he leaned against the wall for support.

"Come on, Sam, pick up!"

It went to the machine again. Shouting over the message, Enrique bellowed, "Pick up, Sam, Alena is in trouble, answer the phone!"

"Enrique? Is that you? I'm up," Sam broke into the message.

A deadly calm flooded Enrique.

"Sam, Alena's in trouble. I don't know how they found her, but I need you to go to their motel and get her and the girls out. Right now."

"Enrique, are you drinking? Where are you?"

"No, Sam! Listen to me, Alena is in trouble. I need you to go and get her and the girls, now!"

Something of Enrique's panic communicated itself to Sam. "Okay, okay, calm down. Where are they? I'll go."

"Do you know Tuckahoe Road? There is a motel there, near the skating rink and a McDonald's."

"Yeah, I know it."

"They are in room 215. Get them and call me at this number. Go!"

Enrique sank to the floor, leaned on his knees, and prayed the only way he knew how.

"Please, God, not Alena, not the girls."

In his mind he kept pace with Sam—*he was out the driveway and at the first light. It was a right turn; he was turning. Surely he had turned already. Was he at the strip mall light yet? Run it, run it, hurry, Sam! Hurry! Not far, up the street a quarter of a mile. Could he be there yet?*

Chapter 32

Sam was pulling into the hotel parking lot, looking for room numbers, when the foreboding enveloped him as well. Turning out his headlights, he parked and rolled down his window. Concentrating on the hotel, he struggled to read the room numbers next to each door.

Out of the corner of his eye he saw something move in the dark: a piece of blackness detached itself near the stairwell, and he watched the shadow flow up the stairs. Sam lost sight of whatever it was when it reached the second floor. Instead of opening his car door, he lifted himself out of the window and jumped lightly to the parking lot. He had left the house without his shoes, so he padded silently in socks as he ran to the stairs.

Something moved at the top of the stairway as Sam reached the stairs. Taking the steps two at a time, he gained the top just as the door to 215 closed with a soft click.

An ear to the door revealed nothing. He moved to the picture window, the curtains were pulled. He looked to see if he could see anything around the edges but it was all blackness and still. Sam's mind raced through his options, and with his ear to the door again, he listened for any disturbance.

This time he heard murmurs from inside the room, and he thought he recognized one of them—he was sure it was his sister. Moving in the shadows, Sam again pressed his face to the window, and this time there was light around the edges of the curtains. Sam could see movement through a narrow opening. Alena was sitting in a kitchen chair and a man in black was using duct tape to bind her to the chair.

"You will sit quietly, or you will wake your daughters. Do you understand English, señora?"

Sam could see a silent struggle that ended with a resounding slap.

A large pistol appeared in the man's hand. Pushing the gun to her neck, he made it very clear in both Spanish and English just what would happen to her daughters if she didn't sit quietly.

Alena nodded and the gun was removed from her neck.

Sam's thoughts churned furiously. Enrique knew his wife was in danger; someone must be using Alena to get to Enrique in some way.

The man in black had a phone out and was talking to Alena. Sam pressed his ear to the window to try and hear the muffled conversation.

"You tell me how to find him or I will wake your daughters and then you will tell me what I want to know." The intruder spoke with a thick British accent.

"I don't know!" Alena said, her voice a terrified cry.

Sam saw Alena look away from the intruder, a look of horror on her face. Sophia had come into the room, rubbing her eyes, a stuffed monkey in her arms.

"Mama?" she said, not knowing what she was seeing.

Alena murmured to her daughter; what she said, Sam could not hear.

"Mama!" Sophia said again. This time she was awake enough to feel terror.

Sophia moved to stand by Alena, clutching pitifully at the tape on the chair. She burrowed her face into her mother's shoulder.

The man in black had watched indecisively, but now he grabbed at the child and pulled her away from her mother. He put his face close to Sophia's, and as he yelled his skin turned a mottled red. He put her roughly on the counter.

"Sit!" he commanded her. He looked at her in warning and she sat stiff and motionless. He turned back to get what he needed from the woman.

Sophia took her focus off the stranger and looked only at her mother. Ignoring the warning she had been given, she tucked her stuffed monkey more securely under her arm and, rolling over onto her stomach, slid off the counter to the floor.

Sam could no longer remain a spectator.

"No, Sophia!" Sam cried. "Go back!"

Sam stood still at the window's edge, watching in horror as Sophia again ran to her mother. The intruder turned from his interrogation in disbelief, grabbed the little girl, and shook her once.

"Stay put, you little brat!" he yelled. Sam watched, helpless, as a large, muscled arm descended in a wide arc and slapped at the six-year-old Sophia. For a single instant she quieted, but fury at the abuse fermented and she lashed out at him. Squirming and flailing about in his arms, he could not catch hold of the moving mass of hysterical child.

She slipped out of his arms and gathered her breath to holler.

"Mama!" she wailed, and ran around the stranger to Alena.

In disbelief, Sam watched as the man in black pulled his pistol from his holster and pointed it at the six-year-old child. Galvanized into action by the sight of the gun trained on the little girl, Sam slammed his shoulder against the window. The thick plate glass was impervious to his attack. Scanning the area, he could see nothing he could use to break the glass.

Sam pounded on the window, screaming, "No, stop!"

Alena's eyes widened in horror, and then a look Sam had never seen came over her face. With a wrench of effort the tape on her legs tore, and she bent at the waist to charge at the intruder. The back of the chair became an oak battering ram. The edge of the chair caught him on the neck. Surprised, Alena looked up and the chair slammed a horrible blow to his chin.

Sam left his lookout then and began pounding on the door.

"Sophia! Let me in. It's Sam, Sophia, open the door." He pounded some more, and finally he heard a chair being dragged across the tile floor; it seemed an eternity before he heard the swing bar moving, and at last he heard the blessed sound of the door handle rattling. Sam grabbed the handle and pushed in. Scooping up Sophia, he ran to the kitchen and looked down upon the intruder.

"I think he is out," Alena said. He turned to her. She was panting with exertion and relief. Tendrils of duct tape trailed from her legs. She sat in the weaponized chair and watched the intruder without blinking.

Sam moved carefully around the man on the floor, found a sharp kitchen knife, and cut Alena loose. He watched her gather Sophia in her arms and then turned and used the roll of duct tape to bind the fallen invader. When Sam was done he found Alena packing, Sophia by her side. Suri was still sound asleep, curled up and sucking her thumb.

They were packed in minutes. They pulled out of the motel parking lot, drove for an hour on a wildly meandering path until they were sure that no one was following, and then stopped at a small hotel and paid cash for a room for the night. It was three in the morning when Sam called Enrique back.

"I got there in time," he said and he handed the phone to Alena.

"Are you hurt?" Enrique asked.

"No, no, we are all fine. Our sweet little Sophia has quite a temper, thank heaven! How did they find us?"

"I hoped we had rounded the bad guys up, but we obviously have not!" Enrique said.

"Are you finished with your job?" Alena asked, tucking the girls in a huge king-size bed in the new room.

"Almost. We were supposed to go upstate this morning, but I don't want to leave you alone now."

"Sam will stay with us, won't you, Sam?" she said, smoothing Suri's hair. "I did call the school yesterday, they were calling my cell phone every day and sounded so worried. I told them where we were and when Sophia would be back to school. I wonder if that number I called was really the school. I wrote it down, but it is back at the other hotel. I won't be tricked like that again! We will be fine for another day or so if Sam can stay with us."

Enrique hesitated. "I love you. Let me talk to Sam, will you?"

Alena handed the phone to her brother and climbed into bed with the girls. They drifted off to sleep holding hands under a mound of warm blankets.

Sam sat in an easy chair turned to face the door, waiting and watching, shaking his head whenever he thought about the thug that decided to take on a six-year-old who was single minded about wanting her mother.

About an hour later, Alena disentangled herself from the little girls and came to sit by him.

"Thanks, Sam. How did you know we were in trouble?"

"That is the first thing I am going to ask that husband of yours when I see him."

CHAPTER 33

Skimming the surface of a blue-green sea, David stared out the window and watched the southern Hebrides island of Islay come into view. A few fat sheep ignored the plane as it swept over the island, leaving them to graze in isolated solitude. The plane had lifted somewhat as it passed over the small island, but it soon dipped again to follow their shadow atop the quiet sea. They would pass to the east of Colonsay and then touch down at Iona.

Camryn sat beside him in the cramped confines of the tiny plane. Something had changed since he had returned. Her ease with him had evaporated, and she prickled with a new tension that puzzled him. It was the purest form of torture to sit beside her, and a part of him wished she had stayed behind. But the bigger part of him wanted to keep her close to him forever. He'd finally fallen, and for a married woman.

It was too noisy in the small aircraft for conversation, but David raised his voice and made the attempt.

"What did Eileen mean when she said that Lucas told you where to find me?" David said to her.

"What?" Camryn asked, leaning toward him.

"When did you talk to your husband?" He raised his voice another level.

"What? I can't hear you!" Camryn yelled back.

David just shook his head and shrugged. It could wait.

The pilot turned in his seat and gesturing to them, pointed out the right window. An island filled the horizon: they had arrived.

The pilot spoke into his radio and banked to the right. They flew over the harbor and passed the dock. The radio squawked, and out the window David could see that the road below was blocked off with a makeshift barrier. They flew along the route, a long lazy tour of the sleepy island that ended up back at the dock. David could feel the airplane shake as the pilot lowered his landing gear. They came at the island one more time. The wharf flashed by as they descended quickly and landed without a glitch on the lonely road outside of the little town.

The pilot spoke into the radio again and a single car drove around the barricade and pulled up to the plane. A small sign on the door proclaimed it as the Iona Taxi. The pilot turned off the prop and the vibration and noise stopped abruptly. He leaned over the empty passenger seat and pulled the lever that raised the door.

"Let me help you out," he said.

Within a minute, Camryn and David had been deposited on the side of the road. They watched the plane wander up the road until the airplane was just a glint in the distance. The sound of the engine revving came at them and they watched the small plane race toward the channel. Lifting into the sky with a small waggle of wings, it headed off toward Glasgow and another engagement. Within seconds the whine of the airplane faded and only the sounds of a sparsely populated island remained to ripple softly on the air.

The driver of the taxi introduced himself as the mayor and offered to drive them to the abbey.

"We don't often get requests to allow a landing like that," the mayor said, patting his comb-over in the mirror and keeping a close eye on Camryn in the backseat. There seemed to be no need to watch the road since there were no other cars on the road. He veered all over the single lane track with his eye fixed on the rearview mirror.

"We thank you then, for letting us invade you this way," Camryn answered.

The mayor swelled and a violent blush crept up his neck and bloomed all the way up to the top of his broad forehead. Seemingly unable to talk after her remark, his Adam's apple bobbed a few times, and he opened his mouth to speak but closed it after several unsuccessful attempts.

David took pity on the gentleman, having been in the same condition himself several times in the past few days.

"Mr. Mayor, what would you suggest we try to see while we are on Iona?"

With a cough to clear his throat, the mayor pontificated, "I would start with the abbey, of course, and the old graveyard. The ancient cairn is close. We also have a lovely choir in for the evening service tomorrow night."

"We are hoping to soak up the history of the place, will those places have guides?"

"If you want history then the abbey is full of it. Let me set you up with MacDougall. He is our local historian and acts as a guide. If he isn't here, we can give him a call up."

They pulled up to the abbey, the mayor parked with a flourish, and they got out of the vehicle to take in the spectacular sight of a medieval stone monolith standing before them. Made of multicolored stone, cut in all shapes and sizes, it rose from a bed of mottled green grass and looked over a peaceful harbor.

The mayor, chest stuck out with officious pomp, marched to the entrance of the edifice and returned with the aforementioned MacDougall.

"Call me Mac, please," he said, hastening to divert them from using his full name. "I understand you were the cause of quite the most exciting event of the week. The schoolmaster let the children take recess when they heard you come in so they could watch the landing."

"Are you free to take these good people on one of your special tours this evening?" The mayor all but twirled a vaudeville mustache in his attempts to be ingratiating.

"If you don't mind waiting, we are scheduled to start a tour just a few minutes," Mac said. When the mayor moved to follow them toward the abbey, Mac intervened.

"The ferry is due, shouldn't you be down there about now to meet them?" he asked pointedly.

"How much do we owe you for the taxi service?" David pulled out a few bills from a brand new wallet.

"Why, it was a privilege to drive you and the young lady," he protested. "Please have MacDougall phone me and I'll be back to pick you up when you are ready to go."

Camryn held out her hand. Hastily the mayor took it before anyone else could usurp his place; bowing slightly, he tucked her arm under his and turned as if to walk off with her.

Camryn, however, didn't budge. "We might want to stay the night. Do you have any recommendations for us?"

The mayor again flushed. This time it was an alarming shade of scarlet, and he gaped at her soundlessly.

"I'm sure your wife would be able to find them a bed and breakfast with a vacancy," Mac broke in.

With that direct reminder of his wife, the mayor flung Camryn's hand away and abruptly left them. They watched his stiff-legged stride take him to the taxi, and with a little spurt of gravel he turned and took the road to the harbor.

Camryn waved goodbye. Mac and David looked at each other and grinned.

"Let's go and see who else is waiting for the tour," Mac said. "It should be about time."

CHAPTER 34

A small group of tourists stood at the gate with their good walking shoes on and umbrellas close at hand.

Mac greeted them and gathered them around to begin the tour.

"I'd like to begin with my compliments, you have obviously experienced our soggy Scots weather." With an eye toward the clouds billowing off the coast, Mac took them around the grounds to begin their tour. His soft Scottish burr transported them to another place and time as he began telling them about the history of St. Columba and the Isle of Iona.

"Saint Columba," he began, "was a man of tremendous energy and strong personality. Born Colum MacFhelin MacFergus in Ireland in 521 AD, he had the natural right to the kingship of Ireland. It would have been offered to him had he not put it from him for God's sake. Instead of king, he became known as one of the twelve apostles of Ireland. It was said that he was a figure of great stature with a powerful build. He possessed a loud, pleasing voice that could be heard from one hilltop to another.

"Can you imagine a man, born to be king, turning from it to serve God?" Mac asked the group. "This man that we call Saint could be stubborn and opinionated. Sounds just like your husband, my dear." Mac looked knowingly at one of the older women in the group and all the women laughed. He then continued.

"Sometime around 560, he copied a holy manuscript owned by his mentor, Abbot Finnian. The Abbot disputed Columba's right to keep the copy while Columba maintained that all people should have access to the wisdom written by holy men. The quarrel led to the terrible Battle of Cúl Dreimhne in 561, during which as many as 3,000 men were killed. The words of the dispute are still quoted in courts today when trying cases of copyright infringement. Yes, he was stubborn and sure of himself!

"Columba's own conscience was uneasy about the part he played in that bloody battle, and on the advice of an aged hermit he resolved to atone for his offense by going into exile and to win for Christ as many souls as had perished in the terrible fight.

"In 563 Columba and a dozen companions set out for northern Britain in a wicker coracle covered with leather here to the beautiful isle of Iona.

"As the king's relation, Columba was well received by the king of the Scots and was allowed to preach and baptize. Here on Iona, Columba founded the monastery, which became a school for missionaries as well as the center of literacy and education in the region. For thirty years, he taught, studied, wrote, and lived here at Iona.

"This abbey is not the original building, but it stands as a monument to all this great man accomplished in his life. We can learn even from his mistakes."

"Are there any questions?"

An older gentleman raised his hand.

"Yes?" Mac asked.

"Is St. Columba the one that drove snakes out of Ireland?"

"No, that is St. Patrick. Beloved of all once a year at least. Is he your favorite then? Green beer can be a powerful reminder of our patron saint! No lad, Columba lived much later." Again the women giggled and looked knowingly at each other.

"You may have heard stories of the miracles Columba performed. Many were relatively simple acts, such as restoring spilled milk to a pail or sailing in contrary winds. Some, however, spread his fame throughout the region. Most famously, his encounter with a beast that some claimed was the Loch Ness creature. It is reported that he banished the ferocious water beast to the depths of the River Ness after it had killed a Pict and then attacked Columba's disciple."

The little group was spellbound by Mac's recitation of the story.

"Any more questions?" Mac asked.

"Wasn't the Lia Fáil brought here from Ireland?" David asked.

"Yes it was, this was the second home to the Coronation Stone, fourth if you count Egypt and Israel. It came to Iona for the coronation of Aidan and stayed until endangered by Viking raids," Mac answered.

"It went to Scone from here?" David asked.

"Well, it ended up in Scone. It was brought to Dunadd from Ireland and then it came here, from here to Dunstaffnage, and in 843, Kenneth MacAlpin was crowned on the stone as the first king of the united kingdom of the Picts and the Scots. One of his first acts as king was to build a church at Scone, where they housed the sacred stone."

"Scone is in Perth, right? Is the church still standing?" David asked.

"I believe the old abbey was burned to the ground, but there is a church built on the same spot like our abbey here.

"But enough of Dunstaffnage and Scone! We have plenty of history here on Iona." Mac led them to the abbey. They were pelted with a few fat raindrops as they went inside for the rest of the tour.

"Why don't you sit for a moment and I'll finish our little history, and then we can walk around this beautiful church," Mac suggested. The group sat on chairs set out for services, and Mac began again.

"Nine years after Columba arrived in Iona, the king of the Scots passed away. Aidan succeeded to the throne and Columba was held in such high regard by the clergy and the people that he was selected to perform the ceremony of inauguration of the new king.

"Columba was unwilling to perform the ceremony because he favored Aidan's brother, but an angel appeared to him during the night, holding a book he called *The Glass Book of the Ordination of the Kings*, which he put into the hands of the saint and commanded him to ordain Aidan king according to the instructions in the book. The angel returned three nights in a row and Columba finally bowed to God's wisdom in this matter.

"Aidan was crowned king of Scotland on the Island of Iona in a coronation rite that has been used ever since by the succeeding monarchs of Scotland and England. The ritual included a consecration declaring the future of Aidan's children, grandchildren, and great-grandchildren."

Everyone was quiet. They could hear the rain lashing the windows, but they were warm and dry in the huge old abbey.

"It was said that Columba was fierce and stubborn, but those traits were for the most part exhibited on behalf of others. Saint Columba died here on June 9 in the year 597. He died at his prayers before the altar in the chapel and his lasts words were a command for his followers to love one another.

"Iona has had a big history for such a small island and we could talk about it for hours, but I know it is suppertime and I don't want to keep you from it." Mac was finished. "Feel free to walk around the chapel and the grounds. If any of you want to walk over to Oran's chapel, I'm going there myself in a few minutes.

"Any last questions?" their guide asked the group.

One woman hesitantly raised her hand. "I have a question," she said, looking at her husband mutinously.

"Yes?" Mac prompted her.

"My husband wants to go to Edinburgh Castle tomorrow, but I have heard stories…" She shivered.

"Yes?" Mac said again.

"I have heard that the castle is haunted by all sorts of beasts"—her words tumbled over themselves trying to get out—"and that a ghost child plays the pipes under the castle looking for a way out. I am not setting foot in that place!"

"Well, yes, I do believe that much of Edinburgh is haunted. But the wee ghosties have never hurt a soul. They just wander the castle and don't even know they are dead," Mac said.

The woman looked vindicated and David very much doubted that the couple would be traveling to Edinburgh tomorrow.

With that question the tour was over.

"Mac, we'd like to walk over to the chapel when you go," David said. "Is there anything important to see?"

"That depends on what you're looking for, sir."

Chapter 35

The abbey gradually cleared out and Mac closed up and turned off the lights. David and Camryn followed him out and into the late afternoon day; the storm clouds had blown far to the east and a cloud of midges had taken their place.

"Come on," Mac said, fanning at the insects and moving quickly.

"What are these things?" David asked, choking on a few that flew into his open mouth.

"I think they call them no-see-ums in the colonies," Mac said. "They are vicious little critters and can be held responsible for the fierce nature of the Scots. Everyone but the most stubborn of us moved out long ago to escape these biting beasties!"

They left the cloud of insects behind and followed a grassy stone road toward a small church.

Camryn reflected, "This feels just like Tara!"

Mac nodded in agreement. "There is a residue of energy here; some say that the door between heaven and earth is cracked open just a bit here on Iona."

They were walking on a wide cobbled track, well defined and lush with grass growing between the stones.

"Be careful about wandering off this track, any track, in Scotland," Mac said. "Are you aware that the thistle is a symbol of Scotland?"

David started to answer, but Mac went on without waiting. "I would only venture into that field wearing boots. The thistle is an ancient Celtic symbol of nobility of character, 'for the disturbing of a thistle will bring severe punishment.' The linking of Scotland and the symbol of the thistle began when an invading Norse army was attempting to sneak up at night upon a Scottish encampment. As they approached the sleeping army, one barefoot Norseman had the misfortune to step on a thistle, causing him to cry out. The cry alerted the Scots to the presence of the Norse invaders. And they soundly defeated the army and sent them home."

"Consider us warned, and thank you very much," Camryn said.

"This path is called the Road of the Dead. It leads from the abbey to St. Oran's church and used to extend all the way to the Port of the Martyrs, where the pier now stands," Mac said.

St. Oran's church was small and old.

"Forty-eight kings of Scotland are buried in this place, including Macbeth of Shakespearean fame. There are kings from Ireland and Norway, all laid to rest in this graveyard."

"So, if the stone that Edward took is not the true Coronation Stone, where is it?" David asked.

"We have stone fanatics come to Iona regularly and I have heard all their theories, but I haven't heard one that is backed by anything other than supposition," Mac said. "Sorry."

"Well." David stood and looked out over the grassy slope that led down to the harbor, and then he turned and looked at Camryn. "I think we should stay here tonight. There is something about this place. What do you want to do?" he said.

"I don't think I ever want to leave!" she said.

"That is because those midges aren't around at the moment," Mac said. "We'll see how you feel when they are back."

"I guess we should find a place to stay, then," David said.

"We do have rooms in the abbey we keep for our volunteers to use during the tourist season. You could be close to the action, as it were. You would have to put sheets on the bed and share a bathroom with anyone else that shows," Mac volunteered.

"That would suit us perfectly, right, Camryn?" She only nodded distractedly.

They walked the Road of the Dead back to the abbey. Thunder rolled back at them from the storm, lightning streaked through the evening sky, and winds stirred and moaned all about them. Something was brewing, and David felt there was an open door between heaven and earth. He was anxious to see what Iona had to offer in their pursuit of the Stone of Destiny.

They went through an unlocked side door into the abbey and into the living quarters of the site. A few modern appliances graced the flagstone kitchen and a long monastery style hallway had the bedrooms and communal bathrooms on each side. There were sheets and pillows in the closets; the rooms were austere and quiet.

"It looks like there are a few boxes of cereal in the cupboard and milk and eggs in the fridge; will that do for dinner?" Mac asked. "I don't know who else is here, but make yourselves at home. There are a few rooms with double beds," Mac offered.

"Oh, we're not married!" David said quickly.

"Well," Mac said, "I guess I'll head home then. I hope you find what you are looking for. There is a small library in the abbey if you want to read about the stone; I am sure we have a few books on the subject, since we get so many people interested in following its history."

Mac turned and left then, and when the door shut, David turned to Camryn.

"What is it, Camryn; what is wrong?"

"Nothing is wrong. What makes you think something is wrong?" She wasn't looking at him so he was free to study her face, her eyes. *It isn't her fault I am hungry for her*, David thought, working hard to remember how married she was.

"Come for a walk, then, and let's see what we can find in their library." He didn't take her hand or he might have noticed her ring was gone, and he just may have asked the question that would have brought them both happiness.

They walked out into the evening light. The sun had just dipped below the horizon and the bewitching hour was upon Iona. It was the time of day when hope grew, peace was restored, and the swarming midges were off inhabiting some other locale.

They walked around the south side of the abbey, the wind blowing against them wildly enough to flatten the grass. The rolling surge of the ocean, birds settling in for the night, and the rustling of the rippling grass were the only sounds that met their ears. The stars were just appearing, clear and emanating peace.

They came to the church doors, thick, weathered dark wood. David reached out and the doors opened easily.

They walked through the dimly lit chapel and into a stone corridor, wandering until they found a small room lined with shelves, and made themselves at home. The thick stone walls kept the abbey chilled and deadened every noise from outside, while every footstep and whisper echoed back to them. Overhead lights brought them back into their own century and they searched the shelves for books on the stone. Skimming the first few books and discarding them, they finally settled in on one book in particular: *Fables and Fancies Regarding the Stone of Scone.*

An hour later, they were deep into the fanciful theories of a stone fanatic.

"I figured it out," Camryn said, breaking the silence that had fallen on them. "The professor—remember he told us we hadn't figured out the right question yet?"

"You think he knows where the Stone is?" David asked.

"I'll bet he knows where it could be. I doubt if anyone really knows where it is after all these hundreds of years," she said.

David was already putting the books back on the shelves. "Let's go call Eileen, then, and see if she will go and ask him what he knows."

They hurried back around the side of the abbey and before long found the door into the kitchen. Sitting on the table was a curled fax, a handwritten note alongside.

I thought you might want to see this, the first ferry is at 5 a.m. It was signed *Mac.*

Unrolling the page, they saw what they had been dreading since leaving Ireland: the captain wasn't going to leave well enough alone. A grainy copy of David's passport picture headed the dispatch. Underneath, it read:

Be aware, the fugitive David Lord is known to have expressed interest in the Iona locale. Please be on the lookout for him and his companion, a woman believed to be one Camryn Brough Lavender. Be advised that she may be traveling with him under duress. He is wanted for questioning in connection to the shooting death of Roger Brough, who has a close association with the crown. Please exercise extreme caution when approaching Mr. Lord.

If he is sighted, contact the SO14 immediately.

"We should be on that ferry," David said. "Only someone who knows what we are searching for would know to send this to Iona."

Dinner was a large bowl of Wheaties and they made up beds in adjoining rooms. Camryn found they had enough cell strength to make a call to Eileen; she left a message, asking her to talk to the professor again.

Unable to sleep, David finally got up and opened his window. The tide had risen and the gentle surf played its endless song. The peace and majesty of Iona swept through and about him.

He sat on the bed and thought through where they should go

tomorrow. If they had time, then Dunadd would help them see the full history of the stone, but if time was growing short, then they needed to hurry. Edinburgh would be the next stop.

It had better be Edinburgh, he thought. David crawled under the covers and slept with the window open, the sounds and scents of Iona imprinting themselves on his soul while he dreamed.

He couldn't control his dreams and in them he found that his heart was eased as he held Camryn and looked on her as his own. The dream faded as he watched her smile and saw that she held a baby in her arms. The baby slept and Camryn smoothed the riot of golden curls that capped the baby's small head.

CHAPTER 36

Mrs. Pilliard lay motionless in the cramped quarters of their bed, waiting for her husband to begin breathing again. The silence seemed endless but eventually he began quivering, drew a loud gasp of air, and, snorting and heaving, he rolled to his side and settled back into a rhythmical snore. The decibel of the snore was enough to wake the neighbors if they had dared to open their windows, but it was infinitely preferable to the absence of breathing. The captain had sinus problems, but since he didn't disturb his own sleep with his labored breathing, he refused to believe that there was a problem at all.

"Ma'am, don't you think that I would be aware if I stopped breathing?" he would ask her, perplexed at her stupidity.

The missus relaxed somewhat when he seemed content to lay on his side, and soon she drifted into a light sleep as far on her side of the bed as she could manage.

The captain eventually fell into a deep sleep and drifted on an ocean of dreams, which, at last, cast him up on the shores of Mullaghmore, County Sligo, in Ireland.

"No!" he muttered, but the protest didn't have enough force to change the direction of his nightmare.

He dreamed of a bluff overlooking a manmade jetty on a glorious summer morning. He was taking his bearings when a white station wagon pulled up close to the harbor and Lord Mountbatten and a few others piled out of the car. A guard's car pulled up behind the wagon and a guard helped Lord Mountbatten down the steps and onto a long green fishing vessel.

The captain groaned in his sleep, "Not again…" Unable to look away, he watched the guard climb aboard and help the party stow and fetch and settle in.

The guard returned to his car and followed the progress of the boat, driving along the shore and keeping a close eye on the party. Lord Mountbatten was at the helm and the Shadow V turned left into the calm blue waters of Donegal Bay and paused at the lobster pots.

The guard got out of the car and watched the boat. The captain tensed in his dream, straining to yell but unable to make a sound. Very suddenly, there was an enormous explosion and a huge mushroom-shaped cloud of smoke rose high above the bay and immediately started to dissipate. Debris rained down on the sea and the guard was hit with an immense plume of sea-spray. The captain held his ears as screams of panic and pain filled the air.

He watched the guard call on his radio for assistance and then drive flat-out back to town to gather help.

On the far side of the bed, Mrs. Pilliard agonized along with her husband as he groaned and whimpered in his sleep. She recognized his rambling and regretful muttering from this constantly recurring nightmare. Would he ever be free of the stigma that attached itself to the noble name of Pilliard that day?

She remembered the captain's father, a clerk, and his drunken explanations of the affair to his son.

"I admit," he had told him, "that I held back a directive to form a SO14 guard for the Lord because of the Irish troubles. I thought I knew best."

In the shuffling of blame that began with the Lord's death, great indignation had spread throughout the service that a single, lowly clerk could play such an ignoble role in the death of two octogenarians and two young boys. The word never got out to the press, but his name was mud in the SO14.

As the father began his rapid decline into abject humiliation, so the son clawed and heaved his way through the minefields of service in the SO14, the royal protection services. But he never felt clean of the tarnished image of his father's legacy.

Mrs. Pilliard's eyes wet the pillow that night as she wept for both men, tears that they would never shed for themselves or each other.

Dean's truck rode with stiff axles over the last hundred yards of their journey.

"I think I am going to sell this beast after this is over!" Dean said, as they pulled up to a sprawling white home. It was saved from being pretentious by a silvered wooden tree house perched in the heights of the roomy branches. A frayed rope dangled to the ground. The mailbox was stuffed to overflowing with mail, circulars, and magazines.

"It doesn't look like anyone is home," Dean said.

Enrique stared out the window, deaf to Dean's observation. He opened his door and pulled out a handful of letters from the mailbox, shuffling through them and reading each address. He looked stunned. Deliberately he put them back into the mailbox and got back into the truck.

"Pull up to the house, will you?"

"What's wrong?" Dean asked, concerned. "You look like you've seen a ghost."

Mac was at the ferry when they got to the harbor early the next morning.

"I think I'd better cross over with you. The Mull police will have gotten the same fax we did. There are only a few routes onto our little isle," he said.

"You hardly know us; and we are deeply in your debt," David said.

"Well, the Scots are hardly mates with British authorities. Clan MacDougall was made custodian of the stone at Dunstaffnage and we never really put down the burden of it, even when it left us for Scone. Keep asking your questions," Mac said.

It was only the three of them that made the trip to Fionnphort; they stood in the bow of the ferry and watched as the harbor came closer and into sharper focus.

"There," Mac pointed, "they are waiting." A pair of blue uniforms stood at the dock, watching the arriving ferry.

Instead of looking toward their destination, David looked at Camryn. Reaching down he tenderly gathered her silky gold hair and pulled the hood of her jacket up to cover her head. Then he did the same with his own hoodie.

"Can you two act like lovers? Please?" Mac had a plan. Camryn moved immediately into his arms and he pulled her into a fierce hug. The ferry pulled to the dock. David leaned against the rail and held on to her.

"Keep it up, we're almost there." Mac murmured to them.

David bent his head to her. She buried her face into his wounded shoulder and he stiffened for a moment in pain.

"Hallo! Mac?" someone called from shore. They bumped gently into the dock and sounds of someone tying them off drifted on the air.

"Hey! Are you coming over to Iona?" Mac called. To David he murmured, "Just walk past them and up the street."

"We are assigned to watch anyone trying to get to Iona. There's this guy…" The policeman's voice trailed off.

Mac spoke up. "These two aren't going to Iona, so they won't be who we are looking for. They are just honeymooners wanting to sail to Fingal's Cave today."

Mac got off the ferry and faintly motioned for David to walk on by. David reluctantly released Camryn. He grasped her hand and, keeping his back to the cops, walked right on up the steps and on toward town.

A quick glance over his shoulder as they reached the first intersection showed that Mac was on his way to meet them. The two police had a white sheet of paper out and they looked like they were arguing.

"Quick, come this way," Mac said as he turned the corner and walked to them. They walked to an alley and Mac pulled out a ring of keys. Sorting through them, fumbling in his hurry, he finally found the right one.

"Come in here." He pushed open the door and they stepped into a packed wooden garage. Camryn swatted at a web that brushed across her face and moved aside to let the men through. Mac shut the door and the room was instantly shrouded in shadows; a grimy window let in a few streaks of sunlight, but it was hard to make out where to move.

"They will be looking for you, I only put them off for a few minutes. This is my brother's place."

"We can't hide in here; we've got to get to Scone," David said.

Mac had left the wall and was shifting things around. "My nephew has been wanting this, why don't you take it to him?"

Their eyes adjusting to the gloom, they could now make out a dusty motorcycle of an indeterminate age propped up in the middle of the room. David moved closer to look it over. "Do you know when was it last started?"

"I rode it up the coast a bit last fall. Did just fine once I got the old gas cleaned out of the lines."

"It doesn't look like there is room for both of us!" Camryn said.

"Well, I'm not leaving you here," David responded.

Mac moved to a bench against the wall, took a key off a nail, grabbed a rag, and handed it to David.

"It is a little dusty, but it is a goer!"

Camryn took the greasy rag from David and tried to wipe down the seat.

"Come and help me with this door, then." Mac threw a bolt and strained to lift the garage door.

They wrangled the door up along its tracks. It groaned and stuck a few times but eventually was open enough to clear the motorcycle. David straddled the machine, pulled in the clutch, and turned the key. With a few kicks it sputtered; he gave it some gas and it rumbled and popped and belched a little black smoke.

"Get on!" he shouted to Camryn. She handed the greasy rag to Mac, and he handed her a business card in turn.

"Call me when you get outside of Edinburgh."

She climbed on the back and hung on.

"Wait!" Mac rummaged through some boxes, against the wall. Holding two helmets aloft like trophies he brought them to the riders.

"How far to Oban?" David shouted over the rumble of the engine.

"About three hours; turn right when you get up to the top of the street—there are signs from there and only one way to the big city. I'll keep them thinking you're still somewhere in town for as long as I can."

Mac slapped the back of the cycle and David gave it some gas, they paused at the end of the alley, looking both ways. As they turned the corner they heard Mac shout a full-throated rebel yell: "Strike for the silver lion!"

CHAPTER 37

I
t was a three-hour trip to Oban, and from there street signs led them onto the road to Edinburgh. The road was a deserted stretch of highway and the motorcycle barely touched asphalt, they flew through the lonely country until it was all a gray-and-green blur. At Kirk Road, David let off the throttle and with a slight dip and a turn, he followed the signs to Dunstaffnage Castle.

We are right here, and we'll be back on the road in thirty minutes, he thought.

They skipped the tour and instead walked around the castle proper, which looked as if it had sprung, full-grown, from bedrock. It was built on a huge rock promontory and the foundations bulged and jutted out toward the sea. Inside the roofless ruins, outlines of walls allowed visitors to imagine life in medieval Scotland. The floors were carpeted with mint-green grass that was as soft underfoot as was the finest wool.

With a pamphlet as their guide, walking around the castle didn't take long. As they retraced their path toward the entrance, they came upon a narrow, unmarked path that wandered into the woods. Three small owls perched on a contorted silver birch just inside the thicket. David and Camryn followed the footpath that led into the forest. The light grew dimmer the farther they walked, and finally, through a shield of trees they discovered a ruined stone church. With a violent flurry of wing beats, the small owls flew through the clearing and landed on a moss covered stone bench sitting beside the church. The owls hooted their mournful tongue and then lifted off to sit above the church.

"I can easily imagine Clan MacDougall guarding the stone here." David climbed the steps to the church and looked in the doorway and wondered if the stone had ever been within these walls. None of the grandeur of London cathedrals was here; a simpler time and people perhaps.

Camryn read out loud from the pamphlet. "There is a very old Scottish tradition that says that if an actual descendant of the Mac-Dougalls with red hair and without freckles would stand in the ancient chapel of Dunstaffnage and shout the battle cry of the Scots, instead of an echo, he will hear an eerie voice say, 'Where is the stone?'"

Leaving the church, David came to the bench and looked down at Camryn for a long moment.

"Do you wonder if we'll ever see the true Coronation Stone?" Camryn asked.

"If we are on a true quest, then like the grail, I expect the stone will find us!"

She patted the bench and David sat by her.

"We should be on the road to Edinburgh soon. Are you with me?"

Camryn just looked at him then, with trust and something else blazing from her gray eyes.

It was a long road to Edinburgh, though not nearly long enough. Camryn held on tight and they flew over the road wending through hills and glens. Just outside of Edinburgh they stopped to call Mac, to find out where they should leave the bike.

"We are getting inquiries and updates every hour now, warning us to watch for you."

"Neither one of us has done anything wrong!" David replied, in an effort to give the old Scot confidence in trusting them.

"Let me just ask you this then, are you searching for the Stone of Destiny?"

"We are."

"For hundreds of years, Clan MacDougall has been watching and waiting for the true Stone of Destiny to be returned to the Scots. If you are seeking the stone, any of us would be honored to offer assistance."

"You all are a fierce bunch, aren't you?" David said.

"Well, I guess you are going to find that out for a fact!" Mac said. "Stay where you are and I'll send my brother to find you, and then you can be on your way. Where are you going next? They have all the tourist sites watched from what I can tell," Mac said.

"We are going to try and get to Edinburgh Castle next. Do you know anyone there?"

"Let me put out the word! Where are you right now?"

"We are getting petrol at the Bearsden exit just off of 82. He can't miss us, we'll be the two fugitives on a motorcycle!"

"I guess the captain knows we're still kicking then," David said to Camryn as he hung up the payphone. "Do you want to go home?"

Camryn just looked at him, her gray eyes no longer gentle, but steely and sure.

They filled up the tank and parked the bike to the side of the parking lot. Presently, a car pulled into the lot and slowly cruised. When it had completed a lap, it pulled up beside them. David raised his arm in greeting before he realized that he was waving to an officer in the uniform of the royal Scottish police driving an unmarked car.

David slowly lowered his half-raised arm and acknowledged that they were caught, when Camryn pushed in front of him, her arm deep inside her purse.

"Why don't you leave him alone?" Camryn shouted at the policeman, still rooting around in the bag. "He's done nothing wrong. You've got the wrong man!"

The overlarge policeman reacted, reaching to his side, when Camryn obviously found what she was looking for and quickly pulled her hand from the depths of the purse. Her face passed from righteous indignation to a moment of determination, right on through to puzzlement as she pulled out a large black pistol and looked at it as if it had appeared out of thin air.

David reached out and engaged the safety before he spoke.

"Look at him, Camryn, I think he's our man." The policeman had pulled his wallet and displayed for them his license. Gregor MacDougall. It was Mac's brother.

"He didn't warn you then? He might have saved us all a heart attack!" Mac's brother exclaimed.

"Where did you get that thing?" David asked, looking at the gun.

"I forgot it was in my purse! Do you want it?" she replied, holding it out to him.

"I'd better keep it for you, since I am sure you are not licensed to carry it," Gregor said.

David looked around, realizing they had attracted some attention. "Can we get out of here?" he asked.

Gregor had not come empty handed. They feasted on fish and chips and pickled onions, all wrapped up in newspaper and still piping hot. He drove while they ate, and when the papers had been crumpled and bundled into the take out bag, they were well on the road to Edinburgh.

"So, what has Mac told you?" David asked their driver.

"He said you wanted to see our Coronation Stone," Gregor answered.

"We're not exactly your typical sightseers," David said. "Do you have any idea if the castle is being watched?"

"It is, but the clans are doing the watching, so I think we'll be all right."

"What do you think of the Coronation Stone? Did the English steal the real thing?" David asked.

"Just wait till you see the display: the Honours of Scotland, the crown jewels, the scepter, the sword, and then this big, ugly hunk of sandstone. It just doesn't feel right, you know?"

"Can we spend a few minutes in the Royal Palace with the Honours and the stone?" David asked.

"You won't be able to touch them—they are in a glass case," Gregor cautioned. "Look, we've arrived."

Gregor parked and made a quick phone call.

"It's Gregor MacDougall, did Mac call you? Yes, we just got here. Should we come in the front gate or through the service gate? Okay, three o'clock?" He looked to David for confirmation. David nodded. "I'll bring them along to the front entrance at three then.

"He says they want us to kick around Edinburgh for a bit. The supervisor is Clan McCormack, and I guess Mac talked to him earlier."

"David, I've been thinking," Camryn said. "My grandfather used a solicitor whose office is on the Royal Mile. Why don't we try and find him? We need to tell someone this crazy story and a lawyer might be a good listener."

David was thoughtful. "A Scots solicitor might be inclined to believe us. Do you remember the name of the firm?"

"I think I would recognize it if I could read through the phone book. Or do you want to drive down that way and we can see what I remember?" she asked Gregor. "I know it was at this end of the mile because you can see the castle from the sidewalk in front of their building."

They pulled out of their parking space and drove slowly off the castle mound; they turned on Ramsey and then onto Market. Camryn kept on twisting in the seat to look back at the castle.

"Pull over!" she said. They were at the intersection of Cockburn and Market. "There it is!" An old building made of the dark gray stone commonly used in old Edinburgh formed a three-story building fronted by a round tower. A sign on the front announced they had arrived at the solicitor's office of 'Buchanan and Black.'

"Do you want me to come in with you?" Gregor asked.

"We can meet you at the gate before three. Would that be easier? It isn't a bad walk at all from here," David said. "I did want to ask you what the powers that are telling the police about us before we walk in to explain our situation."

"At first, they were trying to apprehend the killer of Mr. Brough. Then they were looking for the body of Mr. Lord in the Irish Channel, now they are looking for the two of you for questioning and they have decided that you will be showing up in the vicinity of Edinburgh, Perth, and Iona. I don't think that London gives us provincial Scots credit enough to think we might connect those places with the Stone of Destiny, but we've caught on! I don't think you should be walking around in plain sight, though. I've got my phone and you just call me when you've finished and I'll pick you up right here." He handed David a card. Camryn took it from him and put it in her purse.

They walked into the offices as Gregor pulled onto Market. The stairs were narrow, the walls lath and plaster. It took three turns of stairs to reach the uppermost floor, where a formidable woman sat behind a large desk that must have been built right where it stood. There was no way it could have come up those stairs.

"May I help you?" she asked. She peered over horn-rimmed glasses that were so old they were probably coming back into style and looked them both over from head to toe.

"My grandfather uses the services of Mr. Black and we were wondering if he would be free to see us for a few minutes on an urgent matter," Camryn asked politely and with the slightest suggestion of a highland burr.

"Who might your grandfather be?"

"Gerald Ross."

"Let me see if he is in for you then." The secretary unseated herself and walked down the way to an open office, peered in, and spoke, presumably to Mr. Black. Beckoning to them, she gestured for David and Camryn to enter the office.

"Miss Camryn, how nice to see you. Mr. Lord, how good of you to stop by. I've been watching your exploits on the news and I feel honored you have time for a visit!"

The elder Mr. Black had seen the far side of seventy; he was tall and stooped and had a beautiful head of silver hair combed back in a pompadour. His eyes were keen and twinkled with a ready mirth.

David and Camryn looked at each other.

"Sit, please, and let's have a talk, shall we?" Mr. Black got up and pulled out a chair for Camryn, shut the door, and pointed at the other chair next to it. Then he went back around his desk and sat, leaning back and tapping his fingers together.

"What can I do for you?" he asked.

"Well, I'm not aware of the Scottish laws about representation. In the States I would know what to do. How do we retain your services?" David began.

Mr. Black waved his hand lazily. "I am old enough and rich enough that I can pick and choose my cases. This interests me, so let's dispense with the formalities and get on with the story." He leaned forward in his seat and, focusing on them with an eagle eye, asked again: "What is going on?"

David took a long breath then and started in. He spent quite some time on Roger's recital of the problem, described the letter they had uncovered in Roger's desk, told him all they knew about the search in the States for the woman who had written the letter and described Captain Pilliard and his demented antics in great detail. When his voice cracked, Mr. Black got up and poured him a glass of water and then sat back in his chair and motioned him to continue.

David talked about their search for the Stone of Destiny, from the beginning. Jacob, Moses, King David, Jeremiah, through Spain to Ireland and on to Scotland.

David sat back in his chair, quiet now and relieved to have shared the burden of the task they had undertaken.

Mr. Black turned his chair toward the window overlooking Edinburgh, and, rocking slightly, he tapped his fingers against each other and thought. The room was essentially silent. They could hear the muffled sounds of traffic from the window and the slight creak of the chair as he thought, but that was all.

Presently, the old lawyer shifted again and faced his visitors.

"So, Prince George might have married. No wonder he has put out that he is a confirmed bachelor! What an impossible situation. Someone from the palace is trying to keep any evidence of that relationship hidden. What do you know of this Captain Pilliard?"

"We have been running too hard from him to do anything but react. We know nothing," David said.

Mr. Black turned now to Camryn.

"What, my dear, are you doing in the middle of this?"

"I am in it only because I have been in the vicinity of the events, but I am in it all the way."

"Why did your brother connect the two searches, my dear?" Mr. Black ruminated. "I can't see the connection at all."

David answered, "We have watched for a connection and have not found any. The searches must not be tied together."

Mr. Black was quiet for a moment.

"I think I see my way through, we will start our own investigation and bring our own charges. The law can bring light to the truth, if the players are powerful enough." The solicitor stood and walked to the door.

"Calliope!" he called. She came with a pad of paper and a pen, ready to do battle and anxious to find out what had transpired behind the closed door.

David looked at Camryn with a faint smile—such a name for such a woman!

"First, we need to get these two somewhere safe, immediately. We will need…"

"Sir," David interrupted. "I'm sorry, but that isn't possible. We need to go to Scone and then London, and we will need to leave here soon."

"Well, I can't very well insist, but I would prefer to keep you safe. You will be off then? We will certainly do our part from here. We'll see if we can't get a little ahead of the game." Mr. Black turned to his secretary. "Calliope, we'll need to stay late!"

"Can we have your card?" David asked. Mr. Black pulled out a card from his desk drawer and in a fine hand wrote out a private number.

"I will be dining at The Witchery tonight with my daughter. You do need to eat and you shouldn't leave Edinburgh without seeing it, if you would like to join us."

David just shook his head and stood. The venerable old solicitor came around the desk, shook his hand, and helped Camryn to her feet.

"Well, if you can't join us tonight, let's set a date, and it will be my treat when this is over. Say a month from now?"

David nodded at that.

"All right, I am putting you in my calendar for exactly four weeks from today, say 7 o'clock?"

"I am sure that will be fine! Thank you so much for seeing us," Camryn said to him. "May I use your phone before we go? I need to call our ride."

Calliope took charge and showed her out of the room to a phone.

"When have you last heard from your partner in the States?"

"I need to call him! It was a little over a day since we last spoke," David said.

"He needs to be careful. The captain wouldn't be chasing you at all if it wasn't for that other matter!" Mr. Black said. "Can you imagine the dust up if there was a child?" He shook his head at the thought. "I can almost guarantee that the S014 did not instigate the hunt for you. I would bet that someone else wants to eliminate any rival heirs and is using the captain as the hound dog on the hunt, as it were," Mr. Black said.

"Well, it might seem like a big deal to some, but I am from the colonies, as you put it, and one more prince or princess wouldn't matter a bit to me! Can I use a computer for a minute? I'll check on Enrique and get you a phone number," David asked.

Mr. Black logged onto his own computer and seated David behind the desk.

"I just see this one new message...and here is the email with his cell numbers written down." Camryn came to the door, and David quickly signed off.

"Gregor is pulling up right now so we'd better go."

David hurriedly copied Enrique's cell numbers on a scrap paper twice and tore the paper in half, one to keep and one for Mr. Black.

After handshakes all around and promises to be careful, David and Camryn tread carefully down the steep staircase, out into the streets of Edinburgh, and into the car. "Don't forget, we have a date in four weeks!" Mr. Black called down the stairs to remind them.

"I don't know if that was worth anything, but I feel better having the story in someone else's hands," Camryn said to David. "Is it close to three yet?" she asked Gregor as they slid into the backseat.

"I was just getting ready to come and get you: it is time," Gregor said.

They drove up the mound and parked in a reserved parking place. It was a long walk up the esplanade and over the drawbridge but once they bought tickets the Royal Palace was the first building inside the gate.

"Are there usually this many guards?" Camryn asked.

"I think they are here just for you two, but if you notice they are pointedly looking away."

Gregor opened the door of the Royal Palace and they went inside. The sounds of the outside world drifted in with them and then were shut off completely when the large, thick door slowly closed. Their footsteps echoed on the old floors and they could hear faint sounds of a tour group in the distance.

"Hello!" Gregor called into the hallway. "Hello!" He turned to David and asked, "Do you want to stay here while I go and find our guide? I'll be right back." He walked down the hall and disappeared.

"My grandmother was afraid of Ireland because of the fairies and wouldn't set foot in Edinburgh because of all the ghosts!" Camryn said, a shiver creeping up her back as she spoke.

Captain Pilliard excused himself. "I need to take this call. Carry on, I'll be right back."

"I just saw them enter the palace—they are here!"

"You have done well. I need them brought to me. Do you still think you can get access to the palace while they are inside?"

"There are so many of us watching, no one will notice me leave."

"I will be waiting then and you will be rewarded."

The captain then called his benefactor and left a message. "He has come to Edinburgh, as we hoped."

CHAPTER 38

I don't like waiting here," David said. "Do you want to try and find the room ourselves?"

Their footsteps echoed noisily as they followed the hall. The sounds of the other group had disappeared altogether. They looked into the rooms they passed, sure they would recognize the stone if they saw it.

"Oh look! It's this way." Camryn pointed to a sign with an arrow.

They hurried now, anxious to see if it was the Stone of Destiny for themselves. Finding themselves on the threshold of a dimly lit room, they entered eagerly; no one else was in the room. A large glass case was lighted with a dim glow and a deep blue velvet cloth was the resting place of a small, rich crown, a burnished gold sword, a regal sceptre and a large sandstone block. A plaque in front of the display read:

If fate go right, where'er this stone is found,
The Scots shall monarchs of that realm be crowned.

The stone was rough and unpolished and seemed out of place lying next to the gleaming gold and glittering jewels. A sandstone block measuring 26 inches long by 16 inches wide, and 10½ inches deep, it looked weighty and had a deep groove running down the middle with two old metal rings set into it. Some say they were used to convey the stone on a pole across a continent from Israel. Those who believe the Scots foisted a fake on Edward, the British king, say that the fake stone was used as a lid to the privy and the rings were used to lift it from the cesspit.

"Could it be Jacob's Pillow?" David said. He was drawn to the display case, and barely touching the glass, he pressed his hands on the smooth barrier.

Looking closely at the stone, his thoughts flew to Iona and Tara, to Dunstaffnage and Sinai. There was no witness in the air here, no confirmation of the history and promises made upon this stone.

Finally he spoke. "I'm glad we came. This isn't the Stone of Destiny, is it?"

Camryn moved closer to the case, shaking her head. "No, but I can see the Scots fobbing this off on the English and then not saying a word for hundreds of years!"

As she spoke, David watched the light reflect off gold and the crown of James V glittered on her head, a reflection perfectly placed on her head. He blinked to focus again; she moved and it was gone.

"Well, we need to keep going then. To Perth?" David asked.

There were sounds now outside the room, a door opening and closing, footsteps echoing down the halls, and the hushed atmosphere evaporated instantly. Out of the corner of her eye Camryn saw movement ,but when she turned to see there was nothing there. Again, she saw a quick movement, a flicker of light, but when she turned it was not there.

"What's wrong?" David asked.

There it was again, a large dog sat at attention in the doorway. He whined at them and barked.

"I think he wants us to follow him!" Camryn said.

"What are you talking about?" David asked.

The dog started down the hall, his nails clicking on the floor, pausing once to look over his shoulder to make sure they were following.

"Come on, let's see what he wants." Camryn started out the door and down the hall deeper into the castle. David followed. Behind them they could hear a tour guide leading a group through the castle.

"Up ahead we will be entering the room with the honors of Scotland and the Stone of Destiny. Please wait until after we leave the room to ask any questions."

Camryn followed the ghostly beast, something only she could see, straight into the bowels of the castle.

Enrique and Dean were sitting in the truck across the street from the home and waiting for someone to pull in the driveway. Dean's stomach was grumbling noisily, but they didn't dare leave. They had mounted guard, and instead of enjoying a dinner of burgers and fries, they sat in the truck and kept watch, hoping that no one else knew what they had discovered about the passport switch.

"Okay, Rique, you've been quiet since we got to this house. What gives?"

"Did you notice the name on the mailbox? Can you read it from here?"

Dean squinted and looked. "No, I can't quite make it out."

"It says Lord, as in David Lord."

"You've got to be kidding me!" Dean said.

Enrique just shook his head in disbelief.

"It cannot be a coincidence, and yet, how could the search lead straight back to the man who hired me? I don't know what it all means, but we are going to find out," he said.

A car pulled down the street a little after midnight, slowed as they neared the drive, and stopped at the mailbox. Someone collected the mail and pulled down the driveway, around the house, and out of sight.

They decided to approach the house in the morning. Sleeping in shifts, the night passed slowly. Backs aching, stomachs growling, time hardly seemed to move at all.

Finally, dawn lightened the sky. They waited another two hours but it was still early when they finally knocked on the kitchen door. It was opened immediately by a woman with an apron on and a wooden spoon in her hand.

"Hello, Miss. We are here to see Elizabeth O'Brien, it is now Lord, right? It is on a matter of some importance."

"You aren't here about that business in Ireland then?" the woman asked. "You may as well come in. No one ever tells me anything!" She left them standing by the door and walked purposefully out of the room.

"Mrs. Lord? Elizabeth! You have company." Her voice trailed away as she moved farther into the house.

Enrique eventually pulled out a chair and sat in thought. Dean looked out the kitchen window and then moved toward a set of shelves.

"Is this your Mr. Lord?" he asked. Enrique looked up; there was a shelf full of pictures. The frames were mismatched and in a matter of fifteen pictures the child turned into a man right before their eyes. It was David Lord.

Camryn hustled to follow the dog; the light played tricks on her eyes because she couldn't see him at times and had to listen for his footsteps. Why she was following the dog didn't register, she only knew it was right.

"Do you hear pipes?" she asked.

"What are you talking about? I don't hear any pipes and I can't see what you are following either!"

"Oh, don't be silly!" And she hurried off again, with David right behind her. They came to the next corner, where a wide set of stone stairs descended into the bowels of the castle.

"Hello? What are you two doing here?" A guard was coming up the stairs.

"It's all right, this is who I am looking for." Gregor was right behind the castle guard. "I am so glad we've found you. We need to be gone as soon as we can get to the car. The SO14 is at the front door of the castle right now. Follow me!" They moved quickly down the steps; it got colder and damper the further they went.

"I've found you two guard uniforms. We can walk right out the front door if we want! Did you see what you came to see?"

"Yes, we did. Do you know if the captain is here, or just his men?"

They were nearing the bottom of the stair, and as David asked his question Gregor seemed to change from a civilized policeman into a bloodthirsty clansman.

"Judas!" he said, and they found they were looking into the barrel of a pistol held by another uniformed guard. "You will never walk out of here alive, blood traitor," Gregor spat at the floor in contempt.

The guard seemed to realize that Gregor was right, and the gun popped once. Gregor fell heavily down the last two steps and lay groaning on the floor.

David instinctively went to his aid and Camryn sat on the last step and held Gregor's head in her arms.

"Get up, you two. You are coming with me."

Camryn looked at the guard with disgust. "You think that because you have a gun we will do what you say? You are nothing." She turned her focus back to Gregor. "We are here, don't you worry. We won't leave you," she crooned to him. Then something caught her attention beyond the guard; she nodded and pointed to him and said, "Get him, boy!"

The ghostly dog bristled and growled and charged the guard. This time David could see the faintest outlines of the dog flicker in and out of focus.

The guard could see nothing but reacted in terror as the dog tore at his legs and bit his arm. The guard turned this way and that, and then turning altogether he ran down the hall and into the darkened corridor. Several shots went off, and then quiet settled back over them.

Gut shot, Gregor was bleeding profusely and in shock with intense pain.

"You've got to get out," he stammered.

"We are just fine, don't you worry. We won't leave you," Camryn kept repeating over and over. She cradled his shoulders and was covered in his blood.

"Take my keys and go," he murmured, and he fainted.

"You call an ambulance," she said. "I'll stay here with him."

David stood but didn't leave.

"Go! The number is 999."

They were in the functional part of the castle and he found a phone on a desk by the service entrance.

"Just hurry!" He ended the call. *Now we wait.*

He thought about Roger and knew that Camryn wouldn't leave until someone came to look after Gregor. *And SO14 is waiting for us outside*, he thought.

He hurried back to the stairs and heard sirens in the distance, whether police or ambulance he could not tell. Gregor lay still on a stone floor that had been soaked in blood many times over the hundreds of years since a stonemason laid it. David leaned down and pressed his finger to Gregor's neck, there was the barest suggestion of a pulse. He sat on the stair next to Camryn, unsure of what they should do next.

"You win," he whispered as though the captain could hear him. Camryn gave a tight little shake of her head.

"He will never win while I am alive!" she said.

They sat with Gregor as he passed from this life and into the next. When he had struggled to take his last breath, Camryn gently laid his head on the hard stone floor and they walked away.

"I don't want to do this anymore," David said, weariness lay upon him like a shroud. Camryn took his hand and held tight. They walked solemnly to the service entrance, waiting for the ambulance to arrive.

CHAPTER 39

Elizabeth Lord walked into her kitchen rolling a smart little suitcase behind her. She had on a prim beige suit with the jacket folded neatly over her arm and an airline ticket sticking out of a matching purse.

"How may I help you?" she said to them. "I don't have much time before I need to be at the airport."

Now that she was here, Enrique didn't quite know how to break the news to her.

"Ma'am, I hate to tell you this, but I think you are in danger," Dean jumped in to fill the silence.

"Oh, I don't think so. I'm just an old lady, but they might be after my son," she said, putting her things down, looking at the clock and sitting at the table.

"Who are you?" Mrs. Lord asked. "How do you know of this?"

"Your son hired me to find a woman. He gave me a list and I have been searching for each one and asking them about a child born in 1981. Maeve told us about the passport switch and we drove up to find Elizabeth O'Brien. Do you know what this is about, then? Because we have no idea!" Enrique said. "Did Maeve call you about us?"

"She called me last night and told me everything. Why don't you drive me to the airport and I will tell you what I can about it."

The housekeeper reappeared then and made it clear she didn't want to be left behind, so they took Elizabeth's sedan. Dean drove, and once Elizabeth started talking it all started to make sense.

"It is a convoluted story, and I won't go into all the details now, but David is the son of Prince George. I never told him!" She closed her eyes at that, and they sat in absolute silence for a long moment. As they pulled up to the curb at the airport she seemed to gather her wits enough to speak.

"Tell me how to find David once I am in London—do you know?" she asked.

"You can have my cell phone; he called it once and he said he would call again when he could." Enrique pulled the phone from his pocket. "The charger is in the car but it is fully charged right now. Let me give you an email address we have been using. I'll write him that you are coming and you can check it when you land."

She pulled out some scrap paper from her purse and Enrique wrote out the email address for her.

"If you talk to him, tell him I will look for him in London. I'll be staying at Claridge's. His father always stayed at that hotel, so David might think to look for me there."

Enrique helped Mrs. Lord out of the car and got her suitcase out of the trunk. "I don't think the men sent to find you have tumbled to your existence yet. But until we are sure they are all rounded up you should be careful."

"I don't know how to do that, but I understand your concern and will try," Elizabeth said.

Ellen gave Elizabeth a long hug. "You could have told me, you know," she told Mrs. Lord.

"I couldn't tell anyone; it was not mine to tell," she responded.

"Well, I wouldn't have told a soul!" Ellen said.

"Whatever I did, someone was going to get hurt. So I just waited for something like this to force my hand," Elizabeth said.

Enrique took her hand. It was trembling.

"Do you want someone to go with you?" he asked.

"I'll be all right, just a touch of stage fright is all. I tend to like my privacy and I believe that's about to become a thing of the past."

They watched her roll the suitcase down the sidewalk and into the terminal. She turned to wave before the doors closed and then she walked on and they lost sight of her in the crowds. Ellen pulled out a hankie and sobbed most of the way home, but when they pulled into the driveway she calmed down and with only a sniffle asked them in.

"Mrs. Lord wants me to go and stay with my daughter while she is gone. Doesn't think it is safe to be here until she finds Davy, but I won't be able to leave until tomorrow morning. We have plenty of room here if you would consider staying the night. I'd sleep better knowing someone was here with me."

"That sounds like a great idea, we'll stay with you until your daughter comes," Enrique said.

Ellen dished up ice cream and butterscotch sauce while Dean and Enrique checked the locks on all the doors and windows. They visited until Ellen began yawning and then went to bed.

Enrique couldn't sleep. His thoughts of what they had learned and his feelings about finally going home chased every trace of weariness away.

The ambulance had come and they had pronounced Gregor dead. David answered their questions while Camryn drifted through the ordeal in a bit of shock. She was cold and kept trying to rub the blood-stains off her clothing. Finally, the woman EMS driver took her to a restroom and helped her to wash up a bit.

Camryn came back in a castle guard uniform. Black kilt and jacket, white and red wool socks and shoes, with a tartan wrapped around her shoulders.

"We pitched her clothes; they won't ever come clean, I'm afraid. These'll keep her warm. There's a uniform in the dressing room that'd fit you if you'd like to get out of those bloody clothes."

"Can we ride with Gregor to the hospital?" David asked.

"Well, we're not supposed to take civilians with us, but I think the lads will look the other way this time. Just hurry up and get changed."

He was back in a minute in the full uniform. They jumped in the back of the ambulance and amidst a deluge of swirling lights they started off the castle mound. The ambulance was stopped by the police at a hastily erected checkpoint.

"We are looking for two fugitives and we need to take a quick look in the back of the ambulance," a guard said to the driver.

The lights were off in the back, the EMS sat on a jump seat on one side, David and Camryn on the other. They heard the locks flipping and the guard pulled the doors open, shined a flashlight right at David, and said, "All clear here!" He mouthed a hushed "Conquer or die!" and closed the doors, and the ambulance pulled away.

"Clan MacDougall?" the EMS asked.

"It looks like we have been adopted," David replied. "Can we hop off up here?"

After a hurried conversation on walkie-talkies the ambulance pulled over. Camryn touched Gregor one last time and they were let down into the streets of Edinburgh.

They stood for a moment and watched the swirling lights of the ambulance until it turned the corner. Then, looking around, David said, "Well now, how are we going to get to Scone?"

Camryn fished in her pocket and came up with a bunch of keys. With a look of distaste she handed them to David and said, "Do you remember where he parked the car?"

They were still inside the city when Eileen called back. Camryn picked up the call and David pulled off the road, into a field overlooking the river, and listened in on the conversation.

"I've got the professor right here with me. Can you FaceTime with us? He has something he wants to show you." The video screen lit up and they found themselves looking at the professor seated at his table in the pub.

"So, you figured out the right question. I knew you would get to it." He looked pleased with them. "Just a minute..." They listened to him ordering another large selection of bottles and then he was back on the screen.

"So the quest for the stone has hooked you, has it? Here they come, thank you, Ms. O'Brien." David patted the seat close to him, and Camryn moved closer to him so they could both see the screen. They listened to the professor clear his throat and then watched as he emptied a bottle, and then the phone must have been given over to Eileen. She moved back so they could see the professor and the top of the table.

"Ready?" the professor asked. "This is a bit more complicated than our last session, more interesting if you ask me."

There was already a bottle on the table; he pointed at it and said, "This is Iona, right? You have been there?"

"Just yesterday," Camryn answered for them both. "And Dunstaffnage, we spent an hour there yesterday. We didn't have time to see Dunadd, but we read of its history."

Two more bottles appeared on the table side by side, north and east of the bottle representing Iona. "Very good!" the professor exclaimed.

"We just left Edinburgh a few minutes ago, where does it come in?" David asked.

"Not at all, not at all," the professor said. "The stone was taken to Scone from Dunstaffnage." And a bottle was slammed to the table at the far edge of the table, east of the rest of them. "It never went to London, I'm afraid, but was buried in some lonely spot to hide it from Edward." The professor paused. "But where, you ask! That is the question!"

The video went fuzzy and then they found themselves looking closely at the professor's eyes and nose. He spoke in a whisper. "There are partial documents that seem to indicate it was buried at a bend in the River Tay. There are rumors that it was taken to the Isle of Skye by Robert the Bruce, which is not a possibility. Robert was crowned on another royal chair, not our stone."

"There are stories of it being buried in the dungeons of the castle of Macbeth, a distinct possibility. I have seen a letter quoting an article from the *London Morning Chronicle* of January 2, 1819, saying that workers on the estate were charged with clearing away stones from excavations on Macbeth's land when the ground gave way. They sank six feet into an old vault and discovered a large stone weighing about 500 pounds, of meteorite or metallic substance. The stone was said to have been shipped to London for inspection and hasn't been seen since.

"Wolfram von Eschenbach's account of the stone speaks of a mythical stone, set somewhere on earth, and the stone is linked with the ascent and descent of the angels. He calls this stone the 'Grail Stone' and speaks of it as part of a covenant between man and God, very like the Jewish Ark of the Covenant."

The professor paused again and asked, "Are you following?"

They both nodded, and remained silent, waiting for his lecture to continue.

"Then, there are those that believe that the Knights Templar have been entrusted with the safekeeping of the sacred stone and hold it in an undisclosed location, either in London proper or in Dull.

"And, to add to our theories, many historians insist the stone was removed from Scone Abbey, in Perthshire, by monks and hidden in a cave on Dunsinnan Hill. But there are now those who suggest it could be four miles away in the grounds of Dunsinnan House. A lift operator who worked at the mansion once said he heard the owner say he could reach out and touch the Stone of Destiny whenever he wanted."

At last, the professor seemed to run out of steam. The sounds of the pub filtered through the phone, but the professor had fallen silent. David opened the door and stood at the edge of the field, considering all the professor had told them.

"Are you still there?" he heard Camryn ask.

"Yes," the professor said. They could hear him drinking, and then he spoke to them again. "That is all I have, you have picked my brain clean."

The phone call was ended abruptly and the sounds of the pub

were immediately cut off. David handed the phone back through the window, opened the door, and started the car. They returned to the country Scottish road and followed the signs pointing them toward Scone.

It was still early evening and they drove along the River Tay for quite some time. Several herds of shaggy Scottish cattle grazed on spring grass, and in other fields the first wildflowers were showing their colors. Bathed in the evenings gentle light it was easy to imagine they were just out for a drive on a beautiful day in Scotland. The roads were designed to carry unhurried travelers. They wound around broad hills and through the smallest of villages always hedged with gray rock walls and trimmed bushes. It wasn't long before they reached Queen's Street and turned in to the remnants of a royal park.

The castle was open, so they parked and walked down a gravel path and into the grounds. Camryn picked up a leaflet about the castle from a board at the entrance to the grounds. Pausing for a moment, they studied a map of the castle grounds.

"I know they are waiting for us," David said. "Where will they be?"

"At the church on the Hill of Credulity." Camryn pointed to the spot on the map. "It is the high ground and the oldest structure in the area. They will be waiting for us there."

"What kind of a name is 'Hill of Credulity'? It sounds like a game! Credulity...that means trust, right?"

"That sounds right! It looks like it is also called 'Boot Hill.' It says here that no Scot could be sworn into Parliament on land other than his own. Instead of the king traveling to the far reaches of the kingdom, the lords would put dirt from their estate in their boots when swearing fealty. They would then dump the dirt out after the ceremony, making, over time, Boot Hill," Camryn read. "So, the stone was brought here from Dunstaffnage and was used to crown their kings for another 500 years. After sacking Edinburgh Castle and stealing the Scottish Crown Jewels, Edward made no attempt to hide that he was coming for the Stone of Scone. It took Edward's army three months to make their way to Scone."

"Of course the monks knew he was coming and hid the stone," David said. "When Edward and his army came for the Stone of Destiny they took home that relic sitting in Edinburgh Castle instead of the true Coronation Stone."

David fell quiet, then asked, "Do you think it is here? Do we even want to find it? If revealing the true stone turns into just another reason to fight, it might be better to just leave it lost and forgotten."

They had walked quite a ways without seeing a soul. The castle was ahead and to the left, a hill was just visible to the right. David stopped on the path, looked about, and said, "Let's make for that stand of trees over there."

The day glowed golden, the sun low in the horizon, casting shadows and running upon the heads of the grass. The palace reigned over a deep peace that blanketed the area. The park appeared to be deserted and all was quiet, the evening songbirds and cricket tunes were subdued. An exquisite tension echoed over the expanse.

They could see a faint path through the grass to what looked like an ancient stand of fir trees in the distance.

David said, "To the Scots this stone was as precious as the Holy Grail was to later Christians: it would have been put in a place of absolute security and somewhere well marked. They wouldn't have put the stone at risk in any way. It has to be buried somewhere near the Hill of Credulity. The hill, not the abbey, was sacred to them."

"What about all the places the professor mentioned? Shouldn't we check out those stories as well?" Camryn asked. "Is your heart pounding?" Some power lurked about them, but whether behind them or before them, they couldn't tell, and whether it was friend or foe wasn't clear.

They gained the grove and paused to let their eyes adjust to the light. Rising from the black earth, ancient stone steps led to a large granite pavilion. They climbed five wide, mossy steps to the summit where a stone lion was set to guard the entrance. An eerie silence was broken only by their footsteps on the rock footing.

"What is this place?" David wondered aloud and turned to look around the circular structure. As he turned he watched in disbelief as the stone lion stood and stretch his immense paws and jaws, languidly sniffing.

The lion's tail whipped once and with an effortless leap was before them. The lion looked at David, radiating power and authority. The lion glowed with a silvery moonlight, no longer stone. The initial fear they felt in his presence was gone, replaced by a sense of companionship.

"He guards the stone!" Camryn thought out loud.

The lion turned and sniffed the air and turned back to them. They understood it was time to go on. They walked down the broad steps with the lion leading them. To their right the ground sloped upward and somewhere near that hill was the stone they were seeking. There was no path, the trees were widely spaced, and they walked on a thick carpet of pine needles. The unnatural silence could have been unnerving but for the peace that filled up the space and made its imprint on their ears and heart.

They are here," Kelso spoke quietly into his radio.

"Are they coming toward the church?" Captain Pilliard asked eagerly.

"They turned off into the firs but will have to come up on our men in back of the cemetery, or around to the church. We are in place."

"Go to radio silence. I don't want them to catch wind of us before we have them."

"Yes, sir. Kelso out."

Kelso turned to his men and with hand signals indicated that they were to spread out along the crumbling wall of the ancient cemetery. It was muddy and the men sank to their ankles but they found their positions and held, alert and anxious to go into action.

Now we wait, Kelso thought.

The sun hung in the western sky. It cast the woods into constantly adjusting shadows that flickered and moved with the approaching twilight. His men were trained and watched the darkening woods for the two fugitives, but they were skittish this evening. Maybe it was the utter stillness of the ancient forest, it could have been the mud oozing and sucking at their boots, but they were restless and overreacted to any movement in the woods.

"Steady, men," Kelso called softly to his team. "I think they are here."

A light appeared, moving toward them from deep in the woods.

"It looks like they have a lantern. Don't they know we are waiting for them?"

The men shifted, sinking deeper into the mud every time they moved.

The fugitives drew closer, and as the trees thinned, the squad could see clearly that what lit their way was, in fact, a full-grown lion. It was bathed in silver moonlight and padding quietly toward them as well. Quaking in disbelief, the men watched as the group drew closer to them. The most potent emblem of the Scots walked with David Lord and Camryn Lavender, who were both dressed in kilts and tartans.

Kelso knew his men and dedication to the job would not override the symbolism of what had accompanied Mr. Lord to Scone. Right or wrong was all parsed out in seconds. Kelso was the first to lower his gun, and his men were quick to follow.

"Mr. Lord!" he called quietly. David looked at him warily.

"Well, there you are," he said.

"We've been waiting for you!"

"I got here as fast as I could," Mr. Lord said, resigned to what would be.

Ms. Lavender stood slightly behind David, and showing no fear, she looked at the men and smiled.

"We have come so far and only have a little way left to go. Will you come with us?" she asked them.

"Yes, come with us," David offered. "Your Stone of Destiny is whispering and we are close enough to hear it."

As David spoke a great rushing of wind blew at them from the woods, pushed them and swirled around them. After the tumult died down a profound peace crept in and settled like a fog over the lowest elevations. Deepening, fattening, stretching, and dawning, the power of it towered over them and penetrated into every particle of their being.

Chapter 40

More powerful than anything he had ever felt, David embraced the onslaught of order from chaos to unity and profound peace. He could think of no perfect word to describe what was all about them. But he recognized it. In some measure its echo still rested at Iona and the Hill of Tara. And here now the air itself quivered with the same overwhelming power such that he felt strengthened from bathing in it.

Following an unerring path along a short stretch of the crumbling stone wall, they stepped over the toppled structure and into the ancient graveyard onto sacred soil. It had been given over to an ever-encroaching mass of peat moss; dampness hung in the air and chilled the approaching evening.

David and Camryn stood at the edge of the cemetery and listened, certain that the true Stone of Destiny was close enough to touch.

Headstones and grave markers leaned this way and that and in the corner, looking over the castle, a sloppy mess of mud and bog had taken over completely. Intricate drainage ditches had been poured and abandoned over the years, but it was a lost cause.

The headstones in that particular corner of the cemetery were sinking deeply and the wall was a good two feet lower than it once had been. Camryn left David's side and began walking across the dryer sector of the churchyard, reading the inscriptions.

"Isabella Blair, died 1871. James Clark, April 2, 1877. Maggie Dow, August 18, 1883. These are not ancient at all," Camryn called to David.

Deep in thought, David heard her as if she were speaking from a great distance. He watched the guardian of the stone; the lion paced the width of the graveyard, sniffing the air and tossing his head.

He watched the guards returning to report to Kelso. The men conferred quietly, with a lot of gesturing toward the lion. Finally, they came to an agreement and dispersed again.

"We are finished here." David surveyed the cemetery. Camryn and Kelso both must have noticed the change in his demeanor because they appeared by his side.

"I think we are done here, for now," David repeated softly to them.

240

"How can we leave to best keep you out of trouble?" he said to Kelso.

"We have passed beyond that," Kelso said.

"I am going to talk to the captain. There are some things we need to work out," David said.

"I don't think talking is what the captain has in mind," Kelso said.

"Well, we are nearly finished here, and I am done with his single-minded pursuit of me. I want this finished, one way or another, tonight."

The lion must have sensed what was coming. They watched as he stopped pacing and lay down upon a large stone marker. He grew more and more still until he resembled nothing more than a granite statue, a great beast carved for a lord's grand headstone.

"Let me send ahead then, if you are determined to meet the captain. I should warn the other guards we are coming."

Kelso spoke quietly to two of his men as David and Camryn stepped over the cemetery wall and back onto the palace grounds. They could see the Hill of Credulity rising a short ways in the distance. A small chapel topped the small mound, steep roofed with four small turrets.

"I sent word, they will know we are coming in," Kelso reported.

The guards, in their black uniforms, loosely surrounded David and Camryn and walked across the lawn toward the chapel. As they passed the first line of trees, another group of guards stepped forward. David hesitated, but Kelso motioned to him to keep going. Boot Hill only climbed a few feet and when they were at the top Kelso's radio squelched.

"Yes?" he answered, and listened for a moment. A torrent of words poured from the radio.

"Was that the captain?" David asked.

"No, not yet. Some of the men are just hearing the story of a lion here in Perth."

Soon more men in black emerged from the shadows and joined the vanguard. Finally, Kelso addressed the group.

"Mr. Lord would like to visit with the captain. Is he still alone in the chapel?" Kelso said.

One of the men spoke up: "Cooper is with him. Smyth is waiting in the car."

"Let's go then, you will be safe with us," Kelso said to David.

"I will go alone. I have something to say to the captain, and it would be best if I said it to him without an audience." And without allowing time for discussion he started across the grass to the little chapel.

David opened the door without a sound and slipped inside the chapel. The last few rays of the sun hovered above the horizon, lighting the entrance until the door swung shut and plunged the room back into darkness, no light except that of a few candles lighting the altar.

David found his adversary humbly kneeling at the altar, so deep in communication with God that he hadn't heard him enter.

He waited patiently, sitting quietly on a wooden bench and waiting for an audience with his hunter.

David opened his eyes at the sound of a bullet being pumped into its firing chamber. The captain had evidently risen from his prayers and found his quarry resting in the chapel.

"You are a fool!" the captain gloated, his eyes gleaming weirdly in the eerie candlelight. He held a gun in one hand, and his phone to his ear.

His eyes focused on David, he spoke into his phone: "Yes, it is done. He is standing here at Scone and we are alone." Listening intently, the gun never wavered as he concentrated on absorbing whatever instructions were given. "I will finish this then and meet you in London." The phone was placed in his shirt pocket and the gun was steadied, aimed at David's heart.

The captain sagged somewhat when David stood, his height exaggerated by the shadows thrown by the flickering candles. Clad in the kilt and jacket he looked the part of a fierce lord. But the captain took courage from the cold steel in his hands and pressed on.

"I have pledged my honor on your capture."

"Captain, you murdered my friend in cold blood and have hunted me down for the deed! You can lie to the rest of the world, but you cannot lie to me!"

"Roger Brough wouldn't leave well enough alone! Our job is to protect and serve the royal house, not bring them into public scorn!"

"You and I know Roger was acting on George's orders!" David exclaimed.

"And I act on orders from a higher source than Prince George!" the captain replied.

The captain raised his gun to his shoulder and looking down the barrel sighted David Lord.

"Sometimes the people we are committed to serve can't see clearly. We are left to act in their best interest regardless of what they might think is right," he said. His finger tightened on the trigger.

"You admit to killing my friend?" David asked, his voice stony, clipping every word. "On whose authority did you murder my friend?"

"Roger Brough couldn't be allowed to continue. He was delving into things that needed to be left alone. It is the same, Mr. Lord, with you."

The captain had tensed, his countenance contorted in rising hysteria. Sensing movement at the side of the chapel he turned slightly and then pivoted immediately back to David, who was walking calmly toward him.

"We are going to end this right now, Captain."

The captain took aim once more and pulled the trigger. They heard a loud snap, but no shot was fired. Panicked, the captain shook the gun and took aim. David approached from the front, Cooper appeared at the captain's side, both reached for the gun and quite gently pulled it from his clenched fists. A terrible weariness welled up in the captain's eyes and his carefully maintained façade started to crumble. Cooper turned away to spare the captain his precious dignity, but David watched the painful process unfold.

A pitiful moan escaped from deep in his soul and with a twist of his wrist the captain grabbed for Cooper's holstered pistol. Backing away from his accusers he pointed at one and then the other, once again the carefully maintained veneer began to disintegrate and he was left exposed and vulnerable.

"Who has been calling the shots, Captain?" David asked. "Who has been feeding you information? You don't have to face this alone, if you name your conspirators."

"It's going to be all right, Captain," Cooper soothed.

A look of horror came over the captain. "I am my own man!" he shouted. They watched as the captain looked upon an unbearable future of pity and mortification and a spark of his own brand of sanity returned. Before either witness could react he brought the gun to his head and it went off, echoing loudly in the closed chamber, and he dropped heavily to the floor and after one labored breath lay stilled and inert on the chapel floor.

CHAPTER 41

Elizabeth O'Brien Lord's arrival at the hotel in London had been expected. She was shown to her room immediately to refresh from her travels. Without stopping to consider exactly what she should do, Elizabeth made a call to the offices of His Royal Highness, Prince George. She was shuttled from one operator to another, up the chain of command, until she was told in no uncertain terms that the Prince did not take phone calls but that he would be sure to receive any message she might care to leave.

"Please tell him that Elizabeth O'Brien Lord has arrived in London. I'm sure he will want to schedule something. I can be reached at Claridge's. Thank you very much." She hung up the phone and heard a knock at the door.

"How may I help you, ma'am?" The butler assigned to her suite had been carefully instructed to handle any requests made by Mrs. Lord with the greatest attention.

"I am afraid I am feeling some jet lag, but I am expecting a phone call from my son, so I don't want to lie down until I talk to him," Elizabeth said.

"I can listen for the phone while you sleep," the butler said.

"I am sure you have more important things to do!"

"Let me close these blinds, Mrs. Lord. What time would you like to wake up?"

She finally consented to hand over Enrique's cell phone, with instructions to wake her if anyone called. She slept almost immediately, clutching her purse, which contained a few documents too precious to entrust to the hotel safe.

David woke gradually, slowly recalling the helicopter ride that delivered them to the Brough's back door late last night. Captain Pilliard's pursuit was officially called off, the depth and breadth and height of all involved might never be known. It was hoped that the shooting and chasing and ambushes might be over, but no one could be certain until the investigation was concluded. The perpetrators might never be found, but the SO14 had pulled in all their agents for questioning.

It was only five here, so it was midnight in New York. He'd have to wait until at least six or seven to call Enrique, but he could check their shared email now. He wanted to see the Coronation Chair in Westminster Abbey sometime today. And, most important, he would need some time to think.

He heard a whine at his door and opening it found the dogs, again standing at attention and knowing too much.

"Come on, boys," he said. They followed him to the kitchen, where Lady Brough had a computer set up at a small workstation. While the computer woke up he studied the family pictures arranged on shelves above the desk. There was one of the family when Roger and Camryn were young, a vigorous Mr. Brough and a beautiful Mrs. Brough completed the happy family. A few school pictures, Roger with his front teeth missing, Camryn with pigtails and ribbons. Two sets of grandparents, and a wedding picture: Camryn in an elegant white dress, her husband in a military uniform posed outside in a garden. He reached for the picture and studied Lucas Lavender and then deliberately arranged the frame back in its place on the shelf.

Pulling up the email account, he found a new message dated yesterday. It was a simple mouse click that opened the message; no premonitions gave him pause. The message simply read: Call me, day or night, we must talk now. I found her. A phone number followed the message.

David hesitated a moment at making an overseas call from the Broughs' phone before picking up the house phone and dialing, the urgency of the message causing him to forego the polite formalities. It rang twice before Enrique picked up.

"David?" Enrique answered, still asleep by the sound of it.

"Enrique, I am back in London. You found her?"

"Yes, and she is in London now. I don't know how to tell you this." Enrique paused. "Mr. Lord, it is your mother. Elizabeth O'Brien." The phone lines fell silent.

"But she wasn't on the list!"

"Remember Maeve? She was the last woman we located, and when we talked to her she told us that she and Elizabeth were traveling together that summer. She said that Elizabeth took a side trip to Wales alone. She told us that her flight left a few weeks earlier than your mother's but that Elizabeth got word that her grandfather was failing quickly and so they traded tickets and passports. Maeve was perfectly happy to have an excuse to stay on and didn't travel back to the States until early 1982."

David sat. "It can't be!" he murmured to himself.

"When were you born?" After a long pause Enrique continued, "I talked to her yesterday and put her on a flight to London. She is staying at Claridge's and should be there already. Are you okay? Are we done here? Is there anything else you would like me to do?"

"I can't think of anything; you should probably keep the other women on that list in protective custody for a few more days while they account for all their officers. The person hunting them is dead and the official search has been called off, but we have been told that there are some who might not stand down. I will talk to Mrs. McCombs so you and she can settle up right away." David spoke in a normal tone while reeling from the impact of what he had heard.

"Thank you, Mr. Lord, for letting me work on this. I feel like it has purged my soul somehow. I will bring my family to the city soon and we'll stop by your office and visit. You should see my girls, they are growing so fast." Enrique paused. "Are you still there?"

"What? Oh, I'll be in touch, Enrique." He hung up the phone and sat with his thoughts racing.

My mother, married to Prince George? he thought, his thoughts disjointed and without anchor, cast adrift on an ocean of uncertainty and confusion. *Who is my father?*

The Claridges' butler knocked firmly at Elizabeth's suite.

"Mrs. Lord, it is noon. Did you still want to get up about now?"

Elizabeth answered the door.

"No one has rung up but I think the phone needs to be put on a charger. Is there anything else I can do for you?"

"Thank you for keeping watch for calls. I don't think I would have slept well listening for it to ring," Elizabeth said. The butler bowed slightly as she closed the door.

Davy! Where are you? she worried. David deserved to hear this story directly from his mother and not from any other source.

It felt good to be back in London and as she dressed for lunch she opened the patio doors and let the city sounds flow through her suite. Her thoughts naturally circled back to remember her summer tour.

Was there ever such an innocent caught in such an impossible web!

She had gone to Wales, alone. Maeve elected to stay in London hoping to catch the eye of a certain young man, and Elizabeth was to meet her Irish cousins and attempt a bicycle tour of Snowdon. A trail of bed and breakfast establishments had been arranged to break up the journey. And so, Elizabeth got on the train in London, waved goodbye out the window to Maeve and started on the greatest adventure of her short life.

The train followed the coast and stopped in every small village and harbor, a meandering scenic trek that ended, for Elizabeth, at the foot of Mount Snowdon at Penrhyndeudraeth. The town was built of dark gray stone, simple, earthy, and orderly in stark contrast to a more sophisticated London.

It was short walk from the train station into town for lunch at the pub. Her cousins had sent her a key to an apartment to let, and they were to meet up day after tomorrow to begin their bike tour. She remembered feeling so free, carrying her suitcase down the short flight of stairs and unpacking in the little apartment and then opening every window and flopping on the bed. She was beholden to no one for a whole day!

A sudden groan of truck brakes reverberated through the open patio doors and brought Elizabeth out of her brief reverie and back to her present predicament and London.

Memories that had been nudging her these past few months were now impossible to ignore. The need to find David was pressing on her continuously, but mentally shrugging she tried to put it out of her mind.

She finished dressing and rechecked her purse once again, everything still in place.

Lunch in the foyer tearoom and then I will call Ellen and see if Davy has phoned home.

The stairs to the lobby curved gracefully and landed her right at the entrance to the tearoom. She gave her name to the hostess and sat in a small enclave to wait for a table. Her thoughts flew instantly back again to the memory of that summer, remembering the urgent phone call from her cousin's father, Uncle Wally, that came late in the evening. He called up the landlady and waited on hold while she woke Elizabeth and brought her to the extension.

"There's been an awful car accident, happened on the way to catch the ferry to Wales," he said.

Neither of her cousins would be able to make the trip and he wouldn't hear of her cutting short her adventure.

"They will be in the hospital and convalescing for several weeks; you should stay and use the apartment and then come to stay with us when your week is up. You are traveling with a girlfriend, right?"

He made arrangements to meet the ferry in Dublin in a week. Elizabeth didn't tell him that Maeve was still in London. He didn't need to worry about her right now and she would be fine on her own until Maeve got here. In fact, there was a small part of her that relished the freedom to do as she pleased.

"Elizabeth?" It wasn't her Uncle Wally speaking to her. She shifted focus and found herself looking up at a familiar face, a former business associate of her husband's. "This is an unexpected pleasure and so nice to see you again," he said.

He took her hand and she stood.

"It has been quite a while," Elizabeth said.

"I'd like you to meet my wife, Helen, and my daughters, Slaney and Ryan. We are in town for just the day and the girls decided we had to come for tea at Claridge's!"

Helen was obviously ready to move on but waited patiently through the polite talk. The girls, in their early twenties, looked at their nails, rummaged through their Prada bags, and mentally rolled their eyes, impatient at being kept waiting by this totally uninteresting person.

A stir in the lobby reached their corner and caught the girls' attention.

"I wonder who it is? I heard that Bon Jovi was in town!" They craned to see who was causing the subtle commotion but couldn't see anyone notable enough to send flutters of excitement through the crowded lobby. All they could see was an elderly gentleman dressed in a black wool suit deep in conversation with a younger colleague. They walked through the foyer and the crowd whispered and twittered on either side.

"Who is that?" Slaney asked her sister.

"No one I know," Ryan said, dismissing them.

Elizabeth seemed to realize that something was happening and looking over the crowd brightened instantly.

"David!" she called, moving toward him.

David looked up and saw his mother; a hard look veiled his features for just a moment and then softened somewhat, and he walked toward her.

"How was your trip?" he asked her, with a cool kiss on the cheek.

"You already know?" she asked him, her eyes flooded with sudden tears.

The man in the black wool suit interceded. "Mrs. Lord, I presume? I am Evans Black, and I have come to help if I can."

Conscious of her husband's friends watching the reunion, Elizabeth turned to include them.

"This is my son, David," she said. "David, Mr. O'Connor worked with your father. This is his wife, Helen, and his daughters, Slaney and Ryan."

"We know you," Slaney said, and sparkled at him with all the intensity of a twenty-something beauty. He had seen that look in so many pretty faces, and a great, dark weariness settled on him. It only made matters worse that the girl he could love was taken.

"Here comes Camryn. Have you had lunch yet, Mother?" David asked.

"I just want to talk to you, son," Elizabeth said.

"Is it true?" David asked.

Mr. Black took her arm then and led them to a more secluded sitting area.

"I know this must be painful, Mrs. Lord, but it is best that we know the truth. Your son has hired me to represent you both, I am your solicitor, and I am quite sure that you are going to need one. If you would like to tell your son the details alone I will leave you, but I will need to know it all eventually."

"I would rather just tell it once and have it done." Elizabeth sighed.

They settled in and waited for Elizabeth to begin the story. Finally, she took a deep breath and, looking only at David, began.

"You know my parents immigrated to the US when I was small. The summer after my freshman year at college I decided to visit Ireland. I had a friend that I traveled with, Maeve Larsen. Between us we had places to stay all over the UK. We were supposed to spend a week biking in Wales together, but Maeve wanted to stay in London a bit longer, and my cousins were injured in an accident and they couldn't meet me. I had the apartment to myself. I rented a bike and tackled Mount Snowdon on my own. I was an hour into my ride when the chain came off, and not knowing the much about bikes, I was wondering what to do." Elizabeth was lost in the story: the years seemed to fall away, and it was easy to see her as a young girl.

"I hadn't seen a single car along the road that whole morning, but as I tried to put the chain back where it belonged I heard a car, shifting gears and making the climb. I remember wondering if they would stop to help. It was a little two-seater sports car with the top down, a second car following right behind. A dashing man, much older than I, pulled to the side of the road and got out to help. The other car also stopped but the driver did not get out. It made me feel safe, having them both stop, and when the gentleman offered to take me and the bike to the next village I eagerly accepted. I didn't know at all who my rescuer was; looking back it is easy for me to plead innocence!"

"Mom, I could understand a flirtation, even an affair, but marriage? How did it get to that?"

"It was magic, I was so young and so unsophisticated, and I think the prince fell for me because I had no idea who he was! No idea at all. Pretty soon we were laughing and talking, my hair was blowing and he put up the top. He must have signaled to his guards because the second car passed us after that and we were alone on Mt. Snowdon. Can you imagine how it must have felt for him to be liked for himself by a young girl that had no idea he was a prince?"

She stopped at that thought and was quiet for a moment.

"But marriage, Mom? How in the world did that happen?"

"George drove to the next town and made arrangements for the bike to be fixed while we bought a picnic lunch. I was so flattered by this man who obviously admired me, and several times during our picnic he asked me to marry him. I laughed and flirted outrageously with him, but he persisted and I began to believe he was well and truly smitten. Every girl dreams of such a man falling for her and I was lost and intoxicated by his flattering attention. My bike was fixed but George didn't want the day to end so he rented one as well. I know now that the shop owners and the clerk at the grocery store knew who he was, but this was Wales, and they didn't treat him like a celebrity—only in hindsight of their extreme courtesy can I see that they knew."

"We pedaled the little roads for hours, stopping at scenic lookouts and fabulous fields of flowers. George picked a little yellow flower for my hair and held my hand while we rode. We talked and talked, about what I don't remember, but it was a day I will never forget.

"It was dusk by the time we rode back to his car. We returned the bikes and he drove me home. I let him kiss me goodnight and when he did I swear I saw stars. He asked me if he could see me the next day and, still in a daze, I agreed. He was knocking at my door at 7 the next morning and we spent the day together again. I had begun to think I was truly in love, and he asked me to marry him again and again. It was late afternoon when we came upon a lonely little church. It had a gate with a climbing rose–covered trellis. We walked around the cemetery holding hands, talking. I was wearing a pale yellow dress with a yellow ribbon tying my hair back. We walked to the church and the doors stood open; an organ was playing clearly, a wedding march. Solemnly, George pulled me to him.

"'Don't leave me,' he pleaded. Tenderly, for that is how I felt, I told him that I would stay with him. A wrinkled old priest came to the doors and invited us in. To this day I can see the flowers at the altar, ribbons festooning the pews. The organ continued to play and the priest said, 'Aren't we a bit early? I guess we can get the paperwork out of the way now.'

"'Paperwork?' George had asked.

"He had beautiful manners," Elizabeth said, remembering.

"'Come with me, my young friends.' We followed the priest and didn't realize until he handed us a sheaf of papers that he was functionally blind.

"George looked at me, I am sure I was beaming, and we filled out the marriage certificate together. The priest could hear the scratching of the pen and asked me to show him where to sign. I guided his hand and he signed a shaky signature. His wife, the organist, was the second witness."

"You actually married Prince George?" David asked again.

Elizabeth opened her purse and pulled out an old marriage certificate, filled out by hand. Elizabeth Renee O'Brien and Prince George Mountbatten-Windsor had both signed.

"You can see the hyphenated last name runs into the wording of the document, I thought his name was George Prince."

The certificate lay on Elizabeth's knees until Mr. Black reached out and gently laid it out on the coffee table and studied it. David studied his mother. Camryn studied David.

"And then you had to cut your visit short to attend your grandfather's funeral so you sent your husband a note on pale yellow note paper and left on Maeve's passport for home. The note was mislaid until it was finally delivered to Prince George and I was called in to help untangle the mystery!"

Elizabeth sent her son a searching look; his eyes were hard. "Yes, that is right," she answered.

"And who, might I ask, is my father?" David spoke deliberately. Elizabeth flinched and grew pale.

She pulled out another official document and laid it next to the marriage certificate. It was David's dual-citizenship birth certificate. The father was listed as George Mountbatten-Windsor.

"George is your father." They could barely hear her.

The look on David's face sent a chill through her heart. But she mentally squared her shoulders and pressed on with the story.

"I traveled home from England and slipped into the life of a young girl again. I waited for a response from George, but he didn't call or write. Not long and Phillip Lord came calling; we had known each other for years and I think he sensed a new maturity in me. When he proposed I put him off until I realized that I was expecting. Phillip knew the whole story, and when I realized just who my baby's father was we decided to never tell a soul. That decision has been weighing on me heavily these past few months."

Elizabeth had finished and quiet settled over them.

"Does Prince George know I exist?" David asked.

"No, but in his defense, my disappearance put George in a spot. How could he search for me without raising an uproar? He was trapped by his life as much or more than I was trapped by mine."

Mr. Black was somber as he leaned forward. "I have never heard such a story, Mrs. Lord. Legally there are many options and we will need to talk them all through carefully before you decide what you want to do."

He stood and offered Elizabeth his arm.

"You were waiting for a table when we arrived, we should get you something to eat," he said. "David?"

"Mother," David said, with hesitant tenderness. She looked at him and pulled him into her arms. "I want to belong to Phillip Lord," he said quietly to her.

"You were Phillip's son in every way. He loved you because you were mine, and then of course he loved you because of you."

David drew back and really looked at his mother, measuring her words without speaking for a long moment. Shaking off the thought of his father, he turned slightly to include Camryn and said, "Have I introduced you to Camryn yet? This is Roger's little sister. Camryn, my mother, Elizabeth Lord."

"I am so sorry about your brother, my dear." Elizabeth took hold of Camryn's hand and they walked across the black and white marble lobby floor to the tearoom. David and Mr. Black followed, there would be many lengthy discussions in the weeks to come, but for now they were content to let thoughts and emotions ripen in the privacy of their own hearts and minds.

Mr. Black carried the conversation in the tearoom, ordered a few plates of sandwiches, and had to prompt his companions to eat. When all that was left were crumbs, David put his napkin on the table and stood.

"I have one last place to visit and my search for the Stone of Destiny will be finished, and then I can go home. Camryn, do you want to come?"

"I will have them leave you a key to my room at the front desk," Mrs. Lord said.

CHAPTER 42

There was a taxi at the front door that took them to the abbey. David was quiet during the ride and stood looking at the building for a long moment.

It is time to finish this, he said to himself before they walked across the plaza and in the front doors. Inside, a docent directed them to Edward's Chair, known as the Coronation Throne, and they navigated the course without a guide.

The chair sat on a raised platform in a beautiful ambulatory that filled the enclave with light. Pillars and stone arches created a fitting background for the throne. It was over large and made of old wood with traces of gilding with four carved gold lions, one on each corner, which served as legs. Edward had commissioned the throne to be built to hold the Coronation Stone, as he supposed, a platform was built to house the stone under the seat of the chair.

A tour guide brought a small group to stand near the throne.

"This is the Coronation Throne, built to hold the Stone of Destiny during the coronation of the kings and queens of England. The stone is said to come from Israel and signifies the continuance of the Throne of David, here in England. During WWII when the Germans were bombing London, the Coronation Stone was moved to Gloucester Abbey for safekeeping. The crown jewels were left in place but the stone was moved. You can see the stone in Edinburgh Castle now, but it will be brought back for the next coronation and will sit under this throne as the king is crowned. Behind the throne we can see the tomb of King Henry V."

The tour group moved on, their footsteps echoing and then receding over the stone floors and the enclave grew quiet once more.

A choir began singing. David paced in the ambulatory, his footsteps muted and his thoughts deep. As he passed the throne he stopped and listened.

"What is this song?" he asked Camryn.

"It is called 'Jerusalem'; it is near to being the English national anthem."

255

And did those feet in ancient time
Walk upon England's mountains green:
And was the holy Lamb of God,
On England's pleasant pastures seen!
And did the Countenance Divine,
Shine forth upon our clouded hills?
And was Jerusalem builded here,
Among these dark Satanic Mills?
Bring me my Bow of burning gold;
Bring me my Arrows of desire:
Bring me my Spear: O clouds unfold!
Bring me my Chariot of fire!
I will not cease from Mental Fight,
Nor shall my Sword sleep in my hand:
Till we have built Jerusalem,
In England's green and pleasant Land.

"You are kidding me!" David exclaimed. "Jesus lived in England?"

"I have always been taught that He lived here from about twelve years of age until just before the beginning of His ministry in Israel," Camryn said. "There is also told a story that Mary and one of the disciples were driven into a ship after the death of Christ. They were cast adrift to die in the sea, but the winds carried them to England and she lived out her life here."

"I never knew any of this!" David continued pacing. Camryn sat on a chilled stone bench and waited patiently for him to walk things out.

At length, he lifted his eyes from the floor and found her on the bench.

"What am I to do? I don't belong here, this has nothing to do with me!" he said. "I can give them their stone, but that is all I can give them, and then I will go home!"

"David, you have to wonder why you were drawn into this! You should consider that before you just walk away."

She continued, "I wonder if Roger realized that the two searches were related to each other?"

"No," David said, "it is too farfetched! That the Throne of David was symbolized by possession of the Coronation Stone was one step further than he had taken. I don't believe he had come to the conclusion that the stone was anything more than a possession of the royal family of Britain. That it came from an Old Testament king is just too fantastic. That the lineage of the king of England is traced back to Abraham through King David.... How could Roger have supposed that on his own?"

David sat in silence, Camryn stood, and he was heartbroken as he looked at her beautiful gray eyes. The sun streaming in the windows turned her hair into pure gold and David turned away from her then.

"I know you don't want to be the son of a prince, who in their right mind would? But maybe you have something to offer these people. Maybe you were raised up for this day," Camryn said. "I know you have an important life to go back to, but I think England needs you! Go home, get your fiancée, and then come back and figure out what you have to offer us."

She looked at David leaning over his knees. She reached out a hand for him but then withdrew it before touching him.

"Goodbye," she whispered. He did not move and she turned and walked away. To the soaring walls of the abbey and out the west doors, she hailed a taxi and, leaning against the cool glass of its window, asked him to take her to Victoria train station.

Camryn's words rattled around in his brain—*maybe you were raised up for this day.* What if it were true? He didn't hear the rest of what she said, but visions of this week and everything they had learned tumbled through his mind.

A cloud passed over the abbey and dimmed the light that pooled around him. He looked up and a small door opened at the back of the poet's corner, under the bust of Ben Johnson. Apart from the soaring beauty of the abbey, the shabby little door caught his imagination. David was drawn across the echoing stone floor, and ducking a little, David found himself looking up a narrow circular staircase, a sign read 'to the library roof.' Counting the stone stairs and fighting occasional gusts of wind, he climbed the seventy-six steps to the top. He found himself in a dusty, cluttered attic space. It had windows that looked outside over the square and a large opening looking inside over the nave. A single bar was the only barrier that kept visitors from falling into the chapel floor below.

David looked out over the cathedral to the high altar and found himself listening to a tour guide describe the coronation of a king. Looking over the chapel he could envision the vast throngs of ancient nobles as they sat in the abbey, there to celebrate the coronation of a king.

"The coronation throne is placed near the high altar of the abbey, the Coronation Stone placed beneath the seat. Pouring a small amount of oil on the head of the king, a priest then prayed over him using these words:

"Lord, who from everlasting governest the kingdom of all kings, bless thou this ruling prince. Amen. And glorify him with such blessing that he may hold the Sceptre of Salvation in the exaltation of David, and be found rich with the gifts of sanctifying mercy. Amen. Grant unto him by thine inspiration even to rule the people in meekness as thou didst cause Solomon to obtain a kingdom of peace. Amen.

"Almighty God give thee the dew of heaven and the fatness of the earth, and plenty of seed and wine. Let thy people serve thee and the nations bow down to thee; be thou lord over thy brethren and let thy mother's sons bow down to thee. God shall be thy helper, and the Almighty shall bless thee with all blessings from heaven above, on the mountains and on the hills, blessings of the deep that lieth beneath, blessings of all things that creepeth, and of milk and honey that flow from thy gift. May the blessings of our ancient fathers, Abraham, and Isaac, and Jacob, be confirmed upon thee. Amen.

"Bless, O Lord, the substance of our prince, and accept the work of his hands; and blessed of thee be work of his hand, for the precious things of heaven for the dew, and for the deep that coucheth beneath, and for the precious fruits brought forth by the sun and for the precious things put forth by the moon that rules over us, and for the chief things of the ancient mountains, and for the precious things of the lasting hills, and the fullness thereof; the blessing of Him that appeared in the bush come upon his head; and let the blessing of the Lord be full upon His children; and let him dip his feet in oil, let his horns be like the horns of unicorns, with them shall he push the people together to the end of the earth, for let Him who rideth upon the heaven be his guide and strength forever. Amen."

Feeling a presence behind him, David came to himself abruptly. Standing near the stone staircase, Prince George stood gazing at him with an inscrutable look on his face.

E nrique parked the truck in front of Mr. Lord's building.

"We can't park here," Dean said. "Pull down the street to the parking lot."

"It is time for you to go home, Junior. You have services to plan and a grandmother to look after," Enrique said. "It is time."

Dean paused and adjusted his thoughts and plans.

"If you need anything, any help at all, I want you to call me. I also expect you to let me know when the memorial service is scheduled and I will be there." Enrique leaned over and shook Dean's hand. "Promise?"

"I will. I still need to meet those two little girls sometime," Dean said.

Enrique pulled his backpack onto his shoulder and opened the door.

"I couldn't have done this without you. *Adiós*, Junior!"

Enrique closed the door, and with a final salute, Dean pulled into the New York City traffic toward home. Enrique watched him for a moment and then turned to find Mrs. McCombs holding the door to the building open for him.

D avid watched the prince as conflicting emotions waged for supremacy: curiosity, embarrassment, and yearning. He felt a gust of wind blow through the yawning opening at his back and David retreated until the safety bar pressed against his hips, allowing Prince George time to sort through the conflict.

Finally, the prince advanced, slowly, deliberately until he stood before David.

David could feel the bar at his back giving just a bit, and when George put out his hand, a small part of David wondered for what purpose it was given. He looked at his father's hand for the barest moment and then took it. George pulled David to him, away from the edge of the precipice, and clasped him in a tight grip.

"I hired an investigator to look for her, but they were unable to track her down since she was married by then. She had vanished into thin air and I didn't know how to find her! I thought she had run away from me," he said with a small catch of emotion. "I didn't know how to find her, and gradually, I came to think it was for the best. Life in the public eye, position and power in the royal courts can be a brutal way of life. For her sake, I wasn't sure what to do, who to involve. And so time passed and my chance for happiness was gone." The prince paused, as if considering his words. David watched him in silence. "Then, there are my siblings, who were glad to see me childless. You can't blame them for being ambitious for their own children." David had the feeling that much was being left unsaid. "But now that it has been brought out into the open, I am glad to know I have a son."

"I know there are matters of state to decide, but I will be glad to know you regardless of the outcome," David said.

The two men, similar in bearing and diffidence, moved away from the opening toward the great rose windows overlooking the palace. They talked of years and regrets and Elizabeth for several minutes, until two guards appeared at the top of the stone staircase.

"It is time for me to go," the prince said. "You are staying at Claridge's with your mother?" David nodded. "I would like to present you to your grandparents as soon as that can be arranged."

"You know, sir, I admire you for marrying my mother," David said.

"She wouldn't have had me any other way!" Prince George said.

Their handshake was just a little awkward, but much ground had been covered in the short visit. And David watched as Prince George disappeared down the steep stairway with the guards, leaving David alone in the dusty, cluttered room.

Mrs. McCombs was in no sense a gossip, but her mouth gaped open more than once as Enrique recounted the results of the search for the missing woman and child.

"Our Mr. Lord, the son of Prince George!" she exclaimed, again and again.

When she had finally wrung out the last crumb of every particular, they talked of remuneration for a job well and faithfully done. She accepted back the company credit card and waved off the extra cash still resting at the bottom of the camouflage backpack.

Writing him a check, she said, "You know, Mr. Lord can always use a good investigator. Before you commit to any other employer, please make sure you talk to him about opportunities here."

She waved the check as if drying the ink, and then, handing it to him, she drew him to the window overlooking the front of the building. He could hear the familiar sound of his car idling, the 30/30 roller cam purring with a sound he would recognize anywhere. He looked down on the street and found his car parked against the curb, Mr. Lord's driver leaning against the door.

"You left your keys on the dresser and Arnold was drooling over that car and looking for an opportunity to take it for a drive," she said.

He managed a "thank you," and with a quick embrace Enrique folded the check, shoved it into his back pocket, picked up the box holding two tired kittens, and walked out the office door, back to his family and the chance to build a brand-new life.

CHAPTER 43

While ministers and parliament debated and positioned themselves on the question of the marriage license and birth certificate, the people of the British Isles relished the drama and romance of the new prince, for whatever the politicians decided the people had embraced him as their own.

Stories of the lion appearing to guard him were told and retold, and wherever it was recounted, the Scot's were convinced he was a true Prince of Scotland.

Ireland fell into his camp as the whispered stories of his miraculous return to life from the bosom of the channel swirled through every home and pub and church. The whole of Ireland gave their collective heart to him, the ancient O'Brien family first of all, and the rest following fast on their heels.

Wales claimed his mother with her story of love and separation. The son was quickly taken and harbored in their communal bosom.

The outlying parts of England raised his banner and its citizens flocked to it in droves. No outsider could take the pulse of Cornwall, but the land of pixies and tin mines finally fell hard at the last for the new prince.

London wavered but fear of offending a true prince finally brought them firmly to his side.

The common people had decided this question and were united enough that their rulers thought twice about deciding against them. The parliament followed the will of the people in declaring the marriage valid and David a legitimate heir to the throne.

After the question had been soundly decided, members of the parliament, the royal family, and editors of every media outlet were deluged with letters from the United States. It seems that the story had struck American fancy as well, and letters backing his claim to the throne came in at the rate of 5 to 1.

The headlines of the *Morning Herald* read: *American takeover of British royal house!* and the *Globe* headlines shouted *Britain, the 51st state.* In the furor of the day it was all taken in good fun, by both sides of the Atlantic.

The three nobles, tied to each other by cords of conspiracy and treason against their future king, met once more to speak of what they would do now, if anything. The death of the captain effectively stopped the unraveling of their treachery, and they had not been discovered. Yet, they couldn't help but regret that they had been unsuccessful; George was completely unsuited to be king.

"My sons have been disinherited for a weakling!" the lone woman confederate muttered.

"You sound like an old hag," her brother complained. "You know that any support for our cause has evaporated now that George has got an heir." The two men, rather afraid of their woman counterpart, shifted, moving physically away from her and the venom that ran rich in her veins.

The third of their group reminded them, "We have nothing. And don't underestimate George, he will have us checked and checkmated if we continue to oppose his son. He must know who was behind the captain, even if he can't prove it. He might be weak but he was never stupid."

The woman clenched her fists. The men knew well her towering ambition for her sons and knew that the thwarting of it might easily cause her descent into madness. They looked at each other, understanding that she was now the weak link in their treachery. She could easily be the undoing of them all.

During the days of decision, David stayed cooped up in the hotel suite, not sure at all if he wanted the role that was thrust on him. At times he wanted to lash out at his mother, angry to be so ill used. He had not asked for his parentage and he had many moments he missed New York and passed time by talking on the phone with Mrs. McCombs. It might not have helped that things were running so smoothly without him.

It also didn't help that Camryn had left; although it was certainly for the best, he was at his most sullen when he thought about what she might be doing. His mother seemed to know when he was thinking about her.

"Why don't you call her and have her come to lunch, I'm sure she is wondering how we are doing," Elizabeth would ask.

"She ran out on me and I can't see begging her to come and visit me!" David said, petulance and sadness vying for supremacy in his heart. "She is married, you know, so you can quit getting your hopes up!"

His mother looked at him then with empathy and stopped mentioning her name at all.

At last, when it was all decided, there was a ceremonial visit to the palace and the House of Lords, and so began the parade of the new prince to meet the people who loved him deeply already. He christened ships and spoke at events, and generally felt like he had traded a full and useful life for some sort of glittering consolation prize. Much like a racehorse would feel to be let out for pony rides at the fair.

Among the hundreds of invitations that poured in daily was an elegantly embossed reminder of a previously scheduled dinner in Edinburgh with Mr. Black and his daughter. An invitation to dine at The Witchery a week hence at 7 p.m. Included with the invitation was a note and a newspaper clipping. The note invited him to bring his fiancée with him to dinner if she was available. Puzzled he unfolded the clipping and read all about his supposed engagement to Mimi.

That little social climber! he thought, *taking advantage of my supposed death to get a bit of the spotlight. I am sure she is mortified by my reappearance.*

Putting the clipping aside, he had his secretary send his acceptance to Mr. Black. The reminder the invitation brought of his days of adventure and freedom and danger introduced him to new depths of discouragement and something that approached despair.

In a futile bid for freedom David insisted that he be allowed to take the train to Edinburgh but only ended up being compelled to take a royal rail car for safety.

"It is too hard to ensure your protection on any public transport!" his guards insisted.

The miles flew by the bulletproof glass of the high-speed train and David watched the towns and fields appear and then disappear behind him. People waved at the train as it whistled at railroad crossings and then went about their business with hardly a thought as to who might be trapped inside. At last they pulled into the Edinburgh station; a police escort met the train, and they bundled him quickly into a limousine and sped through the darkening city streets.

"We are close." David leaned and looked out the window of the limo. "I am going to walk the rest of the way." And he opened his door at the light and shut the door on the vigorous objections of his minders. Two guards piled out of the car behind him, following his path through the narrow streets, but they kept a decent distance, which he didn't protest.

The Witchery was on the corner, with the castle as a backdrop in the deepening evening sky. He opened the door and was greeted by a hostess.

"Table for one, sir?" she asked. "Do you have a reservation?"

"I am meeting Evans Black, is he here yet?" David said.

"Your name, sir." A flutter of excitement surged through him; she didn't recognize him!

"That's all right, Susie, he is with me." Mr. Black had just come through the front doors. He swept David into the opulent dining room and they were seated in a private corner where they were swathed in shadows. Rich paneling and silk drapery that pooled on an exquisite oriental carpet muffled any sounds of commerce.

"I could easily be convinced that we had been transported to another century!" David said.

A dignified waiter came to their table and presented a wine list and menu to them and then retreated without a word. Mr. Black obviously reveled in the discrete treatment.

"I am afraid my tastes run to the gracious past," he said.

"Is your daughter joining us?" David asked.

"I couldn't bring myself to inflict a perfect stranger on you tonight. She is more than content to stay home instead of keeping her old father company once in a while," Mr. Black said. "No, I have something I want to discuss with you in private tonight."

"Can't we just sit here and enjoy being two private citizens eating a meal?" David asked.

"That is what I want to talk to you about!" Mr. Black said. "What are you doing, allowing yourself to be paraded all over the country like some prize conjured up out of thin air? Where is the David Lord that took the bit in his mouth and ran his own race?"

"Isn't this what the royals do?" David asked.

"You mean, waste their days on drivel and pomp?" Mr. Black asked.

"I expected more from you, David. A prince of England is not to be showed off like some pretty face but should rather lead the way toward something noble, expecting that the rest of us will follow."

David sat and absorbed the advice.

"How do I shake loose of hundreds of years of tradition, then?" he asked.

"Well, that I will leave up to you. You're an American, sir! I expect great things from you. I don't want to see you at one more tea unless I see that you are out to sway the females of England to some cause!" Mr. Black said. "Now, have you reconsidered eating dinner with me?"

"No, I needed to hear it."

"Good, good. I have something for you then." And he pulled out a note from his black wool suit pocket and, excusing himself, he walked away.

The note was written on the palest yellow paper and scented with the barest essence of lilacs. On the front was handwritten *Hon. David Prince*, and when he turned it over to open the envelope he could make out the faint mark of a kiss sealing the back fold.

His heart leaped with a faint stirring of hope and he carefully opened the note.

My Dearest David: I meant to tell you everything, before doubt crowded out hope. You deserve to know the truth. Lucas has been declared officially 'missing in action' and presumed dead. I nurtured hope that he was only missing but have learned that he has died and am resigned to it.

You truly looked at me from the very first moment the way every woman wants to be looked at by a man. My heart knew what my head tried to deny. Camryn

Alone in his private corner, David closed his eyes against the onslaught of hope that trampled over the past weeks of regret. And when he finally opened his eyes, Camryn was there, watching him. Without hesitation he pulled her close and shared with her a kiss that tasted of eternity. He pulled her on his lap and they talked of hope and regret and misunderstanding, free at last to love and be loved. Their waiter, bless him, did not intrude to offer food or drink.

Enrique pulled into the parking lot of the rundown motel, turned off the purring motor, and climbed out of the car. He spotted Alena and the girls and watched as they realized it was him. Running full out,

Alena reached him first and held on tight. Sophia and Suri hugged his legs and danced around him in a happy jig.

"You are squishing my surprises!" he said, and, disentangling, he solemnly emptied his pockets. Out of one coat pocket, he pulled a bedraggled little black kitten. Sophia didn't utter a word as she lunged for the little thing. From the other pocket he pulled a slightly more plump kitten, as black as night, and handed it to Suri.

"Well," he asked, solemnly, "can I come home now?"

The girls just nodded rapidly, too happy to speak.

"Hey, Rique!" Sam called. "Rique!"

Enrique looked up and, noticing his brother-in-law, started to walk over to meet him.

"We'll talk later!" Sam said, he tossed him a set of car keys to Alena's SUV. "Let me know where you land, and take care of my sister!"

He climbed in his car and shut the door, leaving the little family in their bubble of happiness.

D avid finally noticed the two guards sitting on a red velvet settee in the anteroom, and he called the waiter over.

"Did you drive, Camryn?" She nodded. "Where is your car parked?"

"Right out front," Camryn said.

"Is there a back way out of here?" David asked the waiter.

"Oh, yes, sir! There is an alley for deliveries and discreet getaways."

"Can you take care of these two guards for me then and bill it to this card?" David asked.

The waiter took the card and ran it while David invited the guards to their table.

"Okay guys, have you had dinner?" David asked them. "I don't want you hungry on my account. I also don't want any trouble when I slip out the back, deal?"

"We'll nae stop you," the guard said.

"We are going to Scone, you can meet us there when you are finished eating, and you should probably bring a truck."

Camryn walked out of the front door, found her car and drove around the block to the narrow alley. She barely had time to reach over the seat and unlock the passenger's door before David was opening it and climbing in.

"Go!" he said. She followed the alley until it came out onto the

267

roundabout that led to Lawnmarket. They turned at Ramsey and settled in on the road to Scone.

"What are we doing? Can I ask?" Camryn asked.

"I think I am breaking the traces," said David.

Scone Palace was closed for the night when they arrived, but David didn't hesitate to pound at the front door of the fortress.

"May I help you, sir?" a woman asked him.

"We need to dig in your graveyard. I was wondering if your gardener would have some lights and shovels," David asked, all politeness.

"Are you by any chance . . ." she trailed off as she recognized the new prince. "Let me wake my husband; won't you please come in?"

"We'll just meet you there. We are in no hurry," David said.

As they walked across the velvet grass toward the wall that surrounded the graveyard, Camryn asked, "Do you really think it is here?"

"I know it is!" David answered. "Think about what we know about this stone, the monks only buried it the night before Longshanks came to steal it from them so it couldn't have been far from the abbey. It had to be somewhere perfectly secure, no chance of accidental discovery. And remember one of its miraculous properties?"

"Well, it roars when the rightful king is on it," Camryn said.

"Yes, farther back than that though," David said. They were at the nearest wall and sinking slightly in the mud. David took her arm and they walked around to the entrance of the cemetery.

"Remember, when Israel was camped in Sinai and demanding that Moses supply them with water?" David asked.

"God had Moses strike a rock and it flowed with water! Was it this stone?" Camryn said. "Is it leaking water now, do you think?"

"That is what I want to find out!" David said. A commotion began at the front door of the castle and a gentleman, hastily dressed, appeared to join them. The gardener was not far behind, riding on a small electric cart. His two sons accompanied him to serve as manpower and they jumped from the still moving cart, eager to dig.

Conferring with the gardener and the gentleman who owned the property they decided on the most likely place to dig. David looked down on his evening clothes and dress shoes.

"Would either of you have some work clothes I could borrow?" David asked the men.

The boys began digging while David was fitted with boots and jeans and when he returned the men took turns digging in the swampy ground. Two feet, four feet, still no sign of the stone.

"Do we keep on going or move to a new spot?" the gardener asked.

Camryn decided, "I'd say keep going for a while more."

Five feet and they had to stop and shore up the dirt walls as they were beginning to buckle. As they stopped to take stock again, a gurgle of mud broke through the floor of the hole and began bubbling and belching air, mud, and water into an unholy mess.

"We've found it!" David said.

The gardener called a halt while he and the boys located a winch, and when they returned, David was the first to leap into the hole. They lowered a strap to him, and feeling through the gurgling mud he found a solid mass of rock just a few inches below the floor of the hole.

David called to the boys, "What is your clan?"

"Clan MacDougall, sir!" the older boy answered.

"Then you should do the honors!" They helped David climb out and the boys both eagerly jumped in. Lowering the nylon strap again, they looped it around the top of the stone and tightened it. The bottom of the hole was filling with thick mud now, and it was slick, but the boys easily scrambled out.

"I think we should set a frame over the hole for the winch," the gardener said. "A pair of sawhorses and a plank should do."

"I am not as muddy as the rest of you, I'll go and get it all," the gentleman said, and he drove off in the cart, feeling the hurry that was pushing them all.

He was back in minutes; the hole had continued to fill with bubbling mud, so they hastily set up the makeshift scaffold and set the winch on the top. The men now took turns cranking the winch. It tightened, then strained and sucked at the mud. Something moved to the surface of the hole.

"Whatever we have caught is heavy!" the gardener said.

The strap groaned and creaked, the scaffold creaked and complained, but it held, until with a surge the stone came free and dangled in the air at the bottom of the hole. The men strained along with the winch; the gardener angled the lights to see what had come free. They had found the stone. They couldn't yet see carvings or writings but water bubbled quietly from the stone, washing the mud slowly back into the hole. They had done it.

CHAPTER 44

The guards arrived in a truck soon after the stone was lifted out of the mud and after considerable discussion it was decided that it should be retained for display on Boot Hill for a time.

They raised the winch and tried to back the truck up to the cemetery, but the grounds were still a swampy mess. In the end they rigged up a platform on two rods and carried it on the shoulders of eight men to the top of Boot Hill. Placed on the replica of the false stone, it continued to leak water until a puddle formed beneath its resting place, and it wasn't long before the puddle overran its new quarters and found a meandering path through the grass and down the hill.

A trickle of visitors began at dawn, word spread like wildfire, and cars soon clogged the country roads as people came to see the relic for themselves. The gardener rigged a basin to hold the water; it filled the makeshift cistern and it wasn't long before the throngs of visitors arrived carrying cups.

The water gurgled from the side through a carving of the tree of life. Pure and cold, the heavenly manifestation dispensed so much more than pure water.

Over time proposals were made in an effort to bottle the water and sell it to fill the public coffers, but David resisted the notion and it continued to give itself freely to all who came to drink. The story of the Stone of Destiny was told and retold, and if a true record had been kept of the effect it had on the people of Britain it would have filled the immensity of the grandest library.

Human nature being what it is, once David committed himself by leaving out the back door of The Witchery, rumors and speculation fomented and began circulating immediately. At first it was limited to the people who had witnessed the tender reunion between their prince and Camryn Lavender, but over the next few weeks the wildfire of speculation was fueled by Camryn's near-constant presence in David's company.

Hysteria was raised to a fevered pitch by headlines brandished across the front page of the *London Evening Standard* on a rainy, dreary Sunday afternoon, PRINCE DAVID ENGAGED?

The story went on: We have received reports from several sources indicating that Camryn Brough Lavender, sometime companion to Prince David, is now wearing a large diamond ring! A black-and-white shot of the couple clearly showed a ring glittering on the correct finger of her left hand. Made from Welsh gold given them from the royal vaults, it was breathtakingly beautiful.

The new prince was engaged and the country rejoiced. But the gossip mills, news hounds, and marketing professionals barely had time to gather their wits about them. The wedding would be held six weeks hence.

It was a considerable feat, but the event of the century was held at Westminster Abbey; wrangling for a seat in the abbey became the hottest game in town.

The *London Times* carried stories above the fold with pictures of the bride's simple wedding dress. Reporters pressed informants in an effort to beat the competition to the presses. They worked the twenty-four-hour news cycle to gather every tidbit of information they could uncover, knowing that every household was awaiting the inside information that only they could report.

David's grandfather, the old king, was too frail at ninety-two to do anything more than make an appearance, but Prince George and Elizabeth Lord stood side by side to witness and approve the marriage. A thousand cameras captured their formally polite poses. Most of the throng shook their heads at the diffidence of the Prince George, although a few matchmakers sniffed the air and detected a decided warming between them as the day wore on.

The vows were solemnly pronounced by the Archbishop of Canterbury, and great sigh was heard through the abbey as both the bride and groom answered with the traditional "I do."

Three days later a ring ceremony was held on the Hill of Tara, and as the cars carrying the newlyweds traveled the small lanes toward Tara it seemed that all of Ireland lined the roadway to welcome them home.

Neal O'Brien stood in for the bride's father, Mrs. Brough at his side. And the family head, The O'Brien, Prince of Thomond, Chief of the Name, arrived by motorcar and brought with him the O'Brien plaid, which was draped over Camryn's shoulder for the ceremony.

Before the ceremony began a column of small girls arrived, carrying a woven rope of flowers and laid it with quiet dignity around the couple, encircling them. Together, David and Camryn turned in the circle, a Celtic tradition given as a promise of their unity with each other and with God.

As they turned, the congregation recited an ancient Celtic prayer, a pleading for a blessing on their union.

I bind myself before heaven today
The power of God to hold and lead
His eye to watch, His might to stay
His ear to hearken to my need
The wisdom of my God to teach
His hand to guide, His shield to ward
The word of God to give me speech
His Heavenly Host to be my guard.

Turning to face each other, they exchanged rings and a kiss. Before stepping outside the circle of flowers, they stood and looked over the shoulders of the Hill of Tara, down upon the fields and streams of County Meath, the crooked roads, the farmhouses, and, off in the distance, a church spire.

At one with the soul of Ireland and each other, they were ready to begin a new life together.

The reserved Prince George allowed the barriers erected to protect his heart to be breached on the Hill of Tara. By day's end Elizabeth responded and took his arm as they walked across the grassy hilltop to the motorcade after the ceremony was concluded.

Not a word was spoken in public, but an understanding was reached nonetheless. The lonely prince would be alone no more.

More public ceremonies at Scone and finally the chapel in Snowdon completed the week-long celebration. Eventually the celebrations wound down, and David and Camryn returned to the Mayfair apartment, overcoming the vehement objections of the SO14, who worried about how they would be able to guard them.

The old king had rallied for the celebration but quickly lost ground. He grew feeble and asked to spend time with David. So David made the trip to Buckingham a daily affair. It became a classroom of sorts, and was generally accompanied by a history lesson as well as a lesson of a more general understanding of the role of a royal in Britain.

One sultry afternoon, after spending the morning with the king,

David became lost while trying to find his way out of Buckingham. His footsteps echoed over marble floors and off of towering ceilings. The usual footmen were gone from their posts and he wandered in strange hallways. After a time, he found himself outside the doors of an immense room of books. Floor to ceiling bookcases lined every wall, and curling staircases wound up to the uppermost reaches of the room at every corner.

Drawn in by the wealth of beautifully tooled books, David wandered the bookcases and, wondering if he was allowed to touch the volumes, pulled several books out to scan the titles and open the covers to read a few pages.

The light, streaming from the heights of the library, seemed to gather and brighten for just a moment. Gradually, David became aware that someone else had entered the room and looking up from his reading discovered Phillip Lord, his father, looking intently at him.

"Did you know all of this from the beginning?" David asked him, ire simmering in his veins.

"Yes, my son; is it so terrible to have power to do good?" Phillip Lord said. "You have done well! My commission to help you is almost finished. I have much to tell you, son, so listen and remember all that will be required at your hands."

Standing above the floor, he paid no attention to the rich details of the royal library, made no mention of the lapse of time since they had last met, but looked on his son with an eager attention.

"Your search for the Stone of Destiny has rekindled in the people a desire to be called the people of God, they have been reminded of the noble history of these fair isles.

"Your search has also stirred up the forces that oppose the promise of the Throne of David. It is imperative that you meet the coming days as one, united with your people. They will rally around their new prince, my son. Remember that you were born for this day!

"You must keep the throne secure! It is imperative that the promise of the throne remain free. You were called to be its defender!

"Now, I leave you with a promise that when you are called on to trust, if you will judge with a pure heart you will not be led amiss."

Our new prince opened his mouth to speak, but Phillip Lord held up his hand and motioned for David to be still. Looking as if he were listening to a distant communication, they were quiet in the still library.

"They are coming for you! There is no time. There will come a time that you seek my help again, you will find the help that you need…"

They could hear the heavy footsteps of booted men coming hurriedly down the corridor toward the library.

His father continued, rushing, "You will find the help you need, you are given this promise as a gift. Remember that unity will overcome, David! Farewell, my son, farewell!"

David's gaze flicked to the doorway and then back to the messenger. Phillip Lord was gone.

A cadre of guards stood in the doorway and then quickly surrounded David.

"Your attendance is required now, sir." And they escorted him, closely guarding him to the rooms of the aged king. David's grandfather, the king of England, lay dying and the family stood vigil through the night.

Toward morning, he seemed to gain strength and motioning for Prince George to come closer they spoke quietly for a few moments. The king was pale upon his pillows, his voice too faint to carry, and watching Prince George it was clear that the communication was dire.

When the whispering was ended, the king lay back on his bed, and gasping he drew a shuddering breath and lay still.

No one dared approach the bed. Prince George stood, seemingly stunned into silence. Casting a long look at his father, George gestured the attendants to the bedside, and throwing the bedroom doors open he left the room without a word.

Word spread almost instantly and the country mourned the death of their beloved king. The populace was given time to say a loving farewell and then resolutely turned toward their future; after all, he was beloved by all but from afar. Only those who knew him well would miss his dry sense of humor, his perverse opinions about football, or his sloppy penmanship, all the particulars that made up the very real person that they cherished. Those who knew him well would mourn him until they were reunited again.

There was great speculation about what Prince George would do. A whisper campaign started the rumors flying that George had decided to abdicate in favor of his son. Although David saw Prince George at the funeral, they did not speak.

It was a Tuesday morning that David was finally summoned to

Clarence House. He asked Camryn to come, to be with him at this auspicious meeting with his father.

They were escorted into a large sitting room and they heard the doors click shut as the guards left them alone. Prince George stood at the windows, David's mother was seated on a small settee.

It was silent with a stillness that carried weight.

Finally, Prince George turned to them.

"Your mother and I are going to renew our vows before the investiture and I wanted to ask you, David, if you will approve of our marriage," he said.

"Well, it's about time! I know you have made my mother happy, I approve wholeheartedly," David said, and he kissed his mother's cheek.

"And I will be your matron of honor," Camryn said.

"What is going on, sir?" David asked. "You haven't been ignoring us because of a decision to renew vows with my mother!"

"No," George said, staring at the floor, "this hasn't been about your mother."

He continued, "I have wrestled with something my father confided in me before he died, and I worry about how much to share with you. I have been conditioned to keep things to myself, to trust no one. But your mother has convinced me that I need your help, at the very least, your advice."

Prince George paused again, it was proving difficult for him to speak so candidly. "I know I am doing you no great favor by sharing the burden I carry! We are besieged by insurmountable problems and I want you to know I don't lightly pass them on."

David started to speak but his father motioned for him to stop. With a shudder that shook his whole frame, George continued.

"In a little more than a week I will take up the throne and I ask that you give me your help in bearing up under the burden."

The room grew still again, until Camryn stepped forward. Pulling Elizabeth to her feet she moved to face her father-in-law, and motioning David to her side, she pulled the future king into an embrace. Elizabeth pressed herself against George as well and caught at David's hand, pulling him into the circle.

"We are here, Father, to help you in any way we can," David said for them all.

Chapter 45

The coronation ceremony was held quickly, but it had been anticipated for years and the dignity and pomp that took over the occasion was dictated by hundreds of years of tradition. Anticipation mounted over what role the stone would play in the ceremony.

It was televised, of course, and it seemed that the excitement of the story had reached into every corner of the earth. Anyone with access to TV or radio had been caught up in the story of the Coronation Stone.

Brought in with great ceremony from Scotland for the sacrament, the stone was escorted by the clans, the trickle of water having slowed and then finally stopped only a few days before the ceremony. Anticipation ran high and every expectation was fully realized when the nation witnessed the new king, King George VII, seated upon the Coronation Stone.

A great hush filled the abbey, indeed, the whole land, and the silence stretched out as the people watched with a hesitant hope. Then, it happened. The new king George must have felt it first for a look of wonder passed over his countenance. The roar was felt as much as heard, and for the first time in many hundreds of years the people of the realm witnessed the roar of the Coronation Stone, the Stone of Destiny, the Lia Fáil, or the Pillow of Jacob, approving the coronation of a heaven-approved king.

About the Author

Ann Farnsworth lives outside of St. Louis, Missouri. She studied the classics in school, along with history. The Farnsworths are the parents of ten children and have two perfect sons-in-law and a granddaughter. You can find Ann online at annfarnsworth.com, via email at AnnFarnsworthAuthor@gmail.com, on Twitter @annfarnsworth, or on Facebook at The Throne of David.